Matt Gemmell is a former consultant software engineer, and the author of *Raw Materials*. He lives with his wife in Edinburgh, Scotland, and can be found on the web at mattgemmell.com

KESTREL BOOK ONE

CHANGER

Matt Gemmell

Copyright © 2016 Matt Gemmell
All rights reserved.

This book is a work of fiction. The characters, places and events are either the product of the author's imagination, or are used entirely fictitiously.

Cover design by Stuart Bache at Books Covered.
Cover photography © Shutterstock

*For Lauren, my wife, my love, my life.
Thank you for believing.*

CHANGER

For Liz & Mike,

Best wishes

Matt *[signature]*

Prologue

Osborne was poorly dressed for the icy weather, but he barely noticed the temperature.

Most of his attention was focused on his pursuer, sparing only a little thought for the growing pain across the top of his shoulder where the bullet had nicked him. The wound felt like a razor blade drawn across his skin. He had a stolen gun tucked into one of the deep, wide pockets of his lab coat, but he barely knew how to use it. As a particle physicist, he had no use for firearms.

Until now, he thought, pushing himself onwards.

The sky was brightening towards midday, but no-one else was in sight. He'd hoped the lab coat would conceal him against the winter landscape, but the single shot had been too close. He had underestimated the man who was chasing him, and in this situation, that could be fatal.

The landscape around the facility was thick

woodland, now blanketed in several inches of snow. Several paths wound through the area, but they were all invisible after fresh snowfall a few hours before. His breath came in ragged gasps and he tried to increase his speed while still staying low. The terrain sloped gradually downwards, and the woods became more dense about fifty yards ahead.

Just a little further, he thought, but another voice in his mind — a panicky, shrill voice that no longer sounded entirely familiar — immediately asked the question he couldn't answer.

Then what?

It was a good question. Hide, perhaps? Or fetch help somehow? Escaping on foot was unlikely, and not just because exposure and hypothermia were very real possibilities. The last time Osborne had run more than a few yards was probably more than ten years ago, and his recent exercise regime only stretched to a three (or four, or five) times daily walk to the kitchen area along the corridor from his lab, to fetch some questionable coffee.

His pursuer was an entirely different kind of man.

Merrick, he thought, pushing sharp branches aside with his aching and rapidly purpling hands as he forced himself forward.

Kurt Merrick was one of the two reasons that Osborne was making such a desperate escape attempt. He knew little about the man's background, except that he was clearly ex-military, and was absolutely obeyed within

Prologue

the facility.

Osborne also knew why Merrick himself, rather than one of his dozens of subordinates, was out here chasing him: because he enjoyed the hunt.

And the kill, that same shrill voice in his head whispered, even higher-pitched than before.

Yes, that was probably true. Merrick was not only trained to kill, but no doubt actively enjoyed it.

The sudden impact on his brow seemed to happen at the same instant he heard the whip-crack of a gunshot. He fell forward, jarring his knees because of the slope, and saw a droplet of blood against a patch of snow. It was shockingly bright and red.

Dead dead dead! shrieked the inner voice, and he felt a tear run smoothly from the corner of his eye and down his cheek, slowing in the icy wind. It hung for a moment and then dropped, hitting the ground only a few inches from the spreading red stain. But he was still alive.

Confused, and with his pulse roaring in his ears, he reached up and touched his brow. His fingers came away wet, but not drenched — it was a cut, nothing more. Then he saw the branch lying alongside him.

That's what hit me; not a bullet, he realised.

Where it had once been attached to the bough of a tree, the thicker end of the branch was a shattered ruin. It had been shot off, precisely if not cleanly, from at least a hundred yards away.

The bastard is toying with me, he thought, and a sick, glassy fear sank from his chest into his stomach. It was replaced a moment later by fury.

Osborne hauled himself to his feet, staggering at first before finding his footing on the slope. He wasn't aware of it, but his lip had curled into the beginnings of a snarl; an expression that his wife Susan had never seen in their nearly sixteen years of mostly happy marriage.

How fucking dare you, he thought.

He was being hunted now; hunted to death, because Merrick knew very well what he intended to do: tell the world about the project. To try, using any means necessary, to make people first believe his story, and then do something about it.

The project was a wonderful thing, but it was also terrifying. It wasn't right that only one — what? Company? Government? — should have exclusive control and knowledge of it. Even he, as a principal scientist, was unsure of the exact nature of the organisation that funded the project, or who Merrick's superiors were.

But that didn't change anything; the world had to know what was happening. What was *going* to happen.

This last thought fuelled his anger, and he felt the painfully cold steel of the pistol in his hand before he was even aware he'd taken it from his coat pocket.

He was no marksman, and he knew it, but the anger made it seem unimportant. If Merrick was willing to take a life to maintain the project's secrecy, then Osborne would do the same to ensure the secret was revealed. He had the presence of mind to disengage the safety, just as he'd read about.

Prologue

Keeping the gun low at his side, he started loping forward again, as if continuing his dash for the thicker woods ahead.

Kurt Merrick smiled, though an onlooker would be unlikely to recognise the expression. His lips were pressed together in a thin, blood-red line, and there was no trace of amusement in his ice-blue eyes.

Run, little rabbit, he thought, feeling a dark and humourless anticipation rise from the pit of his stomach.

Osborne, of all people. He'd been on the project when they'd acquired it; one of the original team of scientists. The man knew the importance of the work, and exactly what their goals were. It was intolerable to Merrick that the success of the project hinged on the efforts of people like Osborne — scientists; civilians and liberals without exception — but it was often the case in the modern world.

Such assets were essential, but for all of their education and intelligence, they lacked vision. He thought Osborne might be an exception, but the silent perimeter alarm less than thirty minutes ago corrected that misperception.

Disappointing, Merrick thought. *A small man after all. And not long for this world.*

He saw his quarry begin to move away again. Merrick adjusted his grip on his Sig Elite pistol, and confidently stepped around the claw-like bare branches of an ash tree.

The hunt would be over soon. Osborne was tired, unfit, wounded, underdressed, and had no survival training. Merrick had allowed at least five opportunities for a kill shot to pass by. He wanted to hear the man beg for his life before it was taken from him.

He increased his pace, coming to within fifty yards.

Osborne's anger vied with panic as he exaggerated his stagger, scanning the terrain ahead until he found what he was looking for: a partially-fallen bough, laden with snow, in front of a natural dip. It would have to do.

The smiling face of his wife flashed across his mind, but he pushed the image aside and instead embraced his hatred and fear of the man he knew was getting closer with every passing moment.

As he reached the bough, he took a single, short breath, then stepped down into the slight dip and allowed himself to fall forward heavily, twisting sideways as he went down. His injured shoulder battered mercilessly into a gnarled clump of the tree's exposed roots, and his scream was real.

Merrick's keen eyes noted his quarry's movements, and he anticipated the stumble almost a second before it happened. His training automatically dropped him to one knee, into a firing position, but he had no clear shot.

A sneer of disgust curled the side of his mouth. It seemed that the hunt would end sooner than he anticipated. *Clumsiness. Weakness. Killing you will be an act of mercy.*

Prologue

He moved forward, keeping his pistol trained on a spot just above the rim of the natural depression in the ground ahead. He could hear Osborne groaning, and the snapping of twigs as he presumably rolled back and forth over them.

Merrick reached the edge of the dip, and sighed with contempt. Osborne lay on his back down there, looking up with bright, frightened eyes. He grasped his knee, and there was blood down one side of his face.

"I don't believe I gave you permission to go exploring, Dr. Osborne," Merrick said darkly, and lowered his pistol. "The forest can be a dangerous place."

His accent was unplaceable. For the hundredth time, Osborne wondered if there was a hint of the German origin that the man's name implied, or perhaps even Norwegian. Merrick's voice was quiet and smooth, and was always laden with both threat and disdain. Everything about the man said danger, and he clearly knew it.

"Go to hell," Osborne spat, and he was alarmed to taste blood in his mouth.

The smallest flicker of an almost kindly smile chased across the other man's lips, but it never reached his eyes.

"Not before you, I think," he replied.

Merrick expected a plea at this point, or at least indignation and anger. Those were the two most common reactions. His victims never displayed disbelief, though — he'd yet to see *that* response. They always believed completely in his ability and willingness to kill them, and he always confirmed their conviction.

Osborne, however, remained silent. Merrick raised an eyebrow.

"Nothing to say? So be it. It is time for you to leave this life, Doctor," he said, raising his Sig once more. He registered the movement of the fallen man's hand, concealed beside his knee, at the same time he heard Osborne speak.

"I won't be alone," the scientist said, then he raised the combat pistol he had stolen, and fired.

The gunshot was like a crack of thunder under the tree canopy, followed less than a fifth of a second afterwards by another, as Merrick automatically returned fire.

Osborne felt a hammer-blow to the right side of his chest, and the pistol flew from his grip, bounced uselessly off a small rock, and tumbled away out of sight.

Merrick grinned and lowered his weapon in satisfaction, then his grin faltered. Numbness radiated from a point low on his left side, above the hip, and then a wave of weakness hit him. He fell to one knee as he looked down to see the dark, wine-coloured stain spreading around a ragged hole in his insulated jacket.

Impossible, his mind objected, but he had been shot before, and he was no fool.

"Congratulations... Doctor...," he gasped, putting pressure on his wound with his free hand.

Osborne barely grunted. He was also losing blood, and much more quickly. His vision was already dark around the edges.

Prologue

Merrick got to his feet again with great effort, holstered his pistol and then used his other hand to put additional pressure on the hole in his abdomen.

"A... perforated stomach, and perhaps an artery" he wheezed, "I would die long before help arrived. I congratulate you again."

Osborne could only watch as Merrick suddenly dropped his hands from the wound, wincing as blood flowed freely. His voice became reedy now, but there was a glint in his eyes. He took two pained steps forward, then sank to his knees and placed his hand over Osborne's on the ground.

"You have learned *nothing*," Merrick whispered, and then suddenly Osborne heard a sound. It was like a rush of wind; the sound of stepping into a strong breeze. He thought he saw the scene around him shudder briefly.

Merrick, whose grip he could still feel on his hand, blurred for an instant, and then came back into focus.

"For all your work on the project, you are as ignorant as a child," Merrick said, and his voice was strong again. He stood up, and his jacket showed no sign of any damage. His face had lost its pallor and sheen of sweat, and he moved with ease.

Osborne's drenched brow twisted in confusion, but his vision was rapidly closing in. How could Merrick be uninjured? Osborne had *shot* him — and even seen the wound, and the blood. His eyes flicked downwards to the snow-covered ground. There were boot-prints, but not a trace of blood at Merrick's feet.

The glint of dull midday light on dark metal drew Osborne's final moment of attention. The barrel of the pistol filled his vision.

"This place is the last you will ever see," Merrick said, and then he pulled the trigger.

Osborne saw a flash that lit the universe in blinding white.

Susan, he thought, and then he fell into darkness forever.

PART 1

Chapter 1

It was raining in Edinburgh, and that suited Neil Aldridge just fine. The streets were marginally less busy, and rain had a way of making even a mediocre cup of coffee seem to taste better.

The morning was bleak, and Aldridge already had the beginnings of a headache. He sat in a nondescript corner cafe, about half a mile north of the main shopping thoroughfare of the city. It was Wednesday, and the clock on the wall said 11:24 AM.

The clientele were mostly wearing the telltale department-store business attire and ID lanyards of a major insurance group, whose satellite office was just around the corner. They talked enthusiastically about nothing remotely interesting, spilling crumbs over their tablet computers and, to Aldridge's disbelieving amusement, actual day-planners.

Welcome to the money business of the twenty-first century, he thought, dumping another half-sachet of brown sugar into the robustly burnt Americano in front of him.

Aldridge was a moderately attractive if slightly bookish-looking man, of average height. His build was slim, his messy brown hair clearly not the result of vanity, and his grey-blue eyes currently as cloudy as the sky outside. His clothes had the unmistakable air of well-worn, faded smartness that said *academic* in any language.

He was a lecturer in the School of Physics and Astronomy at the University of Edinburgh, and he was 37 years old. His PhD in theoretical subatomic particle physics entitled him to be addressed as Doctor, but he shunned that appellation. It was too damned pompous by half, and made him feel ridiculous.

He had been back in Edinburgh for almost two years, after leaving his research position in Oxford. Teaching was fulfilling at first, but now... well, now things were a little less clear cut.

He sighed, swirling a slender wooden stirrer through the black liquid.

This is bloody bad timing, he thought. *Or maybe it's perfect, come to think of it.*

He glanced up, looking out the window and across the street. The downpour continued unabated, and there was no sign of the man he was waiting for.

The voicemail was left yesterday, while he was out. There were several seconds of silence, and he had been just about to press the delete button when an anxious-

Chapter 1

sounding and very familiar voice spoke.

"Neil, it's... Peter."

A pause, then a sigh.

"I hope you're well. I'm in town, and I'd like — I need to see you. It's about... work."

Aldridge was immediately concerned. He hadn't spoken to Peter Taylor in two years, and they hadn't parted on good terms. The voicemail ended with Taylor asking Aldridge to meet him in this cafe at 11 o'clock this morning.

And I almost didn't come at all, Aldridge thought.

Dr. Peter Taylor was the senior professor of high-energy particle physics research at the Rudolf Peierls Centre for Theoretical Physics at Oxford University. His list of publications was extensive, and was dwarfed only by the string of awards, grants (including several from various government agencies, both at home and abroad) and glowing testimonials which seemed to accompany every mention of him. His area of interest was a field called theoretical condensed matter physics, and he was one of the world's foremost experts on the subject.

He was also Aldridge's uncle on his mother's side, and up until a year ago, he was the closest thing to a father that Aldridge had.

Until... I left.

He shifted in his seat, frowning as his headache became more insistent. The sudden honk of a car horn startled him, and he glanced out into the street.

A tall, slender man with a bright red backpack scurried across the road, glancing behind him at the angry driver who had nearly hit him. The driver gesticulated and shouted something before driving off.

The tall man's face was hidden by his jacket's rain hood, and he moved quickly out of view after a furtive glance towards the cafe.

The coffee was almost cold, and Aldridge thought that might be a good thing. He sighed deeply and checked his watch. It was almost half an hour after the arranged meeting time. A part of him had suspected that Taylor might not show up, but he was grimly determined to wait it out. He missed the man, and he owed him the benefit of the doubt.

Aldridge didn't even glance up as the chimes above the door tinkled, admitting another drenched prospective customer.

As the clock ticked past 11:37, he was rapidly coming to the conclusion that Taylor had decided against the meeting, and he took out his iPhone to dial into his answering service and check if any new messages had been left. He swiped the slider to unlock the screen, and was just about to tap the Phone icon when he became aware of a shadow falling across the table, and he looked up.

It was Mr. Red Backpack, of nearly-hit-by-a-car fame, but this time his rain hood was down, revealing grey hair that stuck up in various places.

The stark, familiar lines of his face were deeper than Aldridge remembered, and the bruise-like shadows

Chapter 1

under his eyes showed he hadn't been sleeping much lately.

"Hello, Neil," Taylor said. "Thank you for meeting me."

Aldridge's headache had disappeared for the moment as he watched the man sitting across from him, nervously stirring his tea.

They had exchanged some brief pleasantries in a strained, detached way until Taylor's tea was brought to the table, but for the past minute or so the older man had sat in silence, elaborately adding milk and sugar in precise amounts, counting the number of times he stirred almost audibly under his breath. The teaspoon moved in an odd, rhythmic, slow-then-fast pattern.

Obsessive-Compulsive Disorder, Aldridge thought. Taylor had always suffered from the condition, particularly during times of stress. The man's narrow face was pale and drawn, and the two patches of colour high in his cheeks weren't entirely explained by the dreary weather he'd taken shelter from. His gaze periodically darted around the cafe, and every minute or two he'd anxiously glance out towards the street.

"Is someone else going to join us?" Aldridge asked, drawing a moment of intense scrutiny from Taylor before he sighed deeply and shook his head.

"I hope not," he replied, and Aldridge frowned but decided not to press him on the odd remark just yet. Taylor took a sip of his tea, despite it clearly still being steaming hot, and then set the cup down carefully.

"You must be wondering why I'm here," he said, and Aldridge tilted his head to one side, in a gesture that didn't entirely say either yes or no.

Taylor looked down at his tea again, seeming to gather his thoughts.

You look older, Aldridge thought, and then he felt the stab of guilt he'd been anticipating ever since he heard his former mentor's voicemail.

The silver hair around Taylor's temples was thinning, and tufts were sticking out, damp with rain. The lines across his forehead were carved much more deeply than they had been two summers ago, and his beard was thicker and was starting to look unkempt. For the first time in living memory, he looked every one of his sixty-four years.

Aldridge suppressed a sigh, not liking the surge of self-loathing he was feeling. *Did I do that to you?* he wondered, but there was no use pursuing that train of thought. What was done was done.

The last time they spoke, they'd been sitting in the cramped kitchen/dining-room area of the flat Taylor was granted as part of his tenure at the University of Oxford. The accommodation was quaint, if ratty in places, and Taylor was hardly ever in it — most nights, he slept in his office. On this particular night, though, he had invited Aldridge to come over, alone, and talk.

That didn't go well, Aldridge thought, shifting uncomfortably in his seat as he remembered their last conver-

Chapter 1

sation.

The flat was cold, as usual. Taylor never had the heating on, and tended to inhabit only the kitchen and the small, single bedroom. Aldridge tugged his blazer more tightly around him, willing himself not to shiver. The single energy-efficient bulb above the small kitchen table created a puddle of glare, but did little to make the room feel inviting.

"I'd like you to reconsider. Just hear me out," Taylor said, raising a hand to silence the objection that was already on the other man's lips.

Aldridge sighed, shaking his head, but he didn't say anything.

He's got every right to be upset, he thought. This was perhaps the tenth time that Taylor had tried to convince him to stay, but the decision was already made. Everything was booked, and there was no way that Julie was going to change her mind.

They were moving to Edinburgh; both of them. Aldridge had been in a relationship with a journalist named Julie Hollett for the past two years, and her family lived just outside the Scottish capital, including her mother who was now in failing health. The circumstances were unfortunate, but the timing couldn't have been better.

He'd told Taylor that the move was purely so they could be closer to Julie's mother, but truthfully he'd been restless for months. He and Taylor worked side by side at the Rudolf Peierls Centre six or seven days per week, often long into the evening. The work was purely theoretical, and it no longer held the fascination for Aldridge that it once had. The trigger for his dissatisfaction had come when he bumped into an old university friend, and heard all about his career in teaching chemistry at a local high school.

It was something real. Something tangible, with a direct effect on the lives of the young people in the classroom. Teaching wouldn't change the world, but Aldridge had never felt like a world-changing man. He would settle for a sense of purpose. Theoretical physics just felt… empty. It had become a place to hide from life, not to improve it.

He'd voiced his dissatisfaction with Julie, and she'd quickly latched onto it. Edinburgh was his own home city too, after all, where he was born and had lived until not long after that Tuesday morning when he was eleven years old, and had been taken from his mathematics class by the ashen-faced headmistress. The car accident robbed him of both his parents, and he was sent south to Oxford to live with his uncle Peter within a month.

The adjustment was difficult for both of them, but they had found a rhythm with each other, and the boy had quickly discovered that he loved physics almost as much as his newfound guardian did. The rules that made the world work. Dependable, measurable, and sane. They told him the reasons for things, and he need-

Chapter 1

ed to know.

His school results were stellar, and his place at university was guaranteed. A degree, postgraduate studies, an assistantship in his uncle's lab, and finally a Ph.D had all followed naturally.

And he'd been happy, for a while.

He'd never spoken to Taylor about his shifting priorities, and his growing sense of isolation. When it was finally time to tell his colleague, mentor, and surrogate father about his desire to step away from research and re-focus on teaching undergraduates, it had been a shock to the older man. They hadn't spoken for a week, and their next conversation was little more than a shouting match.

As the months rolled on, though, and preparations for the move began in earnest, Taylor became increasingly desperate to appeal to Aldridge's sense of exploration, of wonder, and the thrill of finding profound answers about the nature of the universe. Aldridge tried to humour him at first, but the relationship became more and more strained. The decision was already made, and he knew that most of the frustration he felt was actually thinly-veiled guilt.

The tension sat between them in the room, like a physical thing.

"I understand how you're feeling, Neil — I do," Taylor said, shifting in his seat in the birdlike way he had, "but you have to consider how you're going to feel later."

"Peter—" Aldridge began, but Taylor spoke over him.

"I've been thinking, and I've spoken to the University. They've offered to give you a teaching assignment; it'd be four hours per week, and you'd—"

"Peter, *stop*."

Taylor's mouth snapped shut, and he blinked twice and then huffed in exasperation. Aldridge could see the frustration and desperation in his mentor's eyes, and it only made the guilt inside him twist more painfully.

He took a breath, and tried to soften his tone.

"You know that I'm going," he said. "And you know that this is what I want. Please, let's not go through this again."

Taylor looked away, clearly struggling to find words. After a few moments, he seemed to deflate. "I think you're making a mistake," he said quietly, and Aldridge frowned.

"I know you do. But I've made up my mind. This is what I want."

"Rudimentary work for children barely out of high school? Lectures and marking?"

Aldridge felt irritation rising in his chest, but he pushed it away, reminding himself that the older man was grieving, in a way.

"People," he replied quietly. "Real people. A chance to make a very small difference to a few dozen lives, year in and year out. I know you can't understand, but can you at least accept my decision?"

There was silence for several long moments. Taylor

Chapter 1

reached up and adjusted his spectacles for the second time in as many minutes. His gaze was on the cup in front of him.

"I'm not sure that I can," he said.

Aldridge was suddenly so very tired of this. The worst part was that he *did* feel like he was in the wrong — not for his choice; not at all — but for abandoning this man who had taken him in, given him back his life, and fuelled a passion that had become his career. This man who had given him both love and purpose.

I'm not abandoning him, he thought. *That's just guilty melodrama.*

But it felt that way, and endlessly rehashing it here wasn't doing either of them any good. They'd just have to find a way to mutually make their peace with it.

Aldridge pushed his chair back from the table, and slowly stood up. Taylor's eyes flicked up at the movement, then he once again shook his head and sighed.

"I should be going, Peter," Aldridge said. "There's a lot we still have to do. Julie asked me to tell you you'd be welcome at the gathering we're having next week."

Taylor didn't respond, and after half a minute or so, Aldridge simply nodded.

"Well, goodnight, then."

He moved around the small table and made his way to the door that led to the hallway, pausing for a moment at the threshold.

"I'm sorry, for what it's worth," he said. The words hung in the air in the ensuing silence.

He waited a full minute this time, but again Taylor didn't respond.

Aldridge looked around the shabby but somehow comfortable space, his eyes eventually coming to rest on the bowed head of the other man. Taylor looked small and frail now, sitting alone at the table under the too-bright single bulb overhead.

After another moment, Aldridge turned and left.

Taylor cleared his throat as he glanced around the cafe, and Aldridge noticed for the first time just how pale the man looked. He leaned forward slightly in concern, still silent. He knew from long experience that Taylor would speak only when he was ready.

"I wanted to ask how Julie is doing," Taylor said suddenly, and Aldridge blinked in confusion.

She hadn't been a common topic for them even before the estrangement, and Aldridge had assumed that Taylor probably harboured resentment towards the woman because of her role in his move away from Oxford.

At least we have that in common, he thought, shifting in his seat.

"I'm honestly not sure," he said, seeing a frown immediately crease Taylor's forehead. He groaned inwardly, and decided to get it over with. "We're not together anymore."

Taylor looked worried now, which struck Aldridge as odd.

Just personal concern? But why?

Chapter 1

"I see," Taylor replied, adjusting his spectacles. "Well, I'm sorry to hear that. But... do you keep in contact?"

Now it was Aldridge's turn to frown.

"Not for over a year now. We didn't exactly part on good terms, Peter." He could have been talking about Taylor and himself, instead of he and Julie.

Taylor just nodded, then glanced over towards the large windows all along the front of the coffee shop. He scanned the street outside intently, then turned back to look at Aldridge, seemingly satisfied.

"You need to get in touch with her?" Aldridge asked, and Taylor tilted his head in a gesture that meant neither yes nor no.

"I... yes, in a manner of speaking, but... there's something else."

Taylor reached for his cup, then changed his mind, letting his hand come to rest on the tabletop. It was only then that Aldridge noticed how the older man's hands were shaking.

"Peter," he said, leaning forward and lowering his voice slightly, "what's wrong? What's all this about?"

Taylor looked up again, two points of colour looking unnaturally bright against his pale cheeks. He paused for a single breath before continuing in an even quieter voice that was nonetheless absolutely clear.

"My life is in danger, and we may not have much time."

Chapter 2

"He went into the cafe."

The mercenary with the binoculars sat in the front passenger seat of the black Toyota Sienna, looking out through its heavily tinted windows.

His name was Tepel, and he bore an ugly, curving scar that ran from the corner of his right eye down to his jawline. The man sitting in the rearmost row of seats inflicted it with a combat knife when Tepel was a few minutes late for duty on one evening the previous winter.

They were parked several hundred yards along the road, and they had been following Dr. Taylor all morning.

There were five men in the vehicle, and each one was a trained killer. They could have apprehended Taylor at any point during the past several hours, but their current orders were to observe, and determine the purpose of Taylor's unsanctioned trip to the city of Edinburgh.

Tepel lowered his binoculars and turned his head to make eye contact with the man sitting immediately behind the driver's seat. He was called Aranega, and he served as the technical specialist for the group.

"Nothing," Aranega said, after consulting the device strapped to his wrist, and Tepel nodded, returning his attention to the door of the cafe further along the block.

"What now?" he asked, and there was no question who he was addressing. From the rear seat, icy blue eyes met his in the mirror.

"We wait," Merrick said.

Aldridge's headache had returned in earnest. He frowned at Taylor, who wore an expression of grim resolve on his face, tinged with obvious fear.

"If you're in some kind of trouble, Peter, then the police-"

Taylor cut him off with a huff of exasperation. "Contacting the police is the *worst* thing I could do," he muttered, "but there's more at stake here than my own life. I need your help."

Aldridge paused for a moment, but there was really no decision to be made. "Of course," he replied, lowering his voice. "What do you want me to do?"

Taylor leaned forward, glancing around at the other patrons of the cafe before once again fixing his gaze on Aldridge.

"I want you to tell the world about the clandestine

Chapter 2

project I've been involved in for the past year, the people who control that project, and the colleagues of mine who have been killed to preserve its secret."

Aldridge knew that Taylor was deadly serious, and he felt a chill run up his spine.

"My god, Peter, what have you got yourself into?"

"More than I bargained for," the older man replied, then he reached into his jacket pocket and withdrew a small, plain brown envelope, and pushed it across the table.

"You'll need these," he said. "I have substantial documentation about the project that I've... borrowed. I'll be able to show it to you, but I didn't dare bring it with me today."

Aldridge carefully tipped the contents of the envelope onto the table. There were three objects: a business card emblazoned with the University of Oxford logo, a small and expensive-looking book of matches, and an identification card. The University card was made of basic institutional paper stock, and gave details of Taylor's position at the Rudolf Peierls Centre, but the ID card was very different.

It was equipped with various holograms, a microchip of some kind, Taylor's name and photograph, and the words *Lab 6*. Aldridge turned it over, finding only an unusual barcode-like design on the back.

No organisation or facility details, he noted.

He then picked up the matchbook. The paper was exquisite, inlaid with fine dark threads against off-white backing, with a gold trim. It bore only a single mark across its entire surface: an anonymous logo consisting of several small circles, arranged in a triangular formation.

"The address of where I'm staying is on the back of my card," Taylor said distractedly, and Aldridge flipped over the business card to find the hastily-scrawled address of a hostel here in the city.

"Alright," Aldridge replied, sweeping the objects back into the envelope and pocketing it, "But what is it you expect me to do, exactly? I can't just—"

Aldridge stopped as he saw Taylor's hand tighten abruptly into a fist. He had been looking out the window, and Aldridge followed his gaze just in time to see a black Toyota minivan with heavily tinted windows drive past the cafe. The older man stared after it until it was gone. It was only when he suddenly inhaled loudly that Aldridge realised Taylor had been holding his breath.

"It was just a car," Aldridge said, not unkindly, and Taylor gave him a sharp look.

"Perhaps, or perhaps not," he replied, his face noticeably paler than a moment before. "Just the sort of vehicle that Merrick's associates use."

Who's Merrick? wondered Aldridge, but he thought it was best to let that question wait for a while. He sat in silence for almost two minutes as Taylor anxiously watched the passing traffic outside.

"It's not safe to talk here," Taylor said at last, and it

Chapter 2

was clear that he really believed it. Aldridge couldn't help but feel a twinge of irritation.

"You're not making any sense, Peter," he said, shifting in his seat as he leaned forward. "Do you want *me* to go to the police? And why are you in danger?"

Taylor sighed and shook his head, looking quickly around again for several moments before again leaning forwards. His too-bright eyes were focused on Aldridge now, unwavering.

"Have you…" he began, then he winced before forcing himself to continue. "Has anything happened to *you* recently? Anything unusual? Something you *can't explain*?"

Another chill chased through Aldridge, and an image flashed across his mind. An elegantly curved shape, made of fine crystal, lit only by streetlights. He pushed the thought aside, feeling gooseflesh rise up on his forearms.

"What do you mean, *unusual*?" he asked, in a small voice, and Taylor scrutinised him. They had known each other since Aldridge was a child, and it was almost impossible to hide anything from his man.

Taylor opened his mouth to reply, automatically glancing over towards the windows, but his next words never came. Instead, his sharp intake of breath made Aldridge follow his gaze towards the window.

That's the same vehicle, Aldridge thought, feeling a prickle of unease. It was clearly the same van: heavy tints on the back and front side windows, which was unusual, and a second aerial mounted further back on the roof. Scrupulously nondescript wheel-trims, and bodywork gleaming in the rain. A threateningly anonymous yet authoritarian vehicle. He felt the hairs on the back of his neck stand on end as the van crawled past the cafe on the opposite side of the road.

Aldridge glanced back towards Taylor just in time to see the older man grab his red backpack.

"Peter, wait—" he began, but the academic's too-wide eyes silenced him. It was pitiful to see an old man so afraid.

"I stayed too long," Taylor muttered, half to himself, in a voice that wavered alarmingly. He glanced frantically around the cafe for a moment before fixing his gaze once more on Aldridge.

"There's a phone booth on the corner of the street you live on. Be there this evening. I'll call at eight o'clock, and if there's no answer I'll try once more at eight-thirty. Don't come to the hostel; I won't be there. Do *not* try to find me."

Aldridge opened his mouth to protest, but the naked terror on Taylor's face silenced him. He just nodded.

"I beg you, Neil, *don't* go to the police," Taylor said. "You… you may also be in danger. You might be involved in all of this too."

Aldridge's pulse thudded in his chest. He wanted to respond, but words had temporarily deserted him.

With one final fearful glance towards the front of the cafe, Taylor abruptly turned and ran through the doors

Chapter 2

leading to the kitchen area at the rear.

A young waitress shouted after him and gave chase, only to return less than a minute later, clearly angry.

"Your friend just ran through our kitchen and out the back door!" she exclaimed. "That's trespassing! If you don't pay the bill, I'm calling the police."

Aldridge could only look at her for a moment as he regained his composure, then he made a placating gesture and reached for his wallet. "I'm very sorry for the trouble. Of course I'll pay the bill now."

The young woman gave him a doubtful look, then after a long moment she nodded and went over to the till on the nearby counter, glancing back at him suspiciously as she pressed the keys.

Aldridge looked down at his own hands, his fingers spread out on the cheap tablecloth, and he took a deep breath.

What the hell is going on? he wondered. His headache was suddenly worse than ever, and his heart was still thudding in his chest.

Outside, the light shower had become a downpour.

Chapter 3

"The other one is exiting alone," Tepel said.

Merrick frowned as he glanced up from his laptop and looked out towards the cafe further down the block.

"And where is the good doctor?" he asked, with a note of threat in his voice.

"He hasn't come out," Tepel replied, still scanning the scene.

Merrick turned to Aranega. "Any disturbances?" he asked, and the other man lifted his arm to peer at an elongated screen which was secured in place above his wrist. It showed a GPS map overlay in orange against black, with a superimposed light-blue waveform. Each of the five men in the van wore one. The waveform was shallow and steady. He shook his head.

"Drost, go and see where Taylor went."

The rat-faced soldier in the side jump-seat got up without a word, zipping his jacket halfway up to conceal the shoulder-holster he wore, and was out the side door of the van in a matter of seconds.

And who are you, I wonder? Merrick thought, as the other man from the cafe disappeared around the corner, walking slowly. *You have poor taste in friends.*

The driver, a blonde, muscular Irish psychopath named Finn, was already putting the van in gear before he gave the command.

"Follow him."

Kurt Merrick wasn't accustomed to feeling either chastened or uneasy, and the combination made him furious.

He glanced occasionally out of the windows of the black minivan, but relied on his subordinates to keep him apprised of the situation. Most of his attention was focused on the laptop in front of him, where he was reviewing the current state of the project via an encrypted satellite uplink.

The loss of Osborne two months ago had been an inconvenience, but their recent findings were very promising. They were closer than ever to pinpointing the location of the event. Taylor's escape had been a blow they could ill afford, however. His jaw tightened as he remembered the events of the previous week.

The problem was the technicians, of course.

The nature of Taylor's role on the project required him to work with some very specialised equipment, on a large scale. It was a matter of practicality that he was assisted by almost twenty technicians who, unlike Tay-

Chapter 3

lor himself, were not permanent residents at the facility.

The technicians came and went each morning and evening, supervised by security personnel and various automated systems, but there was a delicate balance to be struck between secrecy and suspicion. Taylor was one of the only senior scientists who was permitted to freely go back and forth between the instrumentation labs where the junior personnel worked, and the high security areas on the facility's several subterranean levels. He had naturally struck up friendships with those who were assisting him, and solicited help to escape.

Luck also played a part. One of the guards on the ground level had chosen a poor time to take a smoking break, leaving an external door in a maintenance corridor ajar. The security logs showed that Taylor used a technician's ID badge to gain access to the corridor, and had slipped out after the guard, actually having the cunning to ask for a cigarette. The guard, thinking his companion was a simple lab assistant, had left him to finish smoking alone, asking the older man to close the door when he came back in.

Taylor had indeed closed the door — from the outside. A soggy but barely-touched cigarette was found in the slush beside the door two hours later, once Taylor had been reported as missing. Merrick's frown deepened as he remembered reviewing the surveillance camera footage.

As far as the other junior staff were concerned, the person who gave Taylor his ID had been fired immediately for breaching the security protocols, which existed purely for the staff's own safety. The guard, whose name was Alexander Berglund, had similarly lost his job and been escorted from the premises.

Security staff were chosen not only based on experience, but also personal circumstances: the majority of guards at the facility were single men with no living family members. No-one would miss them if they didn't come home one night.

The guard was replaced, a security bulletin was circulated to all personnel, and all guards were given mandatory retraining.

In a remote outbuilding, the hazardous waste disposal furnace was seen to be active for an unusually long time that evening.

And then I had to inform him, Merrick thought.

Merrick glanced out at the dark terrain speeding past below without really seeing it.

The helicopter arrived to collect him less than an hour after he made the phone call to report Taylor's escape. He had been given a headset by the pilot, which sat unheeded on the leather seat beside him. He had nothing to say to the lackey, but their mutual master would expect him to be much more forthcoming.

The flight from the facility took about 30 minutes, but it seemed like barely any time had passed before the craft began to descend. He could already see the sprawling, well-lit estate on a long hill by the coast. After an-

Chapter 3

other couple of minutes, a lone figure came into view, standing off to one side of the private helipad.

Merrick's face twisted into a grimace. *The secretary*, he thought with disgust. The man below was actually a combination of personal assistant and manservant, but Merrick enjoyed demeaning him. His name was Fabian, and he in turn also enjoyed taunting Merrick, knowing that his trusted position with his employer kept him safe.

To hell with you, little Frenchman, thought Merrick, feeling both ice and fire in his chest. No-one could be protected forever. Merrick had other plans for the glorious project, and when the time came, Fabian would find himself on the receiving end of a bullet.

But that time had not yet arrived. The helicopter touched down smoothly, and Merrick opened the door and stepped out before the whine of the rotors had even begun to diminish.

"Welcome, Monsieur Merrick," Fabian said, with a hint of amusement. He wore an odiously smug grin. "He will see you in the conservatory immediately. You would be wise not to keep him waiting."

Merrick stepped toward him so their faces were just inches apart. He wasn't much taller than Fabian, but at least a hundred pounds heavier — all of it muscle. Fabian took a half step back, suddenly wary. Merrick scrutinised him in silence for several seconds before speaking.

"You look like someone I once killed," he said.

Fabian's face paled, but Merrick had already turned

and strode away.

The conservatory would have made a city's botanic gardens proud. Almost a quarter of a kilometre long, it was built on two levels, with long, curving walkways suspended fifteen feet above the ground, where its owner could enjoy the upper canopy of the many exotic species of plants that grew there.

Merrick hated the place. It was too hot, and unbearably humid. He was certain that his discomfort was the main reason his employer often insisted on meeting there.

He pushed through the double set of doors which led inside, and looked down the long central pathway towards the rear, where the enormous glass-encased space adjoined one wing of the mansion behind. There was a desk set up there for occasional use, and Merrick frowned again as he saw that it was occupied.

The man sitting at the desk waited in perfect silence as Merrick began walking towards him. He enjoyed making the killer come here, and traverse the entire length of his conservatory in the heat. It served as a reminder for Merrick of who he worked for.

The man's name was Mikkel Balder Anfruns, but the newspapers in Denmark called him *Ørnen*: The Eagle.

They publicly said it was because of the stratospheric heights of success he had soared to, but it was impossible to ignore the prominent hook of his nose, and his sharp, cunning eyes. He secretly enjoyed the moniker, though he would never give anyone the satisfaction of admitting it.

He had been the first of two children born to an accountant and his librarian wife in the town of Holstebro, on the Jutland peninsula in western Denmark. His father found work balancing the books of a local manufacturer of heavy mining equipment, forming a relationship with the founder which was to last for the lifetime of the company. Anfruns's father hired his own wife to help with business administration, which she enjoyed far more than her work in the town library, and when the company's childless owner finally succumbed to emphysema, it was no particular surprise to anyone that the entire enterprise was jointly bequeathed to Peder and Agathe Anfruns.

Peder's role had long since changed to running the company's entire spectrum of business affairs by that point, and the post-war years were to prove very profitable.

As the company acquired others, mining equipment became military supplies, utility vehicles and defensive installations, and the young Mikkel was only too eager to follow in his now powerful and wealthy father's footsteps. When a heart attack claimed Peder's life some twenty years later, his son was already in full control of the company, which was expanding rapidly into scientific research, logistics and weaponry. Agathe followed her husband to the grave only ten months later, never having adjusted to the loss of the man she spent almost every hour of her life with.

Mikkel Anfruns still felt their loss, but he had never looked back.

His younger sister Vibeke was the black sheep of the family, never taking an interest in the business, and she was currently drifting around northern Europe as some sort of artist. He hadn't seen her in almost ten years, nor did he care to. He had more important things to concern himself with.

Anfruns was sixty-six years old, and his parents had been dead for two decades. The company, now called *Anfruns Industrial Technologies*, had interests in weaponry, precision manufacturing, aerospace, and cutting-edge research into dozens of fields including surveillance systems, nanomaterials, quantum computing, and applied particle physics. While most people had never even heard of the organisation, its reach was vast, employing tens of thousands of people all across Europe and beyond.

And then there was *Stille*.

A secret offshoot of the main business, its name meant *Silent*, and its existence was only known to the senior executive board of its parent company, and the security apparatus of various governments. Stille handled a lengthy series of black-budget projects for many of the countries of the European Union, and several outside. As far as those countries were concerned, it did not officially exist. Each of its facilities, which were spread across Europe and the Middle East, had its own cover

Chapter 3

identity. The majority of its employees had no idea who they actually worked for.

It was almost two years ago when Merrick first found himself at this estate, waiting to find out who had summoned him. He had previously been contracted on a short-term job to test a top secret mobile microwave emission weapon, on behalf of an Eastern European government. He believed he was working for an offshoot of their own military, albeit an unscrupulous one — which made sense, since he had been a mercenary for hire since the dissolution of the German Democratic Republic in 1990. He had many talents, and moral flexibility was perhaps the greatest of them.

The weapon had been tested in laboratory settings on sides of beef, a number of inorganic substances, and even to a limited extent on livestock and small primates. But a weapon designed for use against humans ultimately required human test subjects.

Merrick's remit was to deploy the weapon against the inmates of an isolated prison camp, as a false-flag operation in the guise of guerrilla freedom fighters in a troubled former Eastern Bloc territory. He completed the mission with aplomb, and was not troubled by the discovery that the so-called "active denial" weapon, which was intended to make enemy combatants retreat by creating a harmless sensation of burning on the top layer of skin, had in fact caused fourth degree burns to 100% of exposed areas, killing the entire population of the camp. Nor did he hesitate to deploy it against the guards, civilian staff, and kennels, in the spirit of rigorous scientific enquiry.

Anfruns made it a point to notice people in his organisation who could be useful in difficult situations. With black-budget projects for multiple governments, none of whom had the others' best interests at heart, difficult situations were the most common type.

So Merrick was brought into the fold, his true employer revealed, and he was tasked with security oversight of the organisation's largest enterprise to date: the clandestine scientific research project that Brussels called *Destiny*.

"Do you remember the first time I called you here, Kurt?" Anfruns asked, just as Merrick reached the desk.

Merrick's jaw clenched at the older man's continued insistence on using his first name, but he said nothing. He did indeed remember.

That was the day my own destiny changed, he thought, adjusting his weight and closing his hands into fists at his side, settling in for however long this was going to take. He remembered the entire conversation, even though twenty-two months had passed since then.

He had learned what Destiny meant, and why the European Council, the European Defence Agency, and NATO were willing to throw billions of Euros into it. At first he had assumed it must be a weapon, but Anfruns had set him straight.

It was unimaginably worse.

Chapter 3

"I remember," he replied, and Anfruns nodded thoughtfully.

"And so you understand very well what's at stake. Not just for my company, but for the citizens of this country, and yours, and many others besides."

Merrick said nothing, and Anfruns only continued to look at him for several long moments.

"You understand," Anfruns continued at last, "and yet you jeopardise this project with your incompetence."

A vein pulsed on Merrick's forehead. His knuckles were white.

"The security matter has been dealt with, and Dr. Taylor will be found," he replied.

Anfruns's eyes narrowed. "Taylor would be a great loss to the project," he said. "You, however—"

You would be surprised, old man, Merrick thought, keeping his voice calm with great effort. "He *will* be found."

"—could be replaced without trouble," Anfruns continued, as if Merrick hadn't spoken. "You, and your... attack dogs too. And it is I who holds your leash. Need I remind you?"

Merrick knew very well what he meant. Anfruns held in his possession video evidence of what Merrick had done with the microwave weapon. One of the squad members, unbeknownst to Merrick, had been put in place to secretly record everything that took place.

Anfruns had already made it clear that, in the event of any disobedience or failure during the course of the Destiny project, both Interpol and — more troublingly

— the internal security forces of the country in question would be given the entire dossier. Merrick would become a hunted man overnight. Doubtless the same would happen if Anfruns himself were to disappear.

"You do not," Merrick replied, his voice quieter now. He saw one of Anfruns's eyebrows twitch, and he knew the older man was wondering if his change in tone was a note of submission. Let him think whatever he wanted.

There was silence for a moment, before Anfruns spoke again. "Taylor knows everything about our work."

He knows everything that you *know*, Merrick thought. *Which is not the same thing.*

"Any release of information would be very dangerous," Anfruns continued. "There is no room for failure."

"No-one would believe him," Merrick said, and Anfruns abruptly slammed a fist against the smooth mahogany surface of the desk.

"Dr. Taylor is a respected scientist," he barked. "There are those who *would* listen, Kurt, and then ask questions."

Anfruns pushed back his chair and stood up. He was twenty years older than Merrick and slender in comparison, but a lifetime of power and influence sat well on him. He stood ramrod straight, his suit cost more than most family cars, and his eyes were bright with intelligence and unquestioned authority.

Chapter 3

The Eagle indeed, Merrick thought. He yearned to pull his pistol from its holster, but that was for another day.

"Find him and bring him back," Anfruns said, his voice even and cold. It was his boardroom voice; the one that nobody dared challenge. "Or it will be you who must run."

Merrick held his gaze for three measured breaths, and then simply nodded.

Anfruns briefly looked him up and down in unmasked disdain, then he turned and walked towards the doors that led from the conservatory into his mansion.

"Sometimes I don't know why I hired you, Kurt," Anfruns called back in parting, as he grasped one of the ornate handles and pulled it towards him. He did not look around.

"There is a great deal you don't know," Merrick said under his breath, but Anfruns was already gone.

Chapter 4

Merrick was pulled from his recollection by the van slowing to a halt. The side door opened, and Drost climbed in again. He had been gone for less than three minutes.

"Well?" Merrick said impatiently, but Drost shook his head.

"Gone. He went out through the back. There was no sign of him." The soldier immediately looked away as Merrick closed his eyes.

Finn pulled the vehicle smoothly away from the curb and resumed following the other man who had left the cafe.

"Then you should hope his companion will be more helpful," Merrick said, his quiet voice loaded with threat.

He looked out ahead, and saw the man in question. He had turned the corner of the street, and was walking uphill towards the city centre. His pace was unhurried, and he had no idea he was being followed.

Aldridge walked slowly up the hill, lost in thought. There had been no sign of Taylor when he left the cafe, which wasn't surprising, but the genuine terror of the old man was troubling.

The envelope and its contents were tucked inside Aldridge's jacket, forgotten for the moment. The rain had slackened off, but grey clouds remained overhead.

First things first, he thought. *Try to get some more facts.*

But how? Taylor made it clear that contacting the authorities wasn't an option, and there was little else that Aldridge could enquire about. He could try to get in touch with Julie, and show her the ID card, but he had nothing concrete to tell her. He wasn't willing to cross that particular bridge yet, not without a lot more information.

He had the address of the hostel, but Taylor had told him not to go there, and it seemed unlikely that the old man would even be there himself at the moment, given his paranoia about being hunted. And if what he said was true, discretion was clearly in order.

Aldridge frowned. There wasn't a lot more he could practically do before Taylor gave him some new information to work with. He stopped at the junction of Great King Street, and glanced around to check for traffic before crossing.

He saw the black minivan crawling slowly up the hill,

Chapter 4

only about thirty feet away.

His pulse skyrocketed, but he forced himself to turn his head away and continue walking. His feet felt suddenly heavy, and he had an odd pins-and-needles sensation creeping across his scalp.

He remembered reading somewhere that one of the maxims of espionage was that there's no such thing as a coincidence. If you see the same person twice, they're probably following you. Three times, and it's definite.

Or the same vehicle, his mind added, and he quickened his pace without being consciously aware of it. He drew near the next intersection, forcing himself not to look back, then he noticed a removal truck blocking most of the lane in the adjoining street.

They won't be able to follow me along there.

The primitive part of his brain that was focused on survival needed no further prompting.

He drew level with the intersection, and then abruptly turned to the left and ran.

Tepel's eyes narrowed as he watched their quarry walk slightly faster up the hill towards another intersection. "I think he recognised us," he said, turning to glance with disgust at Finn. "I told you to stay back."

"There's fucking traffic," the Irishman spat, clearly annoyed with himself nonetheless. His large fingers gripped the wheel even tighter. Tepel enjoyed taunting him, and Finn had decided that one of these times, if he could get away with it, he was going to kill the bastard.

Finn had spent a number of years in Portlaoise Prison in Ireland (more than one stretch, even), and he could snap a man's neck as easily as he could start an engine.

Still, he'd have to be careful. He had a bloody good thing going here with Merrick, and he loved his work. Merrick was a nutter — a dangerous one, and there was something damned creepy about him — but he had plenty of cash and resources, and someone else was pulling the strings. Finn had a feeling that Merrick wouldn't take too kindly to losing a member of his team, even a prick like Tepel. He also had a distinct sense that losing his job would be the least of his worries if Merrick found out he'd been the one responsible.

There were always ways, though. Accidents happened all the time, especially in this line of work. Tepel was going to find that out sometime. The thought calmed Finn down a bit, and he had just begun to smile when his train of thought was interrupted.

"I told you he saw us," Tepel said, as the man they were following suddenly ran down a side street that was blocked by a removal truck. Finn stood on the brakes, bringing the minivan to a sudden halt just before the intersection.

"Tepel and Aranega, apprehend him," Merrick ordered, his voice as still and cold as a lake in winter, and the two men immediately leapt from the minivan and ran to the intersection, then down the street the man had taken.

"Now find a way around," Merrick said to Finn, sit-

Chapter 4

ting back in his seat and drawing a pistol from his shoulder holster. His expression was unreadable.

Aldridge ran.

His loafers slapped noisily on the damp concrete slabs of the pavement, the sound echoing off the sandstone fronts of old townhouses that were now business premises. A few faces peered from office windows in mild annoyance, but quickly lost interest after he passed by.

He made it to the far end of the street, and paused to catch his breath at a corner which turned up a steep hill towards the city centre. He was breathing loudly, and he rested his palm against the wall to steady himself. *I should really start using that exercise bike again*, he thought.

Suddenly there was a noise, and a puff of brick dust blew out of a small hole in the wall only inches above his fingers.

His brow creased with puzzlement for a moment before his brain reluctantly suggested the explanation.

Was that... a bullet?

As incredible as it was to imagine the idea of gunshots in Edinburgh, he spun around to see two black-clad military-looking types rapidly closing on him, and one did indeed have a handgun drawn.

Fuck, he thought, instinctively ducking down slightly as he threw himself around the corner and ran up the hill, his breathlessness forgotten.

* * *

"Ty chuju!" cursed Tepel under his breath, seeing that Aldridge had taken the uphill path despite the carefully-placed shot to try to make him run in the opposite direction.

Uphill led towards the busy primary commerce hubs of George Street, Princes Street, and eventually the Royal Mile. There would be thousands of people, and no doubt a discreet but regular police presence. There was also no shortage of places where someone could blend into a crowd or duck into a store and disappear.

"Put the gun away, *cabron*," Aranega said with disdain. "Merrick wants him alive."

Tepel gave him an ugly look, but holstered his pistol as they both ran towards the corner. There were other ways to bring a man down.

Aldridge sprinted towards a major intersection, frantically looking around for any patrolling police officers or vehicles.

Never around when you need them, he thought, and part of him was surprised at his own fatalistic attitude. It wasn't exactly an everyday occurrence to be pursued, much less actually shot at, yet he felt a strange exhilaration coupled with a sense of unreality.

He reached the junction and felt relief wash over him. There were at least fifty people within sight, including several groups of tourists. He looked back down the hill and his momentary surge of hope vanished. The two black-clad soldier types were closing on him, though

Chapter 4

now only at a fast walk. One of them had his hand ominously concealed in a pocket.

Aldridge turned to face the road again. There were three lanes of traffic in front of him, and a four-way junction feeding buses, taxis, cars and bicycles in all directions. The crossing signs displayed a red standing figure, meaning Wait.

Easy for you to say, Aldridge thought, then he dashed out into the busy road.

A taxi slammed on its brakes as he ran in front of it, almost hitting him, and the frightened driver sent a choice stream of profanity in his direction.

Aldridge stopped in the middle of the road to allow a bus to sail past, and then hurried forward again, making it to the opposite side of the road after several tense seconds. He glanced back and saw that his pursuers were hesitating on the far side of the road, and one of them glanced warily at something further down the road. Aldridge followed his gaze and saw the reason: a police car.

"Police! Help me!" Aldridge shouted, waving his arms wildly and drawing surprised looks from several nearby pedestrians. He took a step out into the road, still shouting and waving, but his voice was almost lost against the sound of several buses queuing for a stop along the next block. He felt his stomach turn over as the police cruiser whipped past him without the young WPC driver giving him so much as a glance.

This is what happens when the Tories are in power, he

thought, before seeing the two very serious-looking men across the street step out into the road with renewed confidence. One of them withdrew his hand from his jacket pocket, revealing a small black tube clenched in his fist. It looked like the kind of syringe device that people with severe allergies kept with them for emergencies. Aldridge doubted it contained epinephrine.

He turned and ran up the hill, knocking an American tourist to the ground, then he dashed down another side street.

Tepel tightly gripped the auto-injector as he and Aranega ran towards the narrow lane. The device contained a powerful combination of sedative and paralysing agent which was effective within two seconds of administration. He was looking forward to plunging the fine steel needle into their quarry's neck.

Aranega's earpiece buzzed into life. "Status?" barked Merrick's impatient voice, and Aranega winced at the loudness of it in his ear. "He's moving East along, uh-" he glanced at the street sign as they both ran past it, "Thistle Street." His thick accent rendered it as *Tissel*. "We will have him in minutes."

In the van, Merrick nodded in satisfaction. "See that you do," he replied, and the line clicked off.

Merrick glanced at his wrist screen's map, and tapped Finn on the shoulder. "Take the next right, then pull in. It's time to cut off this rabbit's escape."

* * *

Chapter 4

Aldridge's feet pounded against the cobblestones, throwing out sharp echoes which sounded too much like gunshots.

This might have been a bad idea, he thought. The street was deserted, featuring only low-windowed rear walls of shops, sealed loading bays, and locked entrances to upper-floor flats. Several even smaller alleyways split off from it, but some were no doubt dead ends — and in any case, his goal was to get back into the midst of people and further into the city centre, not to hide.

He could hear the muffled thud of his pursuers' boots not far behind, and he urged his aching legs to move even faster.

He was more than halfway down the narrow street now, and he could see a busy thoroughfare up ahead. He knew he was only a minute or so from George Street and its many upmarket department stores. He passed an alleyway without so much as a glance sideways, and was about to make a final desperate sprint for freedom when the black minivan screeched into view a couple of hundred metres ahead, blocking his exit.

Aldridge skidded to a halt, feeling his heart thundering in his chest.

The alley. No other choice.

He turned on his heels and ran back into the alley barely five seconds before Mr. Syringe, who he could now see had a vicious scar on his face, reached the corner with his unpleasant-looking associate.

The alley curved around to the right after only twenty

metres, then veered abruptly left. *Please don't be a dead end*, he thought frantically as he approached the second turn. He could hear an engine, which gave him some hope, but the acoustics in this maze of narrow stone- and brick-lined corridors could be confusing. He rounded the corner, and once again stopped dead in his tracks.

"What do you want with me?!" he shouted, clenching his fists in frustration.

He had come face to face with another van, this one an unremarkable plain white Transit with blacked-out windows. The side bay door was open, and standing beside it were two people. A woman in a tan leather jacket and dark blue jeans, her auburn hair efficiently pulled back into a short ponytail, and an enormous man with sandy-blonde hair, wearing fawn slacks and a button-down Oxford shirt.

Both had sleek but businesslike silenced handguns pointed right at him.

Chapter 5

Tepel rounded the corner to face a completely unexpected sight. The huge man standing near the van smoothly shifted aim to the centre of Tepel's chest, causing him to drop the auto-injector in surprise. The woman had Aranega covered too.

"Out for a fun run, sunshine?" the man asked in the unmistakeable twang of a Welsh accent, and Tepel narrowed his eyes. Their clothes were civilian, but the man certainly had a military bearing. Tepel could hear no approaching footsteps, so it was clear that Merrick had kept Drost and Finn with him in the van, expecting an easy capture. It would not be long before Merrick became impatient and then suspicious.

"I asked you a question," the large man said, taking a threatening step forward, but the woman raised her hand without looking at him.

"You," she said, to the man they had been chasing,

"get over here." Her accent was crisply English, and she was clearly in charge.

Their quarry looked uncertain for a moment, but then he sighed and began to walk forward slowly, his arms partly raised in surrender. After only a couple of metres, his foot caught on the raised edge of a cobblestone, and he stumbled.

Tepel and Aranega moved immediately, sprinting back around the corner. A fraction of a second before Aranega safely cleared the corner, a slash of pain tore across his earlobe, and he heard a small impact on the wall beside him.

He grimaced, feeling blood drip down his neck from the flesh wound to his ear, but there was no time to stop and inspect the injury. Merrick would not be pleased, but the situation had rapidly shifted out of their control.

The surprisingly resourceful little man had some friends, it seemed, but no matter. The next engagement would be on more balanced terms, and the man in the blue beret had a bullet waiting for him.

Aldridge silently cursed his clumsiness as the big man pulled him to his feet and propelled him towards the white van's open side door. "Listen, I don't know what —"

"No time for that, mate. Get in," the other man replied, and Aldridge saw that he must easily have been six foot four. He was still covering the corner with his pistol. The woman nodded to her companion, then she

Chapter 5

climbed into the van.

Aldridge hesitated for a moment, and was roughly shoved through the side door, almost falling to his knees inside the vehicle before scrambling onto a seat. The rear row of seats had been removed to make room for a makeshift work-surface bolted to the floor, which held several laptops and some devices he couldn't identify, all lashed down securely with velcro straps. There was another person there; an olive-skinned woman with large, dark eyes and black hair. She barely glanced at him.

The large man climbed in beside Aldridge and gripped an overhead grab-handle, keeping his gun pointed out the open door towards the corner. The van reversed rapidly, spun around, and accelerated away in the opposite direction with a squeal of its tyres. After a moment, the side door was pulled closed, and the large man holstered his weapon and flipped on a small overhead light.

"Whatever you're thinking, you have the wrong man—" Aldridge began, but the other man only grinned.

"Your pals out there must have made the same mistake," he replied, and Aldridge sighed.

"They're no friends of mine. My name is Neil Aldridge; I'm a physicist at the university," he replied. He was about to say something else when the woman in the leather jacket turned to face him. She spoke with a tone that was both serious and compassionate.

"Mr. Aldridge, don't be alarmed. You're safe now. I'm

Captain Jessica Greenwood, and we're taking you to a secure location."

Aldridge frowned, despite feeling some measure of relief. "You're... British Army? Or from the Security Service?"

"That'd be nice," muttered the vehicle's driver, who Aldridge had only just noticed now — a slender, dark-skinned man whose head was completely bald. He had a strong and familiar accent that Aldridge couldn't quite place. Greenwood gave the man an amused but warning glance.

"No," she replied, "we're attached to something called EUFOR."

Aldridge's eyebrows shot up. EUFOR was the blanket term for the European Union's rapid reaction forces, one of several military forces operated by the EU as part of its Common Security and Defence Policy. He had seen a documentary about Europe's military structure only a few months earlier, focusing on Bosnia.

He knew that the EU had a gendarmerie, a maritime force, and even a standing army called *Eurocorps*, with dedicated battlegroups and specialist teams supplied by various member nations. But he'd never heard of a covert deployment at home.

"*Brussels* sent you?" he asked, incredulously, feeling a sense of unreality beginning to set in that was only partly due to shock.

He could barely imagine a situation where Whitehall would approve the presence of an armed, multi-national

Chapter 5

European special forces team on UK soil, without oversight by the British Security or Secret Services — or even just the UK Armed Forces. Something very unusual indeed was going on.

Greenwood nodded. "We're here under the authority of the European Defence Agency."

"What if I made a quick phone call to the Home Office?" he asked, somewhat petulantly, drawing a surprised glance from the large man beside him.

"Both MI5 and SIS are fully aware of our presence," Greenwood replied tightly. "And neither of them want anyone *else* to become aware of it. We're on the same side, Mr. Aldridge, but you're not going to be making any unsupervised phone calls in the near future." She gave him one last appraising look, and then turned to once again face the road.

The van took two tight turns in quick succession, and at last Aldridge felt the tyres return to solid tarmac instead of bone-jarring cobblestones. The alley had connected with another, and eventually led them out into busy traffic heading south around St. Andrew Square.

"No sign of pursuit," the woman sitting behind him said in a lilting Spanish accent, and Aldridge finally felt the tension start to drain out of him, to be replaced by a very sudden and insistent headache.

"I should bloody well hope not," replied Greenwood without looking round, and the large man grinned. "Let's get back to field base," she said to the driver. "I think it's time I had a chat with our new friend."

The rangy man behind the wheel tipped his entirely shaved head in acknowledgement without speaking, and Aldridge felt the van pick up speed.

Just over twenty minutes later, Aldridge watched as the driver took the turn-off for Edinburgh Airport. The journey had been conducted in silence, with no-one else in the vehicle paying him much attention.

They passed through several roundabouts until they were almost at the terminal itself, then the driver took a left and followed a series of access roads past anonymous, industrial-looking buildings, before finally turning into a gravel-covered lane that ran behind what looked like an old warehouse. The faded signage on the side of the building said *AeroServ Aviation Ground Services - Hygiene Division*.

The van rolled up to a shuttered rear bay, and the driver pressed a button on a small remote control device that he pulled from his jacket pocket. After a couple of seconds, the tarnished, graffiti-covered corrugated shutter slid upwards.

There were no lights on inside the structure, and the driver didn't switch on the van's headlights before they moved forward into darkness. Once the van had cleared the entrance, he again used the remote control, and the shutter descended quietly, locking with an echoing clang when it reached the bottom of its track. At almost the same moment, the building's interior lights came on,

Chapter 5

revealing that the parking bay was surrounded by thick blackout curtains.

The large man beside him pulled the handle and slid the side door open, indicating that Aldridge should follow him with a jerk of his thumb. All five of the vehicle's occupants disembarked and stepped through the curtains into the main body of the building. Aldridge looked around, bewildered.

The entire space had been painted white, and was clearly only dilapidated on the outside. Fluorescent strip-lighting illuminated every inch of the place, and there were a number of utilitarian aluminium benches, desks, lockers, and equipment racks lining two of the walls. A bank of computer displays extended across a row of desks, with a single large screen mounted on the wall above them. A conference table and chairs stood near what looked like a makeshift kitchen area.

An ominous-looking large, black safe-like piece of equipment sat near the far back corner, beside a locked cage with a tarpaulin covering the upper two-thirds of it. Both were bolted to the wall. The floor had been recently swept clean, and the entire place was spotless. It looked as if it'd just sprung into existence that morning.

And I bet they could completely clean it out again in a matter of hours, too, Aldridge thought.

"Welcome to the clubhouse," the large man said jovially, clapping Aldridge on the shoulder, and leading him over to a nearby bench. "My name's Sergeant

Dowling, by the way, but mostly people call me Larry. Now empty your pockets, there's a good bloke."

Aldridge hesitated for only a moment before sighing and removing everything from his pockets. *It's not like they won't search me anyway*, he thought, but it was more than that. These people genuinely seemed to want to help him, and if they were indeed with EUFOR as Greenwood said, then they were presumably on the right side of the law.

The bench now held his mobile phone, wallet, house keys, some pocket change, a Moleskine notebook, a pen, a bus ticket, and the envelope Taylor had given him.

Dowling nodded, then gave an apologetic glance before patting down Aldridge's clothing, checking his pockets, and waving an electronic wand over him. Satisfied, he pointed to a chair at the conference table. "Have a seat over there. The Captain will be right with you."

"You'll want to bring the envelope over," Aldridge said, and Dowling raised one eyebrow before simply nodding.

A few minutes later, everyone was seated around the table. The man who drove the van had come over first, asking if Aldridge had been injured in any way, then checked his blood pressure and heart rhythm. Satisfied, he brought Aldridge a plastic cup filled with water, then simply sat down a few seats away as everyone else stowed various pieces of equipment before coming over to the table. Greenwood, the driver, and the olive-

Chapter 5

skinned woman with the Spanish accent now had laptops in front of them, and Greenwood was staring contemplatively at Aldridge. She was about to speak when he beat her to it.

"I want to thank you for getting me out of there," he said quietly, spreading his hands and glancing around to indicate that he meant the entire team. "Whoever those men were, I think my health and longevity weren't high on their agenda."

Several of the others glanced at him, including Dowling, but Greenwood only looked down at the surface of the desk for a moment before speaking.

"They were mercenaries, Mr. Aldridge," she replied. "Serious people. They're under the command of a very dangerous man."

Aldridge thought back to Taylor's muttered remark in the cafe only a short while before. "Someone called Merrick, by any chance?"

Greenwood raised an eyebrow. "So Dr. Taylor mentioned him to you."

You've done your homework, Aldridge thought. But it wasn't surprising, really — these people would have access to considerable resources across Europe, including governmental records and the sort of biographical details usually only available to law enforcement. Perhaps Merrick could still obtain that sort of information, but surely not as readily.

"I suppose you know just about everything there is to know about me already," he said.

Greenwood tilted her head. "Quite a bit, which is why we've been keeping an eye on you today — and it's a good thing we did. What we don't know, though, is what Taylor said to you this morning, and it's very important that you fill us in. His life is in danger, and apparently yours too."

Aldridge felt his heart drop into his stomach. It was already obvious that Taylor's paranoia this morning was well justified, but something about hearing the truth of it from a third party made the full reality of the situation finally hit him.

"Jesus," he said, looking down at the surface of the table. He absent-mindedly ran a hand through his hair.

There was silence for a moment before Greenwood spoke again. "Can you tell us what the two of you talked about? Every detail might be important, so don't leave anything out."

Aldridge nodded, and clasped his hands on the table. "Well," he began, choosing his words carefully, "I met with Peter this morning, at his request. He was squirrely; jumping at shadows. He said that he was in danger. He ran off when a black minivan drove by the cafe twice. He told me to be at a certain phone booth tonight. I think those men were watching him."

"You're right," Greenwood replied, glancing briefly at Dowling. "Did Dr. Taylor give you this envelope?" She tipped its contents out onto the table as Aldridge nodded in confirmation.

"Yes," he replied. "That's all there was. He didn't

Chapter 5

explain any of it, but he said he had a lot of documentation that he'd show me later."

Greenwood flipped over the University of Oxford business card, noting the address on the back, and then put it down again. Next she picked up the book of matches, and stared at the logo before turning it so that everyone else at the table could see it. "It's the insignia of Anfruns Industrial Technologies," she said.

Aldridge frowned for a moment as he tried to place the name, and then it came to him. "The Danish billionaire on all the in-flight magazines?"

Greenwood tilted her head to one side, as if to say *As good a description as any.* "Do you know why Merrick and his men were after you?" she asked, and Aldridge shook his head.

"I have no idea. The only thing I can think of is that they want that ID card back, or they think Peter already gave me whatever information he says he has."

"Perhaps," Greenwood replied, turning the matchbook over in her fingers. After a moment she put it down, picked up the ID card, and handed it to the man who had driven the van. He inserted it into a device attached to his laptop and began pressing keys, as Greenwood turned her attention to Aldridge once more.

"What *exactly* did Dr. Taylor tell you?" she asked, and Aldridge's brow creased as he tried to remember everything Taylor said.

"Well, something struck me as odd, actually," he replied. "Besides... *everything* he said, I mean. It's just that he started by asking about my ex."

"Wife?" Greenwood asked, and then raised an eyebrow at the momentary look of horror on Aldridge's face.

"God, no," he said. "Girlfriend. We broke up about a year ago. We haven't spoken since. She lives in London now, I think."

"And what did Taylor want with her?" Greenwood asked, leaning forward slightly.

"He didn't say. Just that he wanted to get in touch with her, or something."

Greenwood nodded, looking at him carefully. "You and Taylor are family," she said. "You grew up with him after your parents passed away. And he didn't know you'd broken up with this woman a year ago?"

Aldridge sighed, and then a chill ran up his spine. He remembered Taylor's words to him, just before the other man had ran.

Has anything happened to you recently? Anything unusual? Something you can't explain?

Then the image was in his mind again — another memory, this one from last year. Crystal twinkling in dim light, and the smell of alcohol. Then something that couldn't have happened.

He swallowed, and shifted in his chair. Greenwood frowned, and he hurried to fill the silence.

"The thing is, Peter and I haven't been in touch for a while. We parted on poor terms. I wanted to move back up here from Oxford, to focus on teaching. I think he saw it as a betrayal. That was two years ago. Before he called asking to meet me, we hadn't spoken since then."

"I see," Greenwood replied. "And this ex of yours?"

"Julie," he said. "Julie Hollett."

Now it was Dowling's turn to raise his eyebrows. "The one who writes for…"

"Yes," Aldridge said. "She's a journalist for *The Sentinel*. She's the one who broke the story about the leaked US surveillance files."

"I've seen her on the TV," Dowling said. "She's fierce. And pretty, mind you."

Greenwood and Aldridge both gave him a grave look, and he shrugged then folded his enormous arms. "Well, she is."

"*Anyway*," Aldridge said, "she moved back down south. I suppose that Peter must have wanted her to do something with the information he has. Maybe make it public."

Greenwood paled. "We can't allow that to happen under any circumstances."

Aldridge bristled. "Which side did you say you were on, again? Seems to me like you and this Merrick character might have the same goal after all."

"But not the same methods, Mr. Aldridge," Greenwood said testily, holding his gaze until he finally looked away. She waited a few more seconds before she continued in a softer tone.

"Did Taylor say anything else? You said he had more information for you."

Aldridge nodded.

"He… he said he'd been working on a secret project, along with others, and that some of his colleagues had been killed to keep it under wraps. He said his life was in imminent danger, and that he had a lot of documentation to show me later. He said he'd call the phone box at the corner of my street tonight at eight PM, and then again at eight-thirty if necessary."

"And?"

"And that was it," he replied. "That's when he got spooked, and ran off. So I paid the bill and left, then I noticed the same vehicle following me. They came after me on foot, and then I bumped into you, which was bloody lucky."

The barest trace of a grin appeared on Greenwood's face.

"Luck had nothing to do with it," she said. "We've been watching you since Taylor called you." She quickly held up her hand in a gesture of placation before he could protest. "It was for your own protection, and it probably saved your life today."

Aldridge's mouth, which had opened to angrily say something about breach of privacy, slowly closed. *I'll give you that one*, he thought.

A wave of nausea briefly chased through him at her casual confirmation that he had almost died, and then it was gone. "OK. Fine. So why is Peter so important? Why is a man like Mikkel Anfruns trying to kill a physicist?"

Chapter 5

"We're not convinced that Anfruns entirely sanctions Merrick's methods, but there's a lot we don't know," Greenwood replied. "We're hoping you can help us with that after you meet with Dr. Taylor again."

Greenwood searched Aldridge's face, looking for any sign that he was holding something back. It was difficult to separate the anxiety, shock, anger and indignation from anything else that might have been there. *Alright, Aldridge, that'll have to do for now*, she thought.

"So what's this all about?" Aldridge asked, leaning forward in his seat. "What's this secret project? Why is it important enough to kill for?"

Greenwood glanced down at her hands, now clasped on the table in front of her, as if she hadn't heard him.

"Listen, I was shot at today. In Edinburgh!" Aldridge said, his voice rising. "You might call that Wednesday morning, but I call it above and fucking beyond. I'm a lecturer, for Christ's sake." He took a shuddering breath, and then his eyes narrowed. "I've told you what happened, and I'm grateful you got me out of there, but now you have to give me something to help me make sense of all this. Or just drop me off at the airport up the road, and I can have my next chat with the police."

Greenwood met his gaze again, but her expression was compassionate rather than the annoyance he expected.

"I do sympathise," she said, offering a small smile, "but you have to understand that there are matters of international security involved. I'm not at liberty to fully answer your questions, and the fact that you're already threatening to talk to local law enforcement doesn't exactly put me at ease."

She took a deep breath before continuing, with a look of mild distaste. "In fact, I have to inform you that you're expressly prohibited from disclosing any information about anything related to Dr. Taylor, what he said to you, the materials he gave you, this morning's events, my team, the discussion we're having now, or this location. To anyone, in any form, without limit of time. As a British citizen, the relevant legislation is the Official Secrets Act, under which you're now bound. I can have someone from the UK Home Office provide verification of that fact and my own authority whenever you'd like."

Aldridge blinked, and then slowly sat back in his chair. He felt as if he'd been punched in the gut.

"Having said all that," Greenwood continued, her voice harder now, "there are a few things I *am* willing to tell you. Dr. Taylor was telling the truth when he said that several of his colleagues are now dead."

"At the hands of those men I met earlier?" Aldridge asked, and she tilted her head to one side.

"Amongst others. The two you saw are part of a team, under the command of Kurt Merrick. He's been on our watch list, and those of Europol and Interpol, for quite some time. Taylor and the other scientists were all working on a top secret project of enormous security significance for Europe."

Chapter 5

Aldridge frowned and glanced quickly around the table. He felt his stomach turn over again. "Wait, are you saying—" he began, then paused to get his thoughts in order. "The project, whatever it is, was *for* the European Defence Agency?"

"Yes," Greenwood replied, "but don't get ahead of yourself. Anfruns's black-budget organisation was tasked with control of the project, and many leading specialists in energy research and related fields were brought on board to help. That's where Dr. Taylor comes in."

"So are we talking about *state-sanctioned* killings here? You said Merrick was employed by Anfruns on behalf of the EU!" Aldridge asked, glancing around the table in agitation.

"Don't be daft," Dowling spat, startling Aldridge. The big man cracked his knuckles. "What do you think *we're* doing here?"

Aldridge opened his mouth to respond but Greenwood silenced them both with a look.

"Merrick is a wild card," she said. "We know he's worked for Anfruns previously, in a less-than-legal capacity, but you have to understand the nature of the projects that Anfruns's organisation runs. They're black on black, with a budget that would show just how much of a joke Brussels's austerity measures really are. I'm not going to discuss them with you, but I'm quite sure you can imagine some of the areas of interest."

"I'm *imagining* weapons research, surveillance and

communications technology, and exotic new military vehicles," Aldridge muttered dryly, drawing an amused glance from a couple of other team members at the table.

"You don't know the half of it, I assure you," Greenwood replied. "It's advantageous for both Brussels and for Anfruns's staff to preserve a certain… separation. A need-to-know basis, for both sides." She was looking down at her hands again.

Aldridge blinked, trying to process the information.

You're telling me that Anfruns has carte blanche to do what he likes as long as the work is completed, he thought, and he felt his stomach lurch again.

"The end justifies the means, is that it?" he asked in a quiet voice, suddenly very tired, and Greenwood sighed.

"I'm not any happier about it than you are," she replied, "and there *are* limits. That's why we're here."

Aldridge nodded. "Because killing scientists is a bit beyond the project's remit."

"It's more than that. On the surface, the project is continuing as planned, but the flow of information has slowed to a trickle. Status reports are perfunctory and infrequent. Despite assurances, Brussels is worried. So we were called in several months ago."

The EU is spying on its own project, Aldridge thought. *The newspapers would have a field day with this.*

"You put someone inside," he said. It wasn't a question, but Greenwood bristled anyway.

Chapter 5

"Our sources of information aren't any of your bloody business," she snapped, and now it was Aldridge's turn to be placating; he just shrugged. She paused for several seconds before bitterly confirming his suspicions. "The source was killed while trying to escape."

There was silence around the table, and Aldridge could sense the anger in Greenwood.

"I'm sorry," he said quietly. "I take it... you're certain that he's not just been locked away somewhere? One of the men chasing me had a syringe of some kind. I think they wanted me alive, at least for a while."

She glanced at the shaven-headed man, who cleared his throat before speaking. His English was perfect, but his accent was Dutch. "He had a transponder so we could track his movements; it was inserted into a dental crown. We retrieved it, alongside bone fragments, from an industrial incinerator on the premises of one of Anfruns's labs."

Chapter 6

"My god," Aldridge said, his voice quiet, and Dowling again cracked his knuckles.

"The man had a wife," Greenwood said, "and she's now a widow. As far as she'll ever know, her husband died in an unfortunate car accident while driving from the airport to a consultation on enhanced medical imaging technologies. The car skidded on black ice, went through the guard rail, and down an embankment into a forest. It caught fire and the body was badly burned."

"They even got his height and weight right," the raven-haired woman at the other end of the table said, and Aldridge looked around with surprise. She had barely spoken before, and her dark eyes were intense. "Another widow out there somewhere, I think."

Somebody — Anfruns, presumably — obviously wanted to keep this project shielded from outsiders, even his Brussels paymasters, and he had some very serious people to help him do that.

"So Anfruns has decided to take the project fully private, at any cost," Aldridge said. "Brussels is being shut out. Can he do that?"

"Yes, he can," Greenwood replied, clearly irritated at the fact. "He's enormously wealthy and powerful, he has connections to the military in dozens of countries, and this is the most classified project in the history of any EU member state. They already have the data, the equipment and the personnel, and the work *must* continue. The only recourse Brussels has at this point is beat him to the punch, and to do *that* we need to know what Anfruns has discovered. We need to know why he suddenly decided to wrest control of the project away from the Defence Agency."

Aldridge nodded. "And you're hoping that Taylor can tell you."

"We're hoping so *very much*, Mr. Aldridge. We've been keeping track of Merrick and his team as best we can, and we were intrigued to see a flight plan filed to take them to a private airfield outside London four days ago. We had no idea Taylor had managed to escape the facility. We believe that Merrick was tailing him to try to discover if he was passing information to someone outside the project."

"Like me, for example," Aldridge said, and Greenwood nodded.

"We were at least ahead of Merrick on that aspect. We had a standing alert on any mention of Taylor's name,

Chapter 6

and ECHELON pinpointed his location as soon as he left his voicemail message for you. We were very surprised to find he wasn't still in Denmark, where the project is currently based."

Big brother is listening, Aldridge thought. "Didn't I read somewhere that you need sixty seconds to trace calls? Taylor's message wasn't anything like that long."

"That's a convenient piece of fiction," she replied, "and entirely beside the point. The real issue is that it's now a race. Merrick is aware of us, even if he doesn't know who we are yet, and Anfruns has powerful friends. We don't have much time to find Dr. Taylor."

"I'll do everything I can to help you," Aldridge said, unclasping his hands and laying them flat on the table's smooth metal surface, "but since you brought it up, there's something I don't quite understand. Who exactly *are* you people? I don't remember seeing any mention of this kind of thing on EUFOR's charter."

"We're a covert group," Greenwood replied, "and I said we were *attached* to EUFOR, not part of it. You should consider this information to also be covered under the Act." She paused for a moment, looking around at all of the other faces.

"We're an elite surveillance, infiltration and combat force operating under the direct authority of the European Security Council. Our official title is the European Special Tactical Force, Group One, but anyone who knows that name will deny our existence."

Aldridge nodded slowly, considering her words. It

was no particular surprise that a unified covert special forces team existed within the EU. The Security Council fielded every other type of military unit, and the member states all had their own clandestine intelligence agencies and elite combat groups. It was bureaucratically impressive, but not exactly a shock.

Something about Greenwood's choice of words had piqued his curiosity, though. "You said it was your *official* title. But you don't officially exist. So what's the unofficial one?"

Dowling folded his arms again, looking down at his own biceps, and the woman with the Spanish accent glanced towards Aldridge. Greenwood's eyes flashed, and her gaze didn't waver when she answered.

"*KESTREL*," she said.

Aldridge couldn't help but grin. "How very European. Small but dangerous."

"And bloody *everywhere*," Dowling added in mock-weariness, prompting a quick, amused glance from the shaven-headed man.

"Alright," Greenwood said after a moment, "time for some introductions, I think. I believe you've already met Larry here. He's our specialist in weapons and explosives; things that go bang or boom. We also make him carry the heavy bags."

Dowling gave a brief salute, which Aldridge acknowledged with a bemused nod as Greenwood continued.

"Next we have Lieutenant Gerrit Goossens," she said,

Chapter 6

pointing to the man who had driven the van and later taken his pulse and blood pressure, "but don't call him Gerrit - only his mother does that. To us, he's Goose: our driver, pilot, electronics expert and field medic, amongst other things. You have him to thank for us being able to find you so quickly in that warren of alleys."

"Me and your mobile phone, anyway," Goose said in his lilting accent, with a smile.

Aldridge tipped his head towards the Dutchman in acknowledgement, and was amused to see him give a small bow from the waist. His bald head shone under the harsh lighting.

Greenwood gestured towards the raven-haired woman with the Spanish accent next.

"This is Corporal Alicia Ramos. You'll want to stay on her good side. If you can't, you'll want to stay at least three kilometres away from her *bad* side. She's the best sniper in the business, and our surveillance and infiltration specialist."

Aldridge swallowed audibly. "Pleasure to meet you, Corporal."

"The pleasure is mine, Mr. Aldridge," she said, with an amused glint in her eye, before returning her attention to Greenwood.

Quite the motley crew, Aldridge thought, clasping his hands in his lap, but he felt substantially better than he had an hour ago. He realised that he was starting to feel hungry, and that was usually a good sign.

A series of beeps sounded from the device that Taylor's ID card was plugged into, drawing Greenwood's attention. "What have we got?"

"It's a match for Osborne's card," the Dutchman replied, still looking at his laptop. "Same facility code and encryption, but it has a higher clearance level."

Greenwood nodded. The card wouldn't be of much use to them — Taylor's clearance would surely have been cancelled the moment he went missing — but it at least confirmed that Taylor had access to more sensitive information. *If we can find him before Merrick does, maybe he can share some of it with us.*

"OK," she said, "the clock is ticking. Merrick might have caught up with Taylor already, but let's assume that he hasn't. Alicia, I want you to take another run past the address on the back of Taylor's business card. See if anyone is home. If he's there, we'll extract him. Take Larry with you."

They both nodded.

"Aldridge, you're going to keep that appointment tonight at the phone box," she continued, "and Goose will try to tell us where Dr. Taylor is calling from. If we haven't picked him up beforehand, we'll find him and bring him in. And we'll take a quick look at your flat too, just in case you've had visitors."

"Sounds like a plan," Aldridge replied, pausing for a moment before saying what everyone in the room was thinking. "And if this Merrick character has got to him first?"

Greenwood gave him a hard look, but he could see

Chapter 6

that she shared his concern. Her fist was clenched on the tabletop.

"Then we have a big problem," she said.

Aldridge stood by the kitchen area, holding a rapidly cooling cup of coffee, watching Greenwood talking in hushed tones across the room with Dowling and Ramos. Goose was busily working on a laptop at a table running along the opposite side of the brightly-lit space.

It isn't relevant, Aldridge thought, shifting his weight from one foot to the other. He'd just omitted an inconsequential detail. That was all.

But then he heard Taylor's question again in his mind. *Has anything happened to you recently?*

It was... nothing, he thought. He didn't feel like making a fool of himself in front of these people, or wasting their time. There was enough going on already. Taylor was probably just worried about any signs of surveillance.

Anything unusual?

His stomach clenched.

"Nothing," he muttered. Dowling glanced over towards him, but Aldridge just nodded and then took a sip of his coffee before turning away.

He glanced at the various racks of equipment, but the purpose of most of it was unknown to him. He sighed, running his fingers through his hair.

Something you can't explain?

Again the same image in his mind: soft, amber light,

shining against crystal.

He closed his eyes and allowed the memory to surface.

It had been late February, and still cold. He was standing barefoot at the window of his darkened third-floor flat, staring out over shining wet rooftops bathed in the dirty orange glow of sodium streetlights.

The clock above the fireplace indicated that it was just after 9 PM, and he was smoking, which was never a good sign. He hadn't eaten dinner yet, and indeed he wouldn't actually have anything until the next morning. He *had*, however, drank three bottles of Eastern European beer.

The fucking duck, he thought. *Julie's glass duck.*

He knew very well it was in fact a swan, not a duck. He also knew very well (having been told on several occasions) that it was made of *crystal*, not glass. He once attempted to explain that crystal was really just glass with metal oxides instead of calcium, but that conversation hadn't ended well.

Just like most of them during those final few months.

In any case, the relevant point was that Julie had a glass duck, and she insisted on displaying it on the oak coffee table in Aldridge's living room — which was *their* living room at that point, and continued to be so for a further five weeks and four days after that particular rainy evening.

He supposed he'd been wondering where she was, as

Chapter 6

he looked out over the city. A cigarette hung from the corner of his mouth, bobbing irregularly. She'd been due home for dinner three hours earlier, but this wasn't the first time she'd mysteriously disappeared for several hours after work.

At this point, the question wasn't *Is she having an affair?* but rather *Does she — or do I — care about saving this relationship anyway?*

So, another evening spent standing in the dark, looking out. His stomach had stopped grumbling an hour earlier, as if sensing that it was a lost cause.

He rehearsed all the cutting things he could say when she finally arrived, knowing that he'd say none of them. She would walk in, and look at him with a disgust that he knew was actually mostly directed towards herself. She'd say something like "Don't even *start*," and then she'd go into the bedroom and close the door. And that would be it.

He'd sleep on the couch, and he'd stay there until she left for work the next morning, pretending to be asleep whenever she passed through the room. That's what would happen, and indeed that *was* the essential structure of the remainder of the evening as it played out — except that something else happened first.

It started innocuously, as most disasters do.

After one last drag, he turned away from the window to take the cigarette butt to the kitchen, where he would run it briefly under the cold tap before discarding it in the bin. There was no ashtray in the flat; Julie wouldn't have approved of that.

In the darkness, and after those three beers, he stumbled and his shin collided with the coffee table. The smouldering cigarette flew from his fingers, winking in the gloom like a firefly, and then he heard the sound. It was somehow both weighty and fragile; absolutely unmistakeable.

The duck, sitting on the coffee table and pushed to the edge to make room for newspapers and junk mail, had been knocked off balance.

Aldridge's breath whistled between his teeth as he glanced downwards. The duck rolled towards the edge in slow motion, its inscrutable gaze momentarily meeting his own. *How typical of you*, it said in Julie's voice, but he knew the words were only in his own mind. Even the rain outside the window seemed to have paused to watch the tragedy unfold. He saw himself diving alongside the coffee table before he had consciously decided to do it.

Maybe it won't fall off the edge, an uninterested-sounding part of his mind suggested, but he knew that it was nonsense. In situations like this, things always fell. And when they fell, they always shattered. As if in agreement with his assessment, the duck balanced for an exquisite fraction of a second on the very edge of the table, and then plunged off.

His knees connected painfully with the varnished hardwood floor only half a second before his elbows did, arms stretched out in front of him. His eyes closed

Chapter 6

automatically as his jaw clenched, and then, a tiny miracle: the cold, smooth feeling of glass between his palms; still falling along with his hands, but caught.

Barely a third of a second later, he realised that relief was inappropriate. Momentum still carried him downwards inexorably, and since he was already almost lying full out on the floor, he had no leverage to pull his hands upwards, lifting the ornament away from the floor. His eyes were still closed, but he clearly heard the bright, crisp, almost perversely cheerful crunch-tinkle of glass (*crystal*, his mind nagged) giving way.

His eyes clenched even more tightly shut as the previous cool solidity of the object in his hands changed subtly.

A tremor, a settling, a confusion of small, high-pitched sounds, and the beginnings of disintegration. It all took only a fraction of a second.

FUCK.

The thought was enormous; silent but deafening.

No. NO!

In that moment, the duck *was* their relationship — the perfect symbol of something once thought to be beautiful, then later increasingly pushed aside, until its fragility was forgotten and the inevitable breakage occurred.

His locked jaw had only just begun to relax again when Aldridge felt a sensation he'd never experienced before. It was purely in his mind, and it was almost like alternatively closing one eye and then the other, to see the subtly shifting perspective — but this time, more than the angle of perception was different. Though his eyes were still closed, he saw the scene in front of him perfectly, as if from the point of view of a bystander.

A man lying face-down on the floor, arms outstretched with his hands around two jagged chunks of what was once a glass duck. Many broken fragments lie on the floor below, each glowing like embers in the narrow strips of orange street-lighting from the nearby window.

Then there was a sense of blinking; of closing one eye and opening the other. A shift in perspective.

A man lying face-down on the floor, arms outstretched and bent upwards at the elbows, hands cupping a delicate crystal swan, suspended safely less than an inch from the wooden planks.

He felt a stab of utter remorse inside him, paired with confusion. There was suddenly a sense of urgency — a need to do something. Only moments remaining. The image in his mind, focused on the intact crystal swan which was now strangely beautiful, started to fade until he could again see the broken fragments of the other image showing through.

This time, the thought was quiet and undramatic.

No.

Another sense of blinking, then the image of the intact swan reasserted itself, and a sudden blast of wind seemed to strike his face — but he was aware that this, too, was only in his mind. No actual breeze or physical sensation, but nevertheless a strong sense of stepping briefly into a gale. It passed as quickly as it had begun,

Chapter 6

and he finally opened his eyes.

The duck — *swan*, his mind whispered — looked back at him from his outstretched hands. The smooth and elegant line of its neck curved down towards tucked crystal wings, and the barest notion of tail-feathers. It reflected a thousand points of orange light from the window, and it was perfectly intact.

It seems we have a secret, it said.

Part 2

Chapter 7

"*Idiots!*" Merrick shouted, slamming his fist onto the scarred surface of the desk.

Tepel tensed and lowered his gaze to the floor for a moment before looking up again. The scar on his face was itching unbearably, but scratching it now would be suicide.

Aranega and Drost stood nearby, and Drost was fingering the combat knife on his belt. Aranega's earlobe had a dressing on it, which was stained dark brown with dried blood. Finn sat a short distance away on a broken shipping crate. They were in the office area of a condemned warehouse, on the grounds of a closed down bottling plant about two miles outside the city to the East. Enormous seagulls cawed amongst the broken rafters, keeping their distance since Finn shot one of them earlier. Its mangled carcass lay a few feet away from where he sat, with a discernible boot-print in the pool of congealing blood around it.

Despite more than half an hour of searching street to street afterwards, they had failed to locate Taylor, and Merrick was deeply troubled by the news of the other man being either rescued or captured by an armed team in civilian clothing. Aranega and Tepel had barely managed to escape.

He began pacing across the faded, debris-strewn linoleum, which was worn through in many places to the bare concrete below. "You are certain they wore no insignia at all?" he said, glancing towards Tepel with narrowed eyes.

"None," Tepel grunted in reply, his black hair glinting greasily in the dull light. "But they were military."

"British?" Merrick asked, raising an eyebrow, and Tepel shrugged.

"The woman was English."

"Useless," Merrick spat, resuming his pacing. "It seems Dr. Taylor has far more friends than we knew about."

The situation was spiralling out of control. They'd been lucky to pick up Taylor's trail in London after Anfruns had used his influence in Denmark to determine how Taylor had left the country. They had quietly followed and observed him since then, with the hope of finding out his goal in escaping from the facility. Taylor stopped in Oxford for just over an hour, meeting no-one, and posted a small parcel — but he had been careful enough to use a Post Office counter instead of a

Chapter 7

mailbox. There was no way to retrieve the parcel, and the address label was never visible to binoculars.

Paranoid old fool, Merrick thought bitterly, but a part of him respected the scientist's caution. *It has kept you alive so far, but my patience is wearing thin.*

Taylor left the Post Office and went straight back to the railway station, boarding the next northbound train. It connected in Birmingham for a service to Edinburgh's Waverley Station. Aranega joined him on the journey, one carriage back, while the rest drove. They beat the train to its destination by almost an hour, giving them time to find this temporary base of operations, and send a coded status report to Anfruns.

They watched Taylor for two days after he arrived in Edinburgh. He spent most of his time in the ratty hostel, but he left on a handful of occasions to buy a newspaper and food, always to eat in his room. He also made a phone call from a public call box. Merrick assumed that Taylor was arranging to meet with a contact in the city, but they had been unable to confirm the theory because Taylor was clever enough to place a second call, to the national railway timetables information line, immediately afterwards, rendering the redial button in the phone box useless.

Cunning again, Merrick thought, kicking a rusty old can and sending it clattering across the floor.

They followed Taylor when he left the hostel the next morning, and when Merrick saw him sit down with the other man, it seemed like they were finally making progress. He had not anticipated Taylor finding another exit and disappearing, and things had quickly gone from bad to worse.

Who did Taylor meet? Who were the people who helped him? The worst case scenario was very possible: Taylor had contacted the authorities, and they were taking him seriously.

Merrick had taken precautions against that possibility, of course, by making it clear to the scientists at the project's innermost level that any disclosure of information would be very unpleasant for their families as well as themselves. But there were always a few with principles beyond self-preservation. Those ones were trouble, and Taylor was certainly among them. Merrick clenched his fist in frustration and turned to face his men.

"The man you were chasing; he didn't seem to know his rescuers?" he asked, looking in Tepel's direction, and the other man shook his head.

"No. He looked surprised. He shouted. I think he believed they were with us," Tepel replied. "The woman didn't call him by name."

Merrick nodded. "Then we must assume that these were Taylor's friends, not his own. And Taylor was definitely not with them?" Merrick glanced from Tepel to Aranega, and both shook their heads.

"Very well," Merrick continued. "We must assume that the Englishwoman and her associates have taken Taylor and his contact to safety. This places our operation in unacceptable jeopardy."

Chapter 7

He drew his pistol from the quick-draw holster he wore and disengaged the safety, letting the gun hang at his side.

Tepel visibly tensed, his heart rate skyrocketing. Aranega flexed his fingers over his knife sheath, knowing that he could easily kill Merrick with it from where he stood, but not quickly enough to avoid a bullet. Drost mentally recalled the layout of the room around him, choosing the optimal direction to dive for cover.

Only Finn's facial expression changed, as he cracked the usual sneering grin he wore when someone was about to die. He felt the same bubbling sense of wild excitement he'd experienced ever since he first took a human life at the age of eleven. It was all he could do not to laugh out loud.

Merrick looked down at the gun in his own hand. Each of his men had failed him today. Finn allowed their vehicle to be spotted. Drost hadn't been able to locate Taylor after he left the cafe. Tepel and Aranega failed to apprehend the other man. Rightfully, he should kill them all here and now — and he could do it.

Perhaps they would kill me first, he thought without any concern, *but not permanently*.

The ability was his, now; he had been given the gift of second chances. They had all seen it demonstrated by the various guests in the facility's sub-basement, but no-one on his team knew that Merrick himself also possessed the power. It was an enormous advantage, and to be kept secret until it could be most effectively used.

Not even Anfruns knew.

You wanted it all for yourself, Mikkel, he thought. *To remake the world, and bring you even more wealth and power. But your dreams are too small. This is the power of gods, and only for the strong.*

The certainty and purpose that drove him rose up once again, blazing within his chest.

When your project achieves its goal, I will come to see you one last time. And no power on Earth will stop me.

But that would be another day. For now, Anfruns was still in control, and had told him to provide regular updates on their progress, or lack of it. So be it.

"All of you, go to the hostel again. I doubt Dr. Taylor will return, but I see no other option at the moment. I will stay, and speak with our esteemed paymaster." He had spoken without raising his eyes from the gun.

Tepel's heart thudded in his chest. He glanced quickly at Aranega, who shrugged and then turned toward the door that led from the office area out onto the warehouse floor, where the minivan was parked.

"One other thing," Merrick said quietly, causing the others to freeze where they were. "The next man to fail me will die."

No-one moved for a several seconds, and then one by one they all walked off towards the vehicle, with Tepel glancing back uneasily.

Finn started the engine a few moments later, and as they swung around to drive out past the pulled-aside corrugated shutter that led to the road, Aranega glanced

Chapter 7

back through the panes of broken glass into the office.

Merrick stood there motionless, his gaze still fixed on his gun.

Mikkel Anfruns stared into the crystal whisky glass in his hand without really seeing it. The aroma of the 35-year-old single malt stung his nose pleasantly, but his mind was elsewhere. He stood at the large bay window of his mahogany-panelled study, looking out over the coast and across the dark waters to the horizon.

He had spent the better part of his life waiting for these times. He always knew he was meant for something much larger than himself; a greater fate than other men. He had enjoyed enormous success, of course, but those rewards meant little. Money had long since ceased to matter.

The power to reshape civilisation, he mused. That was what he sought — and now it was within his grasp.

Project Destiny was a gift that was always intended for him. At first, he had seen it simply as a chance to avert a terrible catastrophe, and to put the governments of Europe firmly in his debt at the same time. He had given over almost all of Stille's resources to it, with appropriate funding from the EU.

Then there was the discovery in France.

Even now, it was almost impossible to believe — and yet it was true. When Merrick's report came through, it was the beginning of a new existence for Anfruns. He immediately took steps to contain the knowledge, and draw the project under an even darker shroud of secrecy. And then it had happened again — and again.

The project's scope quickly expanded, and Brussels had no idea of its new purpose. Even the facility itself was off limits to all personnel from the European Defence Agency.

The building was a heavily guarded scientific installation hidden a few kilometres from the Nissum Fjord, a wildlife sanctuary near the western coast of Denmark and the North Sea. It was an unassuming single-storey building in the middle of a patch of snowy woodland, but it also extended four levels below the ground. The lowest level covered more than five times the area of the building's surface extent, and security was kept at maximum levels.

There were fourteen guests in the lowest level now, each one so much more than they appeared to be. A handful of others had already died, either due to Merrick's brutality or from stress or fright, but fourteen remained. They were the subject of multiple tests on a daily basis.

It was necessary. It was *all* necessary. Lesser men would have fallen to their knees upon learning the knowledge he now possessed, but Anfruns saw it for what it was: a calling. His higher purpose, revealed at last.

He took a sip of the amber liquid, allowing it to roll around his mouth for several seconds before swallowing. It burned slowly all the way down his

Chapter 7

throat, blooming in his chest like the bonfires of Midsummer.

The afternoon sky outside was covered in grey cloud, but the scene cheered him nonetheless. Let the millions of ordinary lives churn onward as they always had, unaware of what was coming. It would not be long now.

Everything is moving towards its inevitable conclusion, he thought. *Soon, I will remake the world.*

His reverie was interrupted by a soft chime from a hidden speaker. Anfruns walked over to the enormous desk which dominated the room, and pressed a brass button inlaid into the surface. "Yes?"

"I'm sorry to bother you, sir," came the voice of his personal secretary, Fabian, "but Monsieur Merrick is on the secure line."

"Thank you," Anfruns replied, pressing the button once more to mute the intercom. He sat down in the high-backed leather chair in front of the desk, setting the whisky glass down on a coaster, and entered an eight-digit code on a discreetly-placed keypad on the edge of the desk facing him. A panel of wood on the desk's surface silently sank down, and then slid out of sight. A touch-screen computer monitor rose on a hydraulic arm and angled itself to face him. A moment later, the display lit up.

Anfruns tapped the screen, and heard the call connect. "Progress?" he asked.

"We have a new problem," Merrick said, and Anfruns closed his eyes.

"Explain," he said.

Merrick told him about the events of that morning, including the unknown other team who had rescued Taylor's contact before he could be captured.

"I see," Anfruns said at last, without a trace of emotion. "I have been expecting this."

"Then you believe that these men — these people — were sent by Brussels?" Merrick asked.

"I do," replied Anfruns, "but I will attempt to verify it, discreetly. Where are your men now?"

"They are watching the hostel, in case he comes back."

"And they will continue to do so until he is found," Anfruns said, his voice still even and controlled but with a definite note of warning. "You will not return to the facility without first resolving this matter."

When he responded several moments later, Merrick's voice was tight with rage. *"I will command my men as I —"*

"Kurt," Anfruns interrupted, in a tone that was so intense yet gentle that it could almost be mistaken for being seductive, "you must understand the situation clearly. Destiny is my life's work. No-one and nothing can be allowed to stand in its way."

Anfruns leaned forwards. "That is why I entrusted you and your… animals with matters of security. I don't like your methods, and truthfully I don't like *you*, but you are a tool to be used nonetheless. Unless the day arrives when you are of no further use."

His voice deepened now. "My shadow falls over half

Chapter 7

the world. I deploy you with impunity. Do not forget whose hand holds your reins."

There was a long moment of silence. Anfruns pictured Merrick's clenched jaw and furious eyes, but he also knew that the killer feared him. As he should.

"*I have not forgotten,*" Merrick said at last. "*Dr. Taylor will be found.*"

"Find his contact also, and determine the identity of his companions if you can. Use whatever means necessary," Anfruns said. "You will contact me again tomorrow, and I will be impressed with your progress."

He tapped the screen again to terminate the call, without waiting for a reply.

A crease appeared on Anfruns's brow for a moment, then he picked up the glass of whisky once more, swirling the amber liquid around again and again.

Destiny must succeed, he thought. *No matter what the cost.*

The line went dead in Merrick's hand. The plastic handset creaked as he squeezed it in rage, then he abruptly threw it across the room. In one smooth motion, he drew his sidearm, aimed, and fired.

The phone exploded into a hundred pieces in mid-air, and the fragments scattered across the floor of the warehouse.

Chapter 8

Finn yawned for the third time in as many minutes. They were parked one block down from the hostel, and they'd been sitting there for almost two hours. Taylor had already recognised the minivan, so they ditched it in a supermarket car park and took a dark blue Renault Trafic in its place.

"He's not coming back," Drost muttered, for at least the tenth time, and Finn grinned.

"You'd better hope he does, or scarface here will end up like the fuckin' Joker," he sneered, and Tepel gave him a look filled with hatred.

"Your mother spent too much time on her back, and not enough teaching you manners," Tepel growled, unsheathing his combat knife and leaning forward toward the front driver's seat where Finn sat.

The Irishman turned around in his seat, grinning crazily, and he raised his hands ready to deflect the blow. "That must be why I'm so good between the sheets," he said, watching Tepel's hands carefully.

Aranega snorted a laugh, and then shook his head. They could both kill each other right here for all he cared.

Tepel's eyes flashed as he assessed where to strike. *Maybe you would laugh less with a scar on your face too*, he thought, and he was just about to lash out when Aranega's satellite phone emitted three sharp beeps.

Finn never took his eyes off Tepel, and it became clear after another few moments that there would be no attack to fend off. "Saved by the bell, eh pretty-boy?" he laughed, and Drost wondered if the man was actually insane.

Tepel slowly sat back and sheathed his dagger, still not looking away from Finn, as Aranega answered the phone.

"Yes? Yes, we are there. No sign of him." He listened for a moment, and nodded his head. "*Si*— yes, I understand."

Drost glanced out the window as he listened to the one-sided conversation. *Your threats don't help us, Merrick*, he thought. His gaze roamed aimlessly around the street. An elderly Japanese tourist couple were window-shopping at one of the city's many souvenir shops, perhaps considering buying a beach towel that could be folded into a facsimile of the kilt, Scotland's national dress. A girl who could barely have been 16 was navigating the cobblestone pavement with great care in her

Chapter 8

silver stiletto heels. A fat man in the uniform of a parcel courier, with at least two days' worth of stubble on his cheeks, was repeatedly pressing a doorbell with an air of weary contempt for everything around him.

Drost suddenly felt his pulse quicken. There was a minor junction between the block they were parked on and the one with the hostel's entrance, and there was a newsagent's kiosk on the corner. It had a series of free-standing carousels with postcards, cheap sunglasses (*Optimistic*, he thought) and of course the ubiquitous folding travel-umbrellas. Half obscured by the postcards stand, he saw a familiar red backpack beneath a mop of grey hair.

"Yes, we checked at the desk - he has not returned yet," Aranega said, now holding the handset slightly away from his ear as he listened.

"There he is!" Drost shouted, throwing his arm out in front of Aranega's face to point across the street. All eyes turned in the direction he was pointing, and everyone easily saw the distinctive backpack.

"Motherfucker," Finn said, pounding one fist into his open palm.

"He's here," Aranega said. "We see him. He's on the corner between us and the hostel."

Everyone in the vehicle could hear Merrick's voice over the line this time. *"Then GET him."*

Aranega didn't even bother to reply before ending the call and pocketing the phone. Tepel cracked his knuckles, and everyone except Finn bundled out onto the street.

Drost immediately ran between the lanes of traffic to the other side of the road, and began moving carefully but purposefully closer to the newsagent. Aranega and Tepel strode up the near side instead, until they reached the corner diagonally opposite Taylor. The big Renault pulled smoothly away and rolled up to the junction, waited for a car to pass, and then turned into the alley, coming to a stop a couple of car-lengths down on the left hand side.

Drost glanced at Finn as he drove past, and they exchanged a nod. He then turned to make eye-contact with the other two, and with one more brief glance at Taylor — who was peering up the street nervously at the hostel entrance, oblivious to them all — he reached up as if to scratch his head and then made a quick chopping gesture in the air.

Aranega and Tepel immediately ran out into the street, causing a car to slam on its brakes. Taylor glanced up, startled, and all the colour drained from his face as he saw the two men running directly towards him. He dashed diagonally across the front of the kiosk and made to cross the alley, only to see Drost standing on the nearest corner.

No! he thought, seeing that he was almost cornered. He had nowhere else to go but further into the alley, so he broke into a loping run along the north side, hoping to find an open doorway. He had almost passed a parked dark-blue van when he saw a blur of motion,

Chapter 8

then felt a large fist crunch into the side of his face.

He spun around as he fell, and the back of his head struck the concrete with a thud. He saw a brief flash of light even though his eyes were squeezed shut, and then everything went black.

Taylor gradually became aware of a tapping sound, coming from far away.

He couldn't see anything except vague shadows, and he couldn't move. He wondered if he might be dead. Then an intense pain in his head suddenly welled up, and he groaned.

He remembered the men chasing him in the street, and he felt his pulse stutter for a moment. His eyes snapped open, but the sudden brightness made his head swim and he squeezed them shut again. After a moment, he tried again, slowly.

"Good afternoon, Doctor," Merrick said.

So this is the end, Taylor thought, feeling a tear leak from the corner of one eye. "How nice to see you, *Hauptsturmführer*," he replied tonelessly.

Merrick's jaw tensed, and there was a glint of steel in his eyes. "Your tongue has a habit of causing trouble for you," he said, but Taylor only gave a tired old-man's laugh.

"I'm surprised you don't see the resemblance," Taylor replied. "Kidnapping innocents whose only crime is that they're different from you. Subjecting them to experimentation. Depriving them of their freedom." There was some fire in his eyes now, despite the pain and nausea from his head wound. "You're an attack dog, *Herr* Merrick, and you make me ill. You, and the man who holds your collar."

Aranega, Tepel and Drost stood nearby, and Finn was once again sitting on a crate. Drost glanced curiously at Merrick, and saw that he was completely relaxed.

"The world needs men such as me, Doctor," Merrick said thoughtfully. "You will find out that you, however, are disposable."

Taylor nodded in resignation, causing Merrick to frown slightly. "To you, certainly," the old man replied. "Get it over with, then. I have nothing to say."

"But you've already told us so much!" Merrick said brightly, and Taylor looked up in confusion. "Your visit to the Post Office in Oxford, for example."

They can't possibly know who that package was addressed to, Taylor thought. He allowed his shoulders to slump. "You… have it?" he asked, trying to sound dejected. He found that he didn't have to try very hard.

"We will soon, once you tell me where it was sent," Merrick said, a note of threat slipping into his voice. "To your friend from this morning, perhaps?"

Wrong, you bastard, Taylor thought, but he suppressed any reaction and simply shrugged.

Merrick smiled. "We shall see. Now, to business." He half-turned his head and nodded in the general direction of the others, and Drost walked forward holding a small black leather bag, with a zipper along the top. He

Chapter 8

stopped just in front of Merrick, knelt down and opened the bag.

"This is a medical kit," Merrick said, in an almost kindly tone that chilled Taylor's blood.

Drost reached into the bag and removed a sterile syringe packet and an ampoule of clear liquid. Taylor twitched and his face paled. There were two bright spots of colour on his cheeks, and his forehead looked instantly clammy.

"Do not worry, Doctor — not yet," Merrick said conversationally, "This is just a mild dose of adrenaline. It will ensure you're alert and paying full attention."

Drost prepared the syringe with only half of the ampoule's contents, ensured there were no trapped air bubbles, and injected the fluid into the side of Taylor's neck in one smooth motion.

Taylor felt the effects immediately. His headache increased and he felt his heart begin to beat harder in his chest, but he also felt strangely cheered, and the corners of his mouth curled into the barest hint of a dazed smile.

"Yes, it is a pleasant sensation, isn't it?" Merrick said, as if speaking to a child, but there was no warmth in his eyes. He walked over to a battered desk and picked up an oblong black box made of a carbon-reinforced polymer, about two square inches on the ends and five inches long, with a metal latch halfway down the side. Merrick brought the box back over to where Taylor sat tied to an office chair whose casters had been broken off, and unsnapped the latch.

"This is *not* a medical kit, I am sorry to say," Merrick said. He sounded disinterested, as if he was discussing the weather. Taylor's eyes were wide, and a drop of sweat ran down his neck.

Merrick reached into the box and removed a mostly cylindrical device that had a black resin hand-grip along its lower half, and a perforated metallic barrel and tapered nozzle at the upper end. There was a flat button recessed into the housing halfway up, which Merrick pressed and held for a moment.

Taylor heard the snap of an electrical spark, and then a blue-white flame burst from the device's nozzle, projecting almost an inch into the air. He clenched his fists and tried to wrench his arms free, but they were tied behind the chair with plastic pull-cords that cut viciously into his wrists. He let out a moan of terror.

"We use this device to remove certain barriers in our way," Merrick said. "In a way, it's a key. Today we will be unlocking *you*."

"I won't tell you," Taylor gasped, now shaking in the chair. His face was ashen, and his feet were tapping an irregular rhythm against the dirt-strewn concrete.

"I disagree," Merrick replied, operating a thumbwheel on the device which extended the reach of the flame and made it an even more vivid blue. He nodded, satisfied, and then he unhurriedly took the remaining three steps to Taylor's side.

The seagulls on the roof had quietened, as if listening — or afraid. The only sound was the moan of the wind

Chapter 8

through a dozen broken places in the corrugated metal panels.

Then the screams began.

Merrick stood at Aranega's shoulder as the other man rapidly typed on a laptop. After a moment, a document opened with a photo and assorted biographical information. The data had arrived from Anfruns moments ago.

"Is this the man who met Dr. Taylor?" Merrick asked, and Aranega nodded.

"That's him."

Merrick quickly read the information on the screen. "Neil Aldridge, physicist, University of Edinburgh," he said. "And the good doctor's nephew and former ward, I see."

It was all beginning to make sense. As a family member, Aldridge would not only be a trusted confidant, but he was a physicist just like Taylor himself. He had the background to understand whatever Taylor wanted to tell him about the project, and to make the authorities listen.

Nothing would ever reach the press, of course — the EU would make sure of that — but they would also find out about everything else that had come to light since Stille took the reins of Project Destiny.

That would be unacceptable, he thought. The European Defence Agency would demand an immediate explanation, and Destiny would be taken away from Anfruns's company. There was still too much they didn't know.

They needed more time.

Taylor had been surprisingly resilient during the interrogation. Merrick again felt a grudging respect for the old man. In the end, though, he had told them of his intent to call Aldridge at a payphone that evening, to arrange a further meeting.

And I imagine he won't be alone, he thought.

Taylor refused to tell them where he had sent the package he'd posted, but it stood to reason that he'd sent the stolen material on Destiny to the same man he intended to meet, as a backup in case he was intercepted first.

"Collect Mr. Aldridge's mail," Merrick said, turning his head to look at Finn and Drost, "and get the number of the payphone on the corner of his street." He held out a scrap of paper with an address in the Stockbridge area of the city written on it, and Drost walked over and took it. The two men left without another word.

Taylor had known nothing of the other armed group. It had been very clear that he was telling the truth.

"Well, Doctor," Merrick said, turning around to look across at the pitiful figure still tied to the chair, "I hope you're resting comfortably. Tonight you will make the call you promised, and you will invite Mr. Aldridge to come and meet you in a place where we will have some privacy. His friends will no doubt accompany him. After that, there will be no more distractions."

Taylor's eyes were closed, and his breathing was shallow. His white shirt, hanging open, was stained

Chapter 8

with blood in multiple places, the right side of his face was swollen, and there was an acrid smell of burnt hair and flesh coming from him. Four large gauze pads had been taped to his torso and neck. A faint reddish-purple patch was visible through each one. Merrick looked at him coldly for another moment, and then turned back to look at the laptop screen.

Taylor forced himself to keep his breathing shallow. The pain was still excruciating, but a numbing haze had begun to settle in around the edges of his mind. He knew that he was going to lose consciousness soon, adrenaline or not, and he welcomed it. He was feeling cold and hot at the same time. His chest felt like it had steel bars driven into it.

You didn't get everything, monster, he thought as he started to drift away. He remembered that Merrick had asked him about Aldridge's "friends", and who they were. Could Aldridge have gone to the authorities so soon? Surely he wouldn't have had enough time after leaving the cafe.

He was confused, but his mind could no longer hold onto the thought.

He resisted for one last moment, then everything flew apart like a flock of startled birds, and at last he allowed himself to fall into the sanctuary of unconsciousness.

Chapter 9

Greenwood wasn't happy.

Dowling and Ramos had gone to the hostel, but Taylor was nowhere to be found. They returned after two hours, leaving a card with the clerk at the front desk. Greenwood sent them back again later in the afternoon, but they had no luck then either. They were currently en route back from Aldridge's apartment, where they'd apparently found nothing of consequence.

Aldridge was sipping yet another cup of coffee, looking distractedly at the various pieces of equipment around the room. Goose had shooed him away from the large, black safe-like object earlier, but was now engrossed in something involving a computer and what seemed like a combination printer and laminator. A nearby side-table was littered with takeout containers from their makeshift dinner an hour earlier.

Greenwood's foot tapped rhythmically against the

floor as she stood at one end of the conference table, her chair pushed aside. She was looking at a series of printouts that seemed to show isolated areas of terrain, occasionally dotted with woodland. She also had a tablet computer that showed a series of smaller versions of those same areas, with shallow waveforms superimposed. Aldridge had no idea what any of it meant.

She glanced at her wristwatch — it was nearly 7 PM. Taylor's location had been unknown for almost eight hours now, and she didn't like that at all. She was becoming steadily more convinced that he'd been intercepted by Merrick's men, after their failure to grab Aldridge.

If that's true, then they probably already know who Aldridge is, but we're still a wildcard, she thought. *The question is, do we wait for them to make the next move, or do we force their hand?*

She sighed, absent-mindedly pushing a stray lock of hair back over her ear. There was really no decision to be made until after Taylor's promised phone call. If he did make the call, they could at least determine his location and try to decide whether he was being coerced. Regardless, they would attempt to extract him safely.

If he *didn't* call, things got more complicated. She'd have to place a 24-hour watch on the hostel, and hope for an ECHELON hit or some dumb luck. This game was too dangerous to rely on luck.

Time is running out for all of us, she thought.

The next half hour crawled by. Greenwood instructed

Chapter 9

Goose to give Aldridge an earpiece with a bone-conducting microphone and microwave transceiver so they could listen in to the call. He also wore an ultra-thin Kevlar-weave bulletproof vest under his shirt and blazer. If Merrick wanted to eliminate Aldridge right there in the phone box, there was very little they could practically do about it, but it didn't hurt to take the usual precautions. It was a calculated risk.

The drive to the street where Aldridge lived took only twenty minutes. They parked in a driveway around the corner from his flat, just off Comely Bank Place, and Dowling exited the van. He walked right past the phone box, thirty steps ahead of Aldridge, and strode purposefully down some stairs to a basement-level entrance of the next building, as if he lived there. In a dark jacket, navy jogging trousers and a black woollen cap, he became invisible the moment he stepped out of the murky orange pool of light from the nearest streetlamp.

Aldridge knew that Dowling had a futuristic-looking compact semi-automatic machine gun concealed in a cross-body holster within the jacket, and that if anyone decided to try a drive-by assault, Dowling would rip their vehicle to shreds. There was also a discreet device attached to his jacket that relayed live video and infrared to the van.

Goose was at the wheel, with a 9mm pistol in a quick-draw holster under his left arm. The van now bore the livery of a laundry company, and the license plates had been changed. Goose had driven it along farming backroads for twenty minutes, and its lower half was now filthy. Given the cover of darkness, it would deter casual recognition.

Ramos had got out of the van two blocks away, and by now she'd be in position on the roof of the church which looked directly across onto the junction and the phone box on the corner. In the worst case, if anyone did manage to take out Aldridge from street level, their life expectancy after that moment would be measured in mere seconds.

Greenwood wilfully ignored the tension in her chest. She sat in one of the rear seats of the van, with a laptop perched on her knees. The screen relayed the video feed from Dowling's body camera, and she could hear Aldridge breathing in her earpiece.

OK, Dr. Taylor, let's see if you're going to call.

"Aldridge, it's 7:58. Go to the phone," she said, and a moment later she saw him walk up the adjoining street on the video feed, and cross to the corner.

He went into the red phone box, pulled down the ragged telephone book, and pretended to look up a name. As instructed, he stretched it out as much as possible, not looking at his watch.

"It's 8PM," she said, keeping her voice calm and neutral. "Time to search your pockets for loose change."

Aldridge began to pat himself down, appearing to have forgotten where he kept his coins. It was an adequate performance, if a little theatrical, but then he wasn't trained for this sort of thing.

Chapter 9

8:01PM, she noted, feeling a vague sensation of nausea settling into her stomach. *Come on, Dr. Taylor. Now is a bad time to be late.*

Aldridge's image on the screen flinched in unison with Greenwood as the phone started to ring.

"Alright, everyone; let's pay attention. Aldridge, answer the phone," she said. A distant part of her mind was amused that she could clearly see him gulp on the video image.

Aldridge put the phone book back on its shelf, took a deep breath, and then picked up the receiver. "Hello?"

"*Neil, it's Peter,*" said the voice on the line. "*Thank you for following my instructions.*"

Several panels lit up on the laptop screen, and Greenwood quickly glanced at each of them. One showed a positive voiceprint match for Taylor. The other indicated a high probable stress level, but that wasn't unexpected given the circumstances.

"I wasn't sure you'd call," Aldridge said. He felt panicky. Greenwood had briefed him that it was possible Taylor would be under duress, and he was unsure what to say.

"Keep to the script, Aldridge," Greenwood's voice whispered in his earpiece. "Find out where he is, and ask to meet."

"*Well, I said I would,*" Taylor replied. "*And we didn't have a chance to fully discuss the situation earlier.*"

Aldridge thought he heard a brief, sharp intake of breath on the line, and his pulse accelerated.

"You were right to be worried," he said, trying to keep his tone as calm as possible. "I was chased by some very unpleasant men after I left the cafe."

This was a calculated gambit. It would have been unusual for Aldridge not to mention his frightening experience earlier in the day, and had Taylor indeed been abducted, his captors would be listening in to the call.

"I'm... terribly sorry to hear that," Taylor replied, and it sounded like the meant it. *"I trust you're unhurt?"*

"I'm fine," Aldridge said, "but my concern right now is for you. It's not safe for you to be out and about. We should meet somewhere tonight."

"I agree," Taylor replied. *"I don't dare return to my room. There's a multi-storey parking garage not far from Calton Hill. I'm on the ninth level, at the back. Please come as soon as you can."*

"Tell him you'll be there shortly," Greenwood instructed, and Aldridge nodded without being aware of it.

"Of course, I'll be there as soon as I can, Peter," Aldridge replied.

"Thank you," Taylor said, not sounding very relieved, *"and please come alone. I want to make that absolutely clear."*

"I understand. I'll be there soon," Aldridge said, and then he heard the line go dead. He hung up the phone.

"Alright, Aldridge, well done. Get out of the phone box then tie your shoelace," Greenwood said over his earpiece.

Chapter 9

Aldridge did as he was told, purposefully slowly. He waited for several long seconds, looping and re-looping the shoelace into a bow. There was no other movement on the street.

"Alright, come back to the van," Greenwood finally said, and he finished tying his shoe, stood up, and tried not to hurry too much.

Three minutes later, Ramos slid open the van's side door and got in. Dowling had already returned, and Goose pulled away immediately. Calton Hill was less than a mile's drive, directly across the city to the east.

"Voice stress was high, but it's hardly conclusive," Greenwood said, not looking up from the laptop. "The line wasn't being tapped or recorded either."

"There was no surveillance," Dowling added, and Ramos had already indicated she'd seen nothing from her high vantage point.

"It's a trap," Aldridge said flatly, and all eyes turned to him.

"What makes you so sure of that?" Greenwood asked, her eyes narrowing. Aldridge just shook his head.

"I know his voice," he said. "There was something strange about it. Something wrong. I just... know."

She looked at him for a long moment, and then nodded. "Fine. We're going in on the assumption that we'll face hostile resistance anyway," she said. "Goose, ETA?"

"About two minutes, Captain," he replied, glancing at the sat-nav display mounted in the centre of the dashboard.

"And you're ready for this, Mr. Aldridge?" she asked, raising a questioning eyebrow. He nodded, nervously patting the bulletproof vest under his shirt. Greenwood looked at him for a moment, then she nodded.

"Then let's see what Dr. Taylor is so eager to talk about."

Taylor shivered uncontrollably. Every movement brought jolts of pain through the three burn wounds on his chest, and another on the left side of his neck. Despite the cold, he felt feverish, and knew it wasn't a good sign.

He needed medical attention, but he knew he was unlikely to get it. In the best case, Merrick would take him back to the facility, and he'd be treated there. The alternative didn't bear thinking about.

He was leaning against a drab grey concrete pillar in the most remote corner of the top floor of a multi-level parking garage. The structure was vast, echoing and — on this level at least — deserted. The wind gusted mercilessly through the gaps in the outer wall every few seconds, and the drop to ground level outside was more than seventy feet. The garage was designed for several thousand cars, allowing easy pedestrian access to the main shopping areas in the centre of the city. The bays were tightly packed, and the one-way driving routes were garishly signposted. In the middle of each floor, ramps led up and down. This floor, however, had only one ramp, leading downwards. Fluorescent tubes lit

Chapter 9

most of the area, but several others buzzed, flickered or were dark. There were security cameras mounted regularly throughout the area, but Aranega had already taken care of them, attaching a small device to the trunk cable that looped a pre-recorded segment of video back through to the control room downstairs. They were unobserved.

On the rear wall of each floor there was a lobby area, lit by a security light. There was a door to a stairwell, and two elevators, only one of which was in service. A fire extinguisher was secured to the wall, and there was also a glass-encased trigger for the garage's sprinkler system. The door to the stairwell was wedged open against its retaining arm, and the fluorescent tube at the first landing level lay shattered on the corrugated metal floor.

Drost crouched on the fourth step, occasionally glancing up and around the door frame. He could see Taylor easily from this vantage point, and anyone who came up in the elevators would be facing away from him when they stepped out.

Almost diagonally opposite, sixty feet away, Tepel knelt in the shadows of another pillar. He could see his breath in front of him, and was glad of his combat fatigues and body armour. He held a Heckler and Koch G36 assault rifle, casually resting the magazine on his thigh. It was the A2 German Army variant, complete with short stock, aluminium hand-guard for heat dissipation, and Zeiss red dot sight. It was equipped with a

Navy-style pictographic trigger selector, and was set to continuous fire. It took 5.56 NATO rounds, and everyone on the team was very familiar with it. It was a weapon that excelled at brutal incapacitation but not always immediate death, just as Merrick preferred.

Aranega occupied a similar position in the third corner of the gloomy space, and Finn was two floors below on level seven, in the Renault. He was parked in a spot facing the central ramps, and he was crouched in the back of the van. The side door was open only slightly. In his hands he held a Russian GM-94 grenade launcher.

Merrick stood four metres behind Taylor, out of sight in the corner beside the wall. His 9mm pistol was still holstered, and he was smiling. They would be here any moment.

As if on cue, he heard the sound of an engine coming from below.

Chapter 10

"Everybody keep their eyes open," Greenwood said.

She skilfully manoeuvred the big Transit around the fourth level of the multi-storey's central ramp structure. Despite its mundane appearance, the van was equipped with bulletproof panels in the sides, rear, engine block and chassis, run-flat tyres, and half-inch thick bulletproof glass in the windows. Its position was tracked constantly.

All the same, this was risky. The top floor of the garage was just about the worst possible place for a rendezvous. Difficult to leave in a hurry, unpredictable cover, and only a couple of ways in or out. It wasn't a perfect kill box, but it was close. So Greenwood had taken precautions.

Aldridge was already on his way up in the working elevator. Ramos had again been dropped off before they entered the structure, and she would be in position within the next four minutes. Dowling was making his way carefully up the vehicle ramps on foot. Goose was monitoring everyone from his console in the rear of the van.

They reached the sixth level after only another twenty seconds, and she steered the van into a parking space that had a clear run back towards the ascending ramp.

"I think we're ready," Greenwood said into her microphone. "Aldridge, try to stay calm no matter what happens. Keep him talking, and anyone else that shows up. We're all here with you."

"There's a mirror in this lift, and I can only see myself," Aldridge muttered, clenching and unclenching his fists repeatedly. He felt a droplet of sweat run down his brow, and his breathing sounded very loud in the enclosed space.

"I know this isn't exactly your usual evening, and you're frightened," Greenwood replied, with tension in her voice. "That's a wise reaction. But we're professionals, and we have no intention of allowing anything to happen to you. We're listening and watching, and I'll give you further instructions as we go. Just exercise caution, and you'll be fine."

"Caution is my middle name," Aldridge replied. "Well, actually it's Cameron. But close enough."

Greenwood rolled her eyes, but she said nothing.

Aldridge flinched as the elevator pinged and slowed to a juddering halt. After a moment, the doors slid open, revealing the dark and patchily-lit concrete of level nine.

Chapter 10

I must be insane, he thought, taking a deep and uneven breath, and then he walked out. His footsteps sounded unsettlingly loud. *Note to self: wear trainers when next confronting possible squad of killers*, he thought, but there was nothing funny about this situation. He could taste the bitter, coppery tang of adrenaline in his throat.

There was a sudden flicker of movement in a distant corner, and he froze, his entire body radiating tension. His eyes searched the gloomy expanse, and then he saw Taylor. The old man was leaning against a pillar, and half-heartedly beckoning to him.

Aldridge glanced around, seeing no-one else, and then started to walk cautiously forward. He glanced back towards the elevator, noticing the open door to the stairwell, and felt a little better. He could at least make a run for it back down the stairs, if necessary.

"Nice and easy now," Greenwood said in his ear.

Easy for you to say, Aldridge thought. He instinctively didn't want to shout to Taylor, but he also wasn't keen to go all the way to the opposite side of the garage, far from the elevators and stairwell. He stopped about fifteen feet from the other man.

"Well, here I am," he said, swallowing nervously.

Taylor took a step forward out of the shadow of the pillar, and Aldridge noticed for the first time just how pale he looked. There was a bandage sticking out of his collar on one side.

"Peter...?" Aldridge asked, suddenly very aware of just how far it was back to the exit. "Are you alright?"

"I'm so sorry," Taylor replied in a whisper, and then Merrick stepped into view with his gun drawn.

"So we meet at last, Mr. Aldridge," Merrick said. In the chill of the evening air, his words were punctuated with a visible plume of breath.

"Don't provoke him," Greenwood whispered through the earpiece, then she switched the communications channel to brief the others.

Aldridge raised his hands slowly, palms out. "If this is a mugging, you can have my iPhone," he said, and Merrick gave the barest hint of an amused smile. It didn't reach his eyes.

"I think your attitude will soon change," he replied. "But let me be clear. You are here to tell me what you know about the good Doctor's work, and who you have been sharing information with. Your friends from this morning, in particular."

Greenwood could hear the entire exchange. "You don't know who we are," she coached him over the secure channel. "We dropped you off once we realised you knew nothing."

"I don't know who they were," Aldridge said. "They asked about Peter" — he nodded towards Taylor — "and why your men were chasing me. I told them I'd met him this morning, but had no idea who you were. That was it. They dropped me off."

Merrick looked at him for a long moment before he spoke. "I'm afraid I don't believe you, Mr. Aldridge," he said.

Chapter 10

We're running out of time, Greenwood thought, switching to Dowling's frequency. "We need to get up there, Larry."

After a moment, she heard two dull bumps. It was an acknowledgment signal that meant Dowling couldn't speak at the moment. He'd reached up and tapped the microphone twice to let her know he'd heard her message.

Damn it, she thought.

Merrick disabled the safety on his pistol with an ominous click.

"Shall we try again?"

Dowling lay fully flat on the cold concrete floor. He was underneath the rear of a battered old green Honda CR-V, looking across the end of two rows of vehicles toward the dark blue Renault Trafic that faced the ramps.

He'd noticed the side door was slightly open when he'd carefully checked the floor before leaving the cover of the ramp, and decided to circle back around to investigate. Sure enough, there was a big man inside, holding some kind of heavy weapon — possibly a grenade launcher. He was in a perfect position to provide either escape cover for Merrick's team above, or to destroy Greenwood's van if it appeared.

Dowling was holding an unusual-looking weapon. It was similar to a slimmed-down rifle, with a telescopic sight, an extended barrel, double-barred hollow stock and a grey cylinder protruding from the front of the body. Its body was a dark green colour, with a black trigger and grip. He had loaded an ominous-looking red-backed silver projectile into the housing, and was taking aim.

He could see now that the man inside was James Finn, an especially nasty piece of work. They'd been extensively briefed on Merrick's regular team, and Finn was the subject of special concern. The man was a psychopath, and had been incarcerated several times. He was especially fond of torturing animals, and humans when he got the chance. He liked to get up close and personal whenever possible.

Shame you won't be around for all the fun, Dowling thought, lining up the sight's crosshairs over the area where Finn's head periodically bobbed into view through the open door of the Trafic. *Come on now.*

The front of Finn's red hair caught the light as he leaned forward slightly, and Dowling squeezed the trigger. There was a sharp hissing sound, then Finn fell back inside the van.

Dowling was up and running diagonally towards the rear of the vehicle within a second, reloading the rifle and quickly unscrewing the barrel and stashing it in a belt loop. He stopped about eight feet short of the van, well to the side and out of range of any fire from within. There was a heavy thud and a clank from inside, and it rocked on its springs slightly.

Several seconds went by. Dowling was crouched low at the rear, now holding the rifle close-bodied. He stood

Chapter 10

up silently, and edged towards the still-open side door. There was no sound at all.

He took one measured breath, then quickly glanced through the gap, twisting himself back out of view immediately and dropping below the wheel line.

Gotcha, he thought. He had seen the soles of Finn's boots facing out towards him, and the man was lying awkwardly across two seats. The grenade launcher lay nearby, out of his reach.

Dowling stood up, waited for a beat, then put the rifle's barrel through the gap. The dart he'd fired lay on the floor. Finn had obviously managed to pull it from his neck, but it was far too late by that point. He'd be unconscious for at least an hour. Dowling carefully slid the door further open, and climbed inside.

Let's make that two hours, he thought, and put another dart in Finn's neck. It was risky, but he was a big man and he could probably take it. Besides, it was better than having him wake up too soon.

"Floor seven is clear," he said quietly, knowing his earpiece microphone would relay his voice as clearly as if he were standing next to Greenwood. "I've got their transport. They brought a nice grenade launcher for you, chief."

"I'll have to send a thank-you card," Greenwood replied. "Good work, Larry. We're coming up on foot to meet you."

"Acknowledged," Dowling replied, then he began a quick search of the Renault. Greenwood and Goose appeared at the side of the van within thirty seconds.

"Alright," Greenwood said, "let's make our way up."

Aldridge stared at the barrel of the pistol. His stomach churned ceaselessly, and he thought there was a very real possibility that he would vomit, or maybe faint. A part of his mind remarked on how small and harmless the black cylinder looked, but consciously he knew better. If Merrick pulled the trigger, he was dead.

"Please," he said, trying to sound reasonable and only succeeding in sounding frightened, "I honestly don't know anything about Peter's work. He never had a chance to tell me before he ran off. You must know that if you were watching us."

Merrick only looked at him. Aldridge was babbling, and clearly afraid. *But you still don't truly think that you will die tonight*, Merrick thought. *I will correct that misperception shortly.*

"I believe you," Merrick said, noting the other man's cautious look of relief. "About Dr. Taylor's work, at least. But I think you know more about your rescuers than you admit."

"OK, Aldridge, now tell him the cover story," Greenwood said via his earpiece. It was a move designed to buy just a little more time.

"Alright, alright," Aldridge said. "The truth is, they said they were from the Security Service."

Merrick's brow creased. "Your MI5? I think not. My men know fellow soldiers when they see them. The

Chapter 10

British SAS, perhaps, but not Intelligence."

"I wouldn't know anything about that," Aldridge replied, feeling a large drop of sweat run down his back. "That's just what they told me. I had no reason to doubt them."

"Perhaps, and perhaps not," Merrick replied, "but it seems we won't settle the matter here. We're going to take you on a trip, Mr. Aldridge. When we reach our destination, I will be asking you these questions again."

Greenwood's voice was quiet but firm in his ear. "When I say *DOWN*, you're going to faint. Drop to the floor and lie flat."

Aldridge's throat was dry. "I always like to call my mother before I travel," he said, and again Merrick almost smiled.

You certainly have spirit, he thought, lowering his pistol slightly. "Aranega," he said, in a voice barely louder than he'd been using a moment ago, and in Aldridge's peripheral vision a man suddenly materialised out of the darkness of another corner. He carried a compact machine gun, and his face was alert and devoid of any emotion.

Aldridge turned slightly to look at Aranega, recognising him as one of his pursuers earlier in the day. The other man — the one with the scar — was probably around here somewhere too.

"Take him to the vehicle," Merrick said, and Aranega nodded, gesturing with his gun back towards the elevators.

"Get ready," Greenwood whispered.

"I really don't feel so good," Aldridge said, and it was the truth. His heart was beating too fast, and he felt like his ears needed to pop. A pins-and-needles sensation was crawling across his chest and scalp.

Merrick grimaced with disgust and turned partly away, to look at Taylor. Aranega lifted his gun slightly, his face making it very clear that he had no time for weakness.

"Really, I think, I think I'm going to—" Aldridge said, in a shaky voice, stumbling slightly.

"*Down!*" Greenwood said in his ear.

Aldridge felt his heart flutter, and he didn't know whether it was panic or something else. His legs folded under him and he fell forwards. His knees collided painfully with the concrete, but the sensation was far away and unimportant. He was certain that any moment now he would feel bullets punching through his body.

He let himself topple forward from his knees, and his raised hands barely reduced the impact when his face met the ground. There was perfect silence for half a second.

Then an explosion ripped through the air.

Chapter 11

The sound was too loud. For a moment it seemed to bounce all around the parking garage, filling the entire space. Aldridge flinched on the ground, squeezing his eyes even more tightly shut.

"What the hell was that? Aldridge!" Greenwood's voice came over his earpiece, immediately followed by Dowling's.

"Bloody *fireworks*, chief," he said. "Looks like there's a show on outside."

Sure enough, they could all hear the tell-tale sound of more small explosions outside, and faint red and green light was visible through some of the openings in the concrete wall facing out onto the street below.

Talk about bad timing, Greenwood thought, her pulse racing. She cautiously lifted her head above the edge of the ramp, and saw Aldridge still lying face-down on the floor, with Merrick and one of his mercenaries standing nearby. Taylor was a few feet away, leaning heavily against a pillar.

Greenwood immediately recognised the advantage of the situation: the sound of the pyrotechnics outside would probably mask what was about to happen, at least for a few minutes. *So there's no time to waste.*

She made a small gesture with her right hand, which both Dowling and Goose saw and understood. A moment later, all three of them moved as one, lifting their weapons clear of the top edge of the ramp.

Then everything happened at once.

The gunfire seemed to come from every direction, echoing from a hundred hard surfaces. Aldridge's eyes were still closed, so he only heard Aranega's roar of pain and then felt a thud as the man crashed to the ground just a few metres away.

Greenwood's precision burst of three rounds had taken Aranega in the left shoulder, and she was certain that at least two had hit. Merrick immediately dived out of the way behind a pillar. It was several feet thick, and solid concrete. Any weapon capable of getting through it would also bring the roof down.

Barely a second after Aranega hit the floor, a rapid stream of continuous fire raked across the top edge of the ramp. Dowling, Goose and Greenwood were lying on the last section of the ramp, heads barely above the lip, and they ducked just in time.

"There's another one in the opposite corner," Dowling said, raising his voice to be heard while he switched his

Chapter 11

SIG MPX-K to full auto.

"Take him down," Greenwood replied, just as another boom echoed from the sky outside, accompanied by orange-yellow light.

Dowling waited a moment, then fired a few blind shots in the direction the gunfire had come from. There was no immediate return volley, so he edged up to take better aim. Almost immediately, several rounds from two other directions slammed into the concrete just inches from his head. Merrick and Drost had entered the fray.

"Bloody hell," Dowling cursed, sliding further back down the ramp. "We're pinned down on three sides, chief. They have someone back at the elevators."

"Our priority is extracting Taylor and Aldridge," Greenwood said through gritted teeth. "We can't do that with fire from all sides."

She turned to Goose. "Go down a level and try to come back up the stairwell. Keep your eyes open. Whoever's back there, we need them out of commission."

Goose nodded, and immediately returned down the ramp and then vanished from sight. Greenwood peeked over the upper edge of the ramp back towards the elevators, and ducked back down.

"He's probably on the stairs, Goose," she said. "Open doorway. Be careful."

"Understood," Goose replied. He moved stealthily towards the lobby on the level below, gun drawn, pressing himself against the wall beside the door that led to the stairwell. The door had a rectangular glass panel set into it, and he peered around the edge of it with one eye, for just a moment.

He saw combat boots on the upper section of the final stairway, and he reached carefully behind his back and retrieved a small black canister from his belt.

"One on the stairs," he said in a whisper. "Flashbang in five." Greenwood and Dowling ducked further below the lip of the ramp, screwing their eyes shut.

In a single, smooth motion Goose pulled first one pin and then another from the canister, jerked the door open, and threw the palm-sized cylinder upwards on an arc towards the mercenary above. He then immediately slammed the door closed, turned away from it, and wrapped an arm across his eyes.

No matter how many times you'd experienced a stun grenade before, the effect was the same.

The flash of light was like looking directly into the sun on a clear day, except that it filled your entire field of vision. Seeing anything at all except white was impossible for at least five seconds, and after-images would float through your vision for minutes.

Then there was the sound. A bang that could reach 180 decibels, complete with a pressure wave that upsets the fluid in the inner ear that controls balance. The detonation could ignite flammable gases and liquids, though stun grenades were nominally just for disorientation. People had been known to have heart attacks when one went off close by. Even the fireworks exploding in the

Chapter 11

sky outside were completely drowned out.

Drost barely registered the movement in the corner of his eye before the world exploded in light and sound. The gun flew from his hands as he instinctively leapt backwards, blind and deafened, colliding with the opposite railing of the stairway and then falling off the top step. He landed heavily, his head below his feet, and tumbled down the entire top flight to the half-landing below, his head connecting with the side wall with a dull thud. He vomited spontaneously, and then lost consciousness, with blood oozing from his right ear.

Merrick was behind the pillar again, blinking away the afterimages of the reflected flash.

Aranega was down, Drost was certainly incapacitated, and Finn wasn't responding on the secure communications channel. Things were not going according to plan. There was now only himself and Tepel, facing superior numbers, with no clear exit and unknown transportation status.

We must even the odds, he thought, with a snarl on his face. The opposing force would want to extract Taylor and Aldridge as their top priority. The two men were civilians, and Taylor had valuable knowledge of the project, and expertise in relevant fields. Merrick's eyes glittered. The advantage was still his. These others would not be willing to sacrifice the lives of two innocents, but he had no such scruples.

He glanced over towards Tepel's position, seeing a brief glint of reflected light against metal, and gave a hand-signal that asked for suppressing fire. The flat, rapid staccato of controlled gunfire began almost immediately, and Merrick saw the two heads once again duck beneath the upper lip of the ramp.

Outside in the night sky, the trails of light became an ominous red.

"We need to get out of this pit," Greenwood shouted, and Dowling nodded grimly. Goose had returned moments before, and was now lying prone on the ramp beside them with his weapon drawn. Greenwood glanced briefly in his direction. "Goose, cover us."

Tepel ducked behind the nearby pillar and then crouched down on his haunches as almost fist-sized chunks of concrete were chopped out of its surface by returned fire.

Greenwood and Dowling didn't hesitate, immediately sprinting up the last few yards of the ramp and across to the right. They were out of sight of Tepel, and now less than forty feet from Aldridge's unmoving form on the ground. They knew that Merrick wasn't far behind Aldridge's position, and that he had Taylor at gunpoint.

Goose continued to lay down covering fire as they worked their way quickly from pillar to pillar, closing some of the distance. They had gone nearly half the way towards Aldridge when Merrick stepped out from the shadows, holding Taylor in front of him. The old man was pale and clammy looking, and Greenwood could see his rapid breaths condensing in the chilly evening

Chapter 11

air.

"That's far enough," Merrick called out, and Greenwood and Dowling ducked once more around a nearby pillar, readying their weapons.

"Kurt Merrick, you are surrounded by superior forces, and we've incapacitated three of your men," Greenwood shouted back. "There's nothing to gain from this. Surrender Taylor and Aldridge, and we can talk."

Merrick laughed. It was a cold sound, and it echoed around the blank, rough walls of the place. "I think not, madam," he replied with disdain. "You've gained nothing. Dr. Taylor is far more valuable to you than Aldridge, and I have no intention of letting you retrieve him."

I'm not exactly surprised, Greenwood thought. Her mind raced, trying to work out how to get Taylor away from Merrick without endangering the old man, but the outlook was bleak. Merrick would certainly kill Taylor instead of surrendering him, and it was debatable which of the two could provide the most useful intelligence on exactly what was going on at the project. Merrick was only expendable as a last resort.

Forgotten for the moment in the middle of the floor, Aldridge lay spread out on the cold concrete, absolutely still. He was listening.

Merrick and Taylor were about twenty feet behind him, and he guessed that Greenwood was maybe double that distance in front. *I've got to get out of here*, he thought. He was unlikely to be shot accidentally if he stayed on the floor, but there was every chance that Merrick would put a bullet in him deliberately if the situation deteriorated. *Which it certainly has, for him*, Aldridge thought. He turned his head and opened his eyes, looking towards where Merrick stood with Taylor. His next thought was interrupted by a gunshot.

Dowling swore as he drew his shoulders in behind the pillar, the sleeve of his heavy sweater torn by Merrick's bullet. "Bastard," the big man spat, drawing a glance from Greenwood.

"We can't stay here," she replied. "Let's try to push forward, but keep your fire away from Taylor."

Dowling nodded, took a deep breath, and then spun around in place. He waited a moment, then carefully took aim around the edge of his cover, and fired several times.

The rounds were aimed deliberately high, but not by much. Merrick felt the first shot slice through the air just above his close-cropped hair, and immediately drew his head down behind Taylor's.

Aldridge saw his chance and took it. He thrust himself up from the concrete with his hands and knees, trying to stay as low as he could, and he half-stumbled, half-ran diagonally forwards towards the nearest shadows.

"Cover him!" Greenwood shouted, and both Dowling and Goose obliged with well-placed fire. Fireworks hissed and popped somewhere outside and far above, merging with the snap of gunshots.

Chapter 11

Aldridge covered the distance in less than five seconds, collapsing with relief near Greenwood, who then pulled him to the safety of cover with a furious frown on her face.

"Damn it, Aldridge!" she barked, quickly assessing whether or not he was injured before continuing, "That was one of the most bloody reckless things I've seen in a long time."

Aldridge didn't respond other than to shiver and take several noisy breaths. His heart was pounding, and he was badly frightened. He felt a large hand on his shoulder.

"You just stay right where you are, mate," Dowling said in a voice that was incredibly calm, considering the circumstances. "No more running off now."

Aldridge only nodded, beginning to feel a pleasant fuzziness in his head. He shivered again, but felt warm. All of a sudden, a small, cool hand slapped him hard across the face, pulling him back to reality. A distant boom punctuated the stinging in his cheek.

"No time for shock right now," Greenwood said tensely. "Save it for when you're back in the van."

"Jesus," Aldridge said at last, rubbing his face. "You didn't have to hit me."

"That's what we call field-expedient medical treatment," Dowling said, and Aldridge only grunted.

A rapid series of shots rang out, and both Dowling and Greenwood hunched down. "That's coming from a different angle," she said, and Dowling dared to quickly peek out from cover.

"The other guy is back up," he said grimly. "He's had two shots in the shoulder. I think he's firing one-handed."

Aranega's vision was pulsing, and a veil of unreality seemed to overlay everything. He was dimly aware of liquid dripping down his left arm and pooling on the ground, but his attention was focused squarely on the man who had shot him, now ducking behind cover across the echoing space.

I will take you with me, he thought, and with a snarl he lurched forwards into a loping run, firing blindly ahead with his remaining functional arm.

"He's rushing us!" Dowling shouted, readying his weapon as Greenwood grabbed the neck of Aldridge's shirt to keep him out of the line of fire. Dowling readied himself to make a desperate attempt to cut the other man down, but before he could fire a single shot, the gunfire abruptly ceased.

Aranega ran forward, moving between pillars. He passed across an open area within view of the oblong hole cut into the front of the garage to allow air and natural light in. The edge of the concrete was now faintly lit with a green glow from the fireworks exploding above.

I will have you soon, he thought, completely unaware that it would be his last sentiment on Earth. No-one noticed the red dot dance against his temple for barely a third of a second.

Chapter 11

There was no sound. Aranega's world lit up in white, then went dark. Dowling was bringing his weapon to bear when he saw the man abruptly jerk to the left, a plume of bright red blood jetting from the side of his forehead. Aranega went down like a felled tree, and never moved again.

Across the wide four-lane junction outside, nine storeys high atop a shopping centre and nestled invisibly below neon signage, Ramos worked the action of her rifle to chamber another round. The smooth body of the weapon's scope danced with a reflected kaleidoscope of colours from the spectacle in the sky overhead.

There was a moment of stunned silence before more shots from Tepel gouged out chunks of concrete barely ten centimetres to Greenwood's side.

"What the— what *happened* to him?" Aldridge asked, his tone somewhere between fear and wonder.

Dowling glanced at him briefly. "The Captain told you how good Alicia is with her rifle," he said.

Aldridge's eyes widened, and after a long moment he nodded.

Merrick had seen the whole thing. He pulled Taylor across to partially guard the angle from across the street, and kept his pistol trained on Greenwood's hiding spot.

Could such an injury be reversed? he wondered, but there was no way to know.

He had no interest in undoing Aranega's death. The man had already been wounded, and was a liability. The real question was whether such a catastrophic wound on *himself* could be altered. The brain was the centre of the self, and it was impossible to believe that the ability would survive long enough to be useful in that circumstance.

There is so much we don't yet know, he thought, dragging Taylor closer with a cruel tug of the old man's hair. It was time to find a way out of this place.

Greenwood knew the situation was still unstable, despite their advantages. Her team was intact, Aldridge had been retrieved, and the number of active adversaries was down to two. One of them was Merrick, though, and he had Dr. Taylor. He was also a trained killer, and he was trapped. Things were going to get a lot worse, and soon.

"We've got to get Taylor away from that man," Aldridge said, speaking the words they'd all been thinking.

Greenwood took a quick look around the edge of the pillar and then spoke in a low but resolute voice. "Larry, you and I are going to double back around and take the other shooter out of the equation. Goose, move up and keep your eye on Merrick. Don't endanger Dr. Taylor, but don't let them leave."

Dowling nodded, and Goose immediately darted from his position at the ramp, zig-zagging between pillars to quickly join them. Aldridge gave Greenwood a questioning look, and she nodded at him. "You'll be safe here for now. Just stay low, and follow any instructions Goose gives you."

Chapter 11

"Got it," Aldridge said, feeling sick to his stomach. This situation didn't feel right at all, but these people were trained professionals. Surely Greenwood and the big Welshman could at least deal with the other shooter. *But how are we going to get Peter out of this?*

Greenwood and Dowling exchanged a glance, then struck out at right-angles to Merrick's direction, running while hunched and quickly moving to fresh cover. A few stray rounds sliced through the air behind them harmlessly.

Aldridge watched with mounting tension. He was completely concealed from Merrick's position and from Tepel, but he had a clear view of the route Greenwood and Dowling were taking across the floor. Sporadic fire picked at the open spaces they crossed, but Goose provided cover aggressively, and they were now about a third of the way towards Tepel's position, slowly flanking him.

Somehow Aldridge saw it before Greenwood did.

A telltale rainbow shimmer of light in a shadowed patch of the floor just ahead of Dowling, who was pushing forward in front of Greenwood. It took Aldridge a moment to understand what he was seeing. *That's a patch of motor oil*, he realised. *Someone's car leaked there, and Dowling doesn't see it.*

The big man dashed forward, seeing the next safe area, and Greenwood only noticed the danger when it was already too late. She opened her mouth, but there was no time to say anything before the heel of Dowling's boot came down into the black surface of the almost half-metre-wide puddle. He skated forwards, one leg extended far in front of the other, until his weight overbalanced him and he tipped sideways, toppling out into the open in a rolling motion that faced him in the opposite direction from Tepel.

The mercenary didn't hesitate to find his mark, and pull the trigger. The first round skipped off the concrete only inches from Dowling's head, but the rest were on target.

Two rounds punched through Dowling's throat, spraying a grisly storm of blood, bone and cartilage across the floor for twenty feet, and four more shots embedded themselves in his shoulders and upper back. The body armour he wore slowed the bullets, but didn't stop them.

"Larry!" Greenwood screamed with grief and rage, and Tepel immediately turned his weapon towards the sound. She barely made it behind cover in time, sliding down with her back against a pillar, looking directly back across the garage at Aldridge with wide, shocked eyes. Goose had stopped firing, stunned.

Aldridge looked in horror at Dowling's body. *Oh god no. He can't—*

Suddenly, it was as if a switch had been thrown in his mind. He instinctively reached his hand out towards where the large man lay. The explosions in the sky outside rose to a crescendo.

Then everything slowed to a crawl.

Chapter 11

Another round from Tepel barked off the concrete only inches from where Greenwood sat, but it made a dull, echoing thud instead of the usual ugly pop-snap. Aldridge watched as it ricocheted and sailed off as if it were underwater.

Greenwood flinched without ever breaking eye-contact with Aldridge, but she moved as if she were drugged. Far beyond her, out over the city's rooftops, Aldridge saw a seagull float past, each beat of its wings seeming to take many long moments. Fading streamers of light from detonated pyrotechnics hung motionless high overhead.

No, Aldridge thought.

It was like stepping into a gale, but within his own mind. He closed his eyes, but he could still see the scene before him. It flickered and twisted as if he was looking at it through a storm. His pulse dropped, and he watched.

Dowling runs towards cover, not seeing the patch of oil. His foot skids through the rainbow-slick puddle, he loses balance, twists in mid-air, and he falls. The mercenary takes aim, and fires.

It was happening again, just as it had moments before. It was even more real this time, full of exquisite detail. The sudden look of shock across Dowling's face. His free arm pinwheeling in a futile attempt to regain his footing. A chance gust of wind that caught the edge of a nearby discarded newspaper.

In a strange way, it was beautiful.

Then there was a wrenching sensation, as if the world were a ball attached to elastic, and something had jerked it back abruptly. Aldridge flinched, and the scene in his mind shifted.

Dowling runs towards cover, spotting the reflection on the floor at the last moment. His eyes widen and he shifts his weight, leaping over the oil with only a moment to spare. He takes another long stride, draws up his weapon, and reaches cover behind a pillar.

Aldridge saw it as clearly as if his eyes were open. It not only seemed unremarkable, but inevitable. It *was* reality, every bit as much as the other outcome — he knew it on an instinctive level. It was simply a matter of accepting one fate… or choosing another. And he already knew how to do it.

Change, he thought.

He winced and clenched his fists painfully tight as he felt an almighty snap, as if lightning had struck the ground at his feet. The gale within his mind blasted across him once more, and then it was gone.

He took several rapid, shallow breaths, then he slowly opened his eyes. His arm was still outstretched. Even the night outside was muted for the moment.

Fifty feet away, Greenwood and Dowling crouched safely behind cover, faces pale, both looking at him in awe.

Chapter 12

The silence was short lived. Everyone flinched as Merrick and Tepel's wrist-mounted detectors emitted an overlapping series of shrill beeps which were painfully loud as they echoed across the garage.

Goose took the opportunity to fire a few rounds in Tepel's direction while the other man was distracted, and one bullet nicked the mercenary's forearm, making him lose his grip on the G36. He dived for cover, and Goose held his fire.

Merrick had seen the whole thing. The hairs on the back of his neck stood up as he felt the familiar sense of slowing, but this time it was focused elsewhere, instead of on him.

He saw the large man slip or trip on something, crash to the ground, and die from multiple gunshot wounds. Then the scene had shuddered, and he felt the familiar jolt as the new outcome asserted itself. He risked peering out from cover, towards the two places where the woman's team were now positioned, and had seen only an outstretched hand and the sleeve of a blazer.

Aldridge! he thought. *So he has the ability. No wonder Taylor was so eager to contact him.*

Taylor was delirious with the pain and shock of the burns he'd suffered, but he was still able to discern what had happened. The ghost of a smile flickered across his face before he again winced in agony. *Now you know.*

He felt Merrick's grip on his hair loosen slightly. Before he had made a conscious decision, he lunged forward, away from Merrick, feeling several clumps of his hair ripped painfully out.

The movement caught Greenwood's eye as the old man suddenly staggered into her line of sight, but he was still much too far away.

"*Halt!*" Merrick shouted, raising his pistol, but Taylor's entire focus was on trying to stay upright long enough to escape.

Greenwood raised her own weapon desperately, but she had no clear shot at Merrick. Only Taylor himself was visible, half-running and half-falling forwards. The old man moaned in fear and exertion. It was a pitiful sound.

Aldridge's head whipped around, away from Dowling and Greenwood, and he stuck his head out from cover without even thinking.

"Peter!" he shouted, seeing Merrick levelling his weapon behind him, "Get down!" His last word was

Chapter 12

swallowed by a new barrage of explosions from the sky beyond the concrete walls.

Goose could see Merrick now, but Taylor blocked his shot. It had probably been less than four seconds since Taylor had bolted, but it seemed like an eternity. Again the sounds from outside suddenly faded away.

The gunshot was like thunder.

It was difficult to tell whether Taylor had already started to stumble, but once the shot rang out, he went down heavily onto his knees with a jarring thud that broke both of his kneecaps, and then he fell forward to the ground. Aldridge saw his face, frozen in an expression of mixed surprise and horror. The entire front of his jacket was a nightmare of crimson and tattered fabric.

"*PETER!*"

Aldridge's hand flew up, and he tried to find the switch in his mind that he'd instinctively used before, but it was unreachable now — there was something in the way. He cursed in frustration and grief, but there was nothing he could do.

Greenwood looked desperately at Aldridge, and saw that he was wide-eyed and paralysed. It would seem that miracles weren't going to happen twice tonight.

"Goose!" she shouted, and the other man hauled Aldridge back behind cover.

Jesus, Greenwood thought.

Merrick broke into a sudden run at ninety degrees to where Taylor's body lay, and in a few short seconds he reached Tepel. As if on cue, the whole of the night sky seemed to be torn apart by a minute-long cacophony of explosions, accompanied by every colour of light flickering eerily against the areas of the concrete floor within sight of the openings to the street.

"We've got all we're going to get," Greenwood shouted into her radio mic. "Goose, get Aldridge to the ramp. We're leaving."

The rest of the team acknowledged, and they were all safely retreating down the central ramp within half a minute. They faced only half-hearted fire from Merrick and Tepel, and Greenwood thought she knew why. *Now you want Aldridge more than ever, you bastard.*

Less than a minute later they left the parking garage complex, stopping only for a moment to collect Ramos at the next intersection. They were already a mile away by the time Tepel had quickly stripped Aranega's body of any valuable equipment, then gone to revive Drost in the stairwell.

A gunshot echoed around the concrete surfaces, seeming to come from everywhere. Then there were footsteps, followed by another shot, just as the distant sound of police sirens became evident.

Merrick believed in making it very difficult to positively identify bodies.

Chapter 13

It was only shock that allowed Aldridge to make it all the way back to the warehouse, out of the van, and into the toilet before he vomited.

The image of Taylor's face just after he'd been shot wouldn't leave his mind, and every time it rose up he would retch until his eyes were streaming and he was gasping for breath. He was kneeling on the floor in front of the toilet bowl, shivering despite the relative warmth of the room.

Peter is gone, he thought. *My god. Merrick murdered him, right in front of me, and there was nothing I could do.*

Tears rolled silently down his cheeks, and then his pulse stuttered as he remembered what he'd done moments before Taylor's death, after Dowling—

Aldridge felt his stomach lurch, and he leaned forward just in time.

He'd been in there for ten minutes before Goose

knocked and entered, his own face slightly grey but with a look of compassion. Without any preamble, he took out a small disposable syringe, attached an ampoule, and injected him. Aldridge didn't care.

"This'll help," Goose said, his Dutch accent strangely comforting. "Just a mild sedative and antiemetic."

Aldridge nodded mechanically, doubting that anything at all could possibly help, but after a few moments he did start to feel a little less overwhelmed.

He let out a sigh, and Goose smiled. "There you go. I'm sorry, for what it's worth."

Aldridge nodded again, more sincerely this time. "Do you get used to—?" he began to ask, unable to finish the sentence.

"No," Goose replied immediately, and something dark passed across his face for a moment. "Never. There'd be something wrong if you did."

Aldridge supposed the words made sense, but it was hard to think at all right now. After a moment, Goose walked back out.

"How's he doing?" Greenwood asked from her seat at the conference table, looking up from her tablet computer.

"As you'd expect," Goose replied. "He'll feel better soon. For a while, anyway."

Greenwood nodded, feeling a tightness in her chest. She knew that Aldridge had just been wounded in a way that he would never entirely recover from, but she denied herself the luxury of grief. There were always

Chapter 13

casualties, and it was never fair. Her job was to work out how to continue; how to make the next move. Mourning would have to wait. Anger, however, was harder to defer.

Could have been worse, a rational voice in her mind said. *We could have lost one of our own.*

She glanced around, spotting Dowling over in the small kitchen area. He was standing staring at the coffee pot, motionless. After arriving back at the field base, they had ascertained that he remembered falling, and being shot — and then it was as if he'd been jerked backwards, through moments that had already passed. This time he noticed the pool of oil at the last moment, and as if he was on autopilot, he leapt over it and took cover.

But that's not what happened, Greenwood thought. *At least, not at first.*

Goose saw it too. They saw Dowling being shot — *killed*, her mind corrected — and then there was the strangest sensation. Like a hurricane they felt only in their minds, not physically. A sense that they were watching a replay, or a speculative version of events. Then a wrenching change of gears, or perhaps a feeling like a train jumping points onto another branch of track. The scene before them shuddered, then took the shape of the second outcome, with an almost physical *snap* of abrupt reconfiguration.

It was a frightening thing — there was no point denying it. It felt very wrong, like something that was never meant to happen. It sounded crazy here in the familiar, sane fluorescent light of the field station, but Greenwood intuitively knew that Aldridge's — What? Intervention? — had wider repercussions than its immediate effect. She had no idea *how* she knew it, but it was true nonetheless.

It was just too strange, and there were so many questions.

The door to the toilet creaked open and Aldridge slowly walked out. He looked drained, and his fringe was damp, but he had some colour back in his cheeks now and he moved steadily. Greenwood saw him glance over at Dowling in the corner, and momentarily pale once more.

"Come and sit down, Mr. Aldridge," she said gently, gesturing towards a chair.

He walked over, still feeling a little vague, but noticeably calmer. The image of Taylor's face threatened to rise up again, and he pushed it away. He took a seat two places away from Greenwood, and clasped his hands on the tabletop.

Goose stood nearby, leaning against a workbench, and Ramos watched silently from the edge of the room.

"How are you feeling?" Greenwood asked, and Aldridge looked down at his own hands for a long moment.

"I'm… I don't know," he replied. "I can't believe it."

"Imagine how the rest of us feel," Greenwood said quietly, and confusion was evident on Aldridge's face

Chapter 13

before he blinked.

"I mean about what happened to Peter," he said. "Although the other thing is... did that even happen?"

Greenwood raised an eyebrow. "You mean to say you can't explain what you did?"

Aldridge shook his head. "I wasn't even sure it was me. I mean, I know it was. I know that. But it just seems..."

He tailed off, shaking his head again, and Greenwood considered him for a moment. She exchanged a look with Goose, who gave the barest hint of a shrug, before returning her attention to Aldridge.

"Much as I'd like to tell you otherwise, yes, it happened," she said. "I need to know everything you can tell me about what you did tonight."

Aldridge sighed in frustration and scratched his forehead. "I've already told you. I don't know any more than you do," he said.

Greenwood took a measured breath. "I know this has been a very difficult day," — Aldridge exhaled — "but what happened may be critical to understanding why Dr. Taylor really contacted you, and why Merrick was equally eager to capture you."

Aldridge looked uncertain. He was about to speak when a tablet computer on the workbench beside Goose chimed, drawing Greenwood's attention. Goose picked the device up and examined the display for several moments, then he frowned. He picked up another piece of equipment from the bench — a compact, handheld, box-shaped machine with a thick silver cylinder protruding from its top — then he crossed to the table.

He laid the tablet down in front of Greenwood. She glanced up at him briefly, then inspected the display.

"More information on Destiny?" she asked. "This looks similar to the original phenomenon."

"Similar, but smaller — and a lot nearer. Not just physically, either," Goose replied. "It registered in Geneva just seconds after Mr. Aldridge did his thing back in the garage. He was the origin point."

Greenwood looked up again, this time with an alarmed expression. "What exactly are you telling me?"

Goose was tight-lipped for a moment, and then he spoke. "According to our people, whatever Aldridge did tonight caused an energy signature almost identical to the event. Much, *much* smaller in magnitude, but the same phenomenon."

"So what does that mean?" Greenwood replied. "Is he the trigger?"

"I have no idea," Goose replied truthfully. "All I can say for sure is," he began, lifting the other device to point towards Aldridge and pressing a control, resulting in a series of crystalline beeps, "this man is currently a weak anti-tachyon source. And as far as I knew before tonight, that's physically impossible."

"Wait, I'm a *what*?" Aldridge said, getting up from his chair with a worried look on his face. "What is he saying? There's no such thing as *anti*-tachyons. Is that a radiation counter?"

Chapter 13

"No," Goose said, "at least, not in the way you're thinking. You're not in any danger. As far as I know, anyway." He glanced at Greenwood again, and then returned to the workbench, still watching Aldridge thoughtfully.

Greenwood looked at Aldridge for a long moment, then she laid her hands flat on the table. "There's something you're not telling us, Mr. Aldridge," she said, and he briefly glanced away before meeting her gaze again.

"We're all terribly sorry for your loss tonight, and we're grateful for what you did for Larry," she continued, "but I need to know absolutely everything you can tell me about all of this. The rest of those men are still out there. They know more than we do, and sooner or later you're going to see them again."

Aldridge swallowed, feeling his pulse quicken. Greenwood's expression was compassionate but firm, and he knew that she was telling the truth. He thought that the truth probably came very naturally to her. He found her frankness oddly reassuring.

He exhaled quickly, his breath making a whistling noise, then slowly sat down again. "Fine," he said. "You're right. But I swear I had no idea it was anything more than a delusion on my part before now."

Greenwood leaned forward, and Aldridge began to talk.

It took less than ten minutes to tell her the full story of his own strange experience with the broken ornament, and Taylor's question about whether anything unusual had happened to him recently.

He told Greenwood about the apparent slowing of everything around him when Dowling had been shot, and about how he had acted mostly on instinct. She was silent for a full minute before asking the question on everyone's mind.

"Can you tell me why you didn't… bring Taylor back too?"

Aldridge stiffened in his chair, but he had been expecting the question. He'd asked himself the same thing, subconsciously at least, during the drive back.

"I… just couldn't do it," he said at last. "I mean, I wish I could have. It just didn't happen. There was… I don't know. A wall. A barrier."

"What does that mean?" Greenwood asked, but Aldridge only shook his head.

"I don't *know!*" he barked, pounding his fist into the tabletop. "I don't know how this *works*. Nobody gave me an instruction book. I have no idea what I did, or *how* I did it, or why I couldn't do it twice!"

Dowling walked over to the table and sat down between the two of them. "At least we know what Merrick was after now," he said.

Greenwood looked at him quizzically for a moment before her eyes widened. "The devices on their wrists," she said, and Dowling nodded.

"We all heard them go off right after I—" he broke off for a moment. "After Aldridge helped me. And when they met earlier, Taylor asked Mr. Aldridge if anything

Chapter 13

had happened that he couldn't explain."

Greenwood's eyes sparkled. "You're saying that Taylor had seen the ability before."

Dowling nodded. "It's the only thing that makes sense. And Merrick's team had, too. That's why they had those gadgets on their arms: they were prepared to find him. Or someone like him."

There was a long silence as everyone absorbed the large man's words.

"Destiny has clearly gone far beyond what the EU knows," Greenwood said, then she glanced up when Aldridge tapped his fingers on the table. He cleared his throat, then he began to speak.

"I've told you the truth — all of it — now. But I have no idea what Destiny is, or the project, or what the hell is going on here," he said. His complexion was redder now.

"I've been chased, shot at, and apparently I even somehow saved Mr. Dowling's life tonight." He glanced sheepishly at Dowling, who only looked down at the table's surface. "So how about you return the favour, and fill in the blanks?"

"It's your call, chief, as always," Dowling said languidly, "but I think we're well past the point where it makes sense to keep him in the dark."

Greenwood considered her own hands on the tabletop for a long moment, and then she nodded.

"Alright, Aldridge. I'm going to tell you a story. It's an unbelievable story, but it's true. And you're not going to like it at all."

Chapter 14

Merrick sat in silence, looking out one of the large oval windows of the elegantly decorated Gulfstream G650ER jet at the landscape below. They had taken off immediately after reaching the airfield, and had been airborne for less than fifteen minutes. Scotland was rapidly disappearing behind them.

His three remaining men sat silently in leather reclining armchairs further back in the aircraft's cabin, but Merrick paid them no attention. He mentally tallied the events of the evening.

Aranega is dead. Dr. Taylor is dead. Drost has minor injuries, from which he has already sufficiently recovered.

None of these were of much consequence, though Anfruns would likely be angry about Taylor's death.

Aldridge remains at large, assisted by special forces, and he also possesses the ability.

This was of substantially more concern. It was clear

that the Destiny project's EU paymasters had become suspicious, so the elite team with Aldridge were most likely operating under the authority of the European Defence Agency. They no doubt had considerable resources at their disposal, and a great deal of jurisdictional and operational support.

Merrick frowned. *Very well. What are our remaining advantages?*

Himself, Tepel, Finn, and Drost were all at operational readiness. Dr. Taylor could no longer provide any assistance to Aldridge or his companions. And Aldridge's dramatic rescue of the large man had provided Merrick with an additional set of readings to further refine their estimates.

I consider our mission to have been a success, he thought, practising the words as he'd say them to Anfruns the following morning, after he'd taken care of some business at the facility. The old man would chastise him, but it mattered little. Merrick would be the one to bring the plan to completion, no matter the cost.

He glanced idly at the wrist-mounted detector device he wore at all times, but its screen was dark. His mind again drifted back to his first meeting with Anfruns almost two years before, when his own fate had changed.

The plane banked smoothly and then merged into the clouds.

"Just over two years from now, somewhere in Western

Chapter 14

Europe, there will be a disaster," Anfruns said, his fingers steepled as he sat at his large and ornate desk.

Merrick stood before him, careful not to allow his facial expression to change. He had heard grand claims before, though admittedly never from a man as powerful as this.

"Created by you?" he asked, and the older man frowned.

"I create opportunities, not catastrophes, Mr. Merrick," Anfruns said quietly, with a hint of impatience in his eyes. He was silent for several seconds before continuing. "I don't suppose you have heard of *tachyons*?"

Merrick simply held the other man's gaze, even though the word was vaguely familiar. He had perhaps heard it in passing on television. He thought it had something to do with physics.

"No, I thought not," Anfruns said. "Then a brief lesson is in order."

Merrick resisted the urge to grimace. The old man liked the sound of his own voice, but he was also enormously wealthy and influential, and had not yet revealed his reasons for this meeting. Let him prattle. Merrick would listen carefully, as he always did.

"Tachyons are subatomic particles which travel faster than the speed of light," Anfruns began, his eyes brighter now. "Until very recently, I would have told you that they are purely theoretical. Late last year, unbeknownst to the wider scientific community, their existence was confirmed."

Anfruns paused briefly, perhaps waiting for a reaction from Merrick, but he received none.

"An experiment was devised by CERN — in Geneva; I'm sure you've heard of it — and a sophisticated detector was constructed. The experiment was a success, in more ways than anticipated."

Merrick held the other man's gaze, showing neither boredom nor interest. "Why was the discovery not made public?" he asked.

"The need for confirmation," Anfruns replied. "Science requires verification. Publishing a discovery too early can destroy a career if later proven false. Or destroy a company's stock value. But the point became moot only a few weeks later."

His eyes became unfocused for a moment as he seemed to recall something, then he once again directed his attention toward Merrick.

"The detector made its second discovery while trying to verify the first — which it did, incidentally. A veritable blizzard of particles which at first were thought to be tachyons. And they were, in a way, though with an important difference. They were travelling *backwards in time*."

Merrick frowned. This sounded like science fiction, and was of little interest to a man of his background. "So?"

Anfruns smiled icily. "I take it you are familiar with the idea of radioactive decay? Substances which are

Chapter 14

radioactive *lose* that property over time. We can measure their radiation output, and given knowledge of the substance in question, we can determine precisely how long ago it was formed."

Merrick nodded. Every schoolchild was taught as much. Anfruns was already speaking again.

"A similar thing is true for these time-inverted particles - these *anti-tachyons*. We can calculate when the event takes place that causes their release. They will be produced just over two years from now, at an unknown location within Western Europe."

"And what will produce them?" Merrick asked, interested now despite himself. "Some kind of weapon?"

"We don't know," Anfruns replied evenly. "The event hasn't taken place yet, after all. But when it does, the result will be catastrophic." He paused for effect, for several long seconds. "Our calculations indicate that all of Belgium, Luxembourg, the Netherlands, and much of France, Germany, Switzerland, England, and my beloved Denmark will be purged of all life."

Merrick felt the unfamiliar sensation of a chill running down his spine. *Can it be true?*

"How can you know this for certain?" he asked, and Anfruns sighed.

"These anti-tachyons are produced as the result of a massive release of energy. We know the approximate time of their generation, but not to a useful level of accuracy. As for the place, that is even more complicated. Their individual trajectories in space can be measured with precision, but the particles interfere with each other, blurring their origin, and the effect is compounded over time. We cannot currently be more specific as to the epicentre of the event."

Anfruns leaned back in his seat, his eyes never leaving Merrick's.

"But we do know this: the vast majority of the particles will be generated within one one-thousandth of a second, expelling an energy equivalent to thousands of nuclear warheads. Within the event's radius, there will be only death."

Chapter 15

Aldridge was now even more glad of the sedative Goose had given him.

He was sitting alone at the conference table for the moment. Greenwood had briefed him fully on the Destiny project, Anfruns, and the coming cataclysm.

Sometime soon, a big chunk of Western Europe will be destroyed. It was impossible to believe, but he had no reason to doubt what Greenwood had told him. Even worse, the phenomenon was somehow related to what he had done in the parking garage.

Am I responsible? he wondered. There was no way to answer the question, but it terrified him. Millions of people were going to die, and according to Greenwood, her team wasn't even sure exactly when or where the event would take place.

He was brought out of his reverie when Goose put a steaming mug of coffee in front of him, and a packaged sandwich. Aldridge looked up gratefully. Goose's expression was thoughtful. "There's still time, Mr. Aldridge," he said quietly. "I know what you're worrying about, but there's no reason for pre-emptive guilt. We *will* prevent this."

Aldridge smiled distractedly, and Goose nodded before walking away. Greenwood was over at a desk, wearing a headset and participating in a video conference. The monitor showed a richly-appointed room with a large, curving conference table. There were silver-haired men and women in expensive dark suits, and several military officers in various uniforms. The flags of the EU member states were visible in miniature, positioned beside each delegate. A superimposed readout indicated that the communication channel was encrypted, and was not being recorded. Aldridge didn't even try to hear Greenwood's side of the discussion, and for the most part she was just listening and nodding.

Before she had dialled into the conference, Aldridge overheard her talking to Goose in hushed tones. Something about intercepted local police radio traffic, indicating spent shell casings and blood found on the top floor of a multi-level parking garage in the centre of the city, but no other evidence. Merrick had clearly disposed of both bodies. Aldridge's stomach rolled again, but less than before. He felt a growing numbness inside him.

He ate the sandwich mechanically, then picked up his coffee and started pacing. Everyone else was busy but quiet; efficient and in control. He felt almost exactly the

Chapter 15

opposite. Clueless, unanchored, useless, and maybe even dangerous in some way. He had a sudden agonised longing for the simplicity of just teaching a class at the university, without a real care in the world.

Be careful what you wish for, he thought with a grimace, taking a mouthful of coffee and allowing it to burn his throat. It was funny how quickly life could get out of control. One day you're going through your ordinary routine, and the next you've had enough adventure to last a lifetime, with no end in sight.

If I make it out of this alive, I'm going to cancel my voicemail service, he thought, and then he abruptly stopped in the middle of the room. "Damn it," he muttered, drawing a glance from Dowling who was at a workbench nearby, cleaning and reassembling a pistol.

"Problem?" the big man asked, and Aldridge sighed.

"I have to give a lecture tomorrow," he replied. "I have a class of forty undergraduates. I was going to do the prep work tonight."

Dowling pointed to a phone handset on the bench. "I think you should take a leave of absence for a while, mate. Give your boss a call if you like. That's a scrambled phone. Don't say where you are, or anything else about what's going on. Say your granny is feeling a bit poorly."

Aldridge nodded. Both his grandmothers were long dead, but the head of the physics department didn't know that any more than Dowling did. "Mind if I check my voicemail service too? I can dial in from anywhere," he said, and Dowling shrugged.

"Be my guest. Just use it like a normal phone, but you'll always need an area code."

Aldridge nodded and picked up the handset, dialling the faculty reception's number first. He spoke briefly to the secretary for the head of department, telling the lie that Dowling had suggested, and he promised to be back in touch within a week. He accepted the offered sympathy with a twist of discomfort, then hung up. Next, he dialled his voicemail number from memory. He entered a pin code on the keypad, and the synthesised voice indicated he had one new message.

He pressed the 1 key to play the message, and there was a pause of a couple of seconds at the beginning of the recording. As soon as he heard the voice begin to speak, he instantly tensed up.

"Neil, it's… Julie. Julie Hollett."

Jesus, he thought. *This day just keeps getting stranger.* He hadn't heard from her in a year, and she chooses today of all days to get back in contact. The fact that she used her full name seemed to be a microcosm of their whole relationship.

"I've got something here from your uncle Peter. It was sent to my office. I'm not sure why, but the note said it was for you, and urgent. If you want me to forward it on, just leave a message with the right address to use."

There was another pause, as if she couldn't decide quite what to say. He heard her exhale, and then the message ended.

Chapter 15

Aldridge closed his eyes briefly, pushing down the wave of grief that had surged up when he heard Taylor's name, and then he turned again towards Dowling.

"Listen to this," he said, and pressed a key to repeat playback of the message.

"Mm?" Dowling replied, glancing up from the workbench and then taking the phone. The synthesised voice was just finishing announcing the date and time of the message, which was half an hour ago, and then playback began once more. Dowling listened, then his eyes widened and he made eye-contact with Aldridge. Both men were silent until playback had finished.

"Bingo," Dowling said, clapping a big hand on Aldridge's shoulder and handing the phone back to him. "Bring this over and play it again for the Captain."

Dowling gestured to Greenwood and she asked the other conference participants to hold on for a moment. She listened to the message, and her eyes flashed. "Thank you, Dr. Taylor," she said under her breath, then gave the phone back to Dowling.

"Hollett works at her newspaper's head office in London?" she asked, and Aldridge nodded.

"As far as I know. I assume you can check."

Greenwood turned to Dowling. "Find out where she is, and get the plane ready to take us to the nearest airfield. I want us to be wheels-up in thirty minutes."

"Gotcha," Dowling said, and the room became a hive of activity. Greenwood put her headset back on.

"We have a new lead. I'll report in again when we

land."

Aldridge stood off to one side, feeling like the spare wheel, but also relieved. At least they had something to go on.

He had a sinking feeling in his stomach. Greenwood's most obvious course of action would be to send him to see Julie himself, and retrieve whatever Taylor had sent to her. He wasn't looking forward to that.

But there's too much at stake to care about an awkward meeting, he thought.

He flexed his neck, trying to clear some of the nervous tension. It had been the most exhausting day of his life.

And he had a feeling that tomorrow wouldn't be any easier.

Chapter 16

Aldridge was back in the parking garage. It was much larger this time, stretching all the way to the horizon. The window holes had all been filled in, and there were traffic cones blocking the ramps.

Merrick was behind every pillar. He would pop out from one, and then from another in a different place, like some hellish Jack-in-the-box. Taylor and Dowling both lay dead on the floor in a spreading pool of blood, and Aldridge knew that if his foot touched the liquid, he would slip and fall.

Greenwood was screaming at him. "Why didn't you change it, Aldridge? Why?!"

Aldridge felt sick. He suddenly realised he was wearing a shoulder-holster underneath his blazer, and he reached into it to draw his weapon — but it was only the glass duck. It had a trigger, though, so he pointed it at Merrick anyway, and fired. The duck only clicked, and Merrick's laughter boomed out as he flicked between pillars. "It's a swan, you idiot!"

Now Merrick and Greenwood were both laughing at him, and Greenwood stepped out from cover, but she was actually his ex-girlfriend Julie. She drew her pistol and Aldridge dropped the duck, raising his hands in surrender, but she only shook her head as the ornament shattered into hundreds of pieces against the concrete.

"Don't even start," she said, and then she pulled the trigger.

Aldridge woke up with a jolt, not knowing whether he'd cried out. His brow was slick with sweat, and he was momentarily unsure where he was.

The room was dimly lit by a shaft of bleak daylight coming in through a gap in some tasteless striped curtains. He lay on a single bed near the window, and there was also a double bed nearby. Across from the beds, there was a combination desk and vanity, with a small television perched on top.

He blinked and glanced around, and everything started to come back.

He'd tried to return Julie's call the night before while they were in the air, but she had already left her office for the evening. Greenwood considered finding her home address and approaching her there, but Aldridge strongly cautioned against it. It would be too bold a move, and would instantly heighten her suspicion.

The brief flight from Edinburgh to a private airfield in North London took only 45 minutes, and afterwards they had booked three rooms at a budget hotel about a

Chapter 16

mile from the headquarters of Julie's newspaper, *The Sentinel*. Aldridge went to the tired-looking hotel bar for an hour, drinking three whiskies in silence with Goose and Dowling sitting beside him. After finishing the third, he stood up, nodded to the other men, and then went to his room. Sleep had been a long time coming.

He turned his head to look at the alarm clock on the bedside table, and saw that it read 7:27 AM.

Still can't sleep in, even after a day like yesterday, he thought groggily, and hauled himself out of bed. He was wearing only a pair of boxer shorts, and the room was unpleasantly cold. His stomach started growling almost as soon as his feet hit the floor.

"Shaping up to be another brilliant morning," he muttered to himself, and stepped into the bathroom.

Ten minutes later he was buttoning up his shirt in front of the full-length mirror beside the desk when there was a knock on the door. Aldridge glanced towards it, but it began to open immediately, revealing the large frame of Larry Dowling.

"Ah, you're up," he said, and Aldridge spontaneously yawned so widely that his jaw clicked.

"More or less," he replied. "Any chance of breakfast before people start shooting at us today?"

Dowling smiled. "You'll get your breakfast. The Captain would have a mutiny on her hands otherwise."

Aldridge suspected that Dowling would follow Greenwood until he dropped even if she told him he'd never eat again, but he appreciated the reassurance. "We can go now, if you like," Dowling continued, "then afterwards she wants to see you."

Aldridge nodded, and removed the room keycard from the slot on the wall as he stepped out into the corridor. Goose was waiting a short distance down the hallway, and the three men wasted no time in setting off in search of food.

Half an hour later, after a quick continental breakfast, Aldridge found himself on a different floor of the hotel, being led along a corridor by Dowling, with Goose bringing up the rear. They reached a door marked with the number 621, and Dowling knocked once. The door swung open a few seconds later, revealing Ramos. She nodded towards Aldridge as he passed, with an expression of curiosity on her face, and Aldridge returned the gesture.

This room was larger than the one Aldridge had slept in — it seemed to be a cheap version of a junior suite, with an extended sitting area. There was a coffee table bordered by a sofa and two armchairs, and French doors looking out over a depressing car-park. There was ice on the windows of all of the cars outside. Two pigeons were perched atop a streetlight.

Greenwood sat on the sofa, with a laptop and three tablets on the coffee table in front of her. There were several vending-machine coffee cups and some chocolate bar wrappers, all empty.

"Sleep well, Mr. Aldridge?" Greenwood asked, and he shrugged.

Chapter 16

"About as well as can be expected."

"Good," she said, already returning her attention to the multitude of screens in front of her. "Come and sit down."

Aldridge crossed to one of the armchairs and sat down, folding his arms tightly across his chest. After several moments of silence, he realised that Greenwood was so engrossed in whatever she was looking at that she'd forgotten he was there. He cleared his throat quietly, and she looked up at him, raising an eyebrow.

"Be with you in a moment," she said, the barest note of amusement in her tone, then she tapped on one of the tablet devices briefly before pushing it away from her. "Alright. We've put a trace on Julie Hollett's mobile phone, and she's currently en route to her office."

Aldridge's eyebrows shot up. "You can…?" he began, but he didn't finish the sentence. He glanced over at Dowling, who only shrugged.

"Yes, we can do that," Greenwood said. "And yes, it's a gross invasion of privacy. But we're short of time, and the uniqueness of our mission gives us a certain degree of flexibility. I intend to use it."

Aldridge just blinked, and then nodded in acknowledgement. "Fair enough. She's not exactly my favourite person in the world, anyway."

Greenwood looked at him for a moment before continuing. "You're going to call her in a few minutes, and tell her you got her voicemail. You're in London on business, but only for today, and you'd appreciate being able to collect the package Dr. Taylor sent to her."

Aldridge nodded again, a crease appearing on his brow.

"Problem?" Greenwood asked, and he gave a small sigh.

"No. Just not looking forward to seeing her."

"We'll keep the meeting as short as possible," Greenwood replied. "It's best that way. You're not going to tell her anything. Just arrange to meet — anywhere that's convenient for her — and you'll collect the package, then leave."

"She's going to ask what this is all about," he said. "She's a lot of things, but she's not stupid. And she's nosy, too. It goes with the job."

Greenwood tilted her head to one side. "If she asks about anything, tell her you'll explain when you see her."

"And will I?"

"No. And to make sure you don't, I'll be going with you."

Aldridge sat back in his chair, unsure whether he was relieved or more worried.

Maybe both, he thought.

Goose walked over and placed a mobile phone on the coffee table. "You should use this," he said. "It's untraceable — for most people, anyway. You can keep it with you. We're all in the address book under our initials, and Ms. Hollett too."

Aldridge nodded, and picked up the device.

Chapter 16

"Keep it brief, and be polite," Greenwood said. "I know it's an awkward situation, but we need that package."

"I know," he replied. "Here goes nothing."

Aldridge stood up and walked over to the window, facing away from the others. He scrolled to Julie's initials in the phone's contact list, tapped the call icon, and raised the device to his ear. He immediately felt his stomach twist as he listened.

Three rings. Four. Five. Then a click, and he heard Julie's voice on the line.

"Julie Hollett," she said. Aldridge took a deep breath.

"Hello, it's Neil Aldridge. I got your message."

There was a brief pause.

"Oh, ... hello," she said. *"I've got a parcel here from your uncle Peter. There's a note saying it's for you."*

"Yes, I'm sorry about that. I'd like to collect it, if that'd be alright. I'm actually in London today. I could meet you anywhere that suits you."

Another brief pause. *"I see,"* she replied. *"I suppose that'd be best. I could meet you briefly in about an hour. There's a cafe not far from my office."*

Julie gave him the address, which he noted down on a pad of hotel stationery Greenwood handed to him. Aldridge thanked Julie and said he'd see her in an hour, then he hung up.

"Good," Greenwood said.

"That was the easy part," he replied.

* * *

Fifteen minutes later, they were both almost ready to go.

Greenwood was pleased they wouldn't actually be visiting *The Sentinel*'s offices. She preferred to keep as far away from the press as possible, and there would also be a significant security presence at a major newspaper. The cafe was a much better option. She knew that Hollett's request to meet there was probably just because she wanted to avoid any potentially embarrassing scenes in front of her colleagues, but the reason was ultimately unimportant. It was a small stroke of good fortune, and she'd take it.

Aldridge was wired with a concealed microphone and pinhole camera, just in case. It was unlikely Hollett would say anything of value, but Greenwood liked to be over-prepared. She had an invisible earpiece she could use to stay in touch with the rest of the team, who would be nearby during their meeting.

"She's going to wonder who you are," Aldridge said as he fiddled with his shirt collar, still unsure about the idea of Greenwood accompanying him.

"You can say that I'm your friend Claire," Greenwood replied. "Let her think whatever she likes. We won't be there long enough for her to interrogate you. And remember: don't tell her *anything*."

"You shouldn't underestimate Julie, you know," he said. "She's no fool." He paused for a moment before muttering under his breath. "That was definitely my role in the relationship."

Greenwood chose to ignore the remark. "I'm well

Chapter 16

aware of her reputation as a journalist. As long as we keep it short and sweet, we'll be fine."

Aldridge grimaced, but he made no further argument. Greenwood stood up and walked over to the hotel room's combination desk and vanity unit. A black metal suitcase sat there, just beside a tattered copy of a London tourist guidebook, and the hotel's room service menu. She pressed her right thumb against a small glass panel set into the top edge of the case, and its two locks sprang open.

From behind her, she heard Aldridge speak again.

"Is Claire your middle name?"

She opened the case, removed her pistol, checked the magazine, and slid the handgun into the shoulder holster she wore under her jacket. She didn't even turn her head towards him when she replied.

"Wouldn't you like to know?"

The cafe was called *Ivan's Bistro*, and it was tucked between a locksmith and a nail salon on a wide side-street just two blocks away from the glass and steel monolith that housed *The Sentinel*.

Greenwood and Aldridge arrived early, taking a four-person table near the front, not far from the door. He declined her offer of a coffee, but she brought him one anyway.

"Relax," she said, after they'd sat in silence for several minutes. He glanced up at her, raising an eyebrow, but she only returned the look. "We need this."

"For Peter," he replied. "And... everyone."

She nodded. "Just keep it short and sweet."

"The first part sounds manageable," he said, and Greenwood was about to respond when she saw him tense up. She followed his gaze, and easily spotted the woman walking along the pavement outside, heading for the cafe's door.

Greenwood recognised Julie Hollett from her byline photo at the top of each of her columns in the newspaper. She was fairly tall for a woman — about the same height as Aldridge — and she was wearing fitted trousers, a turtleneck, and a woollen coat, all in dark colours. Her blonde hair was in a severe pixie cut that clearly said just what Aldridge had advised earlier: *don't underestimate me*.

In another context, Greenwood could have admired the woman, but this was no time to let her guard down. Hollett was an investigative political and security journalist, and that made her dangerous. Greenwood consciously relaxed her posture, leaned ever so slightly towards Aldridge, and put a small smile on her face.

"Here we go," she said quietly, giving him a small nod.

Aldridge looked down at the untouched cup of coffee in front of him, steeling himself for the impending encounter.

Just be polite, get the package, and go, he thought. *It's that simple.*

From the corner of his eye, he saw Julie enter the cafe,

Chapter 16

and he thought he detected a brief pause.

Probably wondering who Greenwood is.

A few moments later, Julie approached their table, and he looked up, his expression carefully blank.

"Hi," Julie said.

"Hello," Aldridge replied. "Thanks for coming. I'm sorry about the inconvenience with the package."

"No problem," Julie said, even though her tone implied otherwise. Her eyes were on Greenwood, who simply looked back at her.

"Oh, excuse me," Aldridge said, "Julie, this is my friend Claire. Claire, this is Julie Hollett."

"Pleased to meet you," Greenwood said, extending her hand. Julie shook it briefly, and nodded at her.

"Likewise."

Greenwood watched the other woman, reading the indecision on her face. Hollett clearly wanted to enquire about the package she'd received and the circumstances behind it, but she was thrown off-guard by Greenwood's presence.

Just as I hoped, Greenwood thought.

"Please join us," Greenwood said. "Can I get you something to drink? It's the least we can do, isn't it, Neil?"

Aldridge gave her a brief glance of surprise, then schooled his features once more. "Of course," he replied.

Julie shook her head. "No, thank you," she said, and sat down in one of the vacant chairs and clasped her hands in her lap. She didn't remove her coat.

"How have you been?" Aldridge asked, and Julie shrugged one shoulder.

"I've been well. And you?"

"Fine. Good. Working away, you know," he replied, shifting in his seat. Julie nodded, but he easily recognised the look of curiosity in her eyes. A moment of silence passed, then she reached into her oversized handbag and pulled out a small padded envelope. She placed it on the table in front of her.

Smaller than I expected, Greenwood thought. The envelope was only a few inches on its longest side, and had a pronounced bump in the middle. *Probably electronic data.*

"I'm a little confused about why Peter sent this to me instead of you," Julie said, her hand still resting on the envelope. "Seems like a strange thing to do."

Aldridge simply nodded, and let out a small sigh. "The truth is that Peter and I still hadn't been in touch until very recently."

Julie was silent for a moment. "I see. But you are now?"

Aldridge felt Greenwood's gaze on him, and he kept his expression neutral. "I spoke to him just yesterday, actually, in Edinburgh," he said.

Greenwood leaned forward, gesturing towards the envelope on the table. "Peter felt that Neil might be more likely to accept it if it came via you," she said. "He didn't know that the two of you weren't together anymore."

Julie scrutinised the other woman. Greenwood just

Chapter 16

smiled disarmingly.

"Did he come down with you?" Julie asked, and Greenwood shook her head.

"This is just a business trip — for me — and we thought we'd do some sightseeing while we're here."

"What line of work are you in, if you don't mind me asking?"

"Risk assessment," Greenwood replied easily, and Aldridge finally reached for his untouched cup of coffee.

Julie glanced at the envelope again, running her fingers across its surface. "The note mentioned it was urgent," she said, finally looking at Aldridge again. "You don't know why?"

Greenwood felt her first twinge of irritation. *What business is it of yours, Miss Hollett?* But she knew that confrontation was the last thing they wanted.

"The truth is that, no, I don't know why Peter said the parcel was urgent, or why he sent it to me, or what it is," Aldridge replied.

Julie's brow furrowed. "He didn't tell you when you spoke yesterday?"

Careful, Aldridge, Greenwood thought, ready to jump in at any moment, but Aldridge's expression was as calm as ever.

"Peter and I only spoke very briefly last night. I didn't have the chance to ask, and then Claire and I had our flight to catch. All I know is that, whatever it is, it's important to him that I have it."

Oh, and most of Europe is going to be destroyed soon, he

thought. *But on the upside, I seem to be able to change events that have already happened.*

He sighed, and Greenwood watched as Julie's face pinched slightly. *Getting frustrated. Let's hope that's a good thing.* Greenwood then ventured a quick look towards Aldridge, and she immediately saw he was no longer giving the conversation his full attention. She knew the look well, and had seen it on too many faces over the years.

Aldridge's eyes were more dark-grey than blue at the moment, and unfocused. He was staring in the direction of his coffee cup without really seeing it. She knew that his mind was on Taylor, and what had happened the night before.

Sympathy rose up within her, and her hand twitched on the tabletop before she reined herself in. There was a job to do, and so much more at stake. An idea occurred to her.

Remember your training. Feel whatever you want, but don't let it get in the way. Use it.

She reached towards Aldridge and placed her hand over his, squeezing gently. He glanced first at her hand and then up at her, with the barest trace of a question on his face. There were heavy lines around the edges of his eyes. She simply willed him to remain quiet, and he seemed to understand. Then she turned to look across at Julie, who was watching both of them with a sudden expression of discomfort.

"This hasn't been easy. For Neil, I mean," Greenwood

Chapter 16

said. "We know it's a strange situation, and that this meeting is a little... awkward, but we really just want to find out what Peter wanted to give him, and then put this behind us."

She paused for a moment before once again looking at Aldridge, whose gaze was now focused on the tabletop. When she spoke, her voice was quieter than before, and she was clearly still addressing Julie even though her eyes were fixed on him. "We're not going to be speaking to Peter again for the foreseeable future. So, really... we'd just like to collect the package and be on our way. I'm sure you understand."

Aldridge nodded, still not looking up at either woman. There were lines of tension in his jaw and neck.

There was a long moment of silence, but Greenwood resisted the temptation to look across at Julie and try to assess what she was thinking. Almost ten seconds passed before Julie sighed and then slid the envelope across the table, more towards Greenwood than Aldridge.

"It's encrypted, you know," she said thoughtfully. "There isn't anything on the note about a password. I hope you figure it out."

Greenwood finally looked over at her again, and gave a small smile. "Thank you," she said. Julie nodded and then stood up, picking up her handbag.

Aldridge looked up at her. "Thank you," he said. "I hope everything's going well for you."

Julie returned his gaze, seeming to consider something for a moment. "For what it's worth, you should think about giving yourself a break. About what happened with Peter, I mean. There never was any reason to feel so guilty."

Greenwood's eyes flicked towards Aldridge, and she saw some of the colour drain from his face, then he swallowed and simply nodded.

Julie kept looking at Aldridge for another moment, then glanced briefly towards Greenwood. "It was nice to meet you, Claire," she said. "I hope you both enjoy your time here in London."

"Thank you, and it was nice to meet you too," Greenwood replied, her hand still firmly on top of Aldridge's.

Julie just nodded, and with one last look at Aldridge, she turned and left.

Greenwood at last lifted her hand away and grasped the padded envelope on the table top. She waited a full twenty seconds before speaking, keeping her voice low. "You did well. We got what we came for." She took a sip of her coffee, then pushed the cup away from her.

"It wasn't a lot of fun," Aldridge replied, and Greenwood tilted her head in acknowledgement.

"I know. But that was the easy part."

He glanced at her, raising one eyebrow, and she straightened her jacket.

"Now we have to save the world."

Chapter 17

Aldridge was silent as he and Greenwood walked the short distance back to where Dowling was waiting in a rented people-carrier. She left him to his thoughts, her own mind mostly focused on the padded envelope tucked inside her shoulder bag.

They were back at the hotel within ten minutes, and everyone gathered in Greenwood's room. She emptied the contents of the envelope onto the coffee table. There were only two items: a folded piece of letter paper, and a USB flash drive. Greenwood handed the sheet of paper straight to Aldridge.

Four pairs of eyes were on him as he unfolded it and quickly read the brief note aloud.

"Miss Hollett,
Please ensure this reaches Neil urgently. He will know what to do with it. Tell no-one else about this, I implore you.

Peter Taylor"

There was a sketch near the bottom-right corner of the paper, clearly made in a hurry. It was a rough but charming rendering of a bird, done in quick and confident strokes. It had the quality of a signature, often-practised and as uniquely identifying as handwriting. Aldridge knew it well, and he felt a wave of sadness pass over him.

Goose picked up the flash drive, drawing only the briefest glance and then nod from Greenwood. The Dutchman connected the small device to a laptop, and began pressing keys.

"Hollett said it was encrypted," Greenwood said, and Goose nodded distractedly.

"That's true," he replied, still pressing keys. "There's no way we're getting into this without the passphrase. Not in our lifetime."

Greenwood had expected as much; she knew how encryption worked. You could try to guess the word or phrase used to encrypt the data, but if it was wrong by even a single letter, you'd only get gibberish. There were so many possibilities that even with a skyscraper full of the very fastest computers all working together, it could take decades to discover the correct phrase by guessing.

We don't have that much time, she thought.

"Was Dr. Taylor right?" Greenwood asked, and Aldridge looked up at her, tearing his gaze away from the letter he still held. "Do you know what to do with

Chapter 17

this?"

"Yes," Aldridge replied, then he handed the sheet of paper back to her. Greenwood quickly looked over it, noticing the sketch, then set it down on the coffee table. She quirked an eyebrow at him impatiently.

Aldridge just picked up a small tablet computer from the table and quickly searched the web. After only ten seconds or so, he double-tapped the screen to zoom in on something, then handed the device to Greenwood. She read the text that was displayed.

"The birdwatcher must wait, and look, and see the world as it truly is. His most valuable tools are patience, observation, and complete focus on the present. With this simple act, we can understand the beauty all around us."

— Jeremy T. Henderson, *Henderson's Birds* (Oxford Press, 1966)

Greenwood looked over at Aldridge, and saw that he had a small, sad smile on his face. "This quote meant something to Dr. Taylor," she said. It wasn't a question.

"He had a framed copy of it on the wall of his office," Aldridge replied. "I've known it by heart since I was a boy. He said the same was true for science. It's about understanding beauty by having the patience to really look."

"I suppose that makes sense," Greenwood replied. "And you think it's the passphrase? This entire quote?"

Aldridge nodded. "Peter was a keen amateur ornithologist. He's had an original edition of Henderson's book for as long as I've known him. He took me birdwatching dozens of times over the years. The sketch on that note is sort-of his calling card — it's Peter's reproduction of one of the drawings from the book. It's a common chaffinch, for what it's worth."

Greenwood digested this information and then passed the tablet computer to Goose, who sat it alongside his laptop and immediately started typing.

Dowling had been standing in silence over by the wall-mounted television, and now he cleared his throat. "I get why Taylor didn't send this directly to Mr. Aldridge — too obvious, and easy to intercept — and I can see why he'd want to leak it to the press by giving it to this Hollett woman. What I don't understand is why he didn't give *her* any way to decrypt it herself, just in case Aldridge here went missing first."

"Peter knew that Julie had no interest in science, except as a means to an end," Aldridge replied immediately, looking over at the big man. "There's a chance she would have dismissed it out of hand. But I think the real reason is that he wanted someone who's qualified in his field to interpret all this for her — to make it credible. We have to assume it's about the *Destiny* project, and what's going to happen. It's pretty hard to believe, even for me. I think Peter just... he wanted me to convince her it was real, and important, and something that the public should know about."

Dowling nodded. "And he knew she'd call you, even

Chapter 17

if he never reached you himself."

"But Miss Hollett is never going to get that story," Greenwood said. "Or anybody else, if we can help it. There's no benefit to that. Just a lot of panic."

"It's not like we can evacuate most of Europe," Aldridge agreed. Then he frowned, and looked at Greenwood. "We can't, can we?"

"No," she replied. "That would be hundreds of millions of people. We don't have the resources, or a place for them to go, or probably even the time. It's completely infeasible. And it's our job to make it unnecessary."

No-one had a response to that; they all knew she was right. Greenwood spoke again after a moment, turning her attention back to Goose. "How's it coming?"

Goose drummed his fingers against the laptop's casing on either side of the trackpad area. "It's not the fastest flash drive, and there's a lot of data here. I'll need about half an hour to transfer and decrypt it, then we can see what we've got."

"GCHQ has a team standing by if they can help with the analysis," Greenwood said, and Goose nodded.

"Well then," Aldridge said, stretching his neck and then wincing as it made a loud cracking sound, "I think I'm going to get some fresh air while we're waiting. It's not been the best couple of days. Call me when you've got something for me to look at."

He didn't wait for a reply, simply turning and walking past Ramos towards the door, then slipping quietly out into the corridor.

Greenwood felt three pairs of eyes on her, and she considered her options. There was nothing of value she could do until they knew what was on the flash drive, and Aldridge was still at least theoretically in danger, despite his ability. She also had the feeling that in his current state of mind, it'd be too easy for him to get himself into trouble. She stood up.

"I'm going to keep an eye on him," she said. "I think it's time we moved to a more secure location. Let me know the moment you've decrypted the data. I'll bring Aldridge back here, and you can pick us up outside. Make sure everything is packed."

"Understood, chief," Dowling said, folding his large arms across his chest and leaning back against the wall. "Call if you need anything."

Greenwood left without another word.

It was a clear morning, and bracingly cold. The park was only one street away from the hotel, nestled at the junction of a confusing one-way traffic system that everyone except nearby residents avoided. Most of the trees were bare for winter, but a row of evergreens glistened with frost. There was a duck pond, iced along one bank, and it appeared to be deserted. A solitary cola can bobbed out near the middle of the pond, half submerged, like the periscope of a gaudy submarine.

Aldridge and Greenwood walked slowly along one of the park's several diverging paths, their breath pluming out in front of them. The noise of the city was muted,

Chapter 17

but still comfortingly audible. A jogger in pink lycra ran by in the opposite direction, and her cheeks were the same colour as her leggings. Aldridge recognised the tune buzzing from her white earphones, but the title of the song escaped him.

They had been walking in silence for several minutes when Greenwood spoke without looking round at him. "What are you thinking about?"

Aldridge pushed his hands deeper into the pockets of his insulated jacket. When Dowling and Ramos paid a visit to his flat in Edinburgh, the big man had taken the liberty of haphazardly packing a suitcase of clothes for him, and Aldridge was now very grateful for the inclusion of the goose-down sports jacket and several sweaters.

"Wondering where to go on my next holiday," he replied. "I've always wanted to visit Australia."

Greenwood cast a sidelong glance at him. She was quickly realising that he had two coping mechanisms for difficult times, and he seemed to choose between them randomly: half-hearted flirting, and flippant remarks like the one he'd just made.

We all have our defences, she thought.

"Sorry," he said after a moment, in a quieter voice. She looked around at him again, but he was still facing forward.

"Don't be," she replied. "I can't imagine how you're feeling right now."

Aldridge blew out a long breath and shrugged, coming to a stop a few hundred feet from a grove of rowan trees. "Doesn't really matter, does it?" he said at last.

Greenwood stood beside him, looking off into the distance. "Of course it matters," she said, "even if we can't do much about it."

Aldridge didn't say anything for a full minute, and when Greenwood glanced carefully over at him again, she thought she could see moisture in his eyes. She was about to say something when he surprised her by speaking first.

"They're supposed to fend off evil, you know. Rowans."

He nodded towards the cluster of trees further down the gentle hill, and she followed his gaze.

"We're going to need more of them, then," she replied, and she heard him huff beside her. She wasn't sure if it was a sound of amusement or annoyance, but right now she'd be satisfied with either.

Aldridge just stared up the vivid blue sky. It was a stupidly cheerful colour, as if he hadn't just lost someone dear to him, and as if there wasn't an unimaginable disaster looming over everybody. A crow cawed from somewhere nearby, and he thought the sound was disrespectfully loud.

Half a minute passed, and he didn't realise he'd spoken the thought until he heard his own voice. "I should've—"

"No," Greenwood interrupted, quietly but firmly. "It wasn't your fault. None of it was."

Chapter 17

He sighed. "Maybe. But we hadn't spoken in so long. I should've made the effort. I just... I thought there'd be more time."

People always do, Greenwood thought. *We have to think that. It's what lets us keep going.* She'd had to deliver the news of a death to somebody's loved ones more than a few times in her career, and the disbelief was always the worst part — as if sudden, life-changing loss was an impossible occurrence. She knew it was actually all too common.

"What happened between the two of you?" she asked. "You said you wanted to leave the research behind and teach instead."

Aldridge nodded slowly. It was the truth, but he'd be lying if he said it was the only reason. "Did you always know what you wanted to do with your life, Captain?"

Greenwood tilted her head to one side, considering the question. "I knew I wanted to serve my country," she replied after a moment. "Ever since I was a little girl."

She could see the curiosity in his eyes, but she knew he wouldn't ask more about her past right now, especially since he probably realised that she'd just deflect him.

"Well, *I* always wanted to follow in Peter's footsteps," Aldridge said. "I was fascinated by the work — by physics. It made sense. It was about making sense of everything. And for a long time, that was more than enough."

"But then you started to feel differently," she said, and he frowned.

"I... yes, I did," he replied. "Little by little." He gathered his thoughts for a moment before continuing. "Peter gave me everything, you know. He took me in when I was eleven years old, after my parents died. He gave me a new home, and a new life, and something to hold onto. Do you know how a person can hang their entire life on one thing, when there's nothing else?"

Greenwood did. She nodded.

"Mm," he replied. "Learning about the world — the fundamental forces at work — gave me time to put myself back together. It let me *find* myself, or at least find... someone that I could be. I'm not sure if that makes sense."

"It does," she said. "You were lucky to have him."

Now it was Aldridge's turn to nod. "I know I was. I always knew. I threw myself into physics and I walked his path behind him, and then alongside. We were happy, in our own way. The work was everything to him, and I was content to let it be everything for me too."

Greenwood looked at him again, seeing that his eyes were unfocused, staring off towards the cluster of trees without really seeing them. "What changed?" she asked.

"I did," he replied immediately, then he paused for a moment, assessing the truth of the statement. *Yes, I think that's exactly what happened*, he thought. "I just sort of woke up, over the course of a few months. I realised that I wanted something different, and that the research

Chapter 17

wasn't so much a calling in life as a way to hide from it."

He gave a small, bitter laugh and shook his head. "That sounds... I'm being simplistic, I know—" he glanced at Greenwood, as if expecting her to confirm the judgement, but she only looked steadily at him, "—but that's how it was. It took me *years* to realise it. It seems so obvious now."

"In hindsight, most things are," Greenwood offered, and Aldridge nodded.

They were silent for another few moments. The wind had picked up a little, and Greenwood pulled her jacket more tightly around her. "It must have been difficult to tell him about your change of heart," she said at last.

"He didn't take it well," Aldridge replied. "Peter never really understood; he said he did, but he didn't. It wasn't his fault — he just couldn't see things from my point of view. It wasn't in his nature."

Sounds like any father-figure and his son, she thought. She was about to say it aloud, but Aldridge spoke again.

"Julie was... she was part of it too. She encouraged me to break away, but I'd already made up my mind. All I needed was a push."

"How long were you two together?" Greenwood asked.

Aldridge frowned again, and a dark expression passed across his face for a moment. "About two years, all in. From a little over a year before we moved up to Edinburgh."

"Big step," Greenwood said, and Aldridge shrugged.

"It just made sense, for a lot of reasons. None of them were really about us."

Haltingly, he told Greenwood about meeting Julie in a pub one evening in Oxford after overhearing her Scottish accent, and being struck by her sharp, sarcastic wit and obvious intelligence. They ended up in a good-natured verbal sparring match, and that was the start of it. They were a *de facto* couple within a month.

"It was good for a while. For most of that year, anyway," he said. "I think that… I think we were what each other needed at that time. That was most of it. But it started to change when her mother's health failed."

They decided to relocate back to Scotland so that Julie could be closer to her mother, who lived in a town just outside the city of Edinburgh. Despite the grim circumstances, it had come at the right time. He and Julie had been fighting more and more often about his endless late nights in the lab, and the all-consuming nature of his work. Julie's career was only just ticking along at that point, and she'd come to resent his connection with his uncle — *or father*, he thought — and the work the two men did together.

"I think she felt like she was always in second place," he said, his eyes still focused on the trees in the distance. "She was probably right. And she turned the tables once we'd moved and her mother passed away a few months later."

Greenwood remained silent, only nodding to invite

Chapter 17

him to continue.

"It all happened in the eight months after her mother's death," Aldridge said. "She got wind of the story that ended up making her career — the big exposé, with those documents from the U.S. Justice Department — and then she was the one who was never at home. I got to see exactly what it had been like for her in Oxford, with me. But I was patient. At least, I was at first."

He paused, and Greenwood glanced at him again. This must be the part where he was *the fool in the relationship*, as he'd mentioned earlier that morning. She was curious, even if it had no bearing on their mission. Talking also seemed to be helping him, and until she heard from Goose, she had nothing but time.

"What happened?" she asked, and Aldridge sighed.

"The usual thing," he replied. "It was a big story, so she was teamed up with another journalist. Like Woodward and Bernstein, you know?"

She nodded. "I can see why she'd need a partner. I remember seeing new documents being released for weeks. It must have been a lot to handle."

"Lots of late nights," he said. "And as it turns out, she and her *partner* were handling more than documents."

His tone of voice left little doubt as to what he meant, and Greenwood felt a note of surprise. She hadn't picked up on that vibe at all during their brief meeting with Hollett. *I'd have expected more bitterness, or confrontation. But then, he's just lost the last of his family, and been dragged into the Destiny project.*

"I see," she said. "I'm sorry."

Aldridge tilted his head slightly in acknowledgement, still not meeting her gaze. "It's ancient history. She moved out, then down here to London, to work from the paper's head office. Her career is going from strength to strength, from what I read."

"Do you keep tabs on her?"

"Asks the woman who's tracing her phone."

Greenwood raised a perfectly-sculpted eyebrow, giving him a look that clearly said *You know very well what I mean*, and eventually he gave the barest hint of a tired grin.

"No," he replied. "I try pretty bloody hard not to. That's all done."

He paused for a moment as a thought occurred to him, and again Greenwood saw a dark expression flit across his face.

"But I'm going to have to tell her about Peter at some point. Not right now; I know that. When this is… all over."

"When it's over," Greenwood agreed.

Some of the crows briefly took flight as a wild fox dashed across the grass, but the animal veered away at the last moment and vanished over an embankment. The birds slowly returned to their perches atop the rowan trees.

"What if the data on the flash drive isn't what you're hoping for?" Aldridge asked suddenly. "Peter died to keep that information safe."

Chapter 17

"His sacrifice won't be in vain, Aldridge," Greenwood replied. "One way or another, I promise you that."

She half-turned to face him now. "Dr. Taylor was a very brave man, you know. A lot braver than you probably ever had the chance to see. And regardless of what happened between you in recent years, he obviously cared for you very much."

"I loved him," Aldridge replied, in a quiet voice. "He was my—"

He tailed off. He was going to say *my father*, but that wasn't really true. He'd known his actual father, for eleven good years. He remembered the man vividly, and still loved him every bit as much as he always had. Taylor had been something else. His uncle. His adoptive guardian and parent. His tutor and mentor. His colleague. His family.

"A person can have two fathers," Greenwood said gently, and he looked around at her, startled.

He looked into her green eyes, but her expression was unreadable. Again he found himself wondering about her own background, and what her path through life might have been like. *Maybe I'll ask you sometime*, he thought, and then he nodded.

"My father was a good man too," he said. "His name was Hugh. Great sense of humour. And my mother was Mary; she was a wonderful woman. Had the patience of a saint."

"So did everybody's mother," Greenwood said, and the remark finally drew a genuine smile from him. It lingered on his face for several long moments before fading again.

"I just wish I could have saved Peter," Aldridge said, and Greenwood knew that they were getting to the heart of it now. "And I wish he'd come to me sooner. Maybe he would have, if I'd just reached out to him over the past two years."

Greenwood remained silent. Ultimately, these demons were ones he would have to slay for himself.

"Do you—" he began, but then he paused, a deep crease appearing across his forehead. "Why do you think I couldn't undo what happened to him?"

Greenwood shook her head. "I have no idea. But you tried, I know that much. You'd have saved him if you could. You'd just brought Sergeant Dowling back only moments before. Maybe there's a… I don't know. A recharging period."

Aldridge considered her words, his eyes again focusing on the black shapes of the crows against the distant branches. "Mm," he replied. "Maybe. But you don't think it was because he and I—"

"No," Greenwood replied firmly. "I don't. And neither do you, so put it out of your mind, Aldridge."

Easier said than done, he thought.

The image wouldn't leave him. Taylor making a bid for freedom, and then the sound of the gunshot. The old man falling heavily to his knees, his life blood already flowing freely from him. To dedicate your existence to knowledge and understanding, and to give a second life

Chapter 17

to a boy who had lost everything, only for it all to come to an end on the concrete floor of a parking garage as fireworks lit up the sky outside.

Senseless. Cruel. Unforgivable.

"Merrick is going to pay for what he did."

The words were ridiculous on their own — like lines spoken by a swaggering action-movie hero, not a physicist whose girlfriend had cheated on him and then left him — but for the first time he felt real anger bloom in his chest. He had been confused, afraid, and overwhelmed almost constantly since this all began, but now those other feelings moved into the background.

He was caught in the middle of a situation he wasn't remotely prepared for, and he was still very frightened — a large part of Europe was going to be *destroyed* — but he was also suddenly furious. Merrick had shot Taylor in cold blood. And Dowling had been killed too. But Aldridge changed that.

And he wasn't in this alone. The data was being decrypted even now, and Greenwood would know what to do next. They'd come this far. There was still hope. The thought only sharpened his anger to a fine point, and he saw Merrick's face in his mind.

I have this ability, he thought. *I have no idea what it is, or what it's got to do with the disaster that's coming, but right now I'd just like to meet you one more time.*

Without really thinking about it, he raised his right hand and looked down into his open palm. His jaw was rigid with tension. Then he slowly curled his fingers into a fist.

The fine hairs on the back of Greenwood's neck stood on end. She felt it in the air immediately, like a charge building up. She glanced quickly around, but there was no-one else in sight.

At least eight large, black crows abruptly took startled flight from the trees farther down the hill, wheeling in the air and crying out in harsh, anxious calls.

Greenwood turned to look at Aldridge in alarm, and she saw him raise his gaze from his own fist to focus on the panicked birds in the sky... then everything slowed down.

The birds now moved as if they were underwater, languidly drifting far too slowly through the air. The bare branches of the trees seemed frozen in place. The vague background sound of the city was replaced with the whine of sudden and unnatural silence.

Aldridge was exquisitely aware of the now-sluggish movements of every one of the birds. He found that, if he focused his attention, he could see where they were each going to go next, just for a few seconds ahead. And he knew that he could change it if he wanted to. Reaching into the web of unfolding possibilities, and choosing a pathway through.

Everything around Greenwood was taking place in slow motion, but she felt her own pulse hammering too quickly in her chest. Still the sense of a charge building up in the air. Still the terrible feeling of unnaturalness.

The common crow, Aldridge thought, his eyes easily

Chapter 17

tracking the dreamlike glide of one of the creatures. *Or a chaffinch. Or a... kestrel.*

Greenwood saw a deep frown appear on Aldridge's forehead, and his eyes were dark. She could sense more than feel a deep thrumming all around them now, like a bass vibration underlying the whole scene. She reached out towards him, and it was like trying to move her arm through treacle.

I'm going to find you, Mr. Merrick, Aldridge thought. *I'm going to find you, and then—*

Aldridge flinched as Greenwood's hand grasped his upper arm, and the world around them abruptly snapped back to normal.

One of the crows still wheeling in the sky gave what sounded like a scolding cry, and then one by one the birds settled back onto the branches below.

"Don't do that here!" Greenwood whispered fiercely at him in a tone that was more frightened than angry, and Aldridge met her gaze, all of his anger gone now. He realised that he was shaking, and he thought that maybe she was too.

Everything around them was just as it had been before. The usual rumble of traffic, and the sound of the wind in the trees. Nothing had changed, and no-one had come running. But Aldridge could feel goosebumps all down his arms. He'd been on the brink of using the ability again, almost without realising it.

"Sorry," he gasped, his breath whistling through his nose as if he'd been running instead of just standing there, and he was mildly surprised to realise that he truly meant the apology. "Jesus. I wish none of this had ever happened. I wish I didn't have this… thing."

Greenwood was silent for a long moment, her hand still clasping his arm, and she gave him a hard, appraising look before her expression softened slightly.

"Maybe you'll be glad of it, before this is all over," she replied. "Maybe we all will."

The sound of a ringtone pierced the quiet of the park, and Greenwood reached into her jacket to retrieve her phone. The caller ID read *Goose*, and she felt her pulse quicken again. She touched a button on the screen and lifted the device to her ear.

"What have we got?" she asked, then she listened for several moments. "Alright. We'll be there in a few minutes." She returned the phone to her jacket pocket, and turned to Aldridge.

"Any luck?" he asked, and she nodded.

"They've decrypted the flash drive. We should get back to the hotel, if you're ready."

Aldridge gestured for her to lead the way, and they both set off back up the gentle hill, retracing their route.

They walked in silence for a few hundred metres. Greenwood could sense the tension in him after the new demonstration of his power. She supposed he was struggling to understand why he could call it up so instinctively at certain times, but he'd been unable to use it to save Taylor the previous night.

Chapter 17

I'd like to know that too, she thought. *I hope Goose found something promising. Merrick is even more dangerous now that he knows about Aldridge.*

She also knew that Aldridge could be of great help to them. He was a physicist who worked alongside Taylor for years, after all. Even without his strange ability, he was a definite asset. *And I need him focused for this.*

"At least things are looking up for your next relationship, Aldridge," she said. In her peripheral vision, she saw his stride falter for a moment, but she kept walking.

"Oh?" he prompted, drawing level with her again. She knew he was looking at her now.

"Most men would give anything to be able to undo their mistakes."

He grunted in amusement, shaking his head at the sheer absurdity of his situation. "I'll probably save a fortune in flowers," he replied. "Hypothetically."

"Hypothetically," she agreed.

"Did Goose say anything about the decrypted data?" he asked, feeling the scientific curiosity rising up inside him despite everything that had happened.

"No," Greenwood replied. "He knows not to discuss it over the phone, even on our secure lines. We'll find out soon anyway."

"I'm eager to get a look at it. I should be able to help you there."

That's what I was hoping, she thought. It was also an opportunity to distract him from everything else, and she wasn't above manipulating him to help do it.

"I was wondering about that," Greenwood said, "but we have people too, at CERN and elsewhere. And you've been through a lot already. Maybe you should just step back and let us handle this part."

"I appreciate the concern, *Captain*, but I was a senior research physicist in exactly the same field as Peter," Aldridge said firmly. "I studied under him, worked with him, and we co-authored twenty-six peer-reviewed papers. Whatever he was doing, I can help you understand it. You *need* me. Even without considering… what I can do."

Greenwood was silent for a few moments, pretending to consider his words, but she knew he was right. He was probably one of the best people in the world to help them right now.

"Alright, Aldridge," she said at last. "We'd appreciate any insight you can give us."

"Then it's settled," he replied. They had only walked another ten metres before he added "And *I'd* appreciate the chance to have another conversation with Mr. Merrick. I think there's something I'd like to show him."

Greenwood glanced at him briefly, but she didn't respond.

That's what I'm afraid of, she thought.

Chapter 18

How far we've come, Merrick thought.

He was standing in a small conference room on the fifth and most subterranean level of the facility. It was a little after midday, and Anfruns would contact him via video call within the next few hours.

The old man would be displeased again — furious, no doubt — but it mattered very little. Merrick knew that the setback was temporary, and was in fact an opportunity in disguise. Taylor had ceased to be an asset to the project on the day he escaped, but he would have been a dangerous ally for its enemies. Now he had been neutralised, and whatever information he took with him would only serve to end the status quo of secrecy from the European Defence Agency.

Merrick also knew it was only a matter of waiting for the brown-haired woman and her associates to come to him. They would use Taylor's guidance to recreate the mobile detector technology, and the next time a human-scale event took place, they would inevitably travel to that location just as Merrick himself would. There was no need to even search them out.

"They will come to us, and the outcome will be very different," he said to himself.

He was slightly concerned about Taylor's nephew, however. The man had the ability, and had used it to save his comrade's life. But he'd been unable to repeat the feat when Taylor was killed, so Merrick knew he was inexperienced and operating only on instinct. It was the usual way. The inconsistency could be overcome by learning to focus the mind.

Or with practice, he thought. *Willingly or otherwise.*

He had quickly discovered how the ability manifested itself, especially when his own power became apparent one evening in this very building.

But that was later, some time after he was brought on board.

Once CERN discovered the time-inverted tachyon energy signature, they naturally approached the European Defence Agency with their findings, and soon Anfruns had become involved. Conducting further research into the apparently impending cataclysm was exactly the sort of task that his company's *Stille* group was well equipped for, and their existing black-budget relationship with most of the primary member states of the EU inspired a great deal of confidence.

The entire team from CERN was transplanted to one

Chapter 18

of Stille's locations to continue their work under the utmost secrecy. The project's codename was *Destiny*, and its overriding priority was to identify the event's precise location, date, and magnitude. Wide-scale disaster preparedness plans were already being put in place secretly across Western Europe.

It had been a relatively easy task to build anti-tachyon detection equipment, based on the data from CERN. Characteristic patterns of electromagnetic radiation were highly accurate indicators of the phenomenon, and regional detectors were already in place throughout much of the continent, monitoring the activity of the residual energy patterns from the future event. Work continued twenty-four hours per day, every day. And then the breakthrough occurred, which altered the whole nature of the project.

We found the preacher, Merrick thought.

After weeks of passively monitoring the energy patterns and trying to form a mathematical and physical model, a new, much smaller and completely unexpected burst of anti-tachyons had been detected. They had been so weak that they had decayed almost immediately, indicating that whatever produced them had happened in the present, not the future. The trajectories were coherent, and indicated that the point of origin was a small town about fifty kilometres north-east of Paris, called Oissery.

The corner of Merrick's mouth twitched as he recalled the day.

* * *

Upon arriving in the town, Merrick's team had found the place in comparative uproar. A local clergyman apparently had a profound religious experience, and was currently in seclusion, praying for guidance. This would be remarkable enough at any time, but it had caused him to cancel the Sunday service, perplexing the town. It hadn't taken many discreet enquiries to learn that the priest's spiritual encounter had coincided exactly with the new anti-tachyon burst.

The worried groundskeeper who had broken down the door to the priest's private residence behind the chapel late the following morning had found no trace of the old man. By that time, Merrick had already been and gone.

Merrick didn't even have to drug the holy man. His name was Benoit Tebeau, and he was frightened but also righteously indignant. He seemed to feel almost invulnerable, defiantly describing how he had witnessed a genuine miracle. The night before, around midnight, he had been closing up the draughty chapel before going to bed, and had accidentally jostled an oil lamp with his arthritic fingers. It had begun to topple, and then everything seemed to stop.

"*The Lord showed me the lamp falling,*" he had explained in French, spitting in his fervour. "*It broke against the floor, and I was set ablaze — but then He brought me back! I saw myself catch the lamp instead. I felt the breath of angels, and I reached out my hand, and there it was; unbroken. Mer-*

Chapter 18

ciful Father!"

He had repeated the story when prompted, and then degenerated into repeated affirmations of the glory of his saviour, and his certainty that he had been spared on account of his life of pious service.

Merrick had felt uneasy. He didn't believe the old man's spiritual explanation, but the anti-tachyon readings were incontrovertible; there had even been faint remaining readings from Tebeau himself. The fact that the burst had occurred at the same moment as the old priest's vision or experience had to be significant. Merrick had learned many times that coincidences usually meant danger.

Less than an hour later, Aranega had returned with the oil lamp. It displayed no anti-tachyon activity whatsoever, nor did it show any signs of damage beyond the expected wear-and-tear of long use. An ordinary lamp. Merrick ordered Finn to drive their vehicle up an overgrown farm road leading to a disused barn. They took the priest inside the rickety structure, Aranega began video recording, and Merrick lit the oil lamp. Tebeau's eyes showed first surprise and then fear, and he clasped his hands together in silent prayer.

You are more perceptive than my own men, priest, Merrick thought, then he suddenly threw the lamp under-arm at the kneeling old man.

Tebeau called out *"Dieu, aide-moi!"* in a high, wavering voice as he held both his hands outwards and then closed his eyes.

Merrick watched with cold interest as the lamp flew towards the pitiful figure. Then everything seemed to slow down, and the scene before them split apart somehow, with two different versions of events overlapping each other. In one, the lamp arced over the priest's shoulder, spilling a stream of burning oil that scorched his left ear and cheek. In the other, though, the lamp was safely caught, its trajectory ever so slightly different.

At the last moment, with his eyes still closed, the priest's left arm abruptly shifted in position, without appearing to actually move. He seemed to shimmer briefly, and there was a sensation like a blast of wind through the barn. Tebeau's outstretched hand easily snagged the handle of the lamp, catching it smoothly in mid-air.

Impossible, Merrick thought, feeling a chill race up his spine. In his peripheral vision he saw Tepel crossing himself, and the others glancing back and forth warily between him and the priest. Then they all suddenly flinched as a harsh series of beeps echoed in unison from the anti-tachyon detection displays mounted on their forearms.

The devices were state of the art. Flexible, curved screens made from electrostable liquid polymers, sandwiched between an acrylic composite originally designed for sub-orbital missile casings. The displays were multi-touch capable, tied into military GPS and networked via a briefcase-sized microwave array transponder which Aranega carried on his back at all times. They

Chapter 18

were designed as terminals and location-finders, remotely connected to the primary high-energy particle detector installation in northern Sweden. It had taken less than three seconds for the burst to be detected more than one-and-a-half thousand miles away, and the data relayed back to them.

The displays pulsed into life. The dark blue GPS map backdrop was superimposed with fireworks-like patterns of orange and yellow, radiating outwards in zigzag trajectories from their current location. A red warning pulsed along the bottom edge:

EVENT DISTANCE: 6.7m

Merrick slowly looked up from the display to the priest, who now crouched on the floor almost seven metres away, swinging the lamp gently back and forth with tears rolling down his sallow cheeks. He was muttering a prayer in French, and he looked as if he had already found his Paradise.

"Congratulations, Father," Merrick said contemplatively, walking towards the priest. "Perhaps you do have friends in high places." He took the lamp easily from the old man's hand, and then returned to his previous spot near the barn's entrance. He held the lamp up and Drost passed a series of handheld scientific devices over it: a Geiger counter, a highly sensitive electromagnetic field detector, and a bulky device designed to detect neutrino decay. All three devices remained silent.

"It's *him*, not the fuckin' lamp," Finn said from behind Drost, and spat on the ground. "I don't like this. I was brought up as a fuckin' Catholic. Maybe we should take him back to his village."

Merrick gave him a sharp glance, and Finn looked away. Tepel crossed himself once more, and Merrick sighed in frustration, turning to look at the priest again.

"You must forgive my associates, Father," he said, "They have forgotten that we are men of science."

Tebeau looked up at them through wet eyes, a beatific smile on his face. *"Your soul stands in judgement here, monsieur,"* he said, and Merrick's fist clenched at his own feeling of unease.

"This was an experiment, not a miracle," Merrick continued. "Science demands experimentation." He raised the lamp to head height, illuminating the kneeling priest in eerie relief. Shadows danced around the weather-worn timbers of the old barn, competing with the baleful waning moon that shone through a collapsed section of roofing. Drost's hand moved to his holstered pistol, then he glanced at Merrick and thought better of it.

"In experimentation, one principle holds true above all," Merrick said darkly, and the priest's smile finally faltered. The old man held Merrick's gaze for a long moment, and then gave a barely-perceptible nod. His shoulders fell slightly, and he closed his eyes once more.

"Results must be repeatable," Merrick said, and threw the lamp with all his might.

It tumbled end over end, and an arc of oil sloshed out, spraying the floor and almost reaching Tebeau. The

Chapter 18

lamp itself arrived less than a second later, its ornate glass shattering across his face, breaking his left cheekbone in two places. Then the oil caught fire.

Finn grinned as the old man screamed. Drost wore a grimace of disgust. The others only watched, expressionless. Tebeau was now writhing on the ground, his simple cassock completely ablaze. His hair smoked, and his screaming was now cracked and inhuman.

Merrick glanced casually down at his detector display, as if he was checking the time. Its blue stylised map showed his current location relative to surrounding roads. There was no particle activity. He looked back up just as Tebeau ceased to make any sound at all, and saw that the old man's hair was entirely gone. The exposed skin of his face, neck and hands was now a furious blistered red with strips of black, scaly flesh. Less than two seconds later, the body jerked once and then moved no more.

"It seems your God no longer favours you," Merrick said.

Merrick's eyes darkened at the memory. It was the key discovery, and the timing was perfect.

More anti-tachyon bursts were detected in other places in the weeks and months after he had first brought back the astounding story of the priest's ability to somehow alter the outcomes of unfavourable events. In each case, when seeking out the source of the energy signatures, they found a person with the same ability.

Some of these gifted people had suffered unfortunate fates at Merrick's hands. One — an elderly woman in Venice — had been dead before he even arrived, the shock of the experience no doubt too much to bear.

But most of them still live.

Merrick's own ability first manifested itself during early tests of the extent of the captives's powers. It was pure instinct, and he had reversed a lethal gunshot he inflicted on a retired police officer from Lisbon. The only witness besides himself and the victim was one of the project's research scientists. Merrick killed them both to conceal the secret, but not before the scientist had provided him with the final piece of knowledge he required to plan his insurrection against Anfruns.

Every wielder of this power produces an almost-identical but in fact unique energy signature.

Merrick wasted no time in coercing the scientist to erase the relevant log from the facility's computer system, and block his own particular energy signature from ever being reported again. Since all anti-tachyon detection events were fed to the facility for analysis and redistribution, he could hide any use of his power from the project's staff, and from Anfruns.

It was a potentially devastating advantage, to be kept in reserve until the time came to seize control of Destiny for himself.

"And it was you, Dr. Taylor, who set the timetable," he said to himself, pleased at the fact of it.

Taylor's escape had put everything in motion. Brus-

Chapter 18

sels would very soon know all that Stille had hidden from them about Destiny, if they didn't already. They would immediately intervene. Anfruns was extremely powerful, but he had no standing army to defy the European security infrastructure. Brussels would try to snatch Destiny back from him, but they would fail. Merrick had already seen to that.

"Before they drag you away to prison, Mikkel, we will meet one final time," he said to the empty room, "and then the future will be mine."

Chapter 19

The safe house was a flat above a small cafe that specialised in custom-made marshmallows. The entire building was owned by the British Secret Intelligence Service, and the shopkeeper — a kindly-looking woman in her late forties, who walked with a cane — was also on their payroll. The cafe was currently closed.

Dowling led Greenwood and Aldridge up the external staircase from the lane at the back of the cafe, and when they reached the top he simply stopped, facing the door. There was a peephole set into it, which looked decades old. After a moment, the door swung open to reveal Ramos.

Greenwood noticed how the other woman's eyes flicked towards Aldridge, and she tried to read the expression.

Worry, maybe, she thought. *Let's see what we've learned.*

They all went along a short hallway and into what

was clearly a living room under ordinary circumstances. Today, though, the sofa and armchairs had been pushed against one wall, and there was a dining table in the middle of the floor. On it sat a series of laptops and tablet devices, a small projector, and a few other pieces of technology that Aldridge couldn't identify. All of the windows had blinds pulled down over them. Goose was waiting by the end of the long table.

"Show me what we've got," Greenwood said, and Goose nodded. He stepped over to the laptop that sat nearest the projector, and pressed a key. Dowling was still standing in the doorway, and he flipped the light switch to darken the room. The laptop's screen was mirrored on a blank section of wall where a painting had obviously recently hung.

A series of files were open on the screen, including a video window. Aldridge recognised some of the data. There were equations, topographical charts of parts of Europe, and what looked like employee records. There were also what he knew to be DNA double-helix structure diagrams, and an inventory of some kind. The most prominent window was a document that seemed to be a journal, in Taylor's familiar academic style.

"Peter wrote this," he said to no-one in particular, and Goose looked over at him.

"Yes, he did. It's addressed to you. It's extensive."

"Does it say anything about this thing I can do?"

"Yes, it does," Goose replied, after a moment. "It seems that the Destiny project has evolved quite a bit,

Chapter 19

and the European Defence Agency has been kept in the dark."

Greenwood stepped over beside Aldridge, still facing the makeshift screen on the wall. "Give us an overview, Goose," she said, and the Dutchman nodded once more.

"There are other people like you, Mr. Aldridge," he began, in a grim tone. "Merrick found them accidentally, beginning in France. Whenever they use their ability, it produces the same energy signature as the future disaster, localised wherever they happen to be."

Aldridge was stunned. He hadn't even begun to come to terms with the idea that he had this ability himself, much less that there were others out there who could consciously change the outcomes of events. "Where are the others?" he asked, leaning forward.

Goose frowned. "There are fifteen or so," he said. "Or there *were*, at least. Merrick has been rounding them up and taking them to Stille. It seems Anfruns is convinced they hold the key to averting the catastrophe, and I suppose he might even be right about that."

He paused for a moment, considering his next words carefully. "According to the reports Dr. Taylor copied, Merrick has been experimenting on these people. Testing how far their abilities go. There have been some casualties."

Aldridge felt his stomach clench. "Can't say I'm surprised," he replied. "And how far *do* their abilities go? What does Stille know about all this?"

"Quite a lot," Goose said thoughtfully. "They have no

idea how it works, but they know that each time one of these *changers* — that's what they call them — uses their ability, it affects the energy from the future event. Like a magnet disturbing iron filings. Stille is using these perturbations to more and more accurately predict exactly when and where the disaster is going to happen."

Aldridge felt a finger of ice touch his spine. It was only just sinking in that his ability was somehow intimately connected to the future deaths of millions of people. Greenwood saw his expression change, and she knew exactly what he was thinking.

"And what's this?" she asked, pointing at the video window.

"It's the first one they found — a French priest," Goose replied. "They recorded the whole thing. It doesn't end well."

"Play it," Greenwood said, and no-one spoke for the next few minutes as the video ran its course. The recording shut off not long after Tebeau died, once Drost had taken a final set of readings.

There was silence in the room. Eventually, Aldridge spoke. "There's a genetic component to the ability, isn't there?"

"You can read that?" Goose said, tilting his head towards the DNA helix diagram and another document full of letters that Aldridge assumed was a fully sequenced genome.

"No, but it stands to reason," he replied. "Peter didn't just bring the data to me; he asked if anything unusual

Chapter 19

had happened. He knew that I would have the ability. Or at least, he suspected it was possible."

Goose nodded. "Yes, there's a specific mutation. It's familial, but it's not active in most cases. He was an inactive carrier, and his notes say that he thinks your mother — his sister — was too."

Greenwood took a step towards the display on the wall, peering at the jumble of letters. "How prevalent is the active mutation in the general population? How many people like Aldridge are out there, besides the ones Stille is holding?"

Goose tapped several keys and brought up another display. "It's difficult to know, but the project's biologists believe it's incredibly rare. There might not be any more at all. They've gathered the ones they do have from all over Europe."

"Why just Europe, though?" Dowling asked from the back of the room, folding his large arms against his chest.

"Perhaps the mutation just hasn't spread far enough yet," Aldridge said. "Or perhaps it's only detectable within the radius of the event. If there were others using the ability beyond Europe, I assume Stille's equipment would have picked them up."

Dowling made a small noise of acknowledgement, leaning back against the wall.

"There's a letter for you, Mr. Aldridge," Goose said. "It asks that you corroborate the scientific data in the package, and take it all to Julie Hollett. Dr. Taylor wanted her to publish it."

Aldridge pressed a knuckle to the bridge of his nose for a moment. "I'm sorry, Peter, but I'm afraid it would do more harm than good," he said to himself.

There was respectful silence for a few seconds before Goose spoke again. "He also asked you to bring the data to the European Defence Agency."

"And you did," Greenwood said. "Taylor was right about that part. With this information, the Agency can confront Anfruns about keeping the existence of people like you a secret, and demand to know why."

"Anfruns's plan seems fairly clear to me," Aldridge said. There was a tension in his voice now, and Greenwood didn't like it.

"Oh?" she replied, and he nodded slowly.

"Well, he's going to use his captives to try and stop the event from ever happening — and he'll have no argument from me on that. But I doubt he, or Merrick, intend to let them go afterwards. Think about what this ability means, in real terms. If he has a group of people who can each do what I can do, think what he could use them for."

"Bodyguards?" Dowling asked, thinking of what had happened to him in the parking garage. "He'd be safe from pretty much anything."

"Even a bullet," Ramos said.

"Think bigger," Aldridge said. "Imagine what he could *demand*."

"You're talking about ransom and blackmail," Green-

Chapter 19

wood replied. "Bad things happen, and he fixes them — maybe after causing them in the first place."

Aldridge nodded. After a moment, Greenwood turned to Goose.

"Was there anything on Taylor's flash drive about any other way to stop the Destiny event?" she asked, and her chest tightened as she saw Goose and Ramos exchange a grim look.

"No," Goose said. "And there's more bad news, Captain. It was Taylor's work that allowed Stille to refine the predictive algorithm — the program that uses the anti-tachyon decay data to determine when and where the disaster takes place. They had a very crude version from the beginning, but Taylor's is far superior." He pressed a few keys and a document came to the front, obviously part of Taylor's lab journal.

The uncertain temporal and physical coordinates of the event make preparation difficult. Every occurrence of the small-scale phenomenon, however, further localises the area of our search. There exists the intriguing possibility of being able to predict, with sufficient data, the exact future time and location of the event to within useful accuracy — if a suitable algorithm can be constructed.

"He'd produced the current algorithm within a month of writing that," Goose said.

"And what's the bad news?" Aldridge asked, even though he suspected he already knew.

"The location is still vague, but using the additional data from what Aldridge did in Edinburgh, we now have a specific date and time," Goose replied. "We've triple-checked."

The temperature in the room seemed to drop by several degrees.

"How long do we have?" Greenwood asked.

The Dutchman's brown eyes looked almost black, and too wide. He looked down at the laptop, but it was Ramos who answered.

"About fourteen hours," she said.

Greenwood's training allowed her to control any outward sign of panic, but her pulse thudded in her ears. *Millions of people. My responsibility. No time.* She nodded tightly.

"Get me the Director," she said.

Chapter 20

Anfruns straightened his tie, knowing that it was already immaculate.

The most significant days of our lives arrive with so little warning, he thought.

It had been almost half an hour since the emergency request came in from the European Defence Agency, requiring him to participate in a video conference which would start in the next few minutes. It was easy to guess the purpose of the meeting.

Dr. Peter Taylor had obviously taken information from Stille's facility and despite Merrick's efforts, had managed to bring it to the attention of the Agency. It was only ever a matter of time before Brussels found out just how far *Destiny* had progressed, and it would seem that the day had finally arrived.

So be it.

Everything began anew when Merrick discovered the

French priest, the first of a growing set of guests in the secure facility.

Merrick called them *changers*, in typically Germanic utilitarian fashion. He was as disdainful of them as he was of everyone else, though he understood their importance. Once their ability had been confirmed, a series of tests were devised to provoke the use of their power, and determine its extent. They learned more each week, and Stille's pharmaceutical enterprises had furnished some astonishing drugs which made the subjects much more compliant.

Anfruns profoundly disliked the idea of keeping people captive, and experimenting on them was abhorrent. Europe had seen more than enough of such things in the dark century that only recently ended. But there was no other choice. They were simply too valuable.

Destiny was now proceeding on two fronts: refining the location and precise date of the cataclysm, using a computer model based on anti-tachyon decay which was updated every time a new event was detected, and also secretly finding and capturing these special people. They would be the key to preventing the disaster, and so much more afterwards.

My apostles, Anfruns thought. He would take them all, in the closing hours before much of Europe would be wiped out, to the epicentre of the coming disaster. They would direct all of their abilities towards preventing it from ever happening, and they would succeed. He was sure of it. He imagined himself standing there with

Chapter 20

them, guiding them, *leading* them in the very eye of the cataclysm. They would prevail. But that was only the beginning.

With a secret staff of people who could actually alter events in his favour, however limited the ability's window of opportunity might be, he would have undreamed-of power. Nations attacked each other all over the world, constantly. What could he demand in return if he could actually offer to undo such atrocities? Assassinations. The chemical weapon attacks in Syria. Religious wars. The possibilities were unlimited, and so was the potential. With access to each country's national intelligence apparatus, he could have people in place ready to undo almost any wrong — if his demands were met.

And so a new world will dawn, he thought, straightening the sleeves of his suit jacket. *A world of order, and of peace. A world without deterrents, because governments on all sides will have seen and felt every horror, then been given a second chance.*

That would be his legacy. In time, the world would come to understand that his methods were necessary.

In time, the world would thank him.

"I can assure you, Minister, that Stille has shared all of our findings with your agency. Without exception. These allegations are entirely unfounded, troubling, and hurtful."

Anfruns knew the gambit was almost certainly useless, but he was calm, and his voice was measured. He had learned decades ago that confidence was mostly an illusion projected by unwavering eye contact, a firm voice, well-chosen words, and a dry brow.

The panoramic video screen along one side of his office currently linked him to a meeting in the Brussels headquarters of the European Defence Agency.

Ten grim faces looked back at him, mostly in military uniforms, but it was the woman in the navy suit that Anfruns was focusing all his attention on. Janne Wuyts was Head of Agency for the EDA, and directly responsible for oversight of the Destiny project. She was a slender woman with hazel eyes so dark they were almost brown, and her elegantly-styled hair was pure white. She wore gold-rimmed half-moon spectacles on the end of her nose, and when she wasn't speaking, she sat absolutely motionless. Anfruns could feel Wuyts's eyes boring into him, even over the video link. As chairperson of the Defence Agency's Steering Group, she had enormous influence, and she wielded it at every opportunity.

The meeting was not going well. Wuyts's under-secretary had begun by reading from a classified report that Anfruns recognised as being from Stille, specifically about the captive people who manifested the ability to make localised changes to the outcomes of events. Wuyts herself then took over, asking for Anfruns's explanation. Anfruns maintained that he was ignorant of any part of the Destiny project outside of energy re-

Chapter 20

search, and that he had certainly not sanctioned any covert operations.

"We seem to be making little progress here, Mikkel," Wuyts said in a disinterested voice. Her French accent was barely noticeable, and her voice was almost jovial. She was a dangerous opponent. "Our sources are not in question. Do you mean to tell me you've so completely lost control of your own organisation?"

Anfruns smiled patiently. *Bait me all you like, minister.*

"If, and I do mean *if*, there is a rogue element within Stille conducting unauthorised experimentation, then I can assure the Agency that it will be found and eliminated," Anfruns replied, putting the barest emphasis on the last word. None of the other faces so much as raised an eyebrow. They knew very well what Anfruns was capable of, no matter how much they might politely skirt around it. It was why they had approached him with Destiny, after all.

Wuyts sighed, and made a show of removing her spectacles and polishing them on a cloth she whipped from her suit jacket.

"We're unsatisfied with how forthcoming you're being," she said bluntly, not even bothering to make eye contact. "The time has come for the Agency to assume direct control of Stille's operations under the emergency powers granted to us by the General Council this morning. You'll be receiving a copy of the order — at *all* of your locations — within the hour."

Anfruns gritted his teeth behind his smile, but kept

his face neutral. "I don't believe that is necessary, but I will of course comply with any lawful request."

Wuyts perched her spectacles upon her nose once more, and peered at Anfruns over the video link, as if scrutinising something attached to the bottom of her shoe.

"You will indeed, Mr. Anfruns," she said, then paused for a long moment before glancing off to one side and nodding her head. The video link went dead immediately.

Anfruns exhaled silently, then lifted his arms onto the surface of his desk. Both hands were curled into fists.

Anfruns stood at the large window behind his desk, looking out. His empty chair faced the monitor on which Merrick's face was visible, but he knew that the other man could still hear him perfectly.

"We are wasting time," came the gruff voice from over his shoulder, and Anfruns grimaced in irritation.

"It is you who are wasting *my* time, Kurt," he replied icily. "I have just been told that the European Defence Agency is to assume control of Stille for the duration of Project Destiny. Your continuing incompetence disappoints me."

Merrick clenched a fist but forced his anger down. "I consider our mission to have been a success," he said.

Anfruns turned quickly from the window to finally face the monitor, with a grimace of disgust on his face. "And which part of the fiasco was your greatest triumph? The death of Dr. Taylor? Or losing one of your thugs, perhaps? Enlighten me."

"It was imperative to discover why Taylor chose to seek out this man Aldridge, instead of going directly to the authorities" Merrick said evenly. "We've learned that he has the ability, and Brussels is now fully aware of those like him. Our timetable has changed, but we are in a superior position."

Anfruns considered the other man's words carefully. There was some truth there, but they would also have agents of the Defence Agency — probably with regional law-enforcement support — on their doorsteps at any moment.

"This group you encountered..." he began, raising an eyebrow.

"European special operations," Merrick replied. "I don't have any more specific information at this time. They were certainly military, and well trained and equipped."

"I've been making some enquiries," Anfruns replied. "They were sent by the Security Council, it seems — a covert tactical force, codenamed KESTREL. They are led by one Captain Jessica Greenwood. They do not officially exist, as far as the Defence Agency is concerned."

Merrick considered this information for a moment before replying. "Then I have more respect for those fools and their paymasters than I did yesterday."

"Indeed," Anfruns replied, "and I imagine you will be seeing them again very soon. It's reasonable to assume they now have the ability to track the anti-tachyon patterns much as we can. Our options have become severely limited."

Merrick stared at him implacably, waiting for the inevitable order. It came after less than ten seconds.

"Move our guests to the contingency location immediately," he said, and the barest ghost of a grin passed across Merrick's face.

"They are already en route," he said, taking great pleasure in seeing Anfruns's eyes narrow.

"Then you should join them, and see where we stand with the latest batch of data from your ridiculous performance in Edinburgh."

Merrick nodded in mock courtesy, and reached forward to end the video connection.

"And Kurt?" Anfruns said, causing Merrick to pause.

From this angle, Anfruns was only a silhouette against the large window, lit from behind by the dull light of the cloudy sky. Merrick squinted, but couldn't make out the older man's face. He wasn't even sure if Anfruns was facing towards him, or looking out the window again.

"Be very careful how much initiative you show in future," Anfruns said softly. "You wouldn't want me to find you unpredictable."

Merrick stared at the backlit shape on the screen defiantly for several long moments, but made no reply. *You will find me unpredictable exactly once, old man. It will not be long now.*

Chapter 20

Then he reached forward once more, pressed a button, and the screen went dark.

Chapter 21

The only sound in the specially modified trailer was of the wheels against the road.

From the outside, the vehicle was unremarkable: a haulage truck with the livery of an agricultural chemical company, complete with warning decals and well-worn signage. The driver was an overweight middle-aged man with two days' worth of scratchy brown-grey stubble, a tattered denim cap, and nicotine stains on his fingertips. Just another truck, making yet another long delivery run.

Inside, it was a different story. The entire trailer space had been converted to hold racks of seats, bolted securely to the floor. The walls were battleship grey, and the floor was corrugated metal. Four security cameras monitored the entire space, even though there was nowhere to hide.

Fourteen of the available forty seats were taken, the

occupants all securely strapped-in with belts which criss-crossed their bodies and could only be unlocked with a custom key. All of the passengers were pale, worn, and currently unconscious, their heads lolling down towards their chests.

In an additional single row of seats at the front of the space, six men clad in black tactical gear sat cradling semi-automatic machine guns. On the end of the row, there was also a doctor, nervously flipping through a clipboard full of diagnostic print-outs.

No-one spoke. The orders from Merrick had been terse, and delivered with more than the usual undercurrent of menace. The truck was to stop for nothing, and in the unlikely event of being forcibly halted by the authorities, the mercenaries had been authorised to use lethal force without hesitation.

The fourteen captives each showed multiple signs of abuse. Cuts and bruises, dark shadows under their eyes, and prominent cheekbones were visible on all of them. One, a twelve year old girl, had a long bandage wrapped around her wrist and forearm. An elderly man had a cast around his left shin. A young man in his mid-twenties had gauze over his eyes, and a burn mark on his cheek.

They were being moved to a facility which wasn't listed even on the most classified internal directory of Stille locations. The truck had no GPS unit, and was fully electromagnetically shielded. There were no radios or mobile phones in the vehicle whatsoever, and it had

Chapter 21

stopped to change license plates three times in total during the almost seven hours of the journey.

The mercenaries acting as guards had no knowledge of their final destination, and the driver was being compensated extremely well to make the trip: his wife and daughter would be returned to him that evening.

The anonymous vehicle rumbled on through the grey afternoon, along highways and down country roads, bringing its hidden occupants ever closer to their fate.

"So the time is almost upon us," Merrick mused, looking at a large flat-panel monitor attached to the wall of the makeshift lab at the contingency location.

He had arrived with his team less than thirty minutes before, still several hours ahead of the captive changers, and had wasted no time in securing the new facility. No further anti-tachyon bursts had been recorded since Aldridge's spontaneous demonstration of his power the night before, which also meant that the changers being transported hadn't caused any trouble.

One of the handful of energy research scientists they'd also transported here had asked to see Merrick as soon as he arrived, and Merrick now stood before him.

The noticeably uneasy man had just told him the energy readings from the previous evening had been incorporated into the predictive algorithm, and while the location of the event was still vague, they now knew it would take place much sooner than initially thought: in the early hours of the following day.

"Are you certain you can't also predict the location? Surely at least the region. The *country* of the event's epicentre," Merrick said, not bothering to make eye contact.

"I'm afraid not, uh, sir," the scientist replied, his hands thrust rigidly into the pockets of his lab coat. "The algorithm is based on the relative strength and trajectory of each energy event, and the location and date are independent factors. The location is likely to coalesce rapidly once we have enough samples, but we're not quite there yet. It also depends on the nature of the events. Spontaneous demonstrations of the ability are much more useful to us."

Merrick finally turned to gaze at the scientist. "How many more samples do you require?"

The man flushed, and scratched his head as he scrambled to think. "It's very difficult to say. Sir. There's no way to predict accurately. But as an estimate, I'd say only a handful more, given the proximity of the Destiny phenomenon."

Merrick scrutinised the man as an animal stares down its wounded prey, noting the bead of sweat that ran down from his high hairline and caught in an eyebrow. He was clearly telling the truth, and Merrick wasn't entirely unfamiliar with the basis of the predictive algorithm — he had been briefed on the subject, and had made it a point to keep up to date.

"Very well," Merrick replied, dismissing the man with the barest wave of his hand. The scientist exhaled audi-

Chapter 21

bly, but he didn't make any move to leave. "Was there something else?" Merrick asked.

"I thought you'd want to know that Mr. Anfruns was automatically informed of the revised timetable of the Destiny event," the other man said.

There was a long moment of perfect stillness, and the scientist felt his pulse pounding in his veins. He was well aware of the fates of some of the original captives, and he had heard the whispered rumours that Merrick had even been responsible for Dr. Osborne's disappearance too.

"And what did Anfruns say?" Merrick asked, his voice measured and ice cold, as he returned the scientist's gaze without blinking.

The man cleared his throat, feeling his shirt clinging to him beneath his lab coat. "He, uh, gave an order that no new subjects are to be acquired, even if signals are detected. He told us to block any new signals from the mobile detector units, until further notice."

Understandable, Merrick thought. The Destiny event was mere hours away: time was short, and everything was at stake, especially with the Defence Agency assuming control of Stille's known facilities. If further small-scale anti-tachyon events occurred, Greenwood's team could now track them, and they would inevitably deploy to those locations to seek out more people like Aldridge. *And perhaps in hope of avenging Taylor's death,* Merrick thought. Anfruns knew this, and he had no intention of allowing Merrick to be distracted from their primary goal of using the captive changers to prevent or undo the disaster.

But I have unfinished business with Aldridge and his friends.

"Consider the order countermanded. You will restore the mobile detector functionality immediately," Merrick said. His voice was still calm and even, without a hint of anger. He spoke with absolute confidence. His gaze burned into the other man, who looked away after only a moment.

"Yes, sir," the scientist replied, then he hurried from the room.

Chapter 22

"Incredible," Aldridge said, to no-one in particular.

He was sitting in an armchair that had been pulled into the bay window area of their makeshift command post in the safe house, and he was using a laptop to examine all of the decrypted data from Taylor's flash drive.

He'd been making remarks to himself periodically, sometimes drawing the attention of the others in the room, but mostly they left him to it. It was painful to read Taylor's notes, in his familiar style and addressed to Aldridge himself, but it was also fascinating, and he needed the distraction.

There'll be plenty of time for grief later, he thought. *I hope.*

Greenwood had spoken earlier via video link to the head of the European Defence Agency, and Aldridge knew that Brussels was now moving to seize control of

Stille's facilities throughout Europe. He also suspected that Merrick and Anfruns were a lot more cunning than the Agency was hoping, and that the situation hadn't really improved. The disaster was going to occur the following morning, in the early hours, and they were no closer to knowing what its cause would be, or whether Anfruns's presumed plan to stop it was going to be effective.

"Can I get something to write with?" he asked, gesturing without looking up from the laptop, and Goose got up and walked over.

"Here you go," Goose said, putting a smaller tablet device down beside him. He took a plastic stylus from his pocket and sat it beside the small tablet. "Moving around and zooming work like you'd expect. Write with your finger or the pen. You can flip pages with the arrow buttons, or by swiping. If you need something put up on a larger screen, just let me know. All of Taylor's data is on this too."

Aldridge glanced up a him, momentarily taken aback. "Thanks," he said. "But I was really thinking about a pen and some paper."

Goose nodded apologetically. "Brussels prefers everything to be digitised," he said. "That way they see it a few seconds after we do, and it's backed up automatically. Besides," he added, "the EU loves saving trees." Aldridge just shrugged, and Goose returned to his seat across the room.

There was a table of data on the laptop's screen enti-

Chapter 22

tled *Anti-Tachyon Burst Event Metrics*. The information was a catalogue of all logged anti-tachyon events, and some of the columns automatically updated every second. The smaller events had a negative time-displacement value, indicating that they had happened in the past.

Aldridge highlighted several rows of data then clicked a small icon above the table, and a map overlay appeared with several dated markers superimposed on the familiar outlines of Europe.

When he came to the most recent one, he felt his stomach clench. *City of Edinburgh, Scotland, U.K. Yesterday. 9:12 PM.*

His intervention to save Dowling. Followed by his inability to save Taylor.

The only thing I can do now is find out as much as I can about all this. A memory rose up in his mind. He'd been a moody teenager, watching a news report on television about another atrocity in the Middle East. The sophistication of the weapons of war was already frightening, and he'd known it would only get worse. He'd angrily asked Taylor why he had so much faith in science, when it was so often turned to horrific uses. Taylor looked at him with quiet sympathy, taking his time to find an answer, and then he'd pointed out that science had also allowed the world to communicate, and had let us see just how small and isolated our planet really is, and it had also given us medical technology, and transport, and infrastructure, and most of all hope.

Knowledge is always our best defence — especially against ourselves, he said.

Aldridge as a boy had dismissed the remark as a meaningless platitude and stormed out, but Aldridge as a man knew that there was profound wisdom in it. And now he'd never have the benefit of his adoptive father's insight again. There would never be another conversation. Never another word. What a terrible waste of the last two years.

Focus, he told himself, feeling the moisture gather in the corners of his eyes. *There's work to do.*

He opened another document that he'd noticed earlier, about the biological effects of the ability. Stille had obviously performed extensive medical testing on the people Merrick had captured, and the results were intriguing. Aldridge began to make notes on the tablet as he read.

Blood sugar. Use of the ability seemed to deplete glucose levels in the bloodstream. A suitable diet plan had been created for the captives.

Radius. A changer had to be within a certain radius of the event they wanted to alter, and they had to be present for it taking place. It made sense.

Time limit. There was a window of only a few seconds on either side of an event during which a changer could intervene. It appeared to be impossible to make a change in the past, even if only a minute had elapsed.

There was more — much more. Two different changers wouldn't react the same way to the same stimulus,

Chapter 22

producing different outcomes in each case. The ability wasn't infallible, either, as the recording of the French priest had graphically shown. Despite their power, they could be killed. There were no guarantees. There was also some kind of poorly-understood correlation with emotional stress, which seemed to make it easier to trigger the ability.

"Reading about anything that might help us?" Dowling asked, and Aldridge flinched. He hadn't noticed the big man appearing at his right shoulder.

"Just seeing what Her Majesty's finest nerds managed to decrypt from Peter's flash drive. There's a lot about the ability, and its limitations and effects."

Dowling nodded thoughtfully. "So how does it work?"

Aldridge frowned. "That's one thing Stille doesn't know exactly, but they did find out some things about what's involved." He pushed the laptop away and picked up the tablet device, navigating to a view of the same data he'd been examining on the other device.

"It's like a prevailing wind," he continued. "It's blowing in from the future event, back towards us here in the present. And when it's just at the point of passing by, it can be harnessed."

"So you're a sail? Or what, a windmill?" Dowling asked, and Aldridge frowned.

"The analogy isn't perfect, I admit," he replied. "There's another thing, too. The energy isn't equally distributed in space." He tapped several times on the tablet's screen, and brought up a new overlay of a map centred on Western Europe. Superimposed on the geography was an irregular set of squashed, twisted bands of various colours. They were moving very slowly. The overall effect was of a complex weather-system that changed by the minute. There were several noticeable areas of bright red, which were more stable than the surrounding layers.

"Those red areas are where burst events happened. This is a live graph, using CERN's radiological and meteorological monitoring stations throughout Europe. We can roll it back in time too to see how it changed."

He slid his finger across the screen horizontally, and the bands of colour changed more rapidly, ebbing and flowing. Suddenly there was a bright spike of red over the city of Edinburgh, beginning as a large splash of colour and then tightening down to a point before again expanding and dimming slightly.

"That was last night," he said. "Western Europe is blanketed by the… the fallout, if you like, from what's going to happen tomorrow morning. So I was able to use it when I needed to. It drew inwards around me when I did what I did."

"Saved my bloody life," Dowling said in a sombre tone, and Aldridge just shifted in his chair.

"I don't know *why* I can use the energy, or even how I'm interacting with it, exactly," he said, "but when it's present, and when I'm under emotional stress, and when I'm not too exhausted… I can pull it to me, and

Chapter 22

channel it. On an instinctive level."

"You're a lightning rod," Greenwood said from across the room.

Aldridge glanced up to find everyone else looking at him. There was silence for almost half a minute. Eventually, Dowling cleared this throat and turned to face Greenwood.

"Not to question our esteemed masters, chief, but should we even try to stop Merrick? If those people like Aldridge really can prevent what's going to happen, shouldn't we let them do it?"

"What if Stille is wrong?" Greenwood replied. "What if they somehow cause what's going to happen? And it's wrong, Larry. They can't use human beings like that. There has to be a better way."

She focused her attention on Aldridge. "Now that we know what we're looking for, we can track these anti-tachyon events and we'll know where Merrick is — or where he's soon going to be. He wants you, Aldridge, and I think it's become personal for him. Even if he doesn't intend to use you, I'm betting he'd like another chance to take you out of the picture."

Aldridge gave a barely-perceptible nod. "He might find that tricky." The words were brave, and fuelled by anger, but he knew he'd be a fool to underestimate Merrick. A large part of him dreaded seeing the man again.

"Let's not get over-confident," Greenwood said. "We're on a very tight timetable, and Merrick could bring one of the others like you with him as protection. You've already shown us that your ability can stop bullets, remember. With that kind of help, Merrick would be even more dangerous."

"At least they're not the only ones with that advantage," Ramos said, nodding towards Aldridge. "We have him."

"That's true. He has a remarkable talent," Greenwood said quietly.

"Two, if you count my Sean Connery impression," Aldridge replied, but neither of the two women were amused. Nor was he.

After a moment, Greenwood walked off towards the kitchen, and Ramos took out her mobile phone. Goose walked over to join Aldridge and Dowling.

"What's it like?" the Dutchman man asked quietly, looking intently at Aldridge.

"Being able to…?" Aldridge replied, and Goose nodded.

"It's too much bloody responsibility."

Goose nodded sympathetically. "I'm sure. But even so, it's incredible. It's almost impossible to believe, but it's real."

Aldridge frowned. It *was* incredible, if you thought about it. But if you did think about it, you also had to think about the times it didn't quite work, and how guilty it made you feel, and how totally unequipped you were for all of this.

Then you had to think about how it was connected to

Chapter 22

the upcoming deaths of millions of people. That part wasn't so great.

I don't feel like a hero, he thought bitterly. *I feel like a scared little boy who's been handed a gun he doesn't know how to use, and told to save the world with it.*

"Next time, I'd prefer to be able to fly," he muttered.

Goose gave him a wry smile, which faded after a moment. "If there *is* a next time," he said.

Chapter 23

Aldridge was startled by the shrill sound of an electronic alarm issuing from Dowling's laptop, and everyone in the room looked up in concern.

"Checking," Dowling said, as Greenwood got up from an armchair, discarding the tablet computer she'd been carefully reading. She crossed the room to stand at his shoulder, and after a few tense moments of silence, he spoke again.

"We've got an AT burst event, chief. Smaller than average magnitude. Getting location information now."

Greenwood felt a surge of adrenalin. *Merrick will be on his way.*

"Got it. Location is The Netherlands. City of Amsterdam," Dowling said, filling in details as the location was further refined. "Looks like... canals ring, near enough. It's... huh. Well that's a problem."

"What's a problem?" Greenwood asked, glancing at

the digital city map without immediately seeing what he meant.

"This," Dowling said, tapping a large area that encompassed the pulsing blue dot on the screen, "is *Museumplein*."

"Which means…?" Greenwood asked, only to be answered by Goose, who was sitting near the opposite end of the room.

"Museum Square," the Dutchman said. "There are three major museums there. And the US Consulate too. Sometimes a fairground, or ice rink, and there's a supermarket below it. Lots of people there, all the time."

Greenwood sighed. *Fantastic*, she thought. *Not exactly ideal for a low-profile extraction*.

"Just don't tell me that the signal is in the bloody American Consulate," she said wearily, and Dowling pressed several buttons before shaking his head.

"Thankfully not," he said. "But how do you feel about art, chief?"

"I know what I like," she replied, and Dowling grinned without looking away from the screen.

"Van Gogh?" Goose asked, and Dowling glanced around at him with a smirk on his face. Goose pronounced the name like the Scottish word *loch* but beginning with an 'h', instead of the more common American-style *go*.

"No such luck," Dowling replied, extending his finger towards the digital map. "Our lucky caller is in the Rijksmuseum."

Chapter 23

* * *

The truck had arrived almost an hour ago, and the changers were already in their new dormitories in the grand old building's basement. Merrick walked down the harshly-lit corridor unhurriedly, with Drost and Finn close behind.

Fourteen souls, he thought. *But how many are superfluous?*

It was a difficult question. He had to make sure that enough changers remained to thwart the catastrophe, but it was impossible to say just how many would be needed for that purpose. His instincts told him that only one would be required, and he could serve that function himself. But caution was certainly indicated, given the dire consequences of failure.

Each additional living person with the ability was a potential threat to him, however minor. The power was not meant for ordinary men and women.

There was also the matter of security to be considered. *As soon as any of them use their ability, the Defence Agency will be able to pinpoint our location,* he thought. But there was nothing to be done about that. What could they possibly do?

"We will need transport for our guests, at short notice. Have you secured a jet at the nearest airfield?"

Drost nodded. "It landed thirty minutes ago," he said. "The field is only five miles away. The jet is being refuelled now."

"Destiny occurs in the early hours of tomorrow morning," Merrick replied, and he noticed the other man's step falter for a moment. "Put a new pilot on standby. He is not to leave the airfield for any reason. And refuel the truck."

Drost nodded silently, and turned on his heel and went through a nearby door.

"It is almost time," Merrick said quietly, and Finn glanced at him as they walked, knowing that the words weren't addressed to him.

They had almost reached the large double set of metal doors at the end of the corridor when a klaxon sounded, and Merrick came to a halt. He reached to the lapel of his combat vest and depressed a thumb-switch on the small radio clipped to some webbing. "Report," he said roughly.

A technician's voice replied immediately. "There's been another burst event, sir."

Merrick turned to Finn immediately. "Get Drost and go to the rear bay. It seems we have a detour to make. We leave in ten minutes."

Aldridge stared straight ahead, his eyes unfocused. He had pulled down the shade on the window beside his seat, and could still see the afterimages of the bright sunlight streaming in from above cloud level. It was a short one-hour hop to Amsterdam's Schiphol Airport from the small airfield in London, and they had already been airborne for almost forty minutes.

The small jet looked luxurious from the outside, but

Chapter 23

was functional almost to the point of austerity within. The seats were the usual extravagant leather recliners found on private aircraft, but most of the cabin area was taken up with desks, a bank of computer displays, and a communications station. The wall decor was a mottled grey faux-marble, which was an uncomfortable mix of *nouveau riche* and a military aesthetic. The vehicle had clearly begun life with something very different from KESTREL in mind.

There's another one out there, he thought.

Whoever the changer in the Rijksmuseum was, Goose was now tracking his or her location closely. After a change event, the subject retained a weak anti-tachyon energy signature for hours, and they would easily arrive in the vicinity of the museum in time to pinpoint the individual.

And then what?

The answer was unpleasantly obvious. *Merrick will be there too, and there's going to be more trouble.*

He frowned, running his fingers through his hair for the tenth time since boarding the jet. *Maybe someone will die. Again. Then they'll expect me to fix it.*

He exhaled in frustration, feeling his stomach roll. He still couldn't reliably trigger his ability. He had no idea what would happen the next time he tried to use it, and yet he knew Greenwood was expecting him to. It was damned dangerous, and things were happening too quickly.

"Maybe I'm faulty," he muttered aloud, but his words

were lost in the drone of the turbines.

Greenwood was sitting diagonally opposite, on the other side of the cabin, and she had been scrutinising a tablet computer until she heard Aldridge's frustrated sigh. She had watched him for the last minute or so. After a moment, she unfastened her seatbelt, and moved across to sit in the seat directly opposite him.

"What's on your mind, Aldridge?" she asked.

"Just wondering when they bring the drinks trolley around," he replied distractedly, and she pressed her lips together to stifle a sound of exasperation. *It's a defence mechanism*, she reminded herself. *He's not really being flippant*.

"You're worried about what we'll find in Amsterdam," she said. It wasn't a question, and she was surprised when he shook his head.

"I already know what we'll find," he replied. "A frightened person who has no idea what's happening to them, and who's going to be shot at — and maybe killed — because of something beyond their control."

She was silent as she considered his words, and again she felt the weight of the responsibility that was upon her.

"But something else is bothering you," she said.

Aldridge sighed again. "It's me," he said at last. Greenwood didn't respond, and he raised one of his hands in front of him, palm-up. He stared down at it as if seeing it for the first time.

"This thing that I can do," he said, "it's incredible —

Chapter 23

no question about that. But it's... I don't know. It's a curse too."

She nodded, encouraging him to continue. Aldridge was still staring at his palm, and didn't see the gesture.

"It's connected to what causes tens of millions of people to die tomorrow," he said, unable to suppress a shudder. "And it's inside me. When I hit one of those forks in the road and everything slows down, I have to choose. It's one way or the other. I'm on a conveyor belt towards whatever is going to happen."

He glanced up briefly and saw sympathy in her eyes. He closed his outstretched hand into a loose fist, and let it fall to his lap.

"And you're all counting on it," he said quietly. It was clear he was referring to Greenwood and her team. "We know Merrick will be there, going after another experimental subject. We know what he's capable of. There's going to be another firefight. People are going to get hurt, and it might be *our* people."

"We're going to try to get there first," Greenwood offered, but Aldridge only shook his head.

"It'll only be a postponement, and you know it," he replied flatly.

She nodded, conceding the point. "We're trained for this sort of thing. I'm hoping that it won't be your problem this time."

His brow creased.

"It'll become my problem the moment that one of you gets killed. Again," he said. "You'll expect another miracle. That'll be my cue: abracadabra, and *arise*."

His voice was bitter, and Greenwood opened her mouth to say something, but he continued speaking. His words came in a rush this time, and she knew it was a confession.

"The problem is, it doesn't work that way," he said. "I can't just switch it on whenever I like. I don't even know how it *works*. Peter didn't know either, and I couldn't save him, and there's every chance I won't be able to save the next one either. You all have your training, and your technology, and your guns. All I have is… bloody performance anxiety."

She smiled. "I can imagine. Well, actually I can't. But I do know that we have to try. There are so many people who need us to, whether they know it or not."

Aldridge tilted his head in acknowledgement. "That's the problem, though," he said. "I don't want to be the one to let everybody down. And it could happen, Captain, believe me. It could happen so easily."

I know exactly how you feel, Greenwood thought.

Aldridge huffed and shook his head. There was a self-deprecating half-smile on his face, and he looked tired. He lifted one hand to massage the space between his eyebrows.

"How's that for honesty?" he muttered, and she could hear that he was berating himself for his outburst.

"So maybe you won't be able to change something that happens," she said, "but that's the nature of this phenomenon, not a failure on your part."

Chapter 23

"You might be right," he replied quietly. "But that's not going to make me feel any better." His gaze was fixed on his own upturned palms in his lap.

"*Twenty minutes to landing,*" the pilot's voice suddenly said over the cabin speakers, and they both briefly glanced upwards at the sound.

There was silence for several moments before Greenwood spoke again.

"It's Rose," she said.

Aldridge looked up slowly, confusion evident on his face as he tried to make sense of the words in context.

"My middle name," Greenwood added. She folded her arms and looked across the cabin and out one of the windows for a moment before meeting his gaze again. Aldridge was studying her face carefully. She shrugged.

"Since we're being honest," she said.

Chapter 24

"No change in the energy source's position, Captain," Goose said quietly, speaking into his earpiece microphone. He sat in the back of a brand new, dark grey people-carrier with rental plates, parked in the street less than a block away from the Rijksmuseum.

He had already been into the building, wearing the overalls and tool belt of a maintenance worker, using valid ID that was less than an hour old. He had entered only one small room, away from the public areas of the museum, and it took him barely a minute to open the cover of a switchbox, clip a small device into place at the junction of several cables, then reseal the box and leave the same way he'd entered.

The rest of the team were split into two groups, at different places in the entrance line. Once inside the reception atrium, they would take a service staircase into the museum itself using a staff keycard that had been waiting for them at the airport when they landed, thus avoiding the museum's security bag inspection and metal detectors.

Everyone wore civilian clothes, and a discreet earpiece communicator. Greenwood stood with Dowling, and Ramos with Aldridge. To any onlookers, they were simply two different couples, and each pair ignored the other.

Aldridge kept his expression neutral as he glanced at Alicia Ramos. Her face was a mask of absolute calm, but he could see a hint of amusement in her dark eyes.

"Something on your mind?" she asked quietly, her Catalonian accent rolling the *r* and making the question sound almost like a proposition. Aldridge blinked.

"I take it you didn't bring... it," he replied, and she grinned, knowing full well he was talking about her rifle.

"I have everything I need right here," she said, laying her hand across the top of the bright red handbag she had slung over her shoulder.

Aldridge began to imagine what sort of weaponry or devices of mayhem she might be able to pack into the bag, then he deliberately pushed the thought away. Better not to know.

"I'm sure you do," he said, stretching his neck wearily. "So is this your idea of fun?"

"That's for my wife to know," she replied, never breaking eye contact, and she grinned again when she saw his eyes dart down to her left hand in search of a

Chapter 24

ring. "It throws my grip off," she added, plucking a slender silver chain from the top of her blouse to show him the white gold band attached to it.

Message received, he thought, and nodded.

"If everyone is quite ready," Greenwood said, "once we're inside we'll be going to the end of the corridor on the far left." She appeared to be speaking to Dowling who was standing beside her, but her voice sounded in everyone's earpiece, and Aldridge knew very well the remark was mostly aimed at him.

Aldridge turned towards Ramos and said "Sounds good, sweetheart," and they both immediately heard Dowling snort. Ramos rolled her eyes, readily able to picture the look of vexation she'd seen on Greenwood's face regularly during the last twenty-four hours.

Once inside the Rijksmuseum, they would act like tourists, each heading for a different exhibit, and monitor anti-tachyon activity via their own wrist-mounted devices which had also been waiting for them at Schiphol. Within the museum itself, CERN's readings wouldn't be precise enough, but the wrist devices would at least work like Geiger counters to let them home in on the focal point.

Five minutes later, both teams had bypassed the security area without incident. They walked casually through the many high-ceilinged chambers, past walls full of masterpieces and exhibits of everything from weapons to doll's houses. The collection of artwork was breathtaking, and included Rembrandt's *Night Watch*,

Vermeer's *Milkmaid*, and many more.

The detectors were switched to silent operation, producing a vibration when anti-tachyon emissions were detected. They had been wandering the exhibits for less than ten minutes when Ramos felt a buzz on her left forearm.

"This is beautiful," she said, using the pre-arranged phrase. Aldridge came to a stop beside her, glancing at his own detector as if the device were a wristwatch. The display showed a signal-strength indicator on a ten-bar scale, and a very approximate compass direction, disguised as an analogue watch face. Each detector included a gyroscope and a digital compass, and all of the devices were networked together. Given that the two teams were spread out across the main building, the readings would indicate the direction of the unknown changer with a useful level of accuracy.

"Got a reading from Dowling's and Mr. Aldridge's detectors too," Goose said on everyone's earpieces. "Triangulating. Just a moment."

Greenwood stared at an enormous wooden model of a Seventeenth Century Dutch warship without really seeing it. *Merrick could be in this building right now*, she thought. *Come on, Goose.* A few seconds later, she heard the Dutchman's voice again.

"Cuypers Library," he said. "Rear right of the main building from the entrance, one level above ground. Western chamber."

Ramos tapped Aldridge's arm. "I'd like to see the

Chapter 24

Library," she said, and he nodded. They started towards the south-western exit from the gallery they were in, then Aldridge noticed a discreet sign mounted on a brass-trimmed stand, set just to the side of the double doors.

"If my Dutch is up to scratch, that sign says the Library is temporarily closed for maintenance," he said, a little more loudly than necessary. Ramos glanced at him, cocking an eyebrow.

"But whatever you say, dear," he said wearily. Elsewhere in the museum, Dowling grinned.

Less than ten minutes later, they had all assembled in the Cuypers Library atrium, which was a narrow, glass-walled room that served to further isolate the chamber beyond from the sound of the museum around it. The doors ahead were open, but were blocked with velvet ropes and another sign apologising for any inconvenience caused by the temporary closure.

Aldridge stepped forward and peered into the echoing space. "Not bad," he said.

The Library was vast. A huge, vaulted room with a mostly glass ceiling and dazzling arched windows at the far end, it held three storeys of wooden shelves full of books. An antique spiral staircase climbed from the ground to the topmost level, in the rear right corner. The expansive floor was dotted with reading tables, chairs, desks and booths where patrons could borrow tablet computers to help with their research. A long desk spanned the very front of the central section, and held a row of flat-panel computers, presumably for staff use. Despite the abundance of natural light, the chamber also had a comfortingly warm and secluded ambience. On the top level, everything was illuminated; on the floor, there were many pockets of shadow between the support columns, under the balconies, and in the far corners.

There was a soft noise coming from the other end of the chamber: a swishing sound, with the occasional metallic scrape.

"Goose, we need to blind the cameras," Greenwood said. Her hand was in her jacket pocket, cradling the all-plastic .38 slim-profile pistol she had concealed there. Its magazine held twelve rounds, each made of a carbon composite that was invisible to any metal detector, and only marginally less lethal than conventional ammunition.

"Almost there, Captain," Goose's voice said over the intercom. "And done. They're watching re-runs now."

"Good work," she replied tightly, then she turned to Ramos and Dowling. "Find the signal's source, and keep your eyes open for company."

Ramos nodded, and they both stepped over the red velvet cords and slipped silently into the Library.

"Current location?" Merrick asked, prompting Tepel to type rapidly on a laptop.

"Still moving around inside the museum," the other man replied, not glancing up.

Chapter 24

They were both seated with Drost in the rear of a well-used Transit van marked with the bright insignia of a popular parcel delivery company. Finn was at the wheel, as usual. They were about fifteen minutes from Museumplein.

Captain Greenwood will also be on her way, Merrick mused. He thought back to the encounter at the parking garage the night before, and recalled how shocked Greenwood's team had seemed when Aldridge made the change to restore the life of the large man.

So you had no idea about the ability — at least, not then.

But now they knew everything, and the Defence Agency did too. All of Stille's primary locations were under military control by EDA teams. Merrick knew that Greenwood's team may even be waiting in the museum already.

They must not be allowed to stand in my way, he thought. Aldridge had barely began to discover his ability — that much was obvious when he was unable to restore Taylor's life. The physicist could be an irritation, but surely not a serious threat. Greenwood and her team were a different matter.

Merrick grimaced, bracing himself as the van rounded a corner at speed.

Let them come, he thought. *The countdown has already begun. By morning, we will be living in a different world.*

Merrick and his men arrived at the museum only minutes after Greenwood's team entered, and were steadily making their way through the exhibits towards the rear of the ornate building. Their progress was hampered by the general exodus of tourists as early evening approached.

Finn had been ordered to remain with the vehicle, and was parked directly across from the side entrance, keeping a watchful eye for traffic police and parking wardens.

Inside, Merrick led Tepel and Drost past an array of porcelain sculptures, before finally hearing the sound he had been waiting for. A series of crisp, soft beeps echoed from his detector, and he halted at once.

"West," he said, glancing at the device, and then he strode purposefully towards an antechamber with a sign indicating that the Italian Renaissance collection lay ahead. There were no more tourists in this part of the museum now, and Merrick reached inside his black bomber jacket to withdraw his pistol. Drost and Tepel followed suit.

After they had gone another fifty feet or so, Merrick held up a hand. He could see the shadows of several people being cast across the marble floor in the next chamber.

The Library is just beyond there, he thought. *Perhaps you have arrived ahead of me, Captain.*

Merrick silently gestured to the other two men, and they took up flanking positions along the walls of the long gallery, moving stealthily closer and closer to their prey.

Chapter 25

Ramos glanced quickly around a narrow supporting column, but she saw nothing unusual. The sound wasn't far ahead now, and she could occasionally see Dowling moving between identical columns on the opposite side of the Library.

She moved forward another few feet, and the sound became noticeably louder. Stepping carefully, she edged around a bookcase and caught sight of a middle-aged man of average height, with grey hair and a slight stoop. He was wearing navy blue custodial overalls, and he was mopping a section of the polished floor where a patron had evidently spilled some kind of beverage. The swishing sound came from the long, flat fronds of the mop he held, and the occasional scraping noise was made by one wheel of the small trolley-bucket he periodically pulled across the floor as he moved.

Ramos reached up behind her ear and tapped the leg

of the earpiece sharply three times.

Out in the hallway, Greenwood pointed towards the Library doors, and then stepped over the ropes. Aldridge followed close behind.

"Excuse me," Ramos said, and the man spun around, startled, sending droplets of water scattering in all directions on the floor.

"The Library is closed," he said after a moment, in a heavy Dutch accent, pointing to the floor. "Cleaning."

Ramos smiled and nodded. "I saw the sign. But I wanted to ask you something."

She drew back her sleeve to reveal the anti-tachyon detector which was now buzzing repeatedly on her wrist. The display showed a pulsing blue crosshairs in the centre of the makeshift dial, and the signal strength indicator below was at maximum.

"Yes?" the man asked, clearly confused.

"Can I ask your name?" Ramos asked, sliding her sleeve back down again. Her smile had faded, and her tone was full of authority.

He looked her up and down uncertainly, and seemed to decide that she was probably with law enforcement. He shifted his weight from one foot to the other.

"I… I am Fons Nieboer. *Ik werk hier*. I, ah, work here."

He held up the mop in both hands, as if it explained everything. "I clean," he said simply.

Ramos smiled again, as reassuringly as she knew how.

"Thank you, Mr. Nieboer. There's nothing to worry

Chapter 25

about. We just have some questions."

He looked at her cautiously, putting the mop head into the bucket, and clipping the handle against the trolley's crossbar.

They both heard the sound of approaching footsteps, and Ramos reached casually into her now-unzipped purse. A moment later, Greenwood appeared around the corner of the nearby floor-to-ceiling bookcase. Aldridge followed immediately afterwards, then Dowling melted out of the darkness nearby, and nodded.

Nieboer blinked, glancing quickly from one person to the next, now looking agitated.

"Have I done something wrong?" he asked, looking at Ramos, but it was Greenwood who replied.

"No, Mr. Nieboer, you've done nothing wrong," she said. "We just need to talk to you about something unusual that happened to you earlier today."

His face went pale, and he quickly brought one hand up to cover his mouth. "*Mijn God*" he muttered. "But how can you know this?"

"There's nothing to worry about," Greenwood said, offering him a smile. "We're just here to make sure you're alright. Can you tell me exactly what happened?"

Neiboer was silent, with tension in his jaw. He was clearly afraid. After almost half a minute, his shoulders sagged, and he began to speak.

Merrick listened carefully at the open doors of the Library, easily able to make out the conversation taking place at the far end.

He had watched Aldridge and Greenwood enter just a minute or so earlier, and he assumed that some of the other KESTREL team members were already inside. He silently cursed that Greenwood had been the first to arrive, but he knew it gave him an advantage too: while Greenwood would assume he was on his way or nearby, she didn't know his location. He, however, knew exactly where she was.

He motioned to Tepel and Drost to move further down the gallery leading away perpendicularly from the Library's doorway. Merrick had already consulted a detailed map of the museum, and knew that there were two connecting staircases and a small elevator that led directly to the second and third floors, as well as the iron spiral staircase within the Library itself. They would reach the upper floors without ever setting foot in the Library, and surprise Greenwood easily.

Aldridge is the wild card, he thought. The man's ability was poorly controlled, and he clearly had no experience in life-or-death situations. *But operating on instinct, you can still cause trouble.*

Merrick disengaged the safety on his pistol and motioned his men up the staircase ahead of him.

"It is difficult to explain," Nieboer said, hesitantly. "You won't believe me."

Aldridge stepped forward just as Greenwood opened her mouth to reply, and she decided to remain silent for

Chapter 25

the moment.

"I understand that you're confused, Mr. Nieboer," Aldridge said. "I had a strange experience too, and these people helped me."

Nieboer raised his eyebrows, looking first at Aldridge then at Greenwood, then back again.

He wants to believe me, Aldridge thought. *He wants someone to help make sense of whatever happened to him. Join the club.*

Aldridge decided to draw the other man out, and glanced at Greenwood for approval. She nodded slowly, and he turned his attention back to Nieboer.

"I was at home," Aldridge said, "and I accidentally knocked over an ornament. It was made of glass. It fell to the floor, and it shattered. But then something happened."

Nieboer's eyes lit up, and he leaned forward slightly without being aware of it.

"I could see that it was broken," Aldridge continued, "but I could also see what would have happened if I *hadn't* broken it. I found that I could choose whether it was broken or not. There was a feeling like standing in a strong wind. And then the ornament was there in front of me again, intact."

"Yes!" Nieboer exclaimed, stepping towards Aldridge and gesturing animatedly. "It was the same with me. I saw all of this! And the wind. What does it mean?"

"I can't answer that, but it would help if we understood exactly what happened," Aldridge replied. "Can you tell us?"

Nieboer nodded, taking a ragged breath before beginning to speak. He told them how he had been on cleaning duty as usual, and had been working with another man in the long, z-shaped gallery that housed more than eighty pieces of terracotta sculpture. He was sweeping, while his companion was disinfecting the floor at the other end of the room, around two corners from where Neiboer was. Nieboer could hear the other man working, but his colleague was wearing headphones.

Nieboer had been reaching alongside a display case with the broom and he overextended himself, losing his balance. He fell only to one knee, but the broom head became wedged against the edge of the case, making the handle pivot outwards quickly. It knocked against a preparatory bust of William IV, from 1733. There was a sickening moment of uncertainty as the bust wobbled, and finally fell heavily to the floor, breaking into three pieces.

Nieboer was certain he would faint, but instead he felt the odd sensation of seeing two separate scenes in front of him. There was a sense of being caught suddenly in a strong wind, and then he was standing before the bust, which was unbroken and in its original place. He had crossed himself, dropped the broom and ran to his companion, who had obviously seen nothing. Nieboer excused himself and took his break early, sitting outside in the sunshine behind the museum until his pulse

Chapter 25

finally slowed. He had told no-one about the incident.

He grasped Aldridge's forearm, but his grip was gentle, and his voice was beseeching. "Why did this happen to me?"

"It's because you're special, Mr. Nieboer," Greenwood said quietly. "And so is my friend here. You both have an ability that very few others have, and unfortunately it's not safe for you to stay here."

She paused for a moment, assessing the man's reaction. He looked uneasy, but steady enough, so she continued. "There are others on their way here who also know about you, and they intend to take you away by force. We can't allow that to happen."

Nieboer released Aldridge's arm and took a step back, again glancing from face to face, now alarmed.

"I've done nothing wrong!" he cried. "You are the police — who are these others?"

"We're not the police," Greenwood replied, reaching into her jacket to produce an ID wallet and showing it to the man. "We're with the European security forces. Your government is cooperating fully with our work here."

Nieboer still looked uncertain, but Greenwood's calm tone seemed to reassure him. "And if I don't go with you?"

Greenwood sighed, glancing quickly behind her into the recesses of the Library. "We're not going to force you or arrest you, Mr. Nieboer," she said, "but I promise you that you're not going to like the others who will be here very soon. They're mercenaries, and they've already killed several people."

Nieboer's face paled again, and he glanced at Aldridge for confirmation. Aldridge nodded sadly.

Nieboer looked towards his cleaning equipment. "I have to tell my supervisor."

"Of course," Greenwood said. "We can help you take care of that. Now please, come with us — quickly."

Dowling beckoned the man towards him, and Nieboer took several steps before suddenly jerking backwards and falling bonelessly to the floor. A small, round hole appeared on his forehead, and blood began to ooze from the wound.

Greenwood grabbed Aldridge and shoved him behind a bookcase, just a fraction of a second before she felt Dowling's weight batter into her, driving all three of them to the ground.

Chapter 26

Tepel easily eliminated the janitor who was about to leave with Greenwood's team, then he carefully took aim at Aldridge. The woman was too fast for him, though, and Tepel swung around, trying to get a bead on someone else.

Merrick's team were on the second level of the Library, on the opposite wall, using inspection tables for cover. The railings along both of the upper levels offered any number of vantage points for shooting.

"You are pinned down, Captain," Merrick's voice rang out. "Surrender Aldridge and your men won't be harmed."

A silenced shot glanced off the column just an inch from Merrick's head, and he winced as he ducked behind cover.

"It's not her *men* you should be worried about," Ramos shouted back.

"Kill that woman," Merrick commanded, and both Tepel and Drost began firing on the bookcases below.

"Stay low!" Greenwood shouted, mentally cursing herself for allowing the enemy to approach from higher ground. *That won't happen again*, she thought.

"Check in," she said, then she listened as everyone else reported their status. *At least no-one is injured so far*, she thought. *Except Nieboer*. She could see the man's feet from her position, and she knew that he had been dead before he hit the floor. An innocent man, with an incredible gift. Another senseless casualty of the madman just one floor above them. She felt her stomach clench in anger.

"Larry, give me something to smile about," she said through gritted teeth, and Dowling immediately darted from one bookcase to another, chased by a line of shots that nipped at his heels but never quite reached him before he found new cover.

"Can do, chief," he said, reaching into his backpack and pulling out the sort of anodised metal water bottle that runners often carry with them. It had a large decal on the side showing an athletic figure, and the words *Run For Your Life*. He unscrewed the base, and a small device slid out.

"Aldridge, cover your eyes and get ready to make for the entry corner on my order," Greenwood said. "Ramos, cover them, then get the hell up the outside stairs behind those bastards."

"Understood," Ramos replied, readying her weapon,

Chapter 26

and she could hear Aldridge audibly swallow through her earpiece.

"Flash in three," Dowling said, then paused for a second before pressing a button on the device. He lobbed it high in the air, in an arc that brought it close to the upper balcony. A fraction of a second later, the Library exploded in light.

Greenwood heard one of the men above cry out, and forced herself to wait for a full two seconds before opening her eyes. "Go," she said quietly but firmly, as if she was talking to herself.

Further along the same side of the room, Aldridge sprinted towards the doorway, and Ramos moved like a ghost along the opposite wall, tracking the balcony above with her pistol. Two shots traced down from the upper level, but they were haphazard and only chewed into polished wood, yards away from anyone below.

Silenced shots spat out in return from Greenwood's and Dowling's positions, forcing Tepel and Drost to move further back on the balcony, breaking their line of sight. The two mercenaries were still blinking, and weren't quite steady on their feet.

"Keep moving," Ramos's voice urged Aldridge, and finally he made it to the sheltered corner near the entrance to the Library, ducking behind several metal racks filled with scientific periodicals from around the world.

He gasped for breath, not quite recovered from Dowling's weight crushing him to the floor only a minute earlier.

"Ramos," Aldridge said between breaths, "I can't leave."

He caught sight of her across the room and saw her questioning look. "They might need me. What if somebody gets shot?"

Ramos glanced back towards the other end of the Library, then carefully looked out into the hallway before returning. "Alright," she said. "Stay low. Don't do anything stupid. If you need help, just call."

With that, she crept again to the Library's doorway, peered around it for several moments, then disappeared into the hallway beyond.

Greenwood ducked some return fire and muttered "Come on, Alicia" under her breath. She was just about to line up another shot when a scream rang out.

Everyone's attention was momentarily distracted by the sudden scream from the hallway, but Dowling quickly regained his focus and covered Greenwood as she tried to see who the source of the commotion was. It didn't take long.

A young Asian woman of about twenty-five was standing a few feet outside of the Library in the hallway, with her hands raised in alarm. She was looking fixedly towards the upper balcony on the west side, where Tepel was hanging over the edge, pointing his gun down towards the floor area.

"Bollocks," Dowling said, immediately firing several

Chapter 26

shots up at the mercenary to make sure he wouldn't turn his weapon on the tourist. The woman shrieked again, then ran off down the connecting corridor, out of sight.

Wise move, Greenwood thought, rising from cover to fix her sights on the balcony.

"Kurt Merrick," she called out, "You have less than five minutes before the Amsterdam police surround this building. Put down your weapons and surrender now."

Aldridge heard Greenwood's command over his earpiece and also simultaneously from deeper in the Library.

I doubt it'll be that easy, Captain, he thought, with a sick feeling in his stomach. He knew that time was short, and that Merrick would soon be cornered — which made him even more dangerous.

"There's no way he's surrendering to the police," Aldridge said, knowing the earpiece microphone would carry his voice to the others. "Watch yourself, Captain."

"Thanks for the advice," she replied, distractedly. "Now keep the chatter to a minimum. I'm a little busy."

Aldridge craned his neck around the side of the periodicals rack he was crouched behind, trying to get a better view. His heart was pounding, and he had a sick feeling in his stomach. The whole situation was wrong, and Merrick didn't seem to care about the impending arrival of the authorities.

This is the part where he does something terrible, he thought.

* * *

"Drost, go down and stop them leaving," Merrick said, without looking at the other man. "If you see the woman who screamed, kill her."

Drost immediately pulled himself up into a half-crouch and hurried along the rear wall of the long balcony towards the stairwell, not bothering to reply. He made it to within twelve feet of the door before Ramos leaned quickly around the frame, aimed and fired.

Drost felt like he'd been hit in the chest with a sledgehammer, and he immediately tipped sideways, his momentum gone, and crashed into the iron railings of the balcony. Operating on pure adrenaline, he weakly lifted his pistol and fired two shots towards the doorway, but Ramos was already out of sight. His gun fell to the floor with a dull clatter, and he lifted his hand to the upper right part of his chest. Sweat was already running down his brow as his fingertips felt the warm wetness of his own blood beginning to soak through his shirt.

He clamped his hand over the wound, feeling the end of the shell sticking out slightly from his skin. *A good sign*, he thought. The bullet hadn't fully penetrated his chest, and had been mostly stopped by the ultra-lightweight body armour he was wearing below his clothes. Even so, he was a right-handed shooter, and he was bleeding.

"I'm hit," he hissed into his headset, taking deep breaths to control the pain that was now flaring up in

Chapter 26

earnest.

"Idiot," Merrick snarled in reply, nodding to Tepel. "Stay where you are. Tepel is on his way."

It seems we won't be taking Aldridge alive today after all, Merrick thought. *But I can make sure that you don't either, Captain Greenwood.*

Merrick held up one finger towards Tepel before the other man could respond, his ice-blue eyes utterly devoid of emotion. The message was very clear. *If he's too badly hurt, kill him.*

Tepel nodded, and disappeared into the shadows.

"One down, two left," Ramos said quietly as she retreated back down the stairs to the ground floor, covering the upper doorway until she was out of sight.

"Down permanently?" Greenwood's voice asked on the intercom, sounding neither hopeful nor disappointed.

"Doubtful," Ramos replied. "He's a big man, and the silencer takes some of the punch from these carbon .38s. But I'd say he's not going to be a threat for a while."

"Good work," Greenwood replied. "It's just Merrick and the other one we need to worry about now. Cover the stairs."

"Understood," Ramos replied, taking up a position in the ground floor gallery at the doorway to the stairwell, her weapon trained on the halfway point of the descending staircase. Dowling dashed from his position to an adjacent row of shelves past the next supporting pillar, and then further, trying to get a better line of fire towards the upper level.

Tepel returned with Drost to where Merrick was crouching behind a heavy reading table on the balcony. He lowered the other man to the floor, and took up a firing position.

"Prepare an exit route," Merrick said, and Tepel nodded.

"Service entrance through there, down the back stairs," he replied, pointing towards a small doorway set between two racks of bookshelves, on the entrance wall of the Library. "It goes out to a side street."

"Then be ready for my signal," Merrick ordered, glancing thoughtfully at the nearby reading table then at several others like it, placed at even intervals around the entire balcony level. "Provide covering fire."

Tepel replaced his pistol's magazine, and immediately began taking shots at will towards Greenwood and Dowling. Meanwhile, Merrick crouched low and hugged the side walls as he worked his way around the balcony, edging closer and closer to a point above where Greenwood had taken cover.

Greenwood returned fire, then motioned to Dowling to rejoin her at her position. Dowling was just about to move when they heard a noise from above, and both quickly looked up.

Merrick tipped the reading table away from him so it rested against the waist-height iron railings, then squatted down and hooked his fingers under the bottom edge

Chapter 26

at the front. It was a very solid piece of furniture, made from a thick slab of oak fastened on top of a steel frame. With a grunt, he hefted the entire thing up to a horizontal position overhanging the railing, and then shoved it outwards.

"Look out!" Dowling shouted, but Greenwood was crouched in a narrow alley formed by two bookcases, and couldn't move quickly. The table teetered above for a brief moment, and then plunged over the balcony.

The shout drew Aldridge's attention, and his head whipped around to see a huge object fall from above — then everything slowed down.

He saw the table tumbling as if it was underwater. He could see the whole scene clearly, even though his view was partially blocked from where he crouched. He saw Greenwood's wide eyes staring upwards, and he saw the spreading shadow that the table cast over her as it fell. Dowling sprang up and dashed towards her, but Aldridge knew that the other man was too far away to help.

The table tumbled in mid air, almost level with the top of the ground floor stacks now, and he saw Greenwood throw herself into a dive along the base of one of the bookcases she was hiding behind. Her knee clipped against a shelf, and she pivoted and crashed to the floor, landing on her back.

Aldridge felt all the stress and tension of the situation flow out of him, leaving only stillness. It was as if he had a bird's-eye view of what was about to happen.

The falling table now dropped endwise and glanced off the top of one of the bookcases, shearing off its steel frame and leaving the oak slab to drop unencumbered. It fell like a hammer, instant by instant, as Aldridge patiently watched. Dowling had crossed more than half the distance to Greenwood now, but from Aldridge's perspective he was running through syrup, moving so slowly that he almost seemed graceful despite his size. Greenwood opened her mouth and inhaled deeply, then the oak slab finally impacted.

It caught her diagonally, from her right thigh across to the left of her pelvis, and smashed mercilessly into bone. The snapping sound was deep and hollow to Aldridge, but he knew that Greenwood and Dowling were hearing it at normal speed, and that it would be sharp and sickening.

Greenwood's pupils contracted and her eyes were suddenly all whites. The scream that had been building up died on her lips as all the breath was knocked out of her, and her face immediately went frighteningly pale.

The slab now stood precariously on its end, like an uprooted tombstone. One corner skidded on the marble floor, and the slab started to fall.

No, Aldridge thought.

The scene before him shuddered, and then abruptly reset. The table was back up on the balcony again, balanced precariously. Then Merrick shoved it outwards.

The table teetered for a brief moment, and then plunged over the balcony. Aldridge was distantly aware

Chapter 26

of Greenwood's upturned face and expression of shock, and of Dowling trying to get to her, but his attention was focused on the table itself.

It dropped like a stone, twisting in midair as the much heavier oak surface swung lower than the steel frame. It cartwheeled downwards until it approached the top of the two bookcases Greenwood was crouched between.

Aldridge could feel the weight of it in his mind. He was acutely aware of its surface, its centre of gravity, and the speed at which it was falling. He could almost feel the texture of the wood grain, and the smooth coldness of the steel.

Greenwood threw herself into a languid dive that he knew was actually frantic and desperate, but still his attention stayed on the table.

It swung around now, and this time the edge of the frame caught across the top of the nearer bookshelf, jarring the whole unit. The table jerked sideways, rolled end over end on top of the bookcase, and then fell down the side, crashing to the ground only a couple of feet from where Greenwood lay. The table shuddered, then tipped and fell away from her, landing with a final thud.

Yes, Aldridge thought, and suddenly he felt like he had stepped into a hurricane. He instinctively shut his eyes, even though the gale was only in his mind. His thoughts drifted away into chaos for a second or so, and then just as suddenly as it had began, the rushing sensation stopped. His legs abruptly gave way under him, and he collapsed to the ground behind the periodicals rack.

Dowling reached Greenwood, and fired a covering shot up towards the balcony, but Merrick had already drawn back. "You OK, chief?" the big man asked, and Greenwood just blinked.

"Aldridge. He—" she began, and Dowling nodded vigorously.

"I know," he said. "Hell of a thing. Now you know what it feels like. You sure you're alright?"

"I'm fine, Larry," she said, but her voice was higher than usual. "Keep your eyes open. That was cover for an escape."

"Got it," the big man replied, scanning the upper level for any sign of Merrick. He had a score to settle.

Up above, Merrick pressed himself flat against the side wall. *Impressive, Mr. Aldridge*, he thought. The ordinary-looking man was clearly learning about his ability quickly, and that made him extremely dangerous.

Just as Merrick was about to move to rejoin Drost and Tepel, he glimpsed Aldridge himself, peering out from a hiding place near the Library's main door.

Now I have you, he thought. He stepped forward towards the railing, bringing Aldridge fully into view, and aimed his pistol.

Down below, Dowling spotted the barrel of the pistol, only just visible over the railing. *Take one more step, you bastard*, he thought, nodding to Greenwood to look up.

She followed his gaze and saw Merrick standing

Chapter 26

there, visible from almost the waist up. "Not this time," she snarled, then in one smooth motion, she raised her weapon and fired.

Aldridge became aware of Merrick at almost the same moment that Greenwood pulled the trigger. He barely had time to register any shock at seeing the gun pointed at him before he heard the spit of the suppressed shot.

Something's wrong, Aldridge thought immediately. He could feel the sense of slowing and focusing again, but this time it wasn't centred on him. It was almost like knowing where a sound was coming from, or seeing a distant source of light.

Oh god, he thought. *Merrick. He's a changer!*

Merrick hadn't seen Greenwood fire, but he knew immediately that he was being fatally shot. Everything slowed to a crawl, and he saw the gunshot from an observer's perspective, before the sound carried up to him. He watched the bullet surge upwards towards him in slow motion, and then punch through his right temple. The edges of his vision began to blur, and he instinctively understood that he was experiencing the impending brain damage, before it had even happened. He saw himself crumple to the ground, and his gun spun from his fingers and slipped over the balcony, clattering to the floor far below. The spreading pool of crimson around his head was shockingly bright against the deep green carpeting of the upper floors. Merrick was a moment away from death.

As he had done so many times before, he pushed

aside that version of events, stepping sideways in his mind and asserting a new outcome. The anti-tachyon energy he channeled reshaped the world around him, and he felt the familiar turbulence of the abrupt, traumatic reconfiguration of reality. It was over in less than a second.

The bullet ricocheted harmlessly off the iron railing before it ever reached Merrick, and he sneered, not even bothering to turn and face Greenwood. His weapon was still trained on Aldridge, and his eyes blazed.

I am invincible, he thought.

Aldridge saw exactly what had happened, and he felt his heart leap into his throat. Without even thinking about it, he lifted his arm and extended his palm towards Merrick, as if asking him to stop. He reached into that same place in his mind that he'd found so easily earlier, but this time there was nothing there.

Shit, he thought. Then Merrick fired.

Aldridge flew from his feet and landed heavily on his back, then he blinked several times. *Did he miss me? Did Dowling knock me over again?*

"No!" Greenwood shouted, and she dashed from cover towards the other end of the Library where Aldridge had gone down. Dowling fired several shots towards the balcony, but Merrick had already disappeared from sight.

Aldridge was still lying there when Greenwood arrived a few seconds later, skidding to a halt and falling to her knees beside him.

Chapter 26

"He missed," Aldridge gasped.. "I just... fell over. Let me get up."

Greenwood's eyes were dark and she had two bright points of red on her cheeks as she looked him over. "Just lie still," she said. "I'm afraid he didn't miss you, and you're going to know it very soon."

As if her words had been an incantation, he suddenly felt a line of fire running across the top of his left shoulder. A fraction of a second later, he felt wetness on his skin there.

"Oh christ," he hissed, and a drop of sweat ran from his hairline down past his ear.

"I know. Hurts like a bastard, doesn't it?" Greenwood replied. "And this is going to hurt even more."

She leaned forward and clamped her hand over the wound, pressing down hard. He barked with pain.

"Sorry," she said. "You're going to be OK, Aldridge. Do you hear me? You're going to be fine. I don't think it hit anything important."

"My shoulder — *fuck!* — is pretty damned important to me," he gasped, and Greenwood had to brace her other arm across his chest to keep him from writhing around.

"Just stay conscious, and we'll get you fixed up in no time," she replied firmly, but he could hear a note of tension in her voice as she quickly pulled back his jacket and took a closer look at the wound.

"Like I'm going to fall asleep *now*," he hissed as the fabric moved.

"You'd be surprised what shock can do. But that's not going to happen. You're going to get up in a minute, and we're going to leave. It's a flesh wound. I've hurt myself worse than this in the kitchen."

"With or without the help of a trained killer?" he asked bitterly.

"Without, unless you count me," she said, and he snorted a weak laugh then immediately winced.

Their eyes met, and she could see that he was in pain but trying to contain it. He grimaced strangely, and it took a moment for her to realise it was an attempt at a reassuring smile.

"That's better," she said, nodding in approval.

"Easy for you to say," he replied, trying to turn his head to look at the exposed injury. "Listen, Merrick is… *he's one of them*. Like me. He has the ability."

"I saw," she replied, then she pressed her lips together in a fine line.

Greenwood pulled a compact field dressing from a pocket of her coat and pressed it to the wound, making him gasp again, then she pulled his jacket back into position.

"That'll do for now," she said. "We'll fix you up a bit better in the van, then get you some proper treatment afterwards."

When it became clear she wasn't going to say anything else about this new and alarming discovery of Merrick's own ability, Aldridge just nodded. "Was that true about hurting yourself worse in the kitchen, Cap-

Chapter 26

tain?"

He gave her a piercing look with just a trace of amusement. *That's a good sign*, she thought.

"OK, no," she finally replied. "I was exaggerating."

His brow was clammy, but this time his grin was genuine. "Good," he said.

They heard the sound of a throat being cleared just behind them, and Aldridge glanced over Greenwood's shoulder to see Dowling crouching nearby, with an exaggeratedly innocent look on his face.

"Alright there, Aldridge," he said. "You just love being the centre of attention, don't you?"

Neither one of them replied, and the big man grinned. "I'm not interrupting anything, am I chief? I could just go back over there if you like."

Aldridge closed his eyes, and was immediately poked in the side by Greenwood.

"No, Larry," she replied evenly. "Nice of you to join us. Now help me get him up."

Dowling shuffled forward and leaned down, slipping a muscular arm around Aldridge's back and bringing him carefully up to a sitting position.

"Head OK?" he asked. "Things not spinning around or anything?"

Aldridge slowly shook his head. "No," he replied. "But maybe you should hold onto the car keys."

Dowling laughed. "Mate, you're not even on the insurance."

Greenwood was about to speak when the air exploded with sound.

Chapter 27

Merrick had already rejoined Tepel and the wounded Drost and all three were halfway along the balcony level towards the service door when the shriek of the fire alarm burst from sounders all around the room.

The three men instinctively dropped to a crouch, then paused for a moment.

"Good," Merrick said. "The police will be delayed by tourists leaving the building. Move."

Tepel immediately took Drost's weight again, and they pushed forward. Merrick had radioed Finn to bring the battered Transit van around to the side street, and he knew the Irishman was already in position, no doubt with an unpleasant surprise ready for any pursuers.

Merrick was aware of Tepel's furtive looks towards him, and he knew why. *So now you know of my power*. It was of no consequence. He knew that none of his men would share the information, and it would only make them more afraid of him. *A wise reaction.*

When they reached the door, Merrick kicked through the lock and helped haul the now cursing Drost down two short flights of stairs and along a fortunately deserted service corridor to a small loading bay. Finn already had the rear doors open, and in less than a minute they were gone.

"Put your best *frightened tourist* face on," Greenwood said to Aldridge, who was standing upright now on his own.

"That's my normal face," he replied automatically, watching as she pocketed her weapon while glancing towards the library's atrium to check for any security personnel.

He didn't look too bad, all things considered. Merrick's bullet had gone wide, slicing through the skin on the outside edge of his shoulder but not penetrating bone. There was some blood, but the field dressing was holding well. Greenwood had been carrying a shapeless navy blue rain jacket rolled up in her bag in case of this exact situation, and Aldridge was now wearing it over his own blazer, covering the slice in the shoulder of the fabric and the bloodstain there.

It would probably be good enough to get him out of the museum without undue inspection, and in the worst case Greenwood certainly had authorisation to operate in the Netherlands. All the same, she preferred not to be delayed by swapping credentials with the local police.

Chapter 27

Ramos had been in contact less than a minute ago after she returned to the balcony level and carefully searched it, finding no sign of Merrick and his men. A broken door leading to a second staircase was a sure sign that they had already made their escape.

"Let's move," Greenwood said. "We're going to walk out just like we came in. Everybody act normal."

Aldridge opened his mouth to reply but he was silenced by a warning glance from Greenwood, and he simply shrugged and then winced at the pain that the movement caused.

They walked out into the gallery, seeing a security guard come into view around the far corner, and Ramos quickly rejoined the group. Greenwood nodded towards the exit and strode quickly off with Dowling beside her. Ramos slipped her arm into the crook of Aldridge's elbow on the opposite side from his wound, and tugged him in the same direction.

The security guard slowed his pace when he saw that both couples were moving towards the exit, and Greenwood and Dowling passed him without any remark.

The guard was watching Ramos and Aldridge as they drew alongside him, but he looked harassed rather than suspicious.

"Is there a fire? Is the museum going to burn down?" Ramos asked loudly, looking as alarmed as she could muster.

The guard sighed and shook his head, as if he had been asked the same thing a dozen times already. "The situation is under control, madam. Please continue to the exit by following the green signs."

Ramos only nodded and dragged Aldridge along with her, glancing around exaggeratedly as if to find smoke or flames. Aldridge exchanged an apologetic look with the guard, and the other man smiled wearily.

Once they had walked the full length of the gallery and ducked through an emergency exit, Aldridge glanced sideways at Ramos.

"Pretty good," he said.

"They see what they want to," she replied. "Never forget that. Now let's get to the vehicle."

They quickened their pace along a back corridor that was painted a sickly institutional yellow, and finally exited into the cloudy evening. Tourists were milling around and heading generally towards the designated rendezvous point further up the street, but Aldridge quickly spotted Dowling standing a hundred metres away, beside the open side door of the dark grey people carrier.

They reached the others in a few moments, being careful not to look like they were hurrying, and Dowling took Aldridge's good elbow to help him up into the van. Goose was sitting in the middle row of seats, and already had a small medical kit open beside him.

Ramos climbed in behind them, and Dowling slid the door closed then got into the passenger seat. Greenwood started the engine, and with a last careful look around, she pulled smoothly out into traffic.

Chapter 28

The apartment just off the western stretch of the *Prinsengracht* was cramped, but it was centrally located, and enough for their needs. The people carrier was parked three streets away, and was empty. Sunset had come and gone.

Goose, Ramos and Dowling were poring over Taylor's documents yet again, to see if there was anything at all they'd missed. It wasn't looking promising.

Aldridge was sitting on the couch, drinking a large soft drink from a mini-market on the next street. His colour was good, and he was feeling much more like himself — if a little fuzzy around the edges from the injection of painkillers. He had felt unsteady on the way over and Goose used a small device to sample some blood from his fingertip. His blood glucose levels had crashed, and he was experiencing the beginnings of hypoglycaemic shock. Goose administered glucose then re-checked ten minutes later, and Aldridge had improved considerably.

The television was on, and was tuned to an English-language news channel. *Murder at the Rijksmuseum* was the top story, and likely to remain so for the rest of the week at least. The police were requesting that anyone who was in the area and saw anything unusual should get in touch with them immediately. The media were already reporting that a female tourist saw a single man with a gun on the upper level of the Cuypers Library, and that a member of the custodial staff — who had reportedly been feeling unwell earlier in the day — had been gunned down in cold blood.

A service door on the first floor of the Library was broken, and the killer had presumably escaped that way. Police were inspecting surveillance footage, but the woman who saw the gunman hadn't got a good look at him because of the distance, and there seemed to have been a malfunction with the cameras in that area of the museum at the time of the shooting.

Great stuff for the conspiracy theorists, Aldridge thought. *If only they knew.*

He picked up the remote control and switched off the TV, looking over to where Greenwood was standing at the living room window.

They had tried to contact Wuyts earlier, but she was apparently in a sealed meeting about disaster-preparedness plans. Her secretary promised to have her get in touch the moment the meeting ended.

Chapter 28

Greenwood was looking out at the dozens of small, brightly-painted boats docked along the side of the canal. She hadn't moved in several minutes.

"You alright?" Aldridge asked, and she turned around with one raised eyebrow.

"I should be asking you that," she said. "How's the shoulder?"

"It's alright," he said, "and you're really good at evading questions." The side of her mouth twitched, but her expression remained withdrawn and thoughtful.

"It's the thing, isn't it?" he asked.

"The thing?" she replied, and he tilted his head to one side.

"You know, when I sort of…"

She folded her arms. "When you saved my life back there, you mean," she said.

Aldridge shifted uncomfortably on the couch. "I wouldn't go that far."

"I would," she replied. "Once the table crushed my legs, I don't think he'd have missed the chance to shoot me, do you?"

"I suppose not," he replied after a long pause. He tried to think of something else to say, but nothing seemed appropriate. He sighed.

"Thank you," she said suddenly, and he looked at her with an expression of disbelief. "What?" she asked.

"Well, you're welcome," he began, "but you hardly need to thank me. We both know I'd be dead by now if you hadn't grabbed me in Edinburgh. I'm just glad I had the chance to repay you."

"So we're even," she said. Aldridge wasn't sure if it was a statement or a question.

"Probably not yet," he replied. Neither of them broke eye contact for several seconds.

"You're an unusual man, Aldridge," she said, and he was just about to reply with a quip when Goose spoke up from the other side of the room.

"Incoming call from the Director, Captain."

Greenwood immediately walked over to stand at Goose's shoulder. "Put her through," she said.

Goose's hands flew over the keyboard, switching to an encrypted satellite video communications program. The connection was made within seconds.

Janne Wuyts's face blinked into view on the screen, her hands clasped on the desk in front of her. "Captain," she said. "You have news?"

"Yes, sir," Greenwood replied, motioning for Goose to move out of his chair, then taking his place. She quickly explained what had taken place at the museum, and Wuyts listened carefully. There was no visible change in her expression or posture.

"So Kurt Merrick has the ability. This is a considerable concern," Wuyts said.

"He's an intolerable threat," Greenwood replied, "but that's not our biggest problem."

"I'm well aware of that," Wuyts replied. "The destruction of most of Europe is only hours away. I have aristocrats and royalty quietly leaving almost every NATO

Chapter 28

country, and media blackout notices ready to go into effect. The cover story is an undisclosed but credible terrorist threat."

"Not too far from the truth," Aldridge said, drawing a sharp glance from Greenwood. He hauled himself up from the couch and walked slightly stiffly across the room to stand beside her chair.

Wuyts looked at him for a moment, then back at Greenwood. "And we still have no idea what sets the disaster in motion?"

"I'm afraid not, sir," Greenwood replied.

"If I may, uh, sir," Aldridge said, learning down slightly until his face hovered just over Greenwood's shoulder, "I'm Neil Aldridge, and I—"

Wuyts cut him off. "I know who you are. Continue."

Aldridge cleared his throat and nodded. "Well, I was wondering if the other changers have been secured yet. Did your people find them at Stille's facility?"

"No," Wuyts replied. "We have most of the scientists, but no test subjects. Apparently they were all taken from the holding area hours before we arrived, under Merrick's orders."

One step ahead, he thought, exchanging a worried look with Greenwood.

"We believe Anfruns's plan is to prevent the disaster from occurring, using these people that Merrick has kidnapped," Wuyts said grimly. "Presumably for a price. I'm surprised he hasn't made any overtures yet, actually."

"So it's Europe being held for ransom," Aldridge said, nodding several times. "It makes sense. So if you were going to do that, and you'd been found out, what would you do?"

Greenwood thought for a moment. "I'd feel that my hand had been forced. I'd want to move straight to my end game."

"Exactly. You'd put the changers on a jet, and lay low until you knew where to take then. You wouldn't go to Amsterdam for another one, and you *definitely* wouldn't just kill him on sight."

"You're saying that Merrick may have gone rogue," Wuyts said, and Aldridge nodded.

"Put it this way: there's *no mention* of Merrick's ability in Peter's notes. There's no *data* for any time that he's used the ability, and I can't believe that today was his first try. If I were a betting man, I'd say that we're the only ones besides his own men who know about it."

Greenwood immediately knew that he was right. "He's planning—"

"A coup," Wuyts interjected. "Possibly the most dangerous in history. And he no doubt has control over whatever secret facility the captives have now been taken to."

"He's got armed men, and the ability," Greenwood said. "He must still intend to stop Destiny to save his own skin, but after that…"

She tailed off. It didn't bear considering.

Wuyts peered at them over the tips of her spectacles.

Chapter 28

"Can he actually prevent it? Using these people?"

Aldridge frowned. "I don't know," he said. "When I do it, there isn't any sense of a big change versus a little change — there's just the new outcome. With a few changers all focusing on the same goal, who knows what's possible?"

There was silence in the room. No-one had that answer.

Wuyts looked away from the camera for several seconds, and then clasped her hands again on the polished desk surface in front of her.

"I think I should have another conversation with Mikkel Anfruns."

Chapter 29

"I didn't expect to hear from you again so soon, minister," Anfruns said, his hands clasped on the mahogany surface of his desk. His voice was calm and even as always, but he was puzzled.

The late evening video conference request had been a surprise to him. EDA agents, supported by EUFOR oversight teams, had arrived at Stille's primary locations in Denmark, Norway, Sweden, Germany, France and the UK hours earlier. Project Destiny was being thoroughly scrutinised, and Anfruns had been served with all of the necessary court orders extremely efficiently. It was impressive, he had to admit.

But now Brussels had what they wanted, except the changers who had been moved from the second Danish facility to a secret location, entirely unknown to the EDA. There was no reason for a further meeting today, particularly at such a late hour.

And I still have Merrick to deal with, Anfruns thought, controlling his anger. The mercenary was becoming a serious liability. He was impertinent and vengeful, and far too ready to pull the trigger. Merrick was now more of a problem than a solution, and Anfruns knew that time was becoming short.

"I'm afraid our time is almost up, Mikkel," said Wuyts on the video screen, and Anfruns was momentarily startled at the parallels between her words and his own thoughts.

"Oh?" he said, in as neutral a tone as possible.

Wuyts pulled off her spectacles and set them down on the desk in front of her, then cracked her knuckles. It was an uncharacteristic gesture for a woman who was always so poised and polished, and Anfruns frowned.

What is this about? he wondered.

Wuyts didn't keep him waiting long for an answer.

"Let's stop lying to each other," Wuyts said. "We know about your plan to use Merrick's captives to avert the disaster — perhaps for a price of some kind."

Anfruns didn't allow himself to react, or even to blink.

"We *also* know," Wuyts continued, "that your long-term goals will involve further using these people for personal gain."

Anfruns opened his mouth to speak, and Wuyts simply waved her hand.

"Don't waste my time with a denial," she said. "We're dealing with reality tonight. The problem is, you don't

Chapter 29

know the full story."

"Then educate me," Anfruns replied, leaning forward slightly.

"Are you aware that Kurt Merrick and his men were in Amsterdam a short while ago, where they killed a newly-discovered man who manifested the ability this morning?"

Anfruns didn't reply, but Wuyts could see that he hadn't known about Merrick's trip to The Netherlands.

"And are you also aware that a series of anti-tachyon energy events have been systematically concealed from the project?"

"To what end?" Anfruns asked, and Wuyts paused for several seconds before she replied.

"To hide the fact that Kurt Merrick possesses the ability himself, as he demonstrated today."

Anfruns was stunned. Wuyts was not a liar, and Anfruns had no reason to doubt what he was being told. His hands curled into fists on the desk surface.

"Is it true?" he asked, without any of his usual casual confidence.

"Oh yes, Mikkel," Wuyts said. "I'm afraid you lost control of your project long before we intervened. It was taken from you as quietly as you took it from us, by a man who is far more dangerous than you thought."

"*Min gud,*" Anfruns whispered.

"He or she will be of little help to you," Wuyts replied wearily.

A long moment of silence passed, then Anfruns spoke

haltingly. "Merrick's… guests," he said. "They've been taken to a secret location."

"We deduced as much," Wuyts said. "And there's very little time left for us to find them."

Anfruns closed his eyes. Apparently he had been almost as much in the dark as Brussels was. *I should never have allowed this to happen.*

"Have you discovered what triggers the final energy release?" he asked. Stille had been trying to find an answer to that question for months.

"We don't know," Wuyts replied, "and it might be critically important. It also may be a moot point, if Merrick is allowed to continue. Do you really think he'll walk away once he's averted the Destiny event, if that's indeed within his power?"

"I've summoned him here tonight," Anfruns said, glancing automatically towards the ornate double doors of his office. They were closed.

"We can have a team at your home in less than forty minutes," Wuyts said, but Anfruns shook his head.

"He will be here before then, and this is my doing," he said, looking down at his clenched hands. His voice was suddenly that of an old man, but still resolute. "I will take care of it myself. Or at least try."

Wuyts scrutinised Anfruns's face. Both knew exactly what he was talking about, and how futile it was likely to be.

Anfruns reached forward and tapped a series of on-screen panels below the video window, and a box containing two decimal numbers appeared on Wuyts's display. After a moment, he met her eyes again.

"I'm not a monster," he said. "I never sought to unleash horror on the world."

Wuyts inhaled deeply, then picked up her spectacles. They looked small and fragile in her hand.

"Monsters never do," she said, and then the screen went blank.

Anfruns looked down at the gun he was cradling in his hand. Its ivory handle almost sparkled in the dim light of his office, and he smiled sadly. It had been his father's, and despite being a weapon of death, it still brought forth some fond memories of the old man.

He had been taught from an early age to respect power in all its forms. Humanity's dominion over the animal kingdom, an employer's power over his workers, and the cruel power of a weapon over its victim.

Peder Anfruns had been a peaceful man at heart, but also a pragmatist. Powerful men often had powerful enemies, and it always paid to be prepared. As a boy, Mikkel was taken on hunting trips, and shown the meaning of exercising power over other living things. The first time he shot a roebuck, he had wept bitterly and refused to approach the carcass. His father embraced him, and then took him firmly by the arm and led him over to see the dead animal.

"Why did you bring me here? Why did you *make me do it*?" the young Mikkel had cried, with a red face and wet streaks down his cheeks. "I didn't want to!"

Peder Anfruns put an arm around his son's shoulders and spoke gently. "My son," he said, "that is exactly why you're here. Not to learn how to kill, but why *not* to."

His anger and grief prevented him from seeing the point his father was making, and he had lashed out, punching Peder in the chest. The older man had only taken him into his arms, stroking his hair and allowing the boy to cry.

"All lives must end, Mikkel," Peder had said, pressing a kiss onto the crown of his son's head. "What matters is how we live."

It had taken Mikkel days to understand what his father meant, weeks to fully forgive him, and years before he could admit to being grateful for the experience.

Power is a responsibility, not a goal, he thought now. He could so easily hear the words spoken in his father's voice. Exercising control over others was a last resort, and had far-reaching consequences.

Young Mikkel had learned the lesson well — at least until his father died.

As the years passed, pragmatism had become an increasingly dominant voice in his mind, and there was nothing more pragmatic than consolidating power. Wealth and influence weren't just useful: they were also safe. Anfruns had quickly learned to quieten the voice of morality that his father had taken such pains to implant

Chapter 29

in him.

Stille was now one of the premier weapons research and development companies in the world, and Anfruns didn't hesitate to supply cutting-edge armaments to various parties all around the globe.

A large portrait of his father Peder and his mother Agathe hung on the right-side wall of his office, halfway between the entrance and his desk. He passed it every day, and it always drew his eye. He turned his head to look at it now, and it was as if he was seeing it anew. His father's sharp but kind gaze now seemed to be making a plea.

What have I become, father? he thought. A chill ran up his spine, and he placed the gun back into the desk drawer, leaving it open just enough that he could quickly grab the weapon.

Anfruns felt every one of his six decades of life weighing down on his shoulders. With a heavy sigh, he sat down in the leather chair, and reached for the intercom. His hand paused in midair as he glanced again at the portrait on the wall. This time, his eyes fixed on his mother's face.

"Give me strength," he said, and pressed a button to connect him with his manservant Fabian.

The intercom emitted several soft beeps, but Fabian did not respond. That was unusual, but not entirely unheard of — anyone could be temporarily indisposed, after all.

Anfruns was about to try again when there was a

knock on the doors of his office.

"Enter," he said, and the left-hand door swung open to reveal Kurt Merrick.

The light from the hallway behind plunged Merrick's face into shadow, and Anfruns felt an uncharacteristic ripple of fear. "Come in, Kurt," he said. "We have a lot to discuss."

Merrick crossed the room at a leisurely pace, almost like an animal stalking its prey, without saying a word. He came to a halt beside one of the visitor's chairs, but didn't sit down.

Anfruns stared at him for several seconds before speaking. "How is your man?"

Merrick's eyes narrowed. "Recovering," he said.

"Unlike the last one," Anfruns replied, watching the other man's face carefully for any flicker of emotion. He found none, and he felt isolated and terribly vulnerable in the expansive office, late at night, and on his own.

"You must be wondering why I asked to see you tonight," Anfruns continued, slightly too quickly, but again Merrick made no response.

"There has been a change of plan," Anfruns said, clasping his hands in front of him. "We will be working alongside the Defence Agency to avert the Destiny event."

There was silence for almost half a minute. Anfruns felt a bead of sweat trickle down his back.

"What has Brussels told you?" Merrick asked. His voice was so quiet that Anfruns could only just hear

Chapter 29

him.

"The details are unimportant," Anfruns replied, "but suffice it to say that our best chance lies in allowing the EDA to have access to our guests. The situation has changed."

"For you, perhaps," Merrick replied, turning to examine the large screen on the wall. It was switched off and completely black. Merrick's reflection was only a murky silhouette.

"I didn't ask for your opinion," Anfruns said, with a confidence he didn't feel. "You will return the *changers* to the original holding facility, and turn them over to the EDA authorities there. You will be paid in full, and can go wherever you wish."

"No," Merrick said.

Anfruns unclasped his hands, setting them flat on the near edge of the desk surface.

"I beg your pardon?" he said, but Merrick only smiled.

"I knew this day would arrive, Mikkel," he said. "You're an old man, and you're weak. I will proceed as planned, without you."

"Surely even *you* can understand that we have no way to know if your guests can avert such a catastrophe," Anfruns said evenly, using all his willpower not to glance down at the open drawer on his right side. "I doubt it's even possible."

"I'm sure you do," Merrick replied. "But I know exactly what these creatures are capable of."

Anfruns winced at his choice of words, talking about other human beings as if they were little more than cattle. *You are the animal here, Herr Merrick*, he thought.

"And if they fail?" Anfruns asked, raising an eyebrow. "So much will lie in ruins."

"*If* they fail, I'll do it myself," Merrick said at last, his eyes blazing.

Anfruns felt his heart stutter in his chest. He lifted his right hand slightly from the table top, and Merrick spoke immediately, still not looking around at him.

"If you want to shoot me, by all means take the gun from the drawer," Merrick said.

Ice ran through Anfruns's veins, but he grabbed the gun and pointed it at Merrick's head. The other man turned to fully face him again, seemingly unperturbed.

"You have reached the end of your usefulness, Kurt," Anfruns said, clearing his throat when his voice started to shake.

"Then kill me," Merrick replied. Anfruns tightened his grip on the gun, but still didn't pull the trigger.

"I will *gladly* kill you," Anfruns warned, his voice wavering, and Merrick snorted in disgust.

"It will do you no good, old man," Merrick said, his voice dropping to a whisper. "*I have the gift of second chances.*"

Anfruns's eyes widened.

Merrick took a single step forward, and Anfruns had pulled the trigger before he consciously decided to react.

The gunshot was deafening, echoing around the

Chapter 29

wood-panelled room like a clap of thunder. Merrick disappeared from view immediately, thrown eight feet through the air. The wall-mounted screen was sprayed with a fine red mist of blood, and a large spidering hole appeared near its top right corner.

Anfruns took a rapid breath, and began to rise from his chair, and then the strength left his legs. He dragged himself to his feet only with great difficulty. Suddenly, he seemed to hear a roaring sound, and felt as if he was standing in the face of a storm. The room in front of him wavered and flickered.

Am I having a stroke? he wondered, and then he saw something that made his stomach clench in terror.

The shape that was Merrick suddenly twisted upwards from the floor, seeming to melt and reform, like a nightmare seen through a haze of heat. The bullet hole on the video screen snapped out of existence, and the blood spatter evaporated in an instant.

Merrick's face swam back into view, and a moment later he was standing on his feet once again, unharmed, and staring at Anfruns in triumph.

Anfruns lifted his own pistol again and pulled the trigger, but the gun clicked uselessly. *It jammed*, he thought wildly. *He made it jam. It never fired.*

Somehow, he instinctively knew it was true.

"*Min gud,*" Anfruns whispered for the second time that evening, and he felt a cramp of pain under the left side of his rib cage.

"He stands before you," Merrick said, taking another

step forward and drawing his own weapon.

The ivory-handled pistol fell from Anfruns's grip and clattered onto the surface of the desk, chipping the mahogany and pressing down on the intercom button. It beeped loudly, and Anfruns flinched, but Merrick only smiled.

"This place is the last you will ever see," Merrick said, pointing his gun at Anfruns, and he pulled the trigger.

Anfruns saw the room explode in white light, and felt his feet fly out from under him.

He fell back into his chair, his head lolling. There was a crushing pain in his chest, and he couldn't seem to take a breath. He could feel warm, thick liquid dripping down his chest under his shirt, and he couldn't move.

After a long moment of contemplation, Merrick turned and walked away. His footsteps slowly receded and then were cut off as the door to the office clicked shut.

Anfruns could no longer clearly see the other end of the room. The edges of his vision began to dim and close in, and his eyes flicked to the darkening portrait of his mother and father. Peder's eyes now seemed to hold a final judgement, and Anfruns felt gooseflesh break out all over his body.

All lives must end, Mikkel, the voice in his mind whispered. *What matters is how we live.*

Anfruns groaned — a wet, terrified sound — and felt himself shudder. Another bolt of pain surged through him, then he lost all feeling below his neck. He knew

Chapter 29

without a doubt that the end had arrived.

Father, he thought, and then everything went black.

Chapter 30

Merrick walked past the corpse of Fabian and pushed open the large front door of Anfruns's mansion.

The helicopter was only a short distance away on the helipad, waiting to take him back to the private airfield where one of Stille's jets would return him to the secret facility in northern Germany.

Merrick took out his satellite phone and pressed several keys, then held the device to his ear. The call was answered in seconds.

"Drost," came the reply.

"Status?"

"They have determined the location," Drost said. "It's here."

"Here?"

"Within a half-kilometre radius of this facility."

Merrick's eyes blazed. There would be no need to transport the captives to the disaster's epicentre. *It was going to happen there all along*. He could only guess what it meant, but the fine hairs on the back of his neck prickled with the synchronicity of it.

"Very well," he replied. "Anfruns will no longer be involved in our work."

There was a brief pause before Drost replied. "Understood."

"I'll be with you in ninety minutes," Merrick said. "Maintain order. Soon, Europe and beyond will be ours."

He pressed a key to end the call, and returned the phone to a pocket of his jacket.

It was a cold night, but Merrick felt invigorated. He strode towards the helicopter and climbed in without a word, giving the pilot only the merest glance. The rotors began to pick up speed immediately.

As the small craft lifted off from the pad, Merrick spared one last look at the immaculately manicured lawns, tasteful statues and reflecting pools, evergreen foliage and paved walkways beneath, then he focused his attention on the house itself.

It was ablaze with light, as always, but one particular window stood in contrast. From this vantage point there was only the vaguest suggestion of any illumination from within. Anfruns's office.

Farewell, old man, Merrick thought as a cold smile spread across his face. *Destiny is in my hands now.*

Greenwood speared another *bitterballen* with the tooth-

Chapter 30

pick she was holding and took a bite, chewing without enthusiasm.

It's been too long, she thought. *Wuyts should have heard something by now.*

Aldridge was perched on a stool across the room, in the makeshift kitchen area, watching her intently.

"A watched pot never boils, you know," he said, and he immediately regretted it. She gave him a dark look, then returned her gaze to the screen of Goose's laptop on the table across from her.

Wuyts had scheduled an emergency video call with Anfruns, to warn him about Merrick's ability and appeal to his better judgement. It was a gamble, but not quite a desperate measure. Wuyts had read Anfruns's psychological profile, and his family history.

She believed that there was some good in the man, just buried very deeply under years of pride, privilege, and ambition. Greenwood wasn't convinced.

There's no way Anfruns can talk Merrick out of this madness, she thought. *Whatever kind of man Anfruns is, Merrick can't be controlled. We're losing time that we don't have.*

She sighed, then stood up to stretch her back and neck. Dowling walked over with a mug of steaming hot coffee for her, and she smiled distractedly.

"Thanks, Larry," she said, taking a gulp of the dark liquid. "I want to be ready to move as soon as we hear anything. What's our status on—"

She stopped abruptly as the laptop emitted a distinctive chime, and a message flashed across the screen, indicating an incoming secure communication.

Greenwood handed the coffee back to Dowling without a word, and sat down at the computer. She pressed a key to accept the video call, and Janne Wuyts's face appeared on the screen.

"Captain," she said, and Greenwood nodded.

"What did he say?" she asked, getting straight to the point.

Wuyts's brow furrowed slightly. "When I spoke to Anfruns earlier, he decided to resolve the issue of Kurt Merrick himself."

Wow, Greenwood thought. *Just like that?*

"There's no way he'll be able to do that," she said. "We have to get a team out there. Has he been back in touch?"

Wuyts licked her lips, pausing for a moment before speaking. "No, and I very much doubt he will be."

Greenwood grimaced, waiting for Wuyts to continue, but she already knew what the other woman was going to say.

"CERN detected another anti-tachyon event a few minutes ago, centred on Mikkel Anfruns's estate in Denmark," Wuyts said.

"Son of a bitch," Greenwood spat. "Merrick killed him."

"That's my interpretation too," Wuyts replied grimly. "Merrick will no doubt proceed with his plan, but Anfruns gave me a set of GPS coordinates. It's the facility where they're holding the changers."

Chapter 30

Greenwood's pulse accelerated. "Are you certain of that, sir?"

"Completely," Wuyts replied. "CERN has just informed me that today's demonstrations by Mr. Aldridge and Merrick provided enough data to locate ground zero for the phenomenon. It occurs at almost exactly the same coordinates."

Oh god, Greenwood thought, feeling goosebumps break out all along her forearms. Before she could respond, Wuyts was speaking again.

"I want your team to head to Hamburg immediately, Captain. You'll have precise coordinates waiting on the plane."

"Understood, sir," she said. "We won't let you down." Her voice was steady and determined. She knew exactly what was at stake.

Wuyts nodded, and reached towards a control on her desk to end the call, but Greenwood's voice interrupted her.

"What are you going to do now, sir?" she asked.

Wuyts sighed deeply, and reached up to rub her left temple. After several seconds, she met Greenwood's gaze again.

"Now, Captain," she replied, "I'm going to pray."

Merrick arrived at the secure Stille installation in Hamburg after less than seventy minutes of travel, including a very rough landing at a hidden, makeshift airfield. Drost, Tepel and Finn were waiting for him, in command of a small group of hired mercenaries who had replaced all of Stille's existing security staff at the previous confinement location in Denmark.

The facility was in the basement and sub-basement of a former bank, which had been leased to Stille under the guise of a brokerage firm for commercial shipping equipment. It bordered some warehouses on one side, and a grand but relatively quiet plaza on the other, facing a small park and an imposing gothic cathedral across the square on the far end. Absolutely no-one except Anfruns, Merrick, and this facility's former director knew of its existence during the course of the project. Of those three men, only Merrick still lived.

The changers were currently locked in what used to be the vault room in the sub-basement, and a suite of advanced communications and anti-tachyon monitoring equipment had been hurriedly set up on the primary basement level. Two guards were posted at the top of the internal staircase leading to the lower floors, and two more were at the bottom. The changers themselves remained sedated, and were wearing manacles.

"Sir," Drost greeted Merrick, and the other man nodded.

"This location is secure?" he asked.

"As ordered," Drost replied.

"How fortunate for you," Merrick said, then strode past him and descended the first set of stairs. Drost and Tepel exchanged a glance then followed him, leaving Finn in the entranceway. The Irishman was cradling a

Chapter 30

gun, and seemed to be restless. The guards were pointedly avoiding his gaze every bit as much as they avoided Merrick's.

When Merrick reached the sub-basement, the guards there visibly tensed and straightened, but he didn't even glance at them. He walked across to the vault door and then stopped, raising his hand and pressing it against the cold steel surface.

He had been contemplating objects like this more and more often lately. The steel was at least twelve inches thick, and the door was mounted on steel-cored concrete blocks. Bars thicker than his own arms secured the door to its frame. Stille had paid a fortune to obtain the site with all of its original furnishings and equipment intact.

Yet even this door will not withstand the Destiny event, Merrick thought.

Drost glanced at Tepel, and the other man shook his head once. *Let him be.* It was unwise to engage with Merrick at the best of times, and to interrupt his musings would be suicide — especially now that they knew he also had the strange power that their prisoners could wield.

Merrick ran his hand across the vault door, feeling its contours and edges.

Anfruns had failed the final test of worthiness. The old man's guilt and conscience had hollowed him out from the inside, making him falter and then lose his conviction.

That was the difference between us, Mikkel, Merrick

thought. *Doubt*.

Merrick had no doubts whatsoever that preventing the Destiny event was within his capabilities, particularly with the other changers at his disposal. Europe would be saved, for now. He would finally be in full control of the world around him — the arbiter of its capriciousness and cruelty.

He felt completely free. Free of Anfruns, free of any need for subterfuge, and perhaps even free from mortality. Who could possibly threaten him? He had been shot dead twice in the last twenty-four hours, and yet here he stood, whole and vital. And dangerous.

He began to laugh softly to himself, not noticing Drost and Tepel tense up behind him and exchange a worried glance.

Let KESTREL come. Let them bring all of EUFOR's soldiers if they wanted. Nothing could touch him now.

Because I am a god, he thought. *And a god must inevitably hold the world in his hand.*

He straightened, lifting his hand away from the vault door with one last, almost reverential caress.

"Open it," he said.

Drost stepped forward immediately and entered a ten-digit code on a keypad, then he gripped the large, spoked wheel set into the door and turned it rapidly. There was a metallic clunk from inside the mechanism, and the barest whine from the heavy hinges as the massive door began to swing outwards.

Merrick stepped out of the way, and Tepel and one of

Chapter 30

the guards moved forward with their weapons raised. Drost hauled the door fully open. It moved surprisingly smoothly and easily for its weight.

The inside of the vault was bare, except for clusters of mats, blankets and pillows on the floor, each with an unconscious changer lying on top.

Merrick strolled in, looking around disinterestedly as if he was browsing in a store. His gaze settled on a portly, middle-aged Italian man lying prone nearby. The man's head was almost bald, and an ugly scar ran along the right side of his scalp. His face was pallid, and bore several bruises. A large bandage covered one side of his neck, and his left forearm was in a cast.

I remember how afraid you were, Merrick thought, recalling the many experiments they had performed over the previous weeks and months, trying to determine what made these people unique, and how they performed their small miracles. *I will enjoy seeing that fear again.*

"Him," Merrick said.

Drost lowered his weapon and walked back out of the vault, then pulled a wheeled trolley from one side of the antechamber and rolled it into the vault. The guard helped him pick the man up and dump him onto the gurney, then Drost pushed it back out. Merrick and the guard followed, and the huge vault door swung closed with a muffled thud.

Merrick took a deep and cleansing breath. Something had to trigger the event. It was to take place right here, where circumstance had brought him. It was preordained. All he had to do was live up to the promise of his own fate.

He had been informed of the gathering black clouds on the horizon, pushing in towards the city. Atmospheric pressure was already fluctuating. He glanced over at a wall-mounted clock. It was well past midnight.

The only working theory his own scientists had was that use of the ability itself might somehow cause the phenomenon. It stood to reason, but evidence was non-existent. It didn't matter.

Merrick was more than willing to make sacrifices in the name of science.

"Bring Destiny to me," Merrick commanded. "The time has come."

Part 3

Chapter 31

Greenwood checked and re-checked her weapons, periodically glancing around the administrative outbuilding they were in.

Dowling was packing spare ammunition, grenades and extra wrist-mounted anti-tachyon detectors into a set of black multi-strap backpacks. Ramos was checking and balancing her sniper rifle. She had called her wife fifteen minutes ago, but Greenwood had moved away so as not to eavesdrop.

I hope you weren't saying goodbye, Alicia, she thought. *We're not finished yet.*

Greenwood looked at the final two members of her team. Goose was already fully geared up, as always, and was helping Aldridge position and adjust his headset microphone, and briefly instructing him on the use of a .38 pistol. The weapon was for emergency use; it was unlikely that he'd have either the opportunity or the need for it. Nonetheless, they could use all the help they could get.

When did I start thinking of a physicist as a member of the team? she wondered, but there was no time for those thoughts right now. Aldridge had proven himself extremely valuable, and not just because of his ability. Either they would succeed tonight, at which point she could allow herself to think about what the future may hold, or they wouldn't.

Wuyts had been as good as her word. As soon as their jet landed, a minivan with blacked-out windows transported them the very short distance across the airport to this building, which sat near the end of a runway that wasn't currently in use. They were still on the grounds of Hamburg International Airport, but an access road would take them to their destination in around ten minutes.

The outbuilding had been secured, and besides the vehicle, they found a full cache of weaponry, ammunition, communications equipment and all of the necessary authorisation documents. The local authorities had not been informed, since there was little they could constructively do and their presence would likely only make a bad situation much worse.

Greenwood's team immediately set about preparing themselves for an incursion into the location that Anfruns had provided. The predictive algorithm was almost superfluous at this point, but the scientists in Geneva continued to monitor the developing situation.

Chapter 31

Greenwood wondered what it would be like, standing at the centre of an energy build-up that would eventually explode, destroying so many landmarks. So much history. So many lives.

In the worst case, at least it'll be quick, she thought, then she felt a stab of anger at herself. They would succeed. There were no other options available. Europe would not fall tonight.

She gathered her focus and tapped the screen of a nearby tablet computer, which lit up to show an urban map of Hamburg. Their current location was marked with a pulsing blue dot, and their destination was outlined in ominous red.

Binderplatz.

It was a large plaza a few kilometres to the north of the airport, in a primarily residential belt of the city. There were some commercial neighbourhoods there too, including their destination, but the city centre and its shops and nightlife were elsewhere, making it the perfect place for a seemingly-respectable company to quietly go about its business without scrutiny.

She double-tapped the screen near the west edge of the plaza, and a building zoomed to fill the screen. The municipal database identified it as a brokerage firm, but the company's information trail led all the way to Panama, with no listed directors. The building had been the respected *Friedmann & Gottschalk Mercantile Bank* until fifteen years ago, when an investment scandal ended a family business that spanned five generations.

It had lain empty until three years ago, and then the mysterious brokerage company quietly leased it for a period of ten years, which wasn't unusual for the area and property value. They paid the lease promptly, and the phones were answered by a polite but anonymous secretary who insisted that the firm's business was with established clients only, and that no appointments were currently available.

We're coming for you, Merrick, Greenwood thought, *and this time you're not going to escape justice.*

A large flat-panel display was bolted to the wall above a desk that currently held a selection of microphone headsets, and the screen showed a live overlay of the energy patterns CERN was monitoring, a scrolling feed of local law enforcement information, and a weather map of downtown Hamburg. CERN employed a permanent meteorologist due to the possibility of atmospheric electrical activity interfering with their various particle colliders, and Greenwood had received an unsettling report of a rapidly developing weather system towards the north of the city.

They would be heading into the eye of the storm both figuratively and literally. It couldn't be a coincidence.

Already, the weather display was starting to display red fringes and small triangular alert symbols, and Greenwood knew that the airport would probably put its extreme weather contingency plans into effect before long. Incoming flights would eventually be diverted.

Not that it'll do any good, she thought. *They can't fly far*

Chapter 31

or fast enough if things go wrong tonight. Again she pushed the thought down, and gathered the last of her gear.

"Alright," she said, and four pairs of eyes immediately turned towards her. "Are we ready?"

Dowling folded his arms. "As we'll ever be, chief," he said.

Ramos snapped the scope back onto her sniper rifle, and Goose holstered his .45. Each of them nodded, then Aldridge took a step forward.

"I'm not ready at all," he said, "but I don't really have anything planned for tomorrow, so by all means lead the way."

His words were light, but his pale face was lined with grim determination.

You're tougher than you think, she thought, once again feeling a grudging admiration for the man.

"Let's go," she said.

Chapter 32

Merrick straightened his sleeves as Drost carefully balanced the cruel-looking throwing knife in his fingers, and then threw it across the room towards the terrified Italian man.

This was the fourth time Drost had thrown the weapon, and each time the small man had instinctively deflected it with his ability. He was standing against a bare wall in a storeroom on the basement level, handcuffed on both sides to some piping. Guards surrounded him in a wide semicircle, and Merrick had gathered several of the other captive changers too, to observe. Along another wall, there was a metal trolley with an array of computer equipment, monitoring the spiking anti-tachyon energy readings in the area.

Sweat was dripping from the man's brow, and his eyes showed unrestrained terror. His name was Alfeo Sarni, and before this nightmare he had been a carpenter specialising in bookcases. He was snatched from his workshop two months earlier, just hours after a very strange experience with his circular saw. Since then, he had undergone many medical tests, been experimented on, and tortured several times a week in an attempt to discover why he could perform these feats of self-preservation.

Sarni had no idea what goal his captors had in mind, but he knew he was going to die here tonight. He already felt faint and clammy, and his pulse had become irregular. His hands were shaking. He thought of his two teenaged sons, and thanked the Lord that they had been away when he was taken.

The knife whispered through the air towards him, and yet again he prayed for deliverance. This time, though, nothing happened. All of his strength was spent.

The blade struck him full in the chest, embedding itself between two ribs and piercing his heart. Blood exploded from his mouth, and he sank to the ground with a strangled gasp, falling almost to his knees and then hanging there because of the handcuffs.

"Bring another one," Merrick said calmly, and Tepel nodded, turning to the terrified faces of their captives and taking a step forward.

KESTREL deployed from the van on a side-street one block away from the plaza, and immediately set out cautiously along a connecting alley that would bring

Chapter 32

them to the rear of the old bank building.

Greenwood and Dowling took the lead, with Goose and Aldridge bringing up the rear. Ramos took a vantage point across the square to cover the main entrance.

They had discarded their wrist detectors back at the van, because they were triggering constantly now, and CERN could directly relay any information they might need anyway.

"Almost there," Greenwood said. "Get ready."

The plan was to breach the facility via a service entrance at the rear, where armoured cars had once ferried cash and bonds into and out of the building during its time as a bank. The entrance would no doubt be guarded, but it was their best option. The front of the bank was in full view of the plaza, and the studded double doors were a risky choke-point, as well as being steel-lined.

Dowling would approach first, with cover from Greenwood and Goose, and survey the situation. He carried a portable thermal scanner which they hoped would penetrate the loading door. After finding out as much as possible about the strength of resistance immediately inside the delivery bay, they would enter one by one via a secured single-access door to the side of the bay, which Goose would burn through with thermite.

They would penetrate the building as far as possible, neutralising all resistance on the way, and proceed downwards. The city planning database had supplied blueprints of the entire place, and Greenwood's bet was on Merrick having set up his lab in the lower levels. The anti-tachyon energy patterns were detectable regardless of physical barriers, so the only thing Merrick would need to set up above ground was a communications mast, which was most likely to be on the roof of the building, away from prying eyes.

Greenwood glanced upwards, along the roofline, and spotted it immediately: a short cluster of black antennae attached to a base unit, including a ball-shaped transceiver, with a thick cord running over the lip of the roof and entering the building via a slightly ajar top-floor window. A quick and dirty job, but then Merrick wasn't planning to stay here for very long.

"Alicia, I've got eyes on the comms mast," Greenwood said. "Halfway along the building's west side, just over the gutter line."

There was a pause of no more than three seconds before she heard Ramos's voice through her earpiece.

"Sighted," Ramos said. "Ready to hit it on your signal."

They reached the last corner before the alley joined the access lane which led to the loading area, and Greenwood came to a halt, taking a quick glance around the corner. The area looked deserted. There were three security cameras overlooking the entrance area, and Merrick would certainly have someone monitoring them.

"This is it," she said. "Goose, give Larry a way forward. Larry, you'd better be fast with the breach. We'll

Chapter 32

be right behind you."

"Got it, chief," Dowling said, tapping the pouch attached to his combat webbing, and drawing his pistol.

Greenwood pulled back two metres, then Goose took the lead position at the corner, dropping to one knee. He pulled out a small device that looked like a miniature high-tech telescope with a trigger-grip attached, and carefully aimed it at the topmost security camera.

Dowling moved up behind him, with Aldridge close behind.

"Focused EM pulse," the big man whispered, answering Aldridge's unasked question. "It'll fry the cameras without making any sound."

Aldridge nodded, impressed.

"On three," Goose said, and everyone tensed. "One, two, *three*."

He pulled the trigger, and nothing seemed to happen. He kept it depressed for three seconds, then rapidly targeted each of the two remaining cameras in turn, for the same amount of time. Then, he lowered the device and backed away from the corner. "All yours," he said.

Dowling immediately sprinted across the open area, reaching the secured door beside the bay in less than five seconds.

"Alicia, now," Greenwood said, and barely a second later the cluster of communications equipment on the roof blew apart as if it had been struck with an invisible hammer.

Greenwood and Goose moved up to the mouth of the

alleyway immediately, Goose standing at the edge of the faded red brick wall, and Greenwood took a kneeling position. Each of them had semi-automatic assault weapons, complete with grenade attachments.

"Keep your eyes open, Aldridge," Greenwood said, with tension evident in her voice. "I don't want anyone coming up behind us."

Aldridge drew his pistol and leaned into the wall a couple of metres behind Goose. He looked back along the alley, taking the occasional glance towards the access road. His chest felt tight, and the gun was heavy and unnatural in his hands.

Come on, Dowling, he thought. Someone would notice the loss of the security feed very soon.

The big man worked quickly, with the practised hands of a veteran. He applied thermite to the lock casing and to a higher area of the door, where a securing bar would be slid home in its matching steel slot embedded in the concrete that lay behind the brickwork. He ran magnesium ribbon and a short fuse from both thermite packs, checked his work, then took out a tiny, black handheld gas lighter that would work even in a hurricane. He reached up and tapped his earpiece twice in quick succession, lit the fuse, then twisted his body away from the door.

The thermite flared to life and almost instantly liquefied the lock mechanism and the securing bar, dripping blue-white sparks all over the concrete stoop. Dowling readied his own assault weapon, counted to five, then

Chapter 32

again tapped his earpiece twice.

He took a breath, hooked two fingers of his gloved hand around the door handle, and quickly pulled it open.

The third changer fell to the ground, bleeding profusely from a bullet wound. Tepel watched the young woman's face as her eyes fluttered shut, his own expression unreadable.

Merrick opened his mouth to order another of their captives forward, but he was interrupted by a black-clad mercenary running into the room.

"We've lost the rear security feed on all three cameras, sir," he said tightly, and Merrick smiled.

"They've arrived sooner than expected," he said, turning to Drost and Tepel. "Get Finn and keep them out for as long as you can. Nothing can be allowed to interfere."

The two men left immediately, and Merrick pointed to one of the guards. "Continue this," he said.

The man looked uncertain, and Merrick pulled his gun from its holster, raised it and put a bullet in the guard's head in one smooth motion. He re-holstered the gun, and turned to the next guard.

"*Continue this*," he said, and the man nodded quickly and stepped forward, readying his own weapon. He walked to the middle of the semicircle of restrained captives, choosing one at random, and levelled his assault rifle. The Greek college student from Athens pulled uselessly at the handcuffs holding him to an iron radiator, his eyes wide.

Merrick could feel the familiar charge building in the air, and knew that the guard's first volley would fail. It didn't matter. Eventually, they always tired.

The guard pulled the trigger, and the scene slowed down, just as it had dozens of times over the last hour. The first salvo of bullet flew wide, and then the gun's magazine jammed. Merrick had seen the young man take two bullets to the torso, but that was in another reality now.

"Replace the clip and try again," Merrick said cooly, and the guard complied.

He was just about to open fire when they heard the sudden roar of an explosion from upstairs.

Chapter 33

Dowling was crouched just inside the loading bay's security door, behind a heavy steel dolly loaded with empty cash-carrier boxes. Each one was designed to take multiple gunshots without giving up its contents, so they made for effective cover.

Until the bad guys show up, he thought, endlessly scanning the dimly-lit room for any sign of movement.

Greenwood, Goose and Aldridge slipped into the bay beside him, and took cover. They hadn't been discovered yet, but that was surely only moments away.

Greenwood made several gestures, and both Dowling and Goose nodded once in recognition.

Goose immediately half-ran in a crouch to the opposite wall, where a large set of double-doors led into the depths of the building. From studying the blueprints earlier, he knew that they opened onto a service corridor which would eventually take them to the front of the bank, but what he was really interested in was only halfway along that corridor on the right side: the main stairwell leading down to the basement level.

He rose up to glance through the head-height dusty glass panels set into the doors, and immediately dropped back down. He raised three fingers, indicating three guards in the corridor, and Aldridge felt a burst of adrenaline chase through him.

This is where it gets serious, he thought.

Greenwood gestured to Dowling, and the big man took out a grenade, weighing it in his large fist, then quickly crossed to Goose's position. The Dutchman fell back, readying his assault rifle.

Dowling took a deep breath, raised himself to his full height beside the door, then paused for only a beat before pulling the pin. He slammed his free palm against the nearest door, knocking it flying around on its hinges away from him, then immediately threw the grenade down the corridor before drawing back behind the wall.

Greenwood and Aldridge ducked, and there was a half second of silence before the device detonated.

The shockwave battered the doors open in the opposite direction, into the loading bay, and one was wrenched off its hinges and clattered end over end before falling flat in the middle of the floor. Aldridge could feel the shockwave even from this distance, and there was an unpleasantly sharp metallic smell in the air.

Chapter 33

A plume of acrid white smoke blew through the loading bay and then began to clear. Barely a second later, shots rang out and bullets peppered the shutter-mounted door behind the dolly, only a foot above where Aldridge and Greenwood were crouched.

"Stay low," she said, then snapped off three shots over the rim. Aldridge felt a bitter sense of vengeance when he heard a man's scream from further down the corridor.

Dowling readied another grenade, and Goose covered him with precise shots from ground level towards the mouth of the stairwell. Merrick's guards were taking cover around the edge of the stair entrance, and laying down unbroken suppressing fire.

"Do it!" Greenwood shouted, and the big man didn't hesitate. There was another ear-shattering explosion, making Aldridge wince, and then silence for several seconds.

"Move forward," Greenwood said. "Goose, scout it out, and be careful. Larry, cover him."

Goose moved forward cautiously, his rifle raised and his finger taking up the slack on the trigger. The corridor was dark — the grenades had destroyed the light fittings — and completely silent for the moment.

He froze and dropped to one knee when he suddenly heard heavy boots clumping up the stairs, and Dowling stepped fully into the corridor and trained his weapon on the mouth of the stairwell.

A moment later, a guard burst into the corridor, gun

raised, and fired wildly. The bullets strafed along the left wall barely a metre from Goose, but the Dutchman didn't flinch. He pulled the trigger, and a hole appeared in the guard's head before the man dropped like a stone.

Goose rolled to the right as the barrel of a rifle suddenly snaked around the stairwell entrance, and Dowling snapped off a precision shot, blowing a chunk out of the plaster only an inch from the unseen mercenary's weapon. The gun barrel disappeared in a hurry, and Goose rose then walked carefully backwards along the corridor under Dowling's cover.

"We've got to get down there," Greenwood warned.

The rifle's barrel reappeared and everyone ducked as a hail of fire pinned Goose and Dowling down.

We don't have time for this, Greenwood thought, slinging her assault rifle across her back and drawing her pistol, then she darted forward along the corridor. Dowling's eyes widened, then he fired several shots at the mouth of the stairwell, making sure she wouldn't be cut down as she ran.

Greenwood came to a stop eight feet from the yawning black rectangle, pressed her back against the wall, and she extended her pistol arm fully.

She started counting, and she had reached four when the gunman poked half of his head out to check the situation. She fired without hesitation, and the bullet smashed through the bridge of his nose, killing him instantly.

"Blimey," Dowling said, with respect in his voice.

Chapter 33

"Bloody irregular too, chief, if you don't mind my saying so."

"It's an irregular sort of night, Larry," she replied, motioning for them to join her at the top of the stairs.

Without warning, Drost burst from the stairwell, swinging his weapon like a club towards Greenwood's head. She blocked the blow with her forearm, kicking out with her right leg and connecting with his knee.

Drost tipped to one side, his shoulder making contact with the wall, and struggled to raise his gun. He managed to squeeze the trigger, sending a bullet skipping off the wall half a metre behind her, but then Goose and Dowling appeared in front of him.

The Welshman's enormous fist crashed into Drost's jaw, snapped his head to one side, and he crumpled to the floor, desperately trying to cling to consciousness.

Drost shook his head rapidly, rolling away from the men who loomed over him, and he fumbled for his sidearm. He barely managed to unsnap the holster's latch before Goose's rifle coughed twice, and then he lay still.

Aldridge had been hanging back, searching for any sense that there was a change-point approaching, but none came. He hurried along the corridor to join the rest. As Goose glanced at him, he abruptly raised his own pistol, and pointed it towards Greenwood.

"What the *hell* are you-" Goose began, but he flinched as the roar of the pistol cut him off.

There was a dull thud, and then the sound of something heavy rolling a little way down the stairs before coming to a stop.

Aldridge was breathing rapidly, with his pistol still pointed ahead. Dowling took five slow steps towards him, gave him a questioning look, and then put his hand on the top of the barrel of the weapon, pushing Aldridge's arm down.

"Sorry," Aldridge said, with a tremor in his voice. "It was the other one. He chased me, back in Edinburgh."

Dowling followed his gaze to see a new spatter of crimson on the opposite wall of the stairwell entrance, and Greenwood glanced around the corner, seeing a man's body lying about ten steps down. A submachine gun lay askew on top of his body, held in place by its shoulder strap. The shot had taken him at the base of the neck, just above his armour.

"Tepel," Greenwood said, familiar with Interpol's dossier on Merrick's most trusted lieutenants. "That just leaves Finn, and any more hired help."

Aldridge blinked, looking down at the gun in his hand. It was hard to believe that such a small device could end a man's life so quickly and decisively.

"Are you OK?" Greenwood asked, taking a step towards him, and he exhaled loudly, forcing himself back into the moment.

"Fine," he said. "It's just… that was the first time I've ever shot anyone."

"Wish I could say it gets easier," she replied. "And… thanks. I didn't even hear him."

Chapter 33

Aldridge simply nodded, and Dowling clapped him on the shoulder. Goose was watching him with a contemplative expression, and both soldiers noticed that Greenwood was looking at their civilian companion with an expression of respect.

"Alright," Greenwood said after a moment, "let's do what we came here to do. The clock is still ticking."

Greenwood and Dowling took positions along the wall just beside the stairwell, with Goose and Aldridge clustered behind. There was still light coming up from the lower floor, and now that the corridor was silent they could hear the occasional slightly muffled gunshot from below.

Greenwood frowned. *Single rounds being fired? That doesn't make any sense.* She glanced at Dowling, who shrugged, then she felt a light tap on her shoulder. Aldridge stepped up close behind her.

"He's shooting them to trigger their ability," he said in a small voice, and her jaw tensed. "I can feel it. I think he's trying to make it happen."

"Then I think it's time we stopped him," she replied.

The eight remaining captives cowered against the wall, looking from the guards to the door that led out to the basement hallway. They could easily hear the gunfire from upstairs, punctuated by the occasional explosion.

Merrick had his weapon drawn, and his attention was no longer on the changers in the room.

It seems we'll be meeting again very soon, Captain Green-

wood, he thought. *This is a fine night for you to die.*

He depressed a switch on his lapel radio, and spoke into the microphone.

"Finn," he said, "what is your location?"

The response came immediately. "Still at the front," the Irishman replied, in his usual sniggering tone. "They're about thirty feet away, getting ready to come down to you."

"Delay them," Merrick ordered, and a smile crept over Finn's face that would chill the blood of any sane person who saw it.

Finn unsnapped the safety fastener on his ankle sheath, and drew his precious combat knife. It was a wicked-looking blade, immaculately clean, with a serrated portion and a smooth, curved edge nearer the point. At his last count — which was yesterday, when he had impulsively murdered a passing postman while waiting outside the Rijksmuseum, and stuffed the body into a large glass-recycling bin — the knife had claimed the lives of thirty-seven people. With any luck, tonight he could make it to forty and beyond.

He also drew his Sig Sauer M11-A1 pistol, flexing his fingers around the grip. *Let's dance*, he thought, then he stepped abruptly out into the far end of the main corridor with a wild grin on his face, raised the pistol, and fired at the first target he saw.

Goose spun a hundred and eighty degrees and fell flat along the corridor, feeling like something had exploded in his left thigh. He shouted with pain and surprise, and

Chapter 33

Greenwood and Dowling immediately returned fire.

Finn stepped gracefully back behind the cover of the alcove leading to the bank's old teller room and foyer, glancing over at the two Stille guards who were looking nervously at him.

"I bet that hurt a bit," Finn called down the corridor.

Dowling bristled, gritting his teeth. Greenwood pulled Goose further back towards the loading bay room, and Aldridge came over to help her administer emergency first aid. The shot was off-centre, luckily, and it looked like it had passed straight through the muscle and sinew on the outside of Goose's thigh. The bone was probably intact, and the bleeding could have been a lot worse. She applied a compression strap pulled from her own combat webbing, and latched it around his leg. He grunted in pain at the pressure.

"Alright," Greenwood panted, "you're going to be OK. Hang in there." Goose nodded, wincing in pain, but he didn't make a sound.

She stood up, then pressed a small button on her headset microphone. "Alicia, are you there?" she asked.

"Here," came Ramos's voice without a pause, and Greenwood felt a surge of gratitude at the other woman's utter dependability.

"One way or another, this is all going down in the next five to ten minutes," she said. "Goose is hit — he took a nine mil to the thigh. He's immobile. It's time to invite some friends. Call Wuyts and tell her to get GSG 9 here on the double."

"Understood," Ramos replied, and Greenwood heard a click in her earpiece.

GSG 9, the *Grenzschutzgruppe 9 der Bundespolizei* was an elite federal counter-terrorism special forces unit operating in Germany. They were the best of the best, and were trained to handle hostage situations, penetration and extraction, armed and unarmed combat at the highest levels of skill, and plenty more. Comparable to SWAT teams, the British SAS or the US Navy SEALs, they were a formidable force to have on your side.

They're no match for Merrick's ability, though, she thought. GSG could only serve as support once Merrick's own team had been neutralised. Greenwood would be glad to hand the situation over to them at that point, but the more pressing problem was that the Destiny event was imminent and Merrick still hadn't been secured. She turned to Dowling.

"Larry, we're out of time," she said grimly. "We need to get down there. Deal with him."

"Damned right I will," Dowling replied, marching down the hall with his rifle raised. He saw a flicker of movement around the edge of the wall up ahead and opened fire, tearing a chain of holes through an oak panel that was probably at least a hundred and twenty years old.

Impossibly, he heard the man giggling up ahead.

"You made a mistake there, mate," Dowling said, snapping off another three shots that chewed more holes into the alcove's wooden surround.

Chapter 33

Dowling stopped dead and felt his legs tense as an object flew out from around the corner and hit the floor with a clatter. It was a silver-black 9mm Sig pistol.

"Come on and prove it, then, big lad," Finn's voice taunted from the darkness, in a rough Belfast drawl. "There's my gun. I'm more of a knife man myself."

Dowling took a couple of deep breaths to dull his anger, recognising that the man was clearly insane. He stepped forward cautiously, then thrust his rifle around the corner, taking in the scene within half a second.

Two black-clad guards lay dead, with their throats cut. Standing in the middle of the wide foyer was the man he knew as James Finn. He was spinning a vicious, blood-stained combat knife in his right hand, flipping it under and over his outstretched fingers with an ease borne of countless hours of practice.

Dowling glanced around, seeing no-one else, and no indication of a trap.

You're off your head, he thought, thinking back to the briefing on Merrick's known associates. Finn was one of the worst, and had a criminal record as long as both his arms. He was a killer with an underdeveloped sense of self-preservation, and a pathological need to inflict pain and suffering on living things. Dowling knew very well that Finn preferred a knife fight because it was up close and personal, and that he would enjoy every moment of it.

Keeping his rifle trained on the Irishman, Dowling stepped forward. *Rabid bloody animal*, he thought.

Finn twirled the knife, which glittered as it caught the muted light coming in from the ornate glass above the lintel of the bank's main entrance.

"Put the knife down, and I'll let you go to jail," Dowling said. His eyes were flint, and the tendons on his huge neck throbbed with tension.

Finn spat on the ground, deftly tossing his knife from one hand to the other. "Put the *gun* down, and come over here and make me," he replied.

"You'd like that, wouldn't you?" Dowling replied, advancing another step, his rifle still raised.

Greenwood was listening over Dowling's radio mic. "We don't have time for honour, Larry," she said. "Merrick is still down there, with those people."

Finn watched as Dowling approached. He was still casually spinning the knife. "I'm going to open you up, lad, and then I'm going to go and say hello to that bitch you're with," he sneered.

"Good luck with that," Dowling replied. "But I doubt you'll get the chance."

Finn lost his patience, flicking the knife up in the air and catching it in his fist, point downwards. The he raised his arm and started to circle the other man. "We'll see about that," he spat, a wild grin on his face. "Now put down the *fucking gun*, and let's go!"

Dowling tilted his head slightly to one side, sizing the man up. *Not even wearing armour, and you waltzed into a firefight like it was a birthday party. Mad dog. You're not worth my time*, he thought, and tightened his grip on the

Chapter 33

rifle's barrel.

"I think I'll just put *you* down," he said.

Finn's forehead crinkled in confusion for a moment, then his grin widened ghoulishly just as Dowling pulled the trigger.

The rifle coughed several times, and the sound echoed around the vaulted space. Finn was catapulted backwards, landing in a sprawl on the floor, his clothes torn open in several places. Blood oozed freely from four holes in his chest, and his knife clacked to the marble floor as his grip relaxed.

A bubble of red spit burst on his lips as he tried to speak, and then he stopped moving.

Dowling sighed, then turned on his heel and hurried back along the corridor towards Greenwood and Aldridge.

Chapter 34

"Let's move," Greenwood said, starting down the stairs with Dowling at her side and Aldridge following close behind.

Goose was sitting against the wall halfway along the ground-level corridor, his rifle propped on his leg, with his eyes trained on the stairwell. He was pale, but the bleeding had mostly stopped, and help was on the way. Ramos had been in touch to tell them that GSG 9 would be there in ten minutes, bringing a medical team.

The stairway was foggy with smoke, and their footsteps were muffled. The periodic gunfire from below had stopped, bringing an uneasy silence.

They crept further down the stairs, listening carefully for any sign of resistance. Two thirds of the way down, Greenwood held up her hand. She listened carefully, and heard it again: the barest rustle coming from just below.

She motioned to Dowling to cover the left edge, and trained her own weapon on the right. Gently, she reached into one of the pockets on her armour vest and took out a narrow flashlight. She tossed it underarm towards the last few stairs, and as it struck the concrete with a clink, two guards stepped into view and opened fire.

Their shots were far too low, though, and they had no time to lift their angle of fire before they were cut down.

"Can't be many more," Dowling muttered, moving forwards and downwards again, ahead of Greenwood. They reached the bottom of the stairs a moment later, checking the immediate area for any further signs of life. Greenwood retrieved her flashlight, and used it to sweep the walls of the chamber.

Up ahead, there were floor-to-ceiling steel bars extending the entire width of the far wall, but the large gate in the middle was lying open, swinging loosely on its hinges. Beyond, she saw what must have been the old bank's primary vault. The door was closed.

Suddenly, Ramos's voice burst over the intercom. "Things are happening out here," she said. There was a note of fear in her voice, and she sounded out of breath.

"What is it?" Greenwood asked, feeling ice in her stomach.

"The weather is starting to go crazy," Ramos replied. "Big lightning storm coming in, from nowhere. I'm getting off the roof. I think… it's starting."

Greenwood, Dowling and Aldridge each wore the

Chapter 34

same expression of dread.

"Understood," Greenwood replied. "Hold position on the ground across the plaza, and guide GSG when they arrive. Greenwood out."

She turned to Dowling. "Get us in there," she said, pointing to the vault, and Dowling darted forward, examining the mechanism. He tested the wheel that was set into the door, then pulled gently on it. It moved by a few millimetres.

"It's open, chief," he said, frowning. "I guess that's an invitation."

"Then let's not keep him waiting," Greenwood said. "Aldridge, we might need you in here."

"Oh good," Aldridge replied, feeling sweat drip down his back. She directed him over to the left wall of the antechamber, and they both took up firing positions where they'd be out of immediate sight when the door opened.

Dowling hauled the vault door outwards, staying behind it, and it swung easily on its massive hinges. He stepped out of the way and then put his weight against the smooth metal, to steady it until it had stopped. Then he pressed himself flat against the inside surface, ready to dart into the room beyond.

"Merrick," Greenwood shouted, "You're trapped and federal authorities are surrounding this building. Release your hostages and surrender. It's over."

"My dear Captain Greenwood," came Merrick's voice from within, "I promise you that this night has only just begun."

Greenwood took a deep breath, then she nodded to Dowling and they both stepped into the doorway with their weapons raised.

There were bodies on the floor. Men and women of all ages; about eight in all. At the back of the room, six people stood clad in hospital gowns, looking pale, exhausted and terrified. Behind them, she could see the face of Kurt Merrick. There was no-one else in the vault.

Greenwood took two steps into the room, and a gunshot rang out. A slender elderly gentleman fell to his knees and toppled forward to the floor, blood already soaking through the flimsy material he wore.

"That's quite far enough," Merrick said.

Bastard, Greenwood thought, quickly assessing the surviving hostages. There were two adult women, two men, and a young girl of perhaps eleven years old. The girl was a waif, eyes too bright and her jaw hanging open in the stunned pose of someone suffering from long-term shock. The men looked like they were on their last legs. The women looked defeated, drained and haunted, but still present. Merrick was standing directly behind the younger of the two women, a round-faced brunette of about thirty-five.

Now all we need to do is get them out of here, Greenwood thought, her mind racing. *Or get Merrick out first.*

"What do you want?" she asked, and the hatred in her voice was very clear.

"I want you to drop your weapons, or each of these

Chapter 34

people will die here tonight," Merrick replied.

"Not going to happen," Greenwood said, levelling her rifle. "Let them go, and you'll get a trial instead of a burial."

Merrick laughed. It was a cold sound, and Aldridge shuddered.

"One doesn't bury a god," Merrick said.

"You're no god, Merrick," she replied. "You're a lunatic, and you're playing with millions of lives."

Aldridge stepped into the vault. Merrick's gaze flicked towards him, and a flash of recognition and disdain crossed his features.

"Dr. Taylor's protégé," he said, and his eyes glittered in satisfaction as he watched Aldridge raise his pistol. "Have you learned so little about what I am? Better men than you have tried to kill me, and failed."

And women, Aldridge thought. He knew that Merrick was right. A bullet would be useless in here, and probably only a danger to Greenwood and her team.

He was about to respond when he felt something he'd never experienced before.

He was suddenly aware of something far above him, hundreds of feet over his head, and enormous. There was a pulse to it, like music too faint to be heard. His entire body felt like it abruptly acquired a static charge, and all the hair on the back of his neck stood on end.

Across the small, metal-lined room, Merrick's eyes blazed.

You can feel it too, Aldridge thought. *It's Destiny. It's above us. It's building up.*

"It's starting," the two men said in unison.

Greenwood was looking from Aldridge to Merrick in confusion and alarm. "Aldridge, talk to me," she said. She levelled her weapon at Merrick, and Dowling followed her lead.

There was a moment of silence, then Merrick did something completely unexpected: he pushed the female hostage forward, and she fell to her knees.

Greenwood's eyes widened, but Merrick made no move to shoot. She saw Dowling tense in her peripheral vision, and she hissed *"Hold your fire!"*

What the hell are you doing? she thought, watching for the barest twitch.

"You're all free to go," Merrick said, lowering the pistol he was holding, and re-holstering it at his side. His eyes never left Aldridge, and his expression was dangerous.

"Get them out, now," Greenwood commanded, and Dowling sprang forward, hauled the woman up from the floor and pulled her out of the vault by her upper arms.

He returned to the vault and grabbed each of the two men by their shoulders and tilted his head towards the door. They both blinked and exchanged a look, and then shuffled out as quickly as they could. The remaining woman was more aware of what was happening, and she put her arms around the girl and ushered her out of the room without a word. Dowling gathered them all

Chapter 34

along the right wall of the antechamber, opposite the open vault door, and pointed up the stairs urgently. The second woman nodded, and led the stunned group away.

"Goose, we've got five hostages coming up the stairs," Dowling said into his microphone. "They're unarmed, and they're in a bad way. Point them to the back door, mate."

"Will do," Goose replied, breathing heavily over the communication channel, as Dowling dashed back into the vault.

Greenwood had her rifle pointed at Merrick's chest. The man looked unperturbed, and his arms hung casually at his sides.

"So what now?" Greenwood asked. "That's it?"

Aldridge paled. "No," he said, in a small voice. "It's above us now. I can feel it. So can he. And he's either killed or drained all the people he captured. They can't help anymore. We saw it ourselves, when my blood sugar crashed after the museum."

Merrick nodded, his eyes darkening.

"The event is going to happen," Aldridge continued, "and like it or not, he's probably the only one who can stop it now."

"Or you," Dowling said. "Right?"

"I don't know," Aldridge replied. "Maybe. But he has a lot more experience. You saw that in the Library."

Greenwood's jaw clicked and she forced herself to flex it, taking a step towards Merrick and keeping her rifle trained on his chest. "So do whatever it is you do," she said. "Stop this insanity. Then we can talk."

Merrick smirked. "I think that talking is the last thing on your mind, Captain," he said, "and I'm not one of your soldiers. I'm going to walk out of this building, and you are literally powerless to stop me."

He took a sudden step forward, and Dowling's rifle twitched.

"Don't do it!" Greenwood shouted, a bead of sweat rolling down her temple. "You will come with us and you will prevent the Destiny disaster. You're following *my* orders now."

Aldridge knew the situation was deteriorating, and worst of all, he knew that Merrick was right — there was nothing Greenwood, or KESTREL, or even the Defence Agency could do to stop him. He holstered his own pistol, recognising its uselessness here.

Some part of his mind was aware of the storm gathering outside, high over the city of Hamburg. In some sense he was a part of it, and so was Merrick. He had no idea how, but he knew it as surely as he knew his own name.

"I will not come with you," Merrick said with a sneer, "and you will put down your weapons and stand aside, or you will die here just like these creatures did." He gestured to the bodies on the floor.

Dowling felt burning anger rise up inside him. He had known bullies and criminals all through his childhood, and nothing provoked more fury in him than a

Chapter 34

casual disregard for human life. His grip on his rifle was like iron.

Merrick took another step forward, and Greenwood backed up slightly.

"Stand *down*, Merrick," she said, raising her aim to his forehead, but he only grinned more widely. "It doesn't have to go this way."

Merrick's eyes flashed, and Aldridge felt his heart leap into his throat. *Oh no*, he thought. At the same instant, the obscure part of his mind he'd previously reached into instinctively now opened up fully. Everything became sharper, and brighter. He was exquisitely aware of everyone around him. And he could *feel* the power that was his to wield.

"Captain," Merrick said, "you really must learn when to give up." He suddenly sprang forward, knocking Greenwood off her feet, and Aldridge was about to go to her when the sound of gunfire suddenly filled the room.

Dowling had reacted on instinct, pulling the trigger and sending six or seven rounds directly at Merrick.

Aldridge immediately felt it. Time seemed to *clamp down*, brutally jerking almost to a halt more rapidly than ever before. There was a sense of almost limitless power gathered in the air above them, and Merrick's form blurred and shifted as he immediately asserted the change that would preserve his life.

Dowling's rifle began to backfire, and kick out of his hand. Aldridge watched the scene altering frame by frame, as Merrick instinctively twisted reality into a new shape.

This is how the world ends, he thought, and then he felt himself relax completely. He slowly raised his arm without being consciously aware of it, his fingertips pointing across at the flickering shadow that was Kurt Merrick.

He reached into that part of his mind where the hurricane seemed to come from whenever he made a change, and it was as if he had grasped something — a handle, or a lever, or a trigger of some kind. He focused his attention on Merrick, and he saw Merrick suddenly look back at him.

What are you doing? Merrick thought. The room around them was fluid — in flux, and flickering from the scene of his death to a new outcome where the rifle spun from Dowling's hand harmlessly. But now, it was as if a strong hand had encircled his forearm, holding it back.

Aldridge gripped the handle in his mind, and pulled.

There was an enormous boom of thunder, resonating to the very foundations of the building. The scene around them rolled and stuttered, and the hurricane in his mind sprang into full force, a dozen times stronger than ever before.

Merrick's face twisted in rage and fear as he felt control being torn from him. *Impossible!* he thought, and yet he saw the bullets melt back into existence in mid-air, only a couple of feet from him.

NO! he roared in his mind, focusing every ounce of his rage and pushing back against the gale that wasn't

Chapter 34

really there.

Aldridge felt as if he had been slapped across the face, but he held on and forced the handle in his mind forward again.

The room around them seemed to shatter and then fly back together again, with fragments of both realities bursting against each other. In an instant, everything returned to normal speed.

Dowling's gun coughed and backfired, kicking against his elbow and making him lose his steady footing. He fell sideways, his finger still on the trigger, and just before his hip collided with the wall, the gun went off once more.

A single bullet streaked across the room, going wide but not wide enough. It sliced along Merrick's left cheek leaving a singed gash, and then tore off part of his ear. He staggered backwards in surprise and pain, but he didn't fall. He immediately raised a hand to the side of his head. His fingers came away bloody, and he looked up at Dowling in disbelief.

"*How—?*" he began, but he never finished the sentence.

The loudest sound Aldridge had ever heard suddenly engulfed the entire building. It was thunder on a scale that he'd never imagined, and a fraction of a second later, a bang echoed through the entire structure that set his teeth on edge. The air was filled with an acrid, burning smell.

"You're too late," Merrick snarled, pressing a hand

over his mangled ear, then he suddenly dashed for the vault door and disappeared up the darkened stairs.

Chapter 35

Greenwood reached for her headset, then her hand froze in mid-air. Aldridge nodded at her.

"No point," he said. "Ramos won't be able to hit him either." He looked down at the pistol in his hand. "But I can."

"What *was* that?" she asked, and he met her eyes with a sad smile.

"It was like a light bulb coming on," he replied. "I can fight him now. I can push back against *his* changes. He can't get the upper hand anymore."

Greenwood gave him a long, hard look. "But if we kill him, we all die."

"Maybe, but maybe not," Aldridge said, as another ominous boom shook the building. "This thing that's about to happen... I might be able to stop it myself. It's part of me, or I'm part of *it*. Merrick too. I can't explain it. You're going to have to trust me, Captain."

Dowling and Greenwood exchanged a look, and the big man shrugged. "I don't see many other options, chief," Dowling said.

Greenwood shut her eyes for a moment, then opened them again and set her jaw. "Go after him, Aldridge," she said. "We'll be right behind you."

Dowling clicked his fingers. "Almost forgot your present from Goose," he said, reaching into a flap on his trousers and pulling out an auto-injector. The pre-inserted ampoule was labelled *dextrose saline*. He removed the cap, grimaced apologetically, then jabbed the needle into Aldridge's waist.

Aldridge winced, but said nothing. He understood. *Blood sugar*. He took several deep breaths as the minor pain of the injection rapidly faded.

"There's nothing you can do out there except get killed," he said, looking at Greenwood again, "and we still don't know what actually sets it off. You need to keep your distance. I'll let you know if I think there's a way out of this."

"I need a better contingency plan than that!" Greenwood said, taking a step forward. Aldridge only looked back at her.

"I think we both know what you need to do," he said quietly. "I assume you can contact the German Air Force Command and get a fighter jet here. If it looks like it's not going well… tell them to target my location with the fanciest missile they've got. Then go back to Edinburgh and delete my web browser history."

Chapter 35

Greenwood's breathing was audible. At last, she nodded.

Aldridge held her gaze for three long seconds, then he turned and ran up the stairs.

Merrick ran across the plaza, not stopping at the sight of several armoured vehicles parked along one side. The elite federal response team had clearly been summoned by Greenwood, but they were of no concern to him now.

GSG 9 had formed barricades along two opposing sides of the square and a partial barricade on the third side in front of the cathedral, and there were roadblocks visible further along each of the connecting streets. He knew that many crosshairs were tracking him, but he knew that no-one would shoot. They had better things to worry about.

The sky was on fire.

A truly biblical storm raged and churned in the boiling black clouds that filled the entire visible portion of the night sky. Peals of thunder rattled his teeth as he ran, and he was certain he could feel the reverberations through his boots.

Lightning like he'd never seen before snaked across the clouds, and struck the rooftops of buildings every few seconds. There was no rain, but his ears popped as the atmospheric pressure fluctuated.

We stand witness to the end of the world, Merrick thought wildly. He was breathing rapidly, and what was left of his ear pulsed with an icy pain. His pace faltered and then he came to a stop, looking up at the heavens.

There was so much power there. It was clear that the Destiny event had almost arrived, but not quite. He frowned. What else could be necessary? He knew that the cataclysm was incredibly close, but the final spark hadn't yet taken place.

He heard a sound from behind him, and spun around. Aldridge leapt down the front steps of the bank, a hundred and fifty yards away, and came to a stop.

The two men looked at each other across the plaza's broad expanse of grey slabs.

You, Merrick thought. *We are the final two.*

He glanced quickly over his shoulder, seeing the gap in the not-yet-finished barricade across the square. The cathedral loomed beyond, its craggy spire a nightmare shape against the otherworldly storm.

There could be no other place — here it was at last, the birthplace of a new world. Merrick turned back to face Aldridge, and his mouth curled into a grin that had no hint of humanity in it.

He spun on his heel and ran across the plaza, seeing the elite troops following his movements but doing nothing more.

Over the howl of the storm, he could just barely hear pounding footfalls behind him.

He reached and cleared the barricade in seconds, crossed the empty road and took the front steps of the cathedral three at a time, then put two bullets into the iron padlock that hung on the doorhandles without

Chapter 35

even slowing down.

He pushed one studded oak door roughly inward, and the shadows of the ornate building swallowed him. He knew that Aldridge would be there in less than half a minute. Let him come.

This place is the last you will ever see, he thought.

"*Madre de Dios,*" Ramos muttered, wincing as yet another bolt of lightning struck the roof of one of the grand buildings along the main through-road leading into the plaza.

She could see Goose being loaded into an ambulance at the front steps of the bank, and Greenwood and Dowling were heading in her direction.

The storm was unlike anything she'd ever seen. The sky was churning and twisting, like a sped-up time lapse film. The clouds were changing constantly, erupting like blisters and then re-forming. Eerie blue-purple lightning crackled and hummed over every part of the sky, casting disorienting, jittering shadows all over the ground.

She could feel the energy thrumming through her bones, and she had slung her sniper rifle over her shoulder when she started to get static shocks from its metal barrel. The fine hairs on the back of her neck were prickling constantly, and she felt a deep and almost superstitious sense of dread.

She flinched as she heard a loud voice through her earpiece, between waves of buzzing interference.

"Captain Greenwood," the voice said, almost shouting. *"Are you receiving me? This is Director Janne Wuyts."*

Ramos saw Greenwood reach up to the side of her head and press the earpiece further into her ear.

"This is Greenwood," she replied, just as she and Dowling reached Ramos. She had to raise her voice to be heard over the cacophony that surrounded them.

"What is your status?" Wuyts asked. The interference was getting worse by the moment.

"Five hostages rescued," Greenwood replied. "Merrick's lieutenants are dead, and GSG 9 has the scene. Goose was shot, but he should be OK. Merrick made a run for it, and Aldridge followed. There's nothing more we can do."

She quickly outlined all the important events that had taken place inside the bank, including the entire encounter in the vault room, carefully describing the strange clash between Merrick and Aldridge.

There was silence on the line for several seconds, and Greenwood was beginning to wonder if they'd lost the connection, then Wuyts spoke again. Her voice was faint and now overlaid by a constant rolling buzz of static.

"All flights into and out of Germany have been grounded. No-one has ever seen atmospheric phenomena like those in your vicinity, Captain," Wuyts said. *"I assume that this is the precursor to the Destiny event."*

"It looks that way, sir," Greenwood replied. "It looks… like the end of the world."

Wuyts made no reply.

Chapter 35

"Nobody here can touch Merrick," Greenwood continued. "It's up to Aldridge now."

Ramos's wide eyes met Dowling's, and the big man just nodded slowly. She wasn't sure whether it was a trick of the light from the storm above, but for the first time ever, he looked pale.

"God help us all, then," Wuyts replied finally, and then the line went dead.

Chapter 36

Aldridge peered into the darkness of the cathedral. He was standing in the foyer, just a few feet inside the large doors. One still stood ajar, allowing the fierce winds to gust inside every few seconds.

Enormous stained glass windows ran down the full length of the vaulted space on both sides, leading the eye from the narthex to the nave and then on to the pulpit. A plaster statue of Christ on the cross hung on the far wall. The figure was at least twelve feet high, and it flickered in the incessant flashes of unnatural lightning.

The whole interior of the Gothic building was seething with moving shadows, and thunder now boomed several times every minute. A gale-force blast of wind shrieked through the open doors, and a stack of religious pamphlets blew from a nearby pew and scattered across the cold flagstones.

It was impossible to listen for movement or footsteps as the weather-beaten oak doors creaked under the force of the storm, and the wind rattled the glass of every window.

Aldridge could just barely see a plastic box mounted above the doors on the inside, printed with the word *Notausgang*. He knew it meant *Emergency Exit*, but even the backup electricity supply had apparently failed, because the sign was in darkness. Two oil braziers burned at the other end of the main chamber, perhaps from a service earlier in the evening, but their brightness only threw more parts of the vast, echoing space into deep shadow.

He crept forward, hearing only a low buzz of static in his earpiece. The handle of his pistol felt slippery in his palm, and he knew it was from his own sweat. His heart was pounding in his chest, and he could taste a metallic tang in the back of his throat.

That's the storm, he thought. Everything smelled coppery, and the air itself tasted like burnt insulation.

A particularly violent bolt of lightning hit the ground very close by, perhaps even immediately outside the cathedral, and the sudden glare painted the stained glass figures in vivid purple for an instant. They all looked utterly forlorn, as if their god had abandoned them. The afterimages of the faces danced in Aldridge's eyes, and he blinked them away.

He moved between the pews, expecting Merrick to leap out at any moment. His feet echoed on the stone

Chapter 36

floor, and he almost stumbled on a section where the edge of a flagstone had been worn away by the feet of countless worshippers over the generations.

Another flash of lightning illuminated the interior in ghastly purple light, and Aldridge's eye was drawn to another flicker of torchlight, off to the side about halfway up the nave. It was coming from further back than the elaborate tapestries mounted on the walls, and as his vision adjusted, he realised it was a narrow open doorway. Another oil brazier hung on the wall of the small chamber beyond, and by its meagre light he could just make out a spiral flight of stairs leading upwards.

He's going for the roof, Aldridge thought with certainty. *He wants to get closer to the storm.*

It made sense, in a twisted way. The storm was the manifestation of the impending Destiny event that Merrick seemed to see as his own rebirth into godhood. He'd naturally seek the highest available point.

Aldridge reached up and tapped the small button on his earpiece, but the device only continued to emit its soft buzz of interference. "If anyone can hear me, I'm going upstairs, towards the roof," he said.

He glanced down at the pistol he held, knowing it was almost certainly useless, but he felt comforted by its presence nonetheless. He took one last glance back towards the open door beyond the narthex, and the wind abruptly caught it and slammed it shut with an echoing thud.

That's definitely not a bad omen, he though. *I don't believe in that sort of thing*. But there were a lot of things he hadn't believed in a week ago.

He quickly walked along between two pews and reached the left wall of the main chamber, then crept towards the small doorway set into the stone blocks of the wall. He peered around the edge, grateful for the brazier's light, but his view was cut off by the curve of the stairway. There was a short corridor leading to another door on this level, but it was tightly shut and the strip of carpet in front of it seemed undisturbed.

Now that he was right beside the door, he could see a bloody handprint on the old wood.

A breeze blew down from above, and he shivered. A window must be open further up, or perhaps Merrick had already found his way out onto the roof. Aldridge wondered if there was a dead priest somewhere in the building. He wouldn't have been able to hear a gunshot from outside, in the midst of the incessant noise. But that was a problem beyond his control.

The storm seemed to lessen for just a moment, and he tensed as he heard a distant scraping sound from somewhere above.

Let's go up the dark staircase and chase the madman that guns don't work on, he thought. *Seems like the sensible thing to do.*

"I've seen this film before," he muttered, then he adjusted his grip on the pistol and carefully started up the steps.

* * *

Chapter 36

Merrick watched Aldridge enter the cathedral. The other man's slim form was outlined in the doorway, and he would have been a sitting duck for any marksman.

But bullets are no longer a concern for us, are they, Mr. Aldridge?

Merrick listened to the unnatural violence of the storm outside, and some of its breeze reached him even here, far along the balcony on the level above the sanctuary. He had quickly found a doorway off to the side of the pews in the nave below, and come up to this level to try to find access to the roof.

The storm is Destiny, he thought. *Or it will be.* His own wrist-mounted monitor was useless now, showing a constant maximum anti-tachyon reading. His radio ceased to work properly before he had even left the bank, and there was no-one to contact anyway. He had finally switched off its irritating static and threw it into the darkness of the cathedral before ascending the spiral staircase.

He took out a field medical kit from one of the many pockets on his combat vest, searched for the iodine and quickly found it. Tilting his head, he poured it freely onto his ruined ear, producing an explosion of pain that quickly dwindled into heat and a dull throbbing sensation. He didn't make a sound.

Aldridge had crossed to the side of the nave now, moving out of sight below the overhanging gallery, but Merrick could still hear the man's footsteps. He would reach the door soon, and would no doubt climb the stairs to the gallery if his courage held out.

Merrick knew now that he needed Aldridge to make his plan work. The immediate and violent reaction when Aldridge had somehow *resisted* Merrick's own change was the penultimate clue, and the cataclysmic disturbance in the night sky over the plaza was the final one. The event had been set in motion when they were both trying to create opposing changes simultaneously.

And if such a conflict were to happen again, Merrick thought, his eyes flashing in the darkness of the gallery, *then Destiny will surely be triggered.*

He would lure Aldridge out onto the roof, and then he would attempt to kill him. Aldridge would use his ability to save his own life, but this time *he* would find himself opposed.

And then the world will see just what I am capable of, he thought, drawing back into the deeper shadows as he heard faint footsteps coming up the stairs.

Aldridge reached the top of the spiral staircase after passing two half-height doors set into the stone wall, each locked up tight. He exited onto a gallery that ran along almost the entire eastern wall of the cathedral. Across the gulf of open space beyond the latticework railing, he could see the enormous pipe organ filling the opposite wall, its bank of gold-leaf pipes looking almost organic in the flickering half-light.

The gallery was much wider than it looked from below — at least fifteen feet from front to back. There

Chapter 36

were pews facing outwards towards the nave beneath, but they were cordoned off with dark blue ropes. Stacks of Bibles sat atop a narrow counter near the door, and Aldridge had to blink and look twice before confirming that the other object beside the Bibles was in fact an iPad.

There was no exit from the nearest end of the gallery, as it came to a dead end at another railing that faced a long drop to the foyer. Aldridge peered in the opposite direction, which led into the depths of the old building. There was still no sign of movement, but the creaking sound had definitely come from up here.

He walked carefully forward, and his heart pounded in his chest when he suddenly heard the same creaking sound from underfoot as he stood on a floorboard that had warped with age and the constant tread of worshippers. He froze, his eyes roving frantically back and forward.

More thunder boomed just at that moment, and Aldridge almost dropped the gun in surprise. But there was still no movement.

He inhaled a whistling breath, and then began moving forward again. He had made it only ten feet or so when a shadow stepped silently out into view at the far end of the gallery.

Merrick's entire form was a silhouette, lit from behind every few moments by bolts of purple lightning flashing through the huge stained glass rendering of The Last Supper, on the furthest wall of the cathedral.

Aldridge froze, then instinctively raised the gun. He heard Merrick's soft laughter almost immediately.

"I think we're a little beyond guns, Mr. Aldridge," Merrick said. "The event you're all so afraid of is beginning to happen outside this very building, even now."

"It hasn't happened yet," Aldridge said, feeling anger rising inside him like a wave. *You want to risk destroying the world so you can hold it to ransom again and again*, he thought. *But I'm not going to let you.*

"You can't win, Merrick," he said. "I know how to stop you now. I didn't understand before, but in a way, you showed me."

Merrick's eyes narrowed. "Then you are a faster learner than the others of our kind I've met," he said.

Aldridge felt his gut clench. Merrick had murdered innocent people, all because they exhibited an incredible — but dangerous — ability. He had used them, so that he could take his place as a modern-day god, twisting destinies to fit his own designs and holding a sword over the heads of anyone who wouldn't agree to his demands.

The power to choose twice, instead of once, is the ultimate advantage, he realised. Nations would pay dearly to have Merrick's services available, even if they weren't being actively threatened. The ability to undo events at will had incredible potential — and terrifying consequences in the wrong hands.

Aldridge took another step forward.

"I can't let you do this," he said. There was no menace

Chapter 36

in his voice; only a firm resolution, and a note of sadness.

Merrick raised an eyebrow, appraising the other man. "You could join me," he said. "We both want the same thing, after all: to prevent Destiny from destroying the world. I merely wish to let them see its full horror before we turn the clock back. I want to let them know *just how close* they came to destruction."

Now it was Merrick who stepped forward, out of the shadow and into a sliver of illumination from a window opposite. The shaft of light ran across his body as he moved, and Aldridge could see that he wasn't holding his gun. Both his hands were empty, and one was stained with a dark colour he knew was Merrick's own blood.

Aldridge held his ground. "And then what?" he asked, reaching into his mind so he would be ready if Merrick tried to use his ability again. "Terrorise the world, without consequences?"

Merrick smiled. It was a cold, contemptuous expression that didn't reach his eyes.

"Do you think the world is such a fine place, Mr. Aldridge?" he asked, gesturing around him at the darkened cathedral. "After all, I am part of that world. As is your Captain Greenwood and her associates, who killed my men."

"You killed *innocent people!*" Aldridge spat, incensed at the comparison Merrick was making. "Greenwood only did what you forced her to do. And don't pretend that you give a damn about your men. You'd have killed them yourself if it served your purpose."

"Of course," Merrick agreed, "but then, that is the nature of this world you're so fond of. The strong survive. The weak must inevitably perish. Haven't you realised yet why all of this is happening?"

He pointed vaguely upwards, indicating the vortex of energy filling the sky above the building. The thunder was now an artillery barrage, never letting up for more than a few seconds.

"Because you allowed it to happen," Aldridge said. "You hid information from the European Defence Agency. You tortured those people to test them, and yourself, when we could have been training them. That was you, not the world. Not anyone else but *you*."

Merrick didn't speak for a moment, and Aldridge flinched when several bolts of lightning struck somewhere very nearby. Merrick glanced over towards one of the stained glass windows opposite. It showed the Rapture, with angels escorting hordes of souls into the sky above a burning countryside, going to meet a grim-faced God above the clouds. He felt a thrill of synchronicity that it should be this image, of all those in the cathedral, that his eyes fell upon now.

Without looking away from the glowing sculpture in glass, he spoke again, this time more loudly than before.

"Destiny is *judgement*," he hissed, eyes ablaze now, and Aldridge took a half step backwards. "This world you seem to hold so dear is filled with weakness — with

Chapter 36

worthlessness."

He met Aldridge's gaze again, and Aldridge could see that his fists were clenching and unclenching rhythmically, almost in time with the crashing of the thunder above them.

Merrick advanced another step.

"Do you think that Destiny is an accident?" he asked, his voice wavering with a passion that bordered on madness. His face was a snarl. "Just a *phenomenon* to be studied, prevented, and then concealed?"

Aldridge thumbed off the safety catch of his pistol, feeling a chill run down his spine. *You're insane*, he thought. *I've known that for a while, but this is a whole new level.*

"I think it's a disaster, and I can't understand why you'd think otherwise," Aldridge replied, watching for the slightest movement from the other man. "And who are you to decide who's worthless?"

Merrick grinned widely now, the eerie purple glow of the lightning bouncing off all the lines and creases on his face. He didn't look entirely human.

"The weak must always be judged by their god," Merrick replied.

And there it is, Aldridge thought, every muscle in his body tensing up. Merrick's already unstable personality had been thrown into madness by his ability to change events for his own benefit, even cheating death on several occasions. Megalomania and a sense of invulnerability were the natural result. *Then it's just a hop, skip, and a jump to delusions of godhood. I wish you were here, Greenwood.*

"There's something you haven't considered," Aldridge said, adjusting his grip on the pistol and steadying his stance.

"And what might that be?" Merrick replied, beginning to move steadily forward now, as if stalking his prey.

Aldridge's pulse quickened again. He was breathing rapidly through his nose, and he could feel the constant tension of last few days taking its toll. This wasn't the time to shut down. He swallowed, and raised the pistol, seeing Merrick's eyes flick towards it only briefly.

"The thing about gods is," Aldridge continued, "there's usually only one in each story. You're here, but so am I. And there are five more across the square."

Merrick snorted in derision. "Anyone can pick up a gun and pull the trigger," he replied. He drew himself up to his full height, and now the strange lightning seemed to punctuate his every word. He was only a few metres away, and his eyes were points of light inside coal-black hollows. His voice fell to a whisper, and the thunder all around paused obligingly, allowing him to be heard.

"The mark of true greatness… is willingness to *act*."

Merrick suddenly sprang forward, and before Aldridge could fire, he was knocked backwards, the pistol flying from his grip.

He crashed to the floorboards of the gallery, winded,

Chapter 36

and he had barely drawn in a ragged breath before the shadow fell upon him.

Chapter 37

"Holy hell," Dowling whistled, ducking instinctively as a rumble of thunder louder than a grenade detonation tore across the sky above.

It was followed immediately by more than ten lightning strikes along the roofline, and Greenwood shook her head in disbelief as two pigeons fell to the pavement from the guttering of a neighbouring building, dead before they hit the ground, with smoke rising from their charred bodies.

"It doesn't look like he's doing well in there," Ramos said, her eyes fixed on the brooding cathedral across the square. The building was an enormous black outline against the roiling clouds and otherworldly lightning.

"We don't know that," Greenwood replied, shouting to be heard over the storm. "We're all still here, so that means Aldridge is probably OK too."

Ramos glanced at her doubtfully, but said nothing. A

few moments later, the rear door of one of the GSG operations vehicles swung open, and a commando dropped to the ground then quickly crouch-ran over to their position behind the barricade.

He was carrying a piece of equipment the size of a small briefcase, with a padded shoulder-strap attached. It was a charcoal-grey metal box with reinforced corners, and it had a toughened glass display set into the front, alongside a bank of small rectangular buttons. A set of over-ear headphones hung on a hook fixed to the side of the unit, with a small microphone stalk attached to the left ear-pad.

The commando's German accent was thick, but they could all hear the tension in his voice.

"Someone is calling for you," he said, pointing to the headphones. "You can talk with this."

Greenwood nodded her thanks, and slipped the headphones over her ears. "This is Greenwood," she said, cupping her hand around the microphone against the wind.

"Captain, this is Director Wuyts," came the familiar voice. "It's good to hear you're alright."

"Sir, how did you manage to get in contact with the GSG mobile unit out here?" Greenwood asked. "Nothing is working. Comms are down over at least a ten-block radius, and it's getting worse."

"We used emergency subsurface communication lines to impose on the Chancellor to put us in touch," Wuyts replied, her voice uneven over the static. "She was glad

Chapter 37

to oblige."

I bet she was, when the fate of her country hangs in the balance, Greenwood thought. "Aldridge is still in the cathedral with Merrick. The weather is getting worse — a *lot* worse. It looks like the event isn't far away."

There was a brief moment of silence before Wuyts replied. "I expected as much," he said. "CERN found something interesting. It may be the answer to what will actually trigger the Destiny event."

Greenwood's heart raced. *Better late than never,* she thought.

"I had our tracking lab correlate seismic, atmospheric and anti-tachyon activity with the approximate time of your stand-off with Kurt Merrick in the bank vault," Wuyts continued. "They found something profoundly troubling."

That weird thing where Aldridge almost reversed the change Merrick was making, she thought.

"When Mr. Aldridge discovered that he could influence the changes that Merrick was making, you described a new visual phenomenon," Wuyts said.

"Yes, sir," Greenwood replied. "It was like we could see both... situations at once. They seemed to break apart and then come back together, merged into one. It's hard to describe."

"That event was immediately followed by a massive increase in anti-tachyon energy, far beyond what we've seen before," Wuyts said. "The total energy in your location now is over *four hundred percent* of its intensity before Merrick and Aldridge had their duel."

It's the conflict that causes it, Greenwood thought. Goosebumps sprang up on her skin, and she shivered. "My god."

"Do you understand, Captain?" Wuyts asked, a tremor in her voice. "If Aldridge tries to resist another of Merrick's changes, or vice-versa, then—"

"Everything goes boom," Greenwood replied. "I've got to warn him."

She lifted her hand halfway towards her ear before she remembered that the communications headsets were useless now. Aldridge couldn't hear her.

"Captain, I understand you have two Eurofighter Typhoon aircraft on aerial standby," Wuyts said.

Greenwood felt her stomach turn over, but the military tactician in her knew it was the logical option. Both fighter jets were equipped with a pair of *Storm Shadow* SCALP cruise missiles, each with a specially modified multi-stage BROACH warhead. They were already in the air several miles away, and could come in below the storm if necessary, directly over the city. The pilots were willing to give their own lives to ensure their mission was a success. If even one of the missiles found its mark, the cathedral would simply no longer exist.

"Captain?" Wuyts said, her voice full of authority and impatience in Greenwood's ear. "You have operational discretion. Make a decision, and make it now."

Greenwood locked eyes with Dowling, and the big man smiled.

Chapter 37

"Tell them to hold position," she said.

She didn't wait for a reply, tearing the headphones off and standing up. Dowling jumped to his feet too, looking from Greenwood to Ramos.

"Alicia, Larry and I are going in," Greenwood said. "Keep your eyes open. Merrick and Aldridge can't *both* be allowed to use their ability again like in the bank. If you have a shot, use your judgement."

Ramos's eyes were wide, but she nodded without a word.

Greenwood turned her attention to Dowling. "We need to get to them before they cause this disaster," she said.

"Right beside you, chief," he replied, looping the strap of his assault rifle over his head and around his shoulder.

Greenwood took a deep breath, then she and Dowling vaulted over the barricade and dashed headlong across the plaza, their path lit by the hundred jagged trails of lightning that filled the sky above.

Aldridge barely saw the blow coming before pain exploded across the left side of his jaw.

Merrick had him pinned to the floor, and Aldridge wheezed as he tried to get a breath. Merrick's hands were around his throat now, gripping but not squeezing.

"You're going to help me, Aldridge," Merrick growled, tightening his grip alarmingly. "We're going to show the world the horror of Destiny together, and *then* we're going to sweep it away."

"You can kill me if you like," Aldridge gasped, straining to move Merrick's solid mass even an inch, "but you can't make me help you." He had no idea what Merrick meant, but he would die before he'd do anything that the madman asked of him. He could smell iodine, sweat, and the metallic tang of ozone permeating the air.

Merrick grinned again, and in the half-light he looked utterly insane.

"But that's where you're mistaken," he replied, lifting his fist to hurl another blow.

Aldridge saw his chance and flung his own hand upwards, grabbed the raw edges of the wound that was once Merrick's left ear, and squeezed hard.

The other man roared in pain, springing to his feet and staggering back several steps. Aldridge quickly rolled to the side, underneath two pews, his eyes scanning the floor for the dropped pistol. He spotted it ten feet away, out in the open, a short distance away from the gallery railings. *Too damned far*, he thought.

Fresh blood dripped from Merrick's ear, and he clenched his teeth and cursed his quarry.

"A daring move," he called out, looking around to see where the other man had gone. "But you're wasting your time. You *will* help me trigger Destiny, or you will die here tonight."

I'm pretty sure that's your plan for me anyway, Aldridge thought, crawling on his elbows and knees underneath the dusty pews towards the pistol. It was tantalisingly

Chapter 37

close now, but still not within reach. *And what does he mean, trigger it?*

"Do you realise how *fitting* this is, Aldridge?" Merrick shouted from what sounded like only a few metres away. "Two gods who were once men, doing battle in this grotesque monument to an absent saviour?"

It'd be fitting if you were in a sanitarium, Aldridge thought, *but I'd settle for a graveyard*. The gun was barely five feet away, but he would have to make a break for it and cross the open area of floor first. He drew up onto his haunches, steeling himself for the dash.

"You can't escape," Merrick shouted, anger beginning to show in his voice now. "KESTREL cannot help you. The German *kommandos* outside can't help you. Even the Security Council can't help you."

Aldridge heard Merrick's heavy boots compressing the floorboards, but it was hard to tell where the noise was coming from.

No time like the present, he thought, then he sprang to his feet and made a dash for the gun.

Everything slowed down.

Not again, Aldridge thought. His perspective shifted to outside of himself, watching the scene from a bird's eye view. Merrick wasn't quite as close as he had thought, but the other man had clearly known exactly where Aldridge was going.

The blade of Merrick's combat knife gleamed with reflected purple energy, as if it was lit from within. He had already thrown it. It hung in mid-air, on a sure course for Aldridge's back as he ran.

Aldridge watched the scene unfold.

He runs towards the pistol, taking two, then three, then four long strides before slowing, his right hand sweeping downwards to scoop it up from the floor as he passes over it, still heading for cover. Suddenly, the knife blade strikes him in the upper right quadrant of his torso, and he spins, losing his footing and crashing down against the table stacked with bibles.

He felt the familiar sense of fluidity — the edges where he could grasp the scene and run it backwards, nudging it towards another outcome.

Merrick was smiling. Aldridge could see it clearly. He seemed hungry, and eager.

Something's wrong, Aldridge thought. *He could have put that knife into the base of my skull if he wanted to — and why didn't he? He knows full well I'd prevent it from happening, just like he would. So why the non-lethal wound?*

The scene began to shift in his mind's eye, spreading and flowing like paint in water.

He needs me to help him, Aldridge thought. *What is he so happy about?*

Aldridge could now feel Merrick looking back at him in the same way, outside of physical sight and in this second place.

He felt a sense of urgency, and the scene flickered for a moment, tugging at his mind. He knew he had only moments to choose which version of events would come to pass.

Chapter 37

And that's if Merrick doesn't counter my change, like I did to him earlier, he thought.

He wasn't sure if the lightning flash came from outside or from within.

That was it. The counter-change in the bank vault. *That* was when things had accelerated. That was when the gathering storm outside had turned into something apocalyptic.

Aldridge felt panic lapping around his throat. *He wants to counter me, or me to counter him,* he realised. There was no mistaking the mad eagerness in the mercenary's eyes. *That's what sets it off. It's us.*

The knife was wavering in mid-air now, seeming to shudder and dart forwards, then abruptly jumping back to where it had been a moment before. The fluid state of being between the two possible outcomes was starting to destabilise now. There was a pervasive sense of a build-up of energy that needed a release. Time was almost up.

Aldridge focused his attention on Merrick again, and saw the man's grin waver, to be replaced by a black look of fury.

You can't force a change on something you initiated yourself, he realised. *You threw the knife, so it's up to me to intervene. That's your weak point.*

The scene around him shook, and thunder rumbled ominously — an almost unbearable, long, bass note to Aldridge, with time passing so slowly around him.

I won't help you, Aldridge thought, and he released his

mental grip on the knife.

Time snapped back to its normal pace, and there was a single beat before the knife slammed into Aldridge's right shoulder-blade, twisting him to one side and knocking him off his feet. The wound was shallow as the blade hit bone and rebounded back, but the pain was shocking.

He collided painfully with the table that held the bibles, and several of the well-worn books toppled from its surface and fell to the wooden floor around him. The knife also clattered to the ground, and in a moment of hyper-awareness he saw it had blood along its tip.

That's mine, he thought, still feeling detached from reality.

He heard footsteps behind him, and tried to raise his right hand, which miraculously still held the pistol. His arm didn't budge.

Merrick stood over Aldridge, looking down in disgust. "None of this is necessary," he said. "You can't possibly hope to defeat me."

He bent down and picked up his knife, wiping the blade against his thigh. It still glittered with the reflected purple light coming in through the stained glass windows, and the steel looked hungry.

Aldridge twisted himself around to face the other man, feeling a deep stab of pain in his upper back. He still couldn't lift his right arm, but he could at least feel his fingers now.

"If you're going to kill me, get it over with," Aldridge

Chapter 37

said, staring up at Merrick defiantly. "But if you do that, you won't be able to trigger Destiny."

"You're going to help me whether you like it or not, Aldridge," Merrick said. "We already know it's true. The event *does* take place, and nothing you can do will prevent it."

"I don't believe that, and I don't think you do either," Aldridge replied. "I think you're worried, because there's no way you can win this. If you kill me, you can't trigger the event yourself without any of the people you kidnapped. And I won't use my ability to help you. You're stuck."

The words were brave, but inside he was terrified.

Merrick raised the knife and examined its blade almost affectionately. "You're right that I can't kill you," he said, "but nor can you kill me. My ability prevents it. So it comes down to which one of us is more talented in extracting cooperation from the other."

His eyes turned to Aldridge, and the expression of thoughtfulness that had been on his face vanished immediately.

"You *are* going to help me," Merrick said again. "Your only choice is to spare yourself unnecessary suffering before the time comes."

Aldridge flexed his right arm gently. The movement still produced a dart of pain across his back, and his muscles felt sluggish and weak, but his control of the limb was slowly returning. He glanced over at the door leading to the stairway back down to the ground floor.

"Your friends also cannot help you," Merrick said patiently. "They can no more kill me than you can. If they try, I will prevent them. If you try to counter me, you will bring Destiny down upon us anyway."

Merrick twirled the knife in his fingers. The blade flashed with every rotation.

"You're an intelligent man," Merrick continued in a tone that would have been conversational if it wasn't so cold. "Surely you can see that Destiny will and *does* happen, and the logical choice is to bring it about. You already know that I will reverse the disaster immediately. You can even help ensure that no-one is harmed."

And hand you the world on a plate, Aldridge thought. *No thanks. If the price of stopping you is my life, then it's a pretty good deal.*

"What I see is that you're a manipulative, lying murderer," Aldridge said, as Taylor's face flashed across his mind. "And you're going to kill me anyway. Your threats against the world won't be worth half as much if I'm still around, and I wouldn't even be here right now if you didn't need me. KESTREL will keep the other changers safe from you, and you've lost your own men, your resources, and your connections. You're a wanted man. It's all over for you."

Aldridge took a deep breath, and his mind turned to Greenwood. *Not exactly what you had in mind, Captain,* he thought. *But it's the right choice.*

"Do whatever you want, but you won't make me help you," Aldridge said quietly. "You might as well kill me

Chapter 37

right now."

Merrick's face twisted into a snarl, and he took a step forward.

"You're a fool," Merrick said, "and I promise you that you'll die tonight... eventually." He crouched down and pressed the tip of the knife to Aldridge's cheek, just below his left eye, increasing the pressure until a droplet of blood bloomed on his pale skin.

"You will lose many things before the end," Merrick said, pressing his arm across Aldridge's chest to hold him in place. "Perhaps your sight first?"

Merrick pulled the knife upwards by a couple of millimetres, slicing effortlessly through the taught skin of Aldridge's upper cheek. The point of the blade was now only half a centimetre from his lower eyelid.

Aldridge felt his heart flutter in panic, and he reflexively gripped the pistol that still lay in his right hand, resting alongside his leg.

The blade moved again, and Aldridge winced at the agony of his cheek being opened up, millimetre by millimetre. *He'll get my eye soon*, he thought wildly. *No question that he'll do it.*

He saw Merrick tense, and a wicked grin appeared on the other man's face.

Everything slowed down. Aldridge felt his stomach turn over as he saw the knife cut upwards, piercing his eyelid. There was surprisingly little blood released, but his eye began to fill with red almost immediately, which then leaked out as red tears.

He shuddered, trapped in the moment. *Can't change it because Merrick will push back, and then it's all over*, he thought.

Instinctively, he gripped the pistol. The twang of pain in his back was distant and unimportant. He barely turned the barrel towards Merrick, without raising his arm, and pulled the trigger.

Something was different. Time seemed to pucker and then accelerate as Merrick reacted to the gunshot by trying to alter the outcome. An enormous crash of thunder shook the building, but there wasn't the same sense of fracturing that they'd felt back in the vault room of the old bank.

We're both making separate changes, Aldridge thought. Merrick was altering the gunshot to save himself, which meant he couldn't proceed with his knife attack.

That's it, Aldridge thought. *That's how I can fight back*.

The ability gave them advance warning of a fatal or traumatic event — only a few seconds' worth, but it was still enough. *If I use those few seconds to attack him in a way that makes him use his ability, he won't have the chance to counter any change I make.*

Sure enough, Aldridge watched as Merrick asserted his change on the scene around him. The bullet snapped back into the pistol from mid-air, and then Merrick's hand jogged the weapon, making the shot go wide.

The knife tumbled to the ground, never having reached Aldridge's eyelid even though he'd already seen it happen.

Chapter 37

Lightning flashed outside: once, twice, three times, and then again and again, hammering the earth as if protesting at a twisting of the rules. Merrick and Aldridge both looked around in awe for a moment at the terrible display of power.

At the same moment, Aldridge wrenched the gun upwards towards Merrick's chest, but the trained killer was too fast for him. He caught the barrel and wrenched it around, pulling it from his grasp easily.

He threw the weapon over his shoulder, and Aldridge heard it clatter to the ground somewhere in the darkness.

Merrick grabbed for the knife, and while he was distracted, Aldridge slammed his own head forward, his forehead smashing into Merrick's jaw.

The assassin tumbled backwards, blood spraying from his split lower lip where it had been cut open against his own teeth. Aldridge dragged himself to his feet and backed off several steps.

Merrick was on his hands and knees. He shook his head to clear it, and then spat a mouthful of blood onto the floorboards.

"Brave," he said through laboured breaths, "but pointless."

He got to his feet and raised his hand, which clutched the knife once again. "We will begin again," he said, and he was just about to advance when a gunshot rang out.

Aldridge ducked, but he felt no impact, and the ricochet sounded like it was several feet away.

Merrick dropped to a crouch, immediately pulling his own weapon from its holster and readying it.

"Aldridge?" came Greenwood's voice from the ground level, and Merrick spat out another glob of blood.

"Up here!" Aldridge shouted, and he heard heavy boots moving quickly across the flagstones of the cathedral.

"This changes nothing," Merrick snarled, lowering his gun. "They're still powerless to help you."

His eyes narrowed, and his expression became crafty.

"I was hoping to have another chance to kill Captain Greenwood," he said. "Fortune is smiling on me tonight."

He turned and ran further along the gallery, towards the area Aldridge hadn't yet seen, and he quickly merged into the shadows. A moment later, Aldridge heard another door open, and a shaft of light penetrated the gloom up ahead.

Merrick's shadowy form dashed into the doorway immediately, and Aldridge heard the clank of boots against metal steps.

He's going up, Aldridge thought. He glanced once more to the nearer doorway behind him, leading back down to the entrance level. He could already hear muffled noises from there, as Greenwood was no doubt climbing the spiral stairs.

No time to waste. He tried to find his own pistol that Merrick had thrown away, but it was gone.

Chapter 37

With a groan and another stab of pain from the knife wound in his back, he lunged off into the darkness of the gallery, following Merrick towards the roof.

Chapter 38

Greenwood and Dowling quickly surveyed the entrance level of the enormous cathedral, the constant flashes of bizarre purple lightning providing all the illumination they needed. It was almost impossible to hear any small noises with the storm raging outside.

The sprawling narthex, nave and pulpit all seemed to be empty, but Greenwood knew that Merrick could be hiding almost anywhere.

Where are you, Aldridge? she wondered, still hearing only an infuriating buzz of static in her earpiece. She kept thinking she could hear voices coming from somewhere, but it was impossible to tell where, or even if they were anything more than an illusion caused by the noise of the wind and thunder.

Dowling was close behind, gun drawn, eyes scanning the interior. He was the first one to notice the open doorway along the left wall, and he nodded towards it.

Greenwood glanced up at the long gallery above, then they both moved quickly across the room and into the shadow of the overhang.

Greenwood motioned Dowling to move forwards and check out the door, and she was just about to follow him when they both heard a roar of pain from somewhere above.

"Get back out onto the floor — see if you can get a vantage point," she ordered. Dowling moved immediately.

Greenwood strained to listen, but the storm was howling with unearthly force.

Dowling kept his assault rifle trained on the railings of the upper level as he carefully swept the gallery, but other than the occasional sense of someone speaking nearby, there was nothing up there.

Suddenly, there was a crash from above, and they both tensed. Greenwood crossed the floor to Dowling's position, training her own weapon on the gallery.

"See anything?" she asked, not taking her eyes from the gallery, and Dowling shook his head.

"Not a bloody thing," he said. "But they're up there, chief. I can almost hear voices."

Then every hair on the back of Greenwood's neck stood up as she felt the unnatural but immediately recognisable sensation of time slowing down.

No, she thought. *It can't end like this.*

The moment stretched out, until suddenly everything snapped back into place. Lightning furiously struck the

Chapter 38

ground outside multiple times, and then there were a few seconds of silence.

Greenwood looked over at Dowling, and the big man's face was pale. He shrugged, and she exhaled a long breath she didn't know she'd been holding.

They heard the clatter of metal striking wood, and both immediately recognised it as the sound of a discarded weapon. There was another grunt of pain, and then finally Merrick came into view, staggering back a few paces, facing towards the inner edge of the gallery level.

Maybe I can't kill you, you bastard, but I can distract you, Dowling thought, and fired a single shot deliberately wide of the mercenary's head.

"Aldridge?" Greenwood shouted, straining to hear over a fresh rumble of thunder overhead. There was a tense moment of silence that seemed to last for minutes, then she finally heard him call out "Up here!" in response.

"Move," she said to Dowling, and they both ran towards the doorway leading to the spiralling stone staircase. As they leapt up the steps three at a time, she could hear the sound of receding footsteps treading the floorboards off towards the far end of the gallery.

Good, run all you like, she thought. *We're taking Aldridge and getting out of here.*

They burst onto the upper level with their weapons at the ready, but the only movement they saw was from halfway along the gallery. Dowling tensed, but Greenwood waved her hand to stop him.

Barely visible in the darkness, they could see that it was Aldridge. There were drops of blood every metre or so, leading in his direction, and he was moving away from them slowly but with purpose.

"Aldridge!" she shouted, and saw the man stop and turn around.

She and Dowling quickly joined him, and Greenwood's eyes widened at the blood on his forehead, the cut below his eye, and the way he was holding his right elbow clamped to his side.

"What happened to your arm?" she asked, reaching out towards him.

Aldridge shook his head. "Not my arm. He stabbed me, in the back. He's gone up to the roof. There's another door up ahead." He sounded a little out of breath.

Jesus, Dowling thought, glancing warily around to make sure they were alone.

Greenwood stepped around behind him, seeing a dark patch around a narrow vertical slit in his blazer over his right shoulder blade. She pressed her fingertips to the area, and felt blood.

"You have to take this blazer off," she said, exchanging a look with Dowling.

"No time for that," Aldridge said, his brow clammy, but Greenwood took hold of his upper arm firmly.

"You're not going anywhere until we look at this wound. If your lung is punctured, it could collapse at any moment," she said.

Chapter 38

Aldridge made a sound that was half sigh and half gasp, but he reluctantly shrugged off his blazer with Greenwood's help, wincing as the fabric of the collar passed over his upper back.

Greenwood carefully put her fingers into the tear in his shirt, and ripped the material apart to let her see the wound better. She produced a small metallic flashlight that flickered, but provided enough light to help.

"I think it might have bounced off your shoulder blade," she said. "There's not enough blood for a deep wound. You were lucky."

Aldridge huffed in reply, and Greenwood frowned.

"Actually, you were *bloody* lucky," she continued. "That's what I came to tell you. If you'd used your ability to stop this from happening—"

"Then Merrick would have countered me, and the Destiny event would have been triggered already," Aldridge interrupted. "I know. I figured that out a little while ago. He knows it too, which was why he was trying to provoke me by cutting my eye out."

This time it was Dowling's turn to wince. "Bastard," he muttered under his breath.

"Well, let's get you out of here," Greenwood said. "There's nothing he can do without another changer to counter. The event won't happen."

"I wish it were that simple," Aldridge said. "Look what's already happening outside. He's connected to it just as much as I am. It's still going to happen, somehow, or at least *something* is. We can't just leave him here, and none of you can take him down. We have to do this *now*."

Greenwood considered his words, and was forced to agree. Something was clearly building up out there, and in her gut she knew that the only way to stop it was to remove even the possibility that the two men could trigger the event.

Possibilities and fate, she thought. *Other outcomes. So we have to remove any chance of it.*

"Just go back down there and wait for me," Aldridge said, flexing his right arm tentatively. "Like I said, the only thing you can do up here is get killed."

"We're going up there with you, mate," Dowling said, adjusting his grip on his rifle. "He can shrug off every bloody bullet in this gun, but I'll be damned if I'm letting you go on your own. Begging your pardon, chief."

Greenwood gave a tight smile. "I think we're in agreement there, Larry," she said, then turned to Aldridge. "Are you sure you're up to this?"

"Not much choice," Aldridge replied, looking along the gallery towards the faint light coming down from the roof access door Merrick had disappeared through. A glint on the floor about ten metres away caught his eye. "I wondered where he threw that," he said, jogging across to the source of the glint and bending down to pick up the pistol Greenwood had given him hours earlier.

"I'm ready now," he said, "whatever good this peashooter will do me. The roof access stairs are just up

Chapter 38

ahead."

Greenwood and Dowling joined him once more and all three walked side by side down the gallery towards their fate.

Above, the thunder had returned with a vengeance, ripping across the sky with unrelenting fury. The angels on each stained glass window seemed to cower in dread, their faces saturated in the evil glow of the lightning that heralded a coming disaster beyond imagining.

As they reached the foot of the metal staircase leading upwards and out of sight, the heavy oak door at the entrance to the narthex swung shut with a boom that made all three of them jump. A second later, the shrieking wind tore it open again, swinging wildly on its squealing metal hinges.

There was a moment of silence, and then the large window showing the Rapture suddenly shattered into a thousand pieces, and a bolt of purple lightning forked in through the window frame, striking the pulpit with a sound like the hand of God slapping the old stone with terrible force. The ornamental cloth covering the angled top surface burst into flames and flew across the nave, landing on the cold flagstones safely away from any of the wooden pews. It sputtered and sizzled in the gale for a few seconds, then went out.

Greenwood and Dowling exchanged an awed look, but Aldridge didn't take his eyes from the staircase.

This is the last climb, he thought, and he was unsure exactly what that meant. He took a brief glance around the cathedral, seeing it not for its gothic beauty, but as the grim antechamber before a battle so profound it could almost be found in one of the holy books scattered on the floor not far behind them.

I don't think I'll be seeing this place again, he thought, and then he started up the metal stairs.

Merrick stood under the churning storm, his arms stretched wide. His feet were planted astride the crest of the main roof, about thirty feet in front of the cathedral's soaring bell-tower.

The sky was incandescent, and the roar of the thunder was constant now. Forks and trails of unnatural lightning ceaselessly crawled across the clouds, and then leapt downwards to strike buildings, cars, and open ground. Twice, sizzling bolts hammered into the lightning rods mounted regularly along the roofline of the cathedral, and Merrick felt the impacts through his boots. The thick rubber soles protected him, and he knew he was in no danger — he didn't sense the twisting of time that accompanied a mortal threat.

Magnificent, he thought.

From this vantage point, much of Hamburg was laid out before him, and he could see that several neighbourhoods had been plunged into darkness. A few fires were visible, and he could occasionally hear emergency sirens below the peals of thunder.

Absolutely no-one was visible on the streets. He looked down into the plaza, with its barriers and GSG

Chapter 38

vehicles, and he assumed everyone was cowering inside the vans.

Except Aldridge and his companions, he thought, a smile creasing his face. *Let them come.*

He had only one goal now: force Aldridge to help him trigger the Destiny event. Greenwood had badly miscalculated by coming up here after the physicist. She was now a legitimate target, and Merrick still had his knife and pistol. She was powerless to harm him, but he could certainly harm her — and Aldridge would surely intervene.

Merrick didn't even glance around as he heard the clank of boots coming up the access staircase, which was now fifteen feet below him.

"Welcome to the end of your world, Captain," he called.

Greenwood and Dowling took up positions on either side of the door, shoulders hunched against the screaming wind. Aldridge was a couple of steps in front, looking up at the sky.

"Never going to happen, Merrick," Greenwood replied, but her mouth was dry and she could feel her pulse pounding as she gripped the rifle. *It does feel like the end*, she thought.

Never in her life had she seen anything like the spectacle in the sky above them. It looked like the precursor to Judgement Day, as if vengeful angels would break from the black clouds at any moment, swooping down with flaming swords to strike down all sinners and leave only the righteous still standing.

Dowling could feel an unpleasant buzzing in his jaw, and he gritted his teeth against it. He tightened his grip on his weapon, fixing his gaze on the man standing above them, who had his arms raised insanely towards the maelstrom in the sky.

Suddenly, several bolts of the unnatural lightning lanced down in quick succession, one slamming into the bell-tower and the rest finding ground on the rooftops of neighbouring buildings. A piece of guttering shattered, and the pieces fell onto the slate tiles of the cathedral's roof around them. There was an answering peal of thunder that was so loud it felt like it was inside their chests as well as in the sky.

"Are we too late?" Dowling shouted, his eyes wide. "What the hell can we do about all this?" He gestured vaguely upwards, but Greenwood made no response. She was watching Aldridge, who had taken another step forwards, away from the relative safety of the door to the staircase.

"I can feel it," Aldridge said, raising his voice against the storm.

"We can all bloody feel it!" Dowling replied, feeling his hair prickling with the electricity in the air.

"I mean, I can feel the... the energy," Aldridge replied. "Of the event. It's up there, above us. I can feel it in me too."

Greenwood and Dowling exchanged a look, then she took a careful step forward. "What do you mean by

Chapter 38

that?" she asked, and Aldridge shook his head, with a slightly dazed expression on his face.

"It's incredible," he said. "So much power. I feel like I could do anything. Change anything. I could—"

Greenwood gripped his upper arm hard, and squeezed. "Aldridge, I need you to stay with me here," she said. "We're running out of time, and we need to stop what's going on up there. Focus. Focus on me and Larry."

Aldridge blinked, and looked round at her. His eyes seemed to be filled with the same purple glow coming from the clouds, and Greenwood involuntarily flinched.

It's just a reflection, she told herself, but she wasn't entirely sure. A part of the glow seemed to come from within. She peered into his eyes, but his mind was elsewhere.

Incredible, Aldridge thought. *I never imagined anything could feel like this*. He was connected to the storm, somehow. He was a part of it, and in a way, it was also a part of him. He knew instinctively that he could reach into that place in his mind where his ability seemed to live, and draw the power out.

There was no sense of any limitations anymore. No constraints. He found himself relaxing, and the scene around him began to take on a different character. The sense of urgency and panic he was feeling started to fade.

I could do anything, he thought. *Someone with this ability could do wonderful things*. There wouldn't have to be any more tragedies. No more terrorist attacks. No more plane crashes. No more wars. He sensed that if he reached deep enough into the limitless reserve of power here, he could see it all before it happened. He could intervene. And no-one could stand in the way because he couldn't be killed.

I could fix… everything, he thought, a dazed grin flickering onto his lips.

He turned his head to look at Greenwood, and he frowned in confusion. She was still gripping his upper arm, and for the first time since he'd met her, she looked frightened.

Maybe she doesn't understand what this means, he thought. *She doesn't have the ability herself, after all. She's only—*

Aldridge blinked as if he was waking up from a deep sleep. *Only what?* he asked himself, but he already knew the answer. *Human.*

He shuddered, shaking his head to clear it. *This is exactly what happened to Merrick*, he realised, *and he started off a hell of a lot closer to crazy than I am.*

He looked Greenwood in the eye and nodded at her, and she saw the shame on his face. She breathed a sigh of relief, and gave his arm another squeeze.

"Now you begin to understand, Mr. Aldridge," Merrick said suddenly, and all three heads whipped around to look at him. He was facing them now, his arms lifted only a little away from his sides, but with his palms still upturned towards the sky.

Chapter 38

"The project and this marvel were well named," Merrick continued. "This is *our* destiny. Can't you feel it?"

Dowling raised his assault rifle, and Merrick's eyes blazed as he gave the barest sneer.

"Easy, Larry," Greenwood said, not taking her eyes off Merrick. She took a step forward, stopping at the lip of the angled part of the rooftop that led up to where Merrick was standing.

"You're insane," she said, and Merrick laughed even as the thunder boomed again, rattling the slates he stood on.

"You are a small creature, Captain Greenwood," he replied, with the same purple glow visible in his eyes that Aldridge had. "I don't expect you to understand the affairs of gods."

"You're not a god," Aldridge said firmly, stepping forward to stand beside Greenwood, "and neither am I. We're just men. This ability doesn't change that. Your mistake was believing it gave you the right to make choices about other people's lives."

Merrick looked at him for a long moment, and then shook his head in contempt. In one smooth movement he drew his pistol, keeping it at his side for the moment. Greenwood and Dowling immediately trained their rifles on him. Dowling felt a large drop of sweat run from his brow and down his cheek.

Then the rain came. There was a sudden strong smell of ozone, and then a spatter of raindrops struck their faces. Aldridge swiped his hand across his face, and barely a second later, the downpour began in earnest.

Rain hammered down against the sloping tiles, bouncing off the narrow walkway leading from the access staircase and up to the crest of the roof. Their faces were soaked within seconds, and Dowling could feel water gathering in his hair and eyebrows.

"It's warm!" Aldridge shouted over the din. Greenwood drew her sleeve across her forehead to try to staunch the flow of water.

"Bloody dangerous," Dowling replied, stepping off the metal walkway to join Greenwood and Aldridge on the tiles of the roof. "If one of those strikes comes down on part of this—"

As if he had foreseen it, a vivid bolt of purple lightning arced down and struck the walkway just yards from where he had been standing. The intensity of the light was staggering, and the sound was like a hundred fireworks going off at once. Sparks leapt and sizzled in all directions, and for the briefest moment the walkway seemed to be outlined against the shifting light and shadow of the rooftop, laser-etched into the night.

"Shit," Dowling said. "That was too close."

Merrick's laughter boomed out above them, and again they turned their attention to him.

The front of his tactical vest was already soaked through, and his iron grey hair was plastered to his scalp. He still held the pistol in his hand, but both arms were now once again raised to the sky, as if he was tempting the very heavens to reach down and try to

Chapter 38

strike him.

"I think we've waited long enough, don't you?" Merrick said.

He allowed the rain to beat down on his upturned face for another moment, then he lowered his gaze to the three people below.

Greenwood tightened her finger on her rifle's trigger, but she knew she was powerless to stop the man.

Merrick took one final look from Aldridge to Dowling and then to Greenwood, and his eyes blazed.

Then he whipped the pistol around so it was pointing straight at Greenwood, and he fired.

Chapter 39

Greenwood knew the bullet was coming even before Merrick pulled the trigger. She instinctively threw herself sideways, squeezing off two rounds from her rifle as she moved.

Merrick's bullet missed her by inches, and one of her shots went wide. The other was dead on target, and she felt as well as saw him bat it off-course using his ability, with a wave of his hand.

He's more powerful here, just before the disaster, she thought. *He has much more control.*

The flow of time hadn't slowed as much as it usually did, and there was no sense of a delay. Here, with the Destiny event somehow still looming above them, Merrick seemed to have unrestricted use of his power. A direct attack with firearms was as useless as he had always promised.

I hope you're just as much better at using it too, Aldridge, she thought, searching for cover along the roof. They were cut off from the access walkway and staircase by the electricity that still coursed through the structure. It was earthed via the cathedral's lightning rods, but new bolts hit every few seconds. They couldn't get inside, down the staircase and off the whole metal structure between strikes.

"Best of three, Captain?" Merrick called down at her, aiming his pistol, and he fired again. This time, the shot was on target.

Aldridge saw it unfolding, and he was already reaching into his mind to stop the bullet when he remembered what was at stake.

He immediately released his mind's hold on the bullet, raised his own pistol, and fired at Merrick's chest — an easy target outlined against the insane sky.

Merrick cursed him and deflected the incoming shot, giving Aldridge the moment he needed to grab the bullet heading for Greenwood and make it bounce harmlessly off the access walkway beside her feet.

"Over there!" Dowling shouted, racing towards Greenwood as he pointed to a small, decorative stone tower halfway along the exposed roofline. It was barely eight feet high and perhaps four feet wide, but it would provide some cover, at least for the moment. Greenwood saw and understood immediately, springing to her feet as the big Welshman barrelled past her, grabbing her upper arm as he went. They both reached cover in less than four seconds, leaving Aldridge standing in

Chapter 39

the open.

"That's his weakness," Aldridge shouted, drawing Merrick's furious glare. "He can't counter me if he has to make another change for himself!"

"So what do we do?" Dowling shouted back, his heart pounding in his ears.

"Attack *him* when he attacks one of us," Aldridge replied, levelling his gun at Merrick again. "It'll give me time to prevent any damage he does. And don't give him a target!"

"How long do you think you can keep playing this ridiculous game?" Merrick spat, his eyes now luminescent windows to the storm. He stalked along the peak of the roofline, then clumped down the recessed slats, heading for Aldridge.

Greenwood and Dowling eased around opposite edges of the small tower, taking up firing positions while staying behind cover as much as possible. Dowling glanced up at the raised peak atop the tower, knowing it was a potential lightning strike point.

Not much choice, he thought, taking aim.

At almost the same moment, all four fired.

Three bullets streaked towards Merrick, and one flew towards Aldridge. Aldridge already knew that Dowling's shot was going wide because the wind had blown rain into the big man's eyes at the last moment, knocking his shot off-centre. He also knew that his own shot would punch through Merrick's combat webbing just beside his left hip, but wouldn't hit its target.

That left two bullets: Greenwood's shot at Merrick, and Merrick's at Aldridge. Both were well-aimed, and both were lethal.

Aldridge could see Merrick's rage and frustration as if he was standing right in front of the mercenary. Merrick summoned down the power of the storm to shrug off the bullet long before it could strike his temple, and at the same time Aldridge knocked Merrick's bullet from the air by reaching deep into his own mind.

"Not that this isn't exactly what I'd like to be doing at two in the morning," Greenwood shouted from her position on the left side of the tower, "but how long are we supposed to keep doing this?"

Damned if I know, Aldridge thought, feeling tension course through his body as Merrick swung his pistol around towards the sound of Greenwood's voice. "Watch out!" he shouted. Dowling immediately fired at Merrick, but it was useless. The shells spun away into the storm, over the edge of the roof and downwards out of sight.

The temptation to counter Merrick's changes was overwhelming, but Aldridge clenched his fists. *If I do that, it's all over*.

Merrick levelled his pistol at the sliver of Greenwood's shoulder he could see around the edge of her cover, and at the same time he carefully drew his combat knife from its thigh sheath, balancing the blade in his hand.

It's only a matter of time, he thought to himself, barely

Chapter 39

able to suppress the laughter that was bubbling up inside him as he effortlessly turned aside every bullet that came towards him.

Merrick abruptly fired a precision shot at Greenwood as she drew out to take aim at him, then whipped around and hurled the knife at Aldridge.

Dowling immediately sent two rounds towards Merrick, distracting him as Aldridge mentally reached for the bullet before it could hit Greenwood. In his hyper-aware state, the whole thing seemed to take several long, slow seconds, but in reality everything happened almost simultaneously.

The knife was still slicing through the air, nearly reaching Aldridge now, when he safely deflected the bullet from Greenwood. Dowling fired again as soon as he became conscious of Merrick swatting his first bullet aside, leaving only the knife to deal with.

No, Aldridge thought, allowing himself to draw down some of the vast power from above. Thunder split the sky, and a jagged bolt of lightning arced down and blew the knife out of the air only a metre from his chest.

There was a moment of stillness as Merrick, Greenwood and Dowling all stared at Aldridge in disbelief.

"Impossible," Merrick snarled, swinging his pistol around and pointing it at Aldridge's head. *This situation is getting out of control*, he thought, and he felt the first slipping of his sense of invulnerability. He quickly reloaded his pistol.

Aldridge didn't flinch. He walked forward and started ascending the recessed slats that would take him to the peak of the roof where Merrick stood.

"Damn it," Greenwood said, mostly to herself, but she was aware that Dowling leaned a little further out beyond the shelter of the tower, keeping Merrick in his sights as Aldridge climbed the slope.

Suddenly an alarm went off on Greenwood's wristwatch, and her eyes widened even though she never looked away from Aldridge.

Five minutes, she thought. The alarms had been preprogrammed to the calculated precise time of the Destiny event, and Taylor's algorithm ensured it was accurate down to the second. She had no idea how Aldridge's and Merrick's actions factored into the disaster now, but she also knew it was a future event that in some sense had nevertheless already happened.

"Not much time left, chief," Dowling shouted from nearby, over the howl of the storm. She exchanged a quick glance with the large man, and there was only calm acceptance in his eyes.

"Let's keep him covered," she replied, and Dowling nodded. *Five minutes until the end*, she thought, and shuddered. Crouching up here against the wind and rain, under a furious storm the likes of which she'd never seen, and watching two men who were practically invulnerable face off against each other — she had never felt so powerless.

Greenwood felt a clench of desperation, aware of the city around her in her peripheral vision. So many people

Chapter 39

were out there in the darkness, pulled from sleep by the unprecedented storm raging in the sky above their homes, with no idea what it meant.

If the end did come tonight, at least it would be quick.

Aldridge had reached the peak of the slope, and he saw that the access slats continued along the peak, allowing him to walk across the highest point of this section of the roof. Merrick was fifteen feet away, watching him patiently. Both men held pistols, knowing that they were useless against each other.

"Destiny awaits us, Mr. Aldridge," Merrick shouted over the storm, raising his free hand in a gesture towards the sky.

Aldridge glanced up, taking in the terrible majesty of the spectacle above. As he lowered his gaze again, he saw the scattered fires among the rooftops of Hamburg, and further afield he could see the parts of the city that still had electricity.

So much at stake, he thought, thinking not just of this city but of the entire world beyond. *This has to end now.*

He took a deep breath, locking eyes with Merrick. The storm surged above, and the rain fell even harder. Sheets of water lashed down, and lightning sparked and sizzled high over their heads. The thunder was omnipresent, as if they were standing inside an enormous drum being beaten in a frenzied rhythm.

Aldridge's shoulder and back throbbed, but there was no pain. Even the terror had faded away now, and he felt completely calm. He knew exactly what was at stake, and what he had to do.

The rain soaked his hair, eyebrows, and clothes, and water ran freely down his face. His mouth was filled with the tastes of metal and ozone. His mind was completely focused.

He took one final glance down towards the small tower along the lower roofline, and saw Greenwood's face, lit by the constant pulse of lightning. He gave her a small, sad smile.

Then he ran at Merrick.

Merrick grinned as Aldridge rushed towards him, closing the distance between them in seconds before coming to a halt. Both men brought up their guns, knowing that there was no chance of a miss at point blank range.

They stood barely more than arm's length from each other, the barrels of their pistols almost touching the other's chest.

"What are you waiting for?" Merrick snarled, his eyes wild with savage excitement. "Kill me if you can! You know as well as I do that Destiny is only minutes away."

"Never going to happen," Aldridge said. "One way or another, we're finishing this now."

Merrick rammed the barrel of his pistol hard into Aldridge's chest, and then both men fired.

An enormous bolt of jagged lightning lanced down from the sky and then hung suspended in mid-air, metres from the roof. The thunder boomed but never receded, echoing like a diabolical stuck record, filling the

Chapter 39

world with an unending bass note. Time snapped to a tenth of its usual speed, then hurtled forward, then shuddered almost to a halt again.

Greenwood and Dowling watched in awe.

It was like seeing some kind of apocalyptic ballet. Aldridge and Merrick repeatedly lunged and dodged, firing and then deflecting incoming bullets, the sky pounding and flashing in time with their movements as the flow of time pinched and expanded rhythmically again and again. Greenwood felt her ears pop, and she gripped her rifle even tighter, her knuckles white. Still the lightning bolt never reached the roof.

It was like there was a bubble of time surrounding the two battling men, and everything outside was paused. Flames on a nearby rooftop were frozen in place, wickedly bright but absolutely motionless. Debris in the gale hung mid-cartwheel, a hundred feet above the plaza. Sheets of rain became curtains of water trapped in the breath between two flashes of lightning.

Still Merrick and Aldridge lunged and parried, physically and with their strange power, and the storm built and built. Dowling felt the rising atmospheric pressure pushing on his eardrums, and he seemed to hear a growing high-pitched whine under the cacophony of the storm.

Two minutes, Greenwood thought. She had never been a religious woman, but she couldn't stop herself looking superstitiously towards the spire of the cathedral's belltower. There was no solace to be found there, and the structure itself wavered like a mirage.

It was hard to know how many shots had been fired, as first Aldridge and then Merrick rewrote events again and again, endlessly halting and rewinding a single moment of conflict.

The thunder's sustained bass note had evened out into a constant noise that rattled through Greenwood's skull, and Dowling was now crouched down with his hands pressing over his ears, his rifle hanging slack against his knees.

One minute.

She had no idea how her wristwatch was still functioning, but it counted steadily down as Aldridge and Merrick blurred and shifted on the peak of the roof, sometimes swapping positions.

Thirty seconds.

More shots, seemingly dozens simultaneously. And then, suddenly, they stopped.

Twenty seconds.

The world seemed to inhale and then hold its breath. The sky was a furious mass of energy, suspended in time. Even the sound of the storm had passed beyond her awareness, and Greenwood was exquisitely aware of every drop of rain, every slate of the roof, and even every soaked hair on her head. She felt like the universe was compressed down to a point, squeezed tight like a spring, and now just waiting.

Merrick's eyes shone as he stared at his opponent. "My destiny has arrived," he said.

Chapter 39

And in that moment, Aldridge understood. It was so simple.

Goodbye, Captain, he thought, and he felt only relief.

"Destiny can be changed," he replied, then he placed the barrel of his pistol against his own head, and pulled the trigger.

Merrick's eyes widened as he reached out with his mind to grasp the bullet that hurtled down the barrel of Aldridge's gun and towards the man's head.

You can't escape so easily, Merrick thought, just as he managed to halt the bullet's motion.

Then the shot came. A single high-calibre round, streaking through the air.

Greenwood? Merrick wondered for an instant, but the trajectory was wrong. He struggled to maintain his hold on Aldridge's bullet even as a part of his mind saw the other round coming in from far below, in the plaza.

The other woman on Greenwood's team, he thought. With a monumental effort, he hauled Aldridge's bullet back into the pistol, and desperately reached his consciousness out into the darkness to find the sniper round.

The bullet surged into the barrier of slowed time, punching through the air. Merrick scrambled to find and hold it.

At the last moment, with the bullet mere feet away, he shuddered with effort and pushed his change through. He was about to roar in triumph as the bullet began to slow, and then his eyes widened again in horror.

Greenwood pulled the trigger of her pistol, and her bullet seemed to fracture the entire bubble of frozen time atop the cathedral. Her aim was true, and she was barely aware of a sliver of light bouncing away from the air in front of Merrick's face before her own shot punched through the side of his head.

I am a god, Merrick thought in his final moment, and then the universe exploded into light.

Greenwood's ears popped painfully, and she felt like she'd been punched hard in the stomach. For several seconds she couldn't make her lungs work, and then the sky seemed to finally let out the enormous breath it had been holding.

She looked up again, seeing Merrick's legs buckle beneath him. He fell to his knees then twisted to the side, rolling off the peak of the roof and tumbling end over end to the lip of the guttering, before finally disappearing off the edge.

Aldridge looked over at her and blinked, and then he raised his eyes to the frozen storm above, and the jagged spike of motionless lightning hanging over his head.

The long, rolling bass note of thunder suddenly swelled.

Then the bolt of lightning finally struck.

Epilogue

It was raining in Edinburgh, and that suited Neil Aldridge just fine. The streets were marginally less busy, and rain had a way of making even a mediocre cup of coffee seem to taste better.

He was standing at the window of his third-floor flat, looking out over the wet rooftops and cobbled streets of the city. Buses sailed resolutely by, their drab maroon and tan livery seeming to match the mood of the weather. Pedestrians walked doggedly along, hunched under hoods and umbrellas, not bothering to hurry. It was just after 2 PM, and the working week was well underway.

Aldridge stretched his neck, feeling a twinge from the upper-right quadrant of his back. The knife wound was healing well, and if he was honest, he didn't mind the fading jabs of discomfort it caused. They made the whole thing real.

Almost two weeks had passed since that night on the

roof of the cathedral in Hamburg.

The world's media had tired of the story of the freak thunderstorm very quickly. The city's fire department, power companies, and civic construction departments had been very busy indeed for a few days, but life in Hamburg had largely returned to normal. Plans were already underway to repair the superficial damage to a number of buildings, and an architectural firm had been contracted to tender for the more extensive repair work needed to a beautiful old cathedral in a quiet plaza.

Local residents also assumed that there had been damage to the historic bank across the square, because specialist teams were seen moving in and out of the building constantly during the days after the storm.

Meteorologists worldwide had given their opinions on the possible causes of the unusually fierce thunder and lightning, but a few scattered eyewitness reports of people on the roof of the cathedral during the storm had been dismissed as imagination, fatigue, or a trick of the light.

Finding nothing sensational in unusual weather, the newspapers and TV news shows had quickly moved on, especially when the tragic death of a noted Danish industrialist occurred just two days later. Mikkel Anfruns died peacefully in his sleep at his mansion, of a heart attack brought on by overwork and a developing case of coronary artery disease. The chairperson of the European Defence Agency gave a moving tribute to a man whose life's work was dedicated to technological

Epilogue

progress and the responsible use of power.

Anfruns's estranged sister was currently being sought by the executors of his estate, as she stood to inherit several billion Euros in property and other holdings. When asked by journalists about any other beneficiaries, the executors had merely stated that Mr. Anfruns's will was confidential, but that he had made several large contributions to charities, and also to governmental organisations within the field of European security.

No mention of Merrick, Aldridge thought, taking a sip of his coffee and relishing the bitter taste. *Not that anyone would know who he was.*

Wuyts had said that any further disclosure wasn't in the public interest, and Aldridge had to agree.

Destiny never took place. Once the suspended bolt of lightning struck the roof, throwing Aldridge from his feet, the storm had begun to dissipate as the deadline passed.

The event originally occurred because Merrick and I countered each other's changes, which sent the anti-tachyon energy back in time. That's what started everything off.

But then they'd prevented it from happening. It *had* happened, in the future, but they managed to avert the catastrophe the second time around. Did that mean it had never taken place at all? It made his head hurt.

His ability was certainly gone. He had lost all sense of that place in his mind where he could reach in and take hold of one strand of reality, forcing it to change. None of the other surviving changers had exhibited any trace of their power either. CERN's scientists had a theory that the disaster was somehow the energy source for the ability too, and with it prevented or undone, there was no way to trigger the strange power anymore.

Aldridge felt a profound sense of loss, but he was adjusting. As each new day passed, he wondered more and more often if any of it had actually happened.

But then there was the knife wound on his back, and the gash in his left shoulder from a bullet. The cut below his eye, and the bruises on his ribs. The superficial contact burns on his feet from the final lighting strike, which were healing quickly.

Merrick's smashed body had been recovered from just outside the perimeter railings around the cathedral's entranceway. One of the GSG 9 vehicles had been appropriated to quickly move the body, which had been taken to an unknown location for study and eventual cremation. The file on the Destiny incident had already been sealed.

Aldridge had no memory of what happened after Merrick was shot and the lightning bolt struck. His next recollection was of waking up two days later in a hospital bed in Brussels. He remained there for several more days before being discharged, and KESTREL's jet had flown him directly to Edinburgh the day before yesterday. A memorial service for Taylor would take place in Oxford after the announcement of his death — from a stroke — in a few weeks. Aldridge was trying not to think about that yet.

Epilogue

"How's the packing going?" came a voice from behind him, and he grinned as he turned to greet his visitor.

"Done, I think," he replied. "Wasn't as much as I thought."

Greenwood nodded, glancing around at the surprisingly small number of cardboard boxes in the living room. Several were stacked on a coffee table between the couch and the window, and he saw that she recognised it from his tale about the glass ornament.

"How's Goose?" he asked, and she smiled.

"On the mend," she replied. "He'll be starting physiotherapy soon to get back up to readiness. In the meantime, he's taken an interest in physics."

Aldridge shook his head. "Are you here to rescind the job offer then, Captain? Goose is a clever man."

Greenwood took a few more steps into the room, and put her hands in the pockets of her leather jacket. "I think it'll be a while before he can match your credentials, Aldridge," she said. "And Director Wuyts seems quite fond of you, for some reason. Fair warning, though: there's a lot of travel in this job."

"Maybe for you soldiers out on the front lines," Aldridge said, gesturing towards her with his cup. "I'm looking forward to settling into that lab Wuyts mentioned. I just hope I'll be of some value to you."

He looked down at his coffee cup, swirling the dark liquid thoughtfully.

"It's a changed world out there," Greenwood said

quietly, and his eyes flicked up to meet hers. "No pun intended. We're facing new kinds of threats all the time. Guns and grenades aren't even half the story. I think you'll find some way to make yourself useful."

"I'll drink to that," Aldridge said, taking a noisy slurp from the coffee cup and enjoying Greenwood's weary grimace. He put the cup down and then saw that she was still looking at him, and he raised an eyebrow. Greenwood shrugged.

"It's a good look for you," she said, pointing in the general direction of his face, which he knew still bore a couple of healing scars.

"I'm not sure how to take that," he replied, after a pause. Greenwood didn't respond, but she didn't look away either.

A small beep interrupted the moment. Greenwood took out her mobile phone and read the message on the screen.

"Just Larry downstairs in the car," she said. "I — or I suppose I should say *we* — have a message from Wuyts."

Aldridge nodded. "I'll come with you. Everything is ready for your people to collect."

"Let's go," Greenwood replied.

"What did the Director want?" Greenwood said, slipping into the passenger seat of the big silver Audi that was idling at the kerb just outside Aldridge's building. The windows were heavily tinted, and she blinked to

Epilogue

adjust her vision to the sudden gloom.

Dowling was in the driver's seat, which was pushed all the way back. He had a small laptop perched on his thighs, and he glanced up briefly as Aldridge got into the seat behind Greenwood's and closed the door.

"Encrypted message, coming in now," Dowling said. He sounded cheerful as always. He'd been uncharacteristically quiet for a few days after the Destiny mission, but he seemed to be back to himself now, and raring to go.

The laptop chirped as it received the message, and Dowling handed the device over to Greenwood.

She looked out of the car's windows for a moment from long-ingrained habit, making sure they weren't being observed, and then entered her personal decryption key. A moment later, a document popped up on the screen.

Dowling rested his hands on the steering wheel, allowing her to read the communique in her own time. After half a minute or so, he drummed his fingers. "I should probably iron more shirts for my suitcase," he said, to no-one in particular.

"Well?" Aldridge asked, leaning forward to hover between the headrests of the two front seats. "What's the word?"

Greenwood remained silent for several moments before lifting her head to meet his gaze in the rear view mirror.

"You wouldn't believe me if I told you," she replied,

closing the laptop's lid with a firm click.
   Aldridge grinned.
   "Try me," he said.

AFTERWORD

Dear Reader,

Thank you so much for reaching this page. I'm Matt Gemmell, the author of this book. This letter is for you.

I hope you've enjoyed reading *CHANGER*. I deeply appreciate the investment of time and trust you've made. Writing a novel is a stressful, arduous, and slightly crazy thing to do; what makes it worthwhile is the idea that someone, somewhere, is reading your words.

Today, right now, that someone is you. From one human being to another, *thank you*. You're literally the reason I'm doing this.

If you enjoyed the book, I'd be very grateful if you left a brief review on the online store of your choice. Authors live and die, commercially speaking, by those reviews. A minute of your time would mean a great deal to me.

I'd also love to hear from you, and keep you informed

about new books, behind-the-scenes articles about writing, bonus and deleted chapters, and more. Here's how we can stay in touch:

My web site: mattgemmell.com
My newsletter: mattgemmell.com/news-subscribe
On Twitter: @mattgemmell
On Facebook: facebook.com/MattGemmellAuthor

That's enough from me for now. I hope to talk to you again soon.

Thank you for reading.

Matt Gemmell
Edinburgh, Scotland
17th June, 2016

KESTREL will return.

ACKNOWLEDGEMENTS

Books aren't written in isolation. Well, they *are*, but there's more to it than just the act of writing.

First and foremost, I'd like to thank my wife, Lauren Gemmell, who wore many hats during the creation of *CHANGER*: story consultant, proofreader, wise counsellor, gentle but firm taskmaster, and patient partner. As I assembled the words, she kept *me* together.

To my family and friends, who learned when to enquire and when not to: thanks on both counts. I'll keep you posted about the next one.

I'm grateful to Stuart Bache at Books Covered for his excellent work on the cover design. As I watched the art take shape — over a remarkably short period — the book finally became real for me. And *as without, so within*: my sincere thanks to Patrick Foster for his expert eye on the paperback's typography.

The Rijksmuseum in Amsterdam is a beautiful place,

filled with history and treasures. I'd like to extend my gratitude for being able to stage some mischief there.

I couldn't have written this book without the freedom to dedicate my time to it. For that, my eternal thanks go to the generous not-so-few who are patrons of my writing. You made this journey possible, and this book is yours.

Adam and Grace Jaworski, your faith is humbling. I can only continue trying to earn it.

Cyril Godefroy, the advice was very much appreciated — and timely.

To those who braved less-than-finished versions so that others don't have to, you're my heroes: Relly Annett-Baker, fellow traveller and probably better at this; Mark Aufflick, for the insights and bloody Aussie enthusiasm; Anders Kierulf, valiantly and at the last minute; and of course Lloyd Nebres, who's far away but always comes along for the ride.

Lastly and most of all, my thanks go to you, dear reader. Always you.

Made in the USA
Charleston, SC
14 July 2016